WHEN ANNABELLA LAGRANGE WAS SEVEN

she thought the world a delightful place to live in and only occasionally wondered why her parents never took her outside of their magnificent countryside estate. When she was ten, she decided that the seclusion really didn't matter very much, because when she grew up, she would marry her handsome cousin Stephen and never be lonely again. And when she was eighteen, and learned the circumstances of her birth, her entire world quietly crashed around her.

Catherine Cookson transforms the simple plot of riches-to-rags and back again into a vivid, textured, and highly romantic novel that is not altogether unlike Jane Eyre in its impact.

The Glass Virgin

Catherine Cookson

*This low-priced Bantam Book
has been completely reset in a type face
designed for easy reading, and was printed
from new plates. It contains the complete
text of the original hard-cover edition.*
NOT ONE WORD HAS BEEN OMITTED.

THE GLASS VIRGIN

*A Bantam Book | published by arrangement with
The Bobbs-Merrill Company, Inc.*

PRINTING HISTORY

Bobbs-Merrill edition published October 1969
Bantam edition | September 1970

2nd printing .... May 1971	7th printing .... June 1974
3rd printing .... March 1973	8th printing ...... August 1974
4th printing .... July 1973	9th printing ...... August 1975
5th printing .. November 1973	10th printing . September 1976
6th printing .... February 1974	11th printing .... May 1981

*All rights reserved.
Copyright © 1969 by Catherine Cookson.
Cover art copyright © 1981 by Bantam Books, Inc.
This book may not be reproduced in whole or in part, by
mimeograph or any other means, without permission.
For information address: The Bobbs-Merrill Company, Inc.,
4300 West 62nd Street, Indianapolis, Indiana 46206.*

ISBN 0–553–13937–1

Published simultaneously in the United States and Canada

Bantam Books are published by Bantam Books, Inc. Its trademark, consisting of the words "Bantam Books" and the por-
trayal of a bantam, is Registered in U.S. Patent and Trademark
Office and in other countries. Marca Registrada. Bantam
Books, Inc., 666 Fifth Avenue, New York, New York 10103.

PRINTED IN THE UNITED STATES OF AMERICA

20 19 18 17 16 15 14 13 12 11

Contents

The Glass Virgin

Book One

*MY DARLING
DAUGHTER*

On the eve of her seventh birthday Annabella Lagrange learned that it was wrong for men to ask for a penny a day more for twelve hours' work down a coal mine and also that because of such wrongdoing they were deprived of food and shelter. But she also learned on that day that it was right for her father to take all the clothes off a strange lady, bathe her, then feed her with strawberries.

Redford Hall was situated in the County of Durham, six miles from Newcastle and five miles from South Shields, or Jarrow, depending on which path you took at the crossroads. Its grounds extended to sixty acres, ten of which were given over to pleasure gardens, the remainder to the home farm.

The Hall itself was comprised of two separate houses, the Old Hall and the House. The Old Hall had been built in 1640 of blocks of quarried stone and contained only twelve rooms. The House was built in 1780 of red bricks and timber. It had twenty-six rooms spread over three floors. A long, broad gallery connected the two buildings, its west wall being made up of six arched windows set in deep bays. These overlooked the west drive and gave a panoramic view of the gardens beyond. Below the gallery was a small chapel that had been attached to the Hall.

On wet or cold days Annabella was allowed to play in the gallery. Her favorite game was to run the length of it, from the door which led out of the House to that which led into the Old Hall. When she reached this door, she would throw herself against its black oak face, her arms spread wide as if in an embrace, and like that she would listen for as long as she dared, for she was never alone in the gallery—Watford or old Alice was always present. Sometimes she heard her father's voice calling loudly to Constantine. Sometimes she heard him laughing. She loved to hear him laughing. Once she had fallen on her back when the door was pulled open and the half-caste valet, with his negroid features set on pale skin, had come through balancing a great silver tray laden with breakfast dishes.

Never, not once, had she been past that door. In her prayers at night she sometimes asked God to perform a kind of miracle that would transport her to the other side of the oak door. Of late she had begun to imagine what she would find on the other side, and her imagery always showed her pictures of brightness, color and gaiety.

It was a source of questionable comfort to her that she wasn't the only one who never passed through the black oak door, for her mama never went into the Old Hall, nor any of the servants from the House except Reeves, the first footman, and the second footman, Faill. She did not consider Constantine as belonging to the House because he lived in the Old Hall; he did not even eat in the kitchen with the others.

Her papa spent a lot of time in the Hall. He slept and ate there, except when they had company in the House like Uncle James and Aunt Emma; but then they only came to dinner and never stayed overnight; it was only her papa's friends who stayed overnight. Her papa laughed a lot and was very happy when he had his friends staying with him, but at these times her mama did not even smile. She couldn't say herself that she liked the times when her papa had his friends around him, because at these times he drank a lot and raced the horses over the fells, and they came back sweating. The last time, one poor horse had hurt its leg and they had shot it in the yard, and she had seen them do it. It was on a day when her mama had gone across the park to visit Grandma.

Watford had taken her up into the attics and into her room, and Watford's window overlooked the yard, and that was how she had seen the horse. She had screamed.

Mrs. Page, the housekeeper, had beaten Watford over the head and she herself had cried all the more because of that. Mrs. Page had then said to her, "Now, we won't upset your mama by telling her about that horse, will we?"

She had replied obediently, "No, Mrs. Page," while at the same time knowing that the housekeeper was not so concerned about her mama learning about the horse as about Watford's taking her into her room during the time she should have been resting in the nursery.

Things were never the same in the house when her mama was out; the servants acted differently. They walked much slower and they laughed when they passed each other on the stairs. And it was a sure sign that her mama was out when Ada Rawlings put her head round the nursery door, for then she and Watford would whisper together; and sometimes they would put their heads on each other's shoulders and giggle.

No one giggled or laughed when her mama was about. Yet her mama never raised her voice; she never shouted as Papa did. But then ladies never shouted; only men and servants raised their voices. She loved her mama, and her mama loved her. Even when her mama's love wasn't demonstrated by a quick, tight embrace or a kiss in secret she knew she was enveloped in her love. Yet her mama wasn't happy. Even when they walked hand in hand along the crisscross path in the big wood she knew she wasn't happy, and this hurt her. When she lay awake at nights thinking her strange and wonderful thoughts, she tried to devise ways which would make her mama happy.

The house was different today because her mama had ridden out very early, accompanied by old Alice. She had gone to Durham to visit Uncle James and Aunt Emma. The visit was in some way connected with Papa because she had witnessed the unusual sight of her parents' walking down the main staircase together at the early hour of eight-thirty. Her papa had not been downstairs for over a week because his hip was hurting after a fall from a horse, but with the aid of a stick he was descending the stairs. She stood still until they crossed the wide hall and disappeared into the porch, then she flew along the landing, down a corridor and burst into the gallery, and from the last window, where she pressed her face to the glass, she was just in time to see her papa handing her mama up into the coach.

When she returned to the nursery, Watford wasn't there, but this she didn't mind in the least because being left entirely alone was the one compensation her mama's absence afforded.

The last time her mama had been away for a day she had been alone for a full half-hour; it was a wonderful experience, so much so that she had imagined she was someone else; she had just sat and thought her thoughts with no one to say, "Miss Annabella. Miss Annabella. Miss Annabella."

When Watford returned to the nursery on that particular occasion she had been accompanied by her friend Ada Rawlings, and she had pointed toward Annabella, saying under her breath, "There, what did I tell you, she hasn't moved." And then she had said loudly, "All right, Miss Annabella?" And to this she had answered, "Yes, Watford, thank you."

The two girls had then gone into the day room and continued to talk, but again under their breath, yet she could hear everything they said distinctly. She did not know that her hearing was acute, nor did they, and so she had heard Ada Rawlings say, "Sitting there like an old woman dreaming of her Egypt." And she had pondered this saying. What was dreaming of her Egypt? She knew about Egypt. Mama had come to it in the history lesson. Egypt was a place of sand and stone; the stone things were graves called pyramids and the great stretches of sand were called desert. She was very interested in sand because her papa was interested in sand. You couldn't make glass without sand, he said.

Then Watford and Rawlings had gone on to talk about "the hoppings." They didn't lower their voices very much when they were talking about the hoppings, and the switch-backs, cakewalks, roundabouts, and fisticuff bouts. They always giggled a lot when they talked about the hoppings. One day at the beginning of last month nearly all the staff had gone to the hoppings in Newcastle; they had been driven away on flat carts. Her mama and she had watched them from the gallery window as they drove down the east drive. Her papa, too, had gone to the hoppings, but he had gone, as usual, in his carriage down the west drive. She had asked her mama what a hopping was and her mama had explained that it was a race meeting surrounded by a fair, and she had asked her, "Will I ever go to a hopping?" and her mama had answered quietly, "No, dear; you will never go to a hopping."

She had felt a little sorry about this because for days she had felt a sort of excitement running through the house, and all because of the hoppings. Everybody seemed to be happy at the thought of the hoppings, everybody that is except Alice, and Harris, and Mrs. Page, and the cook, because they, like her mama, were excluded from going to the hoppings.

The day after the hoppings, Rawlings had talked about Cargill putting his arms about her and kissing her. Cargill must love Rawlings. She conjured up a mental picture of Cargill, and she couldn't imagine anyone loving him in return, not even Rawlings.

She was sitting finishing her breakfast when Watford came in, again accompanied by Ada Rawlings, and Watford, looking at her, said, "That's a good girl"; then turning to her friend she added, "She's seven the morrow."

"My! there's an age." Ada Rawlings nodded her round, red face toward her. "Do you feel seven, Miss Annabella?"

6

"I don't know, Rawlings."

"What you goin' to get for your birthday?"

Again she said, "I don't know yet, Rawlings."

"You will tonight when your mama comes back, I expect."

"Yes, Rawlings."

Rawlings nodded at her; then, answering a jerk from Watford's head, she followed her friend into the day room, and Annabella sat listening to their conversation, and although she didn't understand the underlying meaning of what they said, their words troubled her. It was Ada Rawlings who asked, "What's she gone for in such a stew?"

"Your guess's as good as mine; there's only one thing, money."

"Do you think she'll get it?"

"With her uncle hating him as he does, not a hope."

"But it's her own money, isn't it?"

"Aye, it might be, but her uncle's her trustee and will be for another two years. When she's thirty she'll get it—what's left of it."

"You know, Betty, I'm sorry for her at times—you never see her smile. I've been in this house four years an' I've never seen that woman smile."

"Well, it's her own fault; she should never have taken him on, not a fellow like him. He wanted somebody who'd stand up to him. Anyhow, she should have had the sense to know he wasn't marrying her for her looks, or even as a bed warmer."

The two girls began to giggle, and Annabella, who had been staring toward the partly open door, bowed her head and looked down on the breakfast tray, which held a miniature silver coffee service and fragile china. When she next lifted her head it was to the words, "How many do you think he's had?" This was followed by another laugh and Watford's saying, "You askin' me that, and I can only count up to ten!"

"It's a week since he was out, isn't it?"

"Aye; but you saw he managed the stairs this mornin', didn't he?"

"Aye, I know that, but it cost him something. His face was gray. He should have that hip seen to."

"Well, he did, didn't he? An' the doctor said rest. That's all you can do for sprained sinews, rest; but fancy him restin', huh! He must be feeling like a caged lion in there."

"It's a wonder he hasn't had his pals over, especially young Rosier. He's quite a lad."

"Well, I'd say this mornin's trip is the reason why he's

7

behaved hisself. He wanted her to dip into the coffers again, and although she's quiet like, she's stubborn. Oh, aye. Under that 'Come to Jesus' look she's as stubborn as a mule. But oh, if she only knew the half, there'd be some kickin'. Still, what the eyes don't see the heart don't grieve over, so they say."

"Aye, that's what they say, and, God Almighty, it's a good job she can't see everything he gets up to. But you know something, Betty; give me him any day in the week afore her. I'd rather have a bawling out from him than one look from her. And that's what John says an' all. He says he'd rather have a kick in the arse than a hunk of scripture cake any day. He can't stand the damned daily prayers; he says you should be left to make your own mind up for or against."

"Well, he would think like that, wouldn't he: He'd be a hypocrite if he didn't, with the tricks he's been up to. It's a wonder he isn't picked up by the police every time he enters Shields."

"Oh, aye, you're right there. You know, I just thought the other Sunday when I saw the master takin' his place in the pew, I thought, Eeh! God, but you've got a nerve, 'cause John had just told me five minutes afore that he'd driven one home at four o'clock in the mornin'; he was dead beat and in no good mood else he wouldn't have told me. He doesn't tell me everything, you know. . . . Just as well."

Something about this part of the conversation made Annabella rise from the table and push her chair roughly back, and the sound brought the girls to the door, and Watford asked, "You finished, miss?"

"Yes, Watford, thank you."

"You go into the schoolroom and read for a bit and then I'll take you for a walk when the weather clears."

"I'd rather go into the gallery."

Watford paused for a moment, then said, "All right. But mind, just sit still, no runnin' about or playin' games until I come. Don't go past the end window, understand?"

"Yes, Watford."

"Turn round and I'll take your pinafore off."

Obediently Annabella turned round and Watford undid the silk ribbons at the back of the neck and at the waist; then she ran a comb through the long brown hair, while saying to her friend, "If you don't comb it practically every hour, it gets full of knots."

"You have lovely hair, Miss Annabella." Ada Rawlings bent down toward the child and spoke in a loud voice as if to

8

someone deaf, and Annabella replied politely, "Yes, Raw-lings," then after a moment added, as her mother had taught her to do even when talking to servants, "Thank you."

"There you are," said Watford. "Go and get your book, and mind what I told you."

"Yes, Watford."

As she went into the schoolroom, she paused a moment and heard Ada Rawlings say, "Biddable, isn't she?"

"Aye, too biddable; it isn't natural."

"Do you think she carries anything?"

"No. Give her her due, I've never known her to carry a tale. An' she must hear things at times she can't help. An' bet your life, if she did say anything about me, I'd know it from madam. By. Aye. . . . Oh, she's no trouble. As I said afore, the job'd be clover, Ada, except for the feelin' that's about, you know, when the mistress is home. It's just as if somebody's died when she's in."

"Well, the funeral's over for the day; let's make the best of it."

"Aye, you've said it. An' by God, here's one that's going to. There's only dear Auntie Page to keep a weather eye open for, and between us we should manage her."

Annabella could still hear their giggling when she reached the end of the corridor. She stood for a while on the landing. The house seemed very quiet. Mrs. Page would be at breakfast with the butler in her room. The rest of the staff would be eating in the kitchen. She was alone, and she might be alone for most of the day. The prospect brought the strange feeling into her body again, a feeling that made it light and happy, a feeling that urged her to lift her feet high from the ground, to jump and run, and even shout.

As the clock in the hall boomed nine she entered the gallery. The rain had stopped and the June sun was flooding the place with light. The binding of the books in the glass cases that lined the long wall stood out like freshly ironed velvets and satins, and this morning she was drawn immedi-ately to them and not toward the windows. All the cases were locked. When she had asked why, her mama had said it was because most of the books were about the history and making of glass and were irreplaceable.

But all the books weren't about glass. She had stood on the library steps and read titles out loud to show her mama how clever she was. The plays and sonnets of William Shakespeare. Who was William Shakespeare?

9

He was a playwright and poet, her mama had said, but his writings were much too old for her yet.

Paradise Lost.

How had paradise come to be lost, Mama?

It was because the gentleman had done wrong. When people did wrong, they lost the good things in life. The more you read your Bible, the more you will come to understand it.

She had brought her Bible with her today and also her French book. Her mama wrote her a little letter in French every day and she wrote one back to her. She had already read this morning's letter. It began: "Mon cher enfant," then said simply, "I wish you a happy day, your loving Mama."

Before her mama had left her this morning she had set her a lesson for today. It was to try to translate parts of the "scripture cake" into French. It didn't matter how many mistakes she made, she said. But she didn't suppose she would make many because she was so good at French.

She and mama spoke in French quite a lot. She couldn't remember a time when they hadn't conversed in French. Nor could she remember a time when she hadn't been able to read or write. Her mama said she was a very clever girl.

She now took out a card from the front of her Bible. The card was headed "SCRIPTURE CAKE" and below were the following ingredients:

4½ cups I Kings 4:22.
1½ cups Judges 5:25, last clause.
2 cups Jeremiah 6:20, 2nd item.
2 cups I Sam. 30:12, do.
2 cups Nahum 3:12.
1 cup Numbers 17:8.
½ cup Judges 4:19, last clause.
2 tablespoonsful I Sam. 14:25.
Season to taste, II Chron. 9:9.
Six of Jeremiah 17:11.
A pinch of Leviticus 2:13.
Two tablespoonsful Amos 4:5 (B. powder).

Follow Solomon's prescription for making a good
girl (Prov. 23:14) and you will have a good cake.

And so taking her seat on the velvet-padded sill that ran the length of the five windows she began to translate:

I Kings 4:22 read: "And Solomon's provision for one day was thirty measures of fine flour, and threescore measures of meal." Then she translated Judges 5:25, and omitting the first clause—"He asked water, and she gave him milk"—she trans-

10

lated the last one, "she brought forth butter in a lordly dish."

She had reached Samuel when Watford came into the gallery. "You all right, Miss Annabella?"

"Yes, Watford, thank you."

"Would you like anything? A cake? Cook's made some lovely meringues."

"Thank you, Watford; I'll have some with my milk."

With sudden, strange tenderness Watford ran her hand over the long brown hair, then said, "Very good, miss."

Watford could be nice at times. When she was happy, she could be very nice. Why weren't people always happy?

The black oak door at the far end of the gallery opened and brought her head jerking round to see Constantine entering with a great bundle of soiled linen tied up in a sheet. As he passed her he smiled widely in her direction, saying, "Mornin', missie."

"Good-morning, Constantine."

Constantine always smiled at her and spoke to her. She liked Constantine, but this was something she had to keep to herself because her mama didn't like the black man. She called him a black man, but it was only his hair that was really black.

After Constantine had returned and disappeared through the black oak door again and Watford had brought her milk and meringue, there unfolded in her a feeling that was quite the reverse of that which she had experienced when she entered the gallery. It was a dull, listless, heavy feeling. She did not put the name of boredom to it; she only knew she didn't like it and that it made her lose interest in her lessons. It made her look out of the window, even stand on the sill to get a better view. She was doing this when she saw the children.

She knew they were children because they didn't look the size of gardeners, more the size of rabbits, and like rabbits that had been startled, they kept disappearing into the hedge that bordered the orchard. When they were lost to her sight, she whispered aloud, "Oh, let them come back." She hadn't seen any children since her cousin Stephen had come to dinner, and that was weeks ago. But Stephen wasn't children, he was quite grown-up; he was fourteen and went away to school, and he slept there, too. That must be very exciting, she had said to him, and he had laughed. She liked her cousin Stephen, she liked him very much. He had gentle ways, very much like those of Mama. Mama said his father, her only brother, who had died, had been like Stephen, gentle

11

in everything he did, and she had added that God always took those he loved when they were young.

But now here were real children, right here in the garden. Swiftly she jumped down from the sill, ran along to the end of the gallery nearest the oak door, and from a shelf attached to a bookcase she lifted from its stand the spy glass. The spy glass wasn't forbidden her; sometimes her mama said, "Would you like to play with the spy glass?" and looking through it, she had brought the birds on the far trees right up to the gallery windows. And so now, clambering back onto the sill, she supported the heavy long glass against her right eye; then, closing her left, she focused on the orchard. And then she saw them, the children, quite plainly, as if they were in the court below. There were two girls and a boy and they were all without stockings. She couldn't see if they had shoes on because their feet were buried in the grass. But the girls' dresses were short and ragged, hanging just below their knees, and the boy had one trouser leg longer than the other.

The glass became so heavy that she had to lower it from her eye. When she next looked through it, she saw the smaller girl ramming strawberries into her mouth. She didn't seem to be stopping to take out the stalks, just pulling them from the plant and ramming them into her mouth. But the boy was piling them into his cap, then emptying them into the bigger girl's pinafore. As she watched them, there returned to her the nice feeling, and she wanted to jump, jump right from the sill, over the gardens and the lake, right into the strawberry field that bordered the orchard.

How long would it take her if she ran all the way from the side door? Five minutes perhaps, less if she ran by the middens. But she wasn't allowed to go down by the middens; even Watford had forbidden her to go down that path when they were playing hide and seek; yet it would cut the distance by half and she could say hello to those children and be back here within a very short time.

Without stopping to consider further, she was out of the gallery and running down the long corridor; she paused before crossing the landing, but there was no one in sight, and then she was going down the back staircase. She had come to know the back staircase during those periods when her mama was absent from the house, for then Watford used it as a shortcut to the kitchen.

She paused before opening the door that led into the side courtyard. When cautiously she peered round it, there was

12

no one in the yard, only the sound of voices coming from the stables at the far end. Her feet, as if borne on wings, carried her through the archway and down the pagoda walk, at the end of which she swung left and through a narrow opening and onto a pathway that led in one direction to the middens, in the other back to the main courtyard.

The middens turned out to be a series of big holes in the ground and a number of mounds, and she knew as she passed them why the place was forbidden her. She nipped her nose and put her head down and ran on until she came to the stream which took the overflow from the pools, and which, until twenty years ago when the well was sunk, had been the main source of water supply for the Hall. Once across the stream, she ran up the steep incline, and on reaching the top she paused a moment and looked down. And then she saw them. They were no longer picking the strawberries but sitting under the hedge eating them as fast as they could.

She did not want to startle them, so she kept on the other side of the hedge until she came to the orchard; then going through the same gap by which they had entered the field, she made her presence known to them by simply standing and smiling at them over the distance.

The result of the apparition on the three children had differing effects. It made the boy dive headfirst into the hawthorn thicket in an effort to escape. It made the smaller girl cry out, "Ma! Ma!" But it reduced the older girl into a fear-filled trance from which she neither spoke nor moved, only stared unblinking at the silk-clad, ribbon-bedecked girl of her own age.

"Do . . . do you like strawberries?" The voice and what it said stopped the boy's struggling limbs; it stopped the child crying; and it caused the elder girl to come slowly out of her trance.

"May I help you to pick some?"

"Whoyou?"

She was well accustomed to the Northern idiom, but she had difficulty in making out what the girl was saying. Then the boy was standing up making the question plainer. "You from here?"

"You mean, do I live here? Yes." She inclined her head politely toward them. "My name is Annabella Lagrange."

The boy and the girl looked at each other; then the boy, looking at Annabella again, said in thick, guttural tones, "You say we can pick some?"

"Yes, yes, of course, as many as you want. They get sick

13

of them, I mean the servants. Watford says they feed them to the pigs." She smiled widely. It was nice talking to someone of her own age.

When the three pairs of eyes continued to stare at her, she said, "I would help you but I have to get back; I'm doing my lessons." That was a better explanation than saying she was afraid that Watford would miss her.

When they didn't speak, she asked, "Where are you from?"

The boy and the girl again exchanged glances before the boy answered, "Rosier's village."

"Oh, Mr. Rosier's village. Oh, I've driven through there. My papa knows Mr. Rosier."

"Aye, we do an' all." This retort came quickly and with such bitterness that it turned the boy's voice into that of a man and it stilled the happy feeling inside her; and she stared back into their eyes and after a moment asked, "Are you hungry?"

And now it was the girl who replied, "Yes, miss, all the time. They're on strike and we've been turned out; the Irish are in."

She couldn't quite follow this. The only thing of which she was aware was that the three faces that were looking at her were hungry faces. She had never glimpsed such faces before; even when she went out in the carriage with her mama and had seen poor people, they hadn't looked as these children looked. She said now quietly, "If you went up to the house and asked cook, I'm sure she would give you something to eat."

The boy's voice came again, thick, bitter and hesitant now. "You can't go nowhere near that back door unless you've got a penny."

"A penny?"

"Aye, the bits 'ave got to be paid for there; an' we haven't got no money, now."

When she moved a step nearer to them, they backed as one toward the hedge, and she said, "You mean you have to give cook a penny before she will give you any food?"

"Aye, that's what I mean, scraps."

She said now slowly, "I have my dinner at three o'clock, but I've got to rest after; could you come back at half-past four and I will bring you some of it?"

When they didn't answer her, she said, "If I'm very late and you can't wait, I could put it"—she looked around, then pointed to the hedge where the boy had tried to get through—"in there. I would wrap it in a napkin. But I've got to go now." She paused and looked from one to the other. "Good-bye."

Not one of them spoke and she turned from them and went through the gap and up the incline and down the other side, past the stream and the sewers, and entered the house by the way she had left. But she hadn't run one step of the distance, and she didn't mind if anyone saw her or not; but she met no one until she opened the gallery door, and then she saw Watford.

Watford was standing with her hands cupping her face and staring toward the oak door at the far end of the room. And now she turned toward her and she jumped and was as startled as the children had been at the sight of her, and then she had her hands on her shoulders as if she were going to shake her, but instead she gasped, "Where did you get to?"

Her mama said it was wrong to tell a lie. If you couldn't speak the truth, you had to be silent. But this was an occasion when she couldn't speak the truth nor yet could she be silent. This was an occasion for—what was that word?—diplomacy. "I went to the closet," she said, "and then I wanted another book." It was better to give two places. "I'm sorry I've worried you."

"You went to the closet by yourself? Are you clean?" Watford pulled her round a little and looked at the back of her dress as if seeking for evidence.

"Of course, Watford." There was a slight note of indignation in the reply, and Watford smiled, drew in a deep breath and said, "Of course you would be, you're a good girl. But eeh! I was worried. I just couldn't find you. I went to the classroom an' to the nursery an' you weren't there."

"I—I came round the long corridor. I like to look at the pictures there." Once started on this diplomacy, it was quite easy. One had only to be—what was that other word?— inventive. She said now, "Do you think I could have another meringue, Watford, please? Or perhaps two?"

"Oh lor', miss, yes. Aye, of course. I'll go and get them right away; cook'll be over the moon 'cause you like them."

Annabella now said, "Please tell cook I like them very much. And—and, Watford, if—if there's an apple or any fruit, I would like some; it's a long time until dinner."

"Why, miss—" Watford bent down and looked into her face as she said, "I'll bring you anything you want. Would you like a tray?"

"Oh yes, Watford. Thank you very much."

A few minutes later Watford, her hand raised in the air, exclaimed to cook, "What did I tell you? Her dull appetite's all because the child's fed on the Bible and such like; she's not like a child of seven at all, more like one of ten, or twelve, sometimes like an old professor. 'May I have a meringue, Watford?' she said. 'Two,' I said; 'the cook will be over the moon.' I tell you, once she's left to me on me own, she's different. I've always said it." She leaned over the table. "Make her a plate up of ham and tongue, an' a piece of that Camembert on it. Give her a treat." Suddenly dropping onto a chair, she exclaimed with slow, weighed words, "Lord! I'm tellin' you, cook, I nearly had a fit. I tell you I nearly died. I thought she had gone through the door at the other end."

At one o'clock Watford took her for a walk in the garden. The sun was out and the ground was steaming, and the smell from the rose gardens was as drowsy-making as a drug, and Watford blamed the atmosphere for Annabella's lethargy, for she didn't want to play ball or hide-and-seek, all she wanted to do was to sit and talk, and all about the strangest things; about the people who lived outside; about Mr. Rosier's village. She had never mentioned Mr. Rosier's village before, not to her knowledge, but then, of course, her mother and she might talk about it, Rosier being a friend of the master's. And, as she related to Ada Rawlings afterwards, she had the wits startled out of her when the child asked, "Do you know what it feels like to be hungry, Watford?" and she had replied truthfully, "No, miss, I don't."

Thank God she had never been hungry. And that was partly owing to having Mrs. Page for a great-aunt and her being housekeeper in the Hall for the past eighteen years. She didn't like her aunt, she had never liked her, but she had her to thank for this grand job and, moreover, for never being hungry. Having been born and bred in the village of Jarrow with its fluctuating fortunes, its coke ovens and salt pans disappearing, and men having to learn new trades, like building iron ships—and who had ever heard of anybody building an iron ship?—work came and went, and food came and went much more quickly. Oh aye, she and her family had a lot to thank their Aunt Eve for, so she could truthfully say to Miss Annabella she had never been hungry. But what a question to be asked! And, as she said to Ada, on a steaming hot day an' all.

At three o'clock Watford, assisted by Cargill, the third

16

footman, brought her dinner up to the nursery day room and laid it out on the round inlaid mahogany table. Uncovering the first dish, she smiled at her charge and said, "There, a little sole with cream, it's lovely."

"What else is there, Watford?"

"What else, miss? Oh!" Watford seemed pleased at her young mistress's sudden interest in food. "Well now, knowing that you've got an appetite, I've brought you some veal fillet an' braised ham an' a little breast of cold fowl and three vegetables. Now, how's that?"

"Very nice, thank you, Watford."

"And there for your dessert"—she pointed to a cut-glass dish—"is an iced puddin' all for yourself."

"Thank you, Watford; it's very kind of you."

"That's all right, miss; I'm glad you're eatin'."

"Watford!"

"Yes, miss?"

"I can see to myself; you can go and have your own dinner."

"You can, miss? Do you think you can manage?"

"Oh yes, yes, I'm sure I can, Watford."

"Well, miss, if you're sure. Now, you're positive?"

"Yes, I'm positive, Watford. You go and have your dinner."

Watford stared down at her charge, into the green eyes half-shaded with the long, dark lashes, and as she stared she thought, She's a nice lass, an' she could be pretty, but at this moment she could go either way. And what if the religion she's having pumped into her doesn't catch on and she takes after him an' turns out a devil? Eeh! because no matter which way you look at it, he is a devil. The mistress not being out of the house a few hours and his order coming downstairs for a plentiful meal to be taken up. They all knew what a plentiful meal meant, enough for two, if not three. But no, it would only be two today. And he ordered his bath water up at half-past three. Of course, he took baths at all hours of the day, that was no surprise, but to have his dinner at five he was cutting it fine, when the mistress could be home any time after six. But then she came by the west drive and the master's visitors always came by the east drive, and then only halfway along it; and when the carriage stopped, they had to walk the rest of the way. He was careful in his ways was the master, and being a gentleman he didn't flaunt his pastime openly. If the mistress knew what was going on, it was more by guesswork than anything else, she surmised. It was an odd setup in this house altogether, religion in one side and whoring in the other. But she wasn't going to grumble about either, oh no. With ten pounds a year and an extra allowance made for tea, sugar and beer, she was in clover, and if she knew anything, she was going to stay in clover.

"Is there something wrong with my face? Have I got a speck on it?"

"No, no, miss; I was just lookin' at you. You're seven the morrow, you're growing up."

"Yes, Watford, yes, I'm growing up. I may have a governess soon."

"What!" It was a high exclamation, almost a shout. "Who said? Who said you were going to have a governess?"

"Papa said I should, but Mama isn't in agreement."

"Oh! Well, get your dinner, eat it all up." She turned about and went hastily out of the room. A governess. That would change the situation, and not for the better. But still, if the mistress was against a governess and wanted to go on doing the teaching herself, there was hope that it would come to nothing, for whereas the master's word was law in everything in the house, it was tempered toward the upbringing of his daughter. And that was funny when you knew the ins and outs of the whole affair. Yet she supposed, as they all supposed down below, that he had to temper the wind to the shorn lamb. And he was a shorn lamb pretty more often than not where money was concerned. As Mr. Harris said, you'd have to have a gold mine an' minting it on the premises to keep up with the master's wants. Sometimes she thought that the butler didn't like the master; likely this was because he had served the mistress's father for years, having started like Cargill was now, third footman; but he, too, knew on which side his bread was buttered and had the sense to see his feet were placed right, one in each camp.

After dinner it was the rule that Annabella should rest on her couch for a while, but today she had taken advantage of the situation and asked Watford if she could return to the gallery, there to pursue her books, and Watford had been very agreeable. And so it was that she watched Faill and Cargill carrying the great copper cans of boiling water along the gallery and leaving them outside the oak door, from where Constantine picked them up and took them into the mysterious depths beyond.

After making their sixth journey with the cans, Faill said

to Constantine, "How's that? Enough?" and the Negro nodded his head and said, "Enough."

When the green-liveried, silk-stockinged men had gone back through the door into the House, Annabella watched Constantine lift two of the remaining cans, and with his buttocks thrusting out, he pushed the door wide, then taking two steps he flicked back his leg and aimed his heel at the bottom of the door, which action, up till now, had closed it.

Annabella waited for the door to close softly as it always did, but today it didn't close. Getting off the sill, she hurried up the gallery. When she reached the door, it was in a position she had never seen before, one third open. Greatly daring, she put her head on one side and looked through the opening, and there, stretching before her, was a fairy-tale hall of enchantment. Numbers of glass chandeliers hung from the ceiling; not just four as in the hall of the House, but eight, twelve, she couldn't count, and the wall that she could see to the right of her was alive with color; great portraits in gold frames covered the walls right up to the ceiling. The carpet was a warm glowing red, not faded like the one in the gallery. In the few seconds during which she had taken in the spectacle, she had also been watching Constantine's back, and it was at the moment that she saw him disappear into a room halfway down the hall that she heard her father's laugh. It was soft and thick and happy. He always laughed like that when he was happy; he must have a friend with him, perhaps Mr. Rosier. Her papa had introduced her to Mr. Rosier once. If she saw Mr. Rosier today, she would ask him why the people in his village were hungry. No one should be hungry, and if Mr. Rosier couldn't feed people, her papa would. Look at all the food that was in the larders and cellars below; whole beasts, and pigs, eggs by the hundred and milk by the gallon. She felt that it was only her father's ignorance of the matter that caused it to exist; once he knew people were hungry, he would feed them. Her father was kind.

She didn't remember stepping over the threshold; it only came to her that she had done so when Constantine's steps, coming muffled from the distance, created the instinct to hide, and quickly she pushed open the first door she came to and went inside. She did not quite close the door after her but held it ajar, and, peeping through it, she saw Constantine passing up the hall carrying the last two cans. After that, she turned and, with her back to the door, looked about the room. It was very disappointing because all the furniture was shrouded in dust covers; but here, too, the walls were thick with paintings, and on one wall, opposite a big open fireplace, the sun was shining full on the pictures and the people in them seemed to be alive. Slowly she walked toward the wall and looked upwards, until her mouth fell into a most unladylike gape. She was looking at lots of ladies and a gentleman, but they were different ladies from any she had ever seen, and the gentleman wasn't really a gentleman, he was all hairy and frightening, but they were dancing and drinking and they were uncovered.

Never before had she seen any part of a human body except the face, hands and feet. She had never seen her own body because Watford, after taking off her dress and top petticoats, put over her head the linen cape and took off the remainder of her things in this manner, and in the morning she again put on the linen cape before she took her night-dress off; old Alice had shown Watford how it should be done. She couldn't remember at what age she had commenced this form of dressing and undressing, but she remembered the old woman demonstrating it to the new nursemaid. And then there was the bathing. Some part of her objected to the practice that was imposed on her when she had a bath, but she did not protest against being blindfolded before her drawers and linen stays were taken off, because to protest, she felt, would be a form of sin, sin against something. What this something was she wasn't quite sure, not yet. This sense of sin weighed heavily on her and frightened her in the night when she put her hands under her nightdress and felt the contours of her stomach and the parts where her legs were joined to it.

As if in a trance, she moved on along the wall until she was brought to a halt by the picture of a little girl kneeling at a couch with a woman standing to the side of it rolling up her sleeves. These two figures were well in the background but they drew her attention immediately because she saw herself as a little girl and the figure as retribution for sin. The little girl was going to be smacked, perhaps because, like herself, she had been looking at the lady in the front of the picture. The lady was lying on a white couch and at her feet was a little dog. This lady, too, was uncovered; but she did not look as if she were afraid of sin; she looked happy. She moved farther toward the picture and read the tablet beneath it: "The Venus of Urbino." What was a Venus? A

lady likely, a lady with no clothes on. And who was Titian?
Slowly she moved away and looked at other pictures, and
there was the name again, Titian, and it came to her that he
was the gentleman who had painted these ladies. He must
have been a very sinful man, like some of the men in the
Bible.

She stood in the middle of the room now and looked about
her. It wasn't as big as the drawing room in the House, but
it was nicer somehow, warmer, even though the rough stone
walls could be seen all around the fireplace and windows.
But why was the furniture covered up and not the pictures?
She felt it was the pictures that should be covered up. It was
very puzzling.

And then the sound of her father's laughter came to her
again, muted and far away, and it drew her moving slowly
and cautiously into the hallway.

There were pictures here too, but these were pictures of
blue- and scarlet-robed people sitting stiffly in chairs. There
was a battle scene with men on horses, but on closer in-
spection she found the riders were only chasing ladies; but
these ladies had clothes on.

She had reached halfway along the hallway when it came
to her, and forcibly, that she shouldn't be here at all. Her
mama had warned her never to pass beyond the oak door.
"Annabella," she had said, "you must not. Now listen to me.
You must not, never, never, go into Papa's house," and she
had answered, "Yes, Mama," but had dared to add, "But if
Papa took me in that would be quite in order, Mama, wouldn't
it?" And her mama had looked away and said, "Your papa
will not take you in; it is a house just for grown-ups, for your
papa and his friends. He thinks the same as I do; he has no
wish that you should go into his private house. Anyway,"
she had ended, "you can see all you want of Papa here."

But she never saw enough of her papa, and something
warned her now that her papa would not wish to see her
today, not when he was with his friends.

She was about to turn and hurry back toward the oak door
and to the safety of the gallery again when she saw Constantine passing along a passage at the far end. He was
carrying a tray of cutlery, and if he had turned his head
just the slightest, he would have seen her. She didn't know
whether he was going into a door opposite or coming toward
her, but in real fright she darted toward a door on her left,
and, pressing herself against the deep lintel, she remained

21

tautly still for a moment. Unconsciously her hand had gripped the knob of the door, and now she was turning it. The next second she was inside, and again she was gaping.

She was in a bedroom, a beautiful bedroom. It must be her papa's bedroom. There, in the middle, was a four-poster bed draped in blue silk curtains. The carpet, too, was blue, but the furniture was all gilt with rose upholstery. It was very, very beautiful. Her papa wouldn't mind her looking at his bedroom.

As she slowly walked toward the bed, she became aware of the big white sheet lying at the foot of it and, standing on it, the porcelain bath. This, too, was covered over with a sheet through which the steam was slowly evaporating. What she should have noticed right away but what was just dawning on her now was that all the blinds were drawn and the room was lit by two glass candelabra, each holding at least twenty candles, and these were standing on tables at each side of the bed head. Her papa, too, then had to have his bath in the dark; well, not in the black dark as she endured her bathing. But perhaps, just before he took his clothes off, Constantine would extinguish the candles. Her stomach began to tremble. She must get away. If her papa found her in his bedroom and he about to bathe, he'd be very angry.

When her father's voice, the words smothered in laughter, came to her from a door to the right of the bed, she turned so swiftly about that she tripped and just saved herself from falling into the bath itself. But she was on her knees when the door opened and with the scurrying movement of a frightened beetle she scampered on all fours up by the side of the bed and toward the shelter of a screen in a corner of the room. Having reached safety, for a moment she lay on her face, her hands pressed tightly over her head and ears.

What brought her hands from her ears was not the sound of running feet, but the vibration that passed through her body from the floor. Slowly she raised her head and looked toward the light streaming through the fretwork of the screen, and as she had put her eye to the spy glass earlier in the day, she now put both eyes to two holes in the screen and witnessed a most unusual sight. Her papa, dressed in a long green robe with a high collar, was chasing a lady around the room. He was still making use of his stick and limping, but he ran at times. They were playing a game of tag, and every time her papa caught the lady, he took off one of her garments and put a strawberry in her mouth, until at last she had nothing on but her stays.

22

Now the lady was standing with her back to the screen, blocking out the light. She could see nothing of what was happening now, she could only hear. The lady was laughing softly and her father was talking, but they were strange words, words that she hadn't heard before, and she couldn't understand them. Then the light was 'in her eyes again and she saw the lady once more. She was just like the one in the picture in the room along the hallway, except that she was younger.

She kept her eyes riveted on the lady, finding it impossible to look away; that was until she saw her father fling off his robe and lift the lady into the bath.

The sight of her father's bare legs and buttocks caused her whole body to shrink away from the screen, and again she was lying with her face to the floor, one hand pressed tightly against her mouth in case she cried out.

Her papa was wicked, he would go to hell; everybody who looked at his own body was destined for hell. Old Alice said that over and over again. She felt sick with fear, fear for her father, and fear of him. Her body was wet with perspiration. She was going to have a fainting seizure like her mama had. She wanted her mama, oh, she wanted her mama; she was going to be sick, really sick. Yet she hadn't eaten much food at dinnertime; she had hidden two-thirds of it away in napkins to take to the children. The children! They would be waiting. They would think she hadn't meant what she had said. Her mama had impressed on her never to promise anything unless she meant to keep her promise. Oh! Oh! she was going to be sick.

When the food regurgitated into her mouth and spewed through her fingers she pushed helplessly against the screen with her other hand, and when it toppled she saw through her misted eyes the contorted figures of her papa and the lady on the bed. Their limbs were locked together but their faces were turned toward her, staring at her as if she herself were a devil.

She fainted away on a high, cursing scream that not only vibrated through the Old Hall but penetrated into the House and brought figures flying from every direction.

She was brought partly out of her faint by the cries of Constantine, whimpering, frightening cries, and she raised her heavy lids and looked up into the face hanging over hers. It was the face of the lady, and she was praying, saying, "Oh, my Gord! oh, my Gord!" And it came to her that she couldn't be really wicked if she prayed. Then she heard Con-

23

stantine's voice again, coming in protesting moans, and she saw her father punching at the Negro while the man cowered against the wall, and when he slid to the ground, her father grabbed something that had been hanging on the wall and beat him with it.

When next she regained consciousness she was in her own bed and her father was sitting by her side. His face was not angry-looking, nor was his voice harsh. She tried to recollect what she had seen and for the moment could think of nothing but that she must have been dreaming, one of those dreams that fade away when you open your eyes, and her father immediately confirmed this. As he stroked the hair back from her brow, he looked straight into her eyes and said, "You've had a bad dream, You ate too much at dinner and were sick. You've had a bad dream, Annabella."

"Yes, Papa." Her voice was faint and, even to herself, far-away-sounding.

"Your mama will be very angry with me when she comes home. She will think that she cannot leave you for a day but that you must take ill, and she will blame me."

She didn't say, "Yes, Papa," or "No, Papa, she won't," she just lay looking up at him. He was still dressed in his blue robe and she wondered if he had put on any clothes underneath; then she chastised herself strongly: she must not think like that. If she thought about what she had seen, it would make her papa wicked, and he wasn't wicked. She looked from one feature of his face to another, from his fair hair still unruly as it had been when she saw him on the bed, the light gray eyes, the long straight nose, the wide full mouth, the lips gleaming softly with saliva as he kept rubbing his tongue over them. Her father was beautiful. She loved looking at his face; he couldn't be wicked—yet he was. She knew he was.

"You've had a nasty dream, haven't you, Annabella?" The gray eyes were staring down into hers and she looked back at them for a long while before she said, "Yes, Papa."

"And we'll say nothing to Mama about it?"

Again time elapsed before she answered, "No, Papa."

"We wouldn't want to distress your mama in any way, would we?"

"No, Papa."

"Do you know what I'm getting you for your birthday?"

"No, Papa."

"A pony."

24

"Thank you, Papa."

"Aren't you excited?"

No, she wasn't excited, because she was afraid of ponies and horses. Her mama knew she was afraid and had said she was too young to have an animal, but her papa had just laughed and said every child loved to ride. And now her papa was talking about the pony in order to make her forget that she had seen a strange lady in his bedroom. He was telling her that she had dreamed everything that had happened. Her papa was wicked, but how she wished he wasn't, oh, she did, she did, because she loved him.

He bent and kissed her now and said softly, "Do you love me, Annabella?"

There was no hesitation now. "Yes, Papa."

He stroked her cheek softly as he muttered low in his throat, "Go on loving me; never stop loving me."

And, shutting out the past hour, she said fervently, "I won't, Papa, ever."

Then in the next minute she stopped loving him, because when he went into the day room, she heard the sound of a ringing slap and Watford cry out; this was followed by a dull thud as from a fist against padded flesh. Then her father's voice low, almost a whisper, but to her acute hearing still audible, said, "She's had a bad dream, remember, she's had a bad dream. If one word of this leaks out to your mistress, you'll find yourself outside those gates, and you won't get into service within six counties, I'll see to that. Do you understand?"

It was some time before the whimpered reply came, and then the day-room door banged.

When she rose from the bed and put her feet on the footstool, she still felt a little dizzy and sick and she had to remain quiet for a moment before she could step down onto the floor.

On entering the day room she saw Watford with her head resting on her arms on the table and her shoulders shaking with her smothered sobbing. As she put her hand on her shoulder, Watford almost jumped from the chair, and, licking at the tears raining down her face, she gulped, "Oh, miss. Oh, miss, get back into bed. You shouldn't; you shouldn't."

"It's all right, Watford. Sit down, and please—please don't cry."

Watford sat down, and, cupping her inflamed cheek with one hand, she rocked herself as she said, "Oh, miss, you shouldn't have—" cutting off the sentence in drooping her

25

head. But her head jerked up immediately when the child before her said solemnly, "I went to sleep and had a bad dream, Watford."

The effect of this statement was to make Watford again lay her head on her arms and cry even louder, and all the while Annabella stood by her side and patted her shoulder. She had a desire to put her arms about Watford and comfort her, but somehow she thought her mama would not have approved.

Watford was again brought into an upright position when her charge said simply, "Papa is a wicked man, Watford."

"Oh, no, no, miss." Watford now caught hold of both of her hands and shook them up and down in agitation. "You must never, never say that. Oh, no. No. The master's not wicked, no, no, miss."

"But—but he struck you, Watford."

Watford shook her head several times, finding speech at the moment impossible, and then blurted out, "He didn't hit me, miss, not the master; no, no, the master's a good man. Always remember that, he's a good man."

"But Watford—"

"Look, miss." Watford got to her feet. "I'll wash your face and hands; it'll freshen you up a bit. You've been upset, you've—you've had a bad dream as you said, but—but remember"—she bent down to Annabella—"remember, the master—your papa is a good man. He's a gentleman and gentlemen are not bad, not gentlemen like the master. No matter what they do, they're not bad. Remember that, Miss Annabella, gentlemen are never bad."

After Watford had washed her face and hands and dabbed eau de cologne on her brow and wrists, changed her dress and pinafore, combed her hair and put fresh ribbons in it, Annabella said to her, "Would you take me for a walk to the strawberry field, Watford?"

"You want some strawberries, miss?" Watford managed to smile.

"No, Watford; but—but I've got to see someone."

"See someone?"

As Annabella looked up at Watford she became aware of new emotions, new trends of thought. She wouldn't be seven until tomorrow, but in the last hour she had grown up a great deal. She had discovered that you could love someone one minute and not love them the next, then love them again; you could have feelings that were not love but which were nice, and kind, like those she had for Watford. Yet at one

26

and the same time there was this new feeling, this feeling that put her in a position of power. She realized, without fully understanding, that the events of the past hour had given her power, not only over this woman, and not only over the other servants in the household, but over her father. She held a secret, a dream, that could make people do what she wanted. She said now quite quietly, "There are some poor children, they are very hungry, they were eating strawberries because they hadn't anything else. I've saved half of my dinner; I want to take it to them."

"Po-po-poor children? How do you know any p-poor children?"

"I told you a lie this morning, Watford. I said that I had been to the closet and the schoolroom when I had really gone outside. I saw the children from the gallery and ran out to speak to them. They were very frightened and very hungry."

"OH, MY GOD!"

These were the same words as the lady had used, but Annabella now knew that they were not said in the form of a prayer.

Watford had moved two steps away from her and was looking at her most oddly, and then she said, "What's come over you, miss, what's come over you? You've never been like this afore."

"Will you take me down or shall I go myself?"

Annabella watched Watford put her fingers tightly across her mouth; then she said almost in a whimper, "They're scum, miss, those brats. They're from the fells livin' wild. Their folks neither work nor want; they're from Rosier's village. If they would do what they're told and not strike, they'd have food and shelter. They're bad, miss, they're very bad."

"Will you take me down, Watford?"

Again Watford used the expression that wasn't a prayer, and then she swallowed deeply and said, "Where did you put the food?"

"In one of the cabinets in the gallery under the bookcase."

Ten minutes later Watford informed a glaring, greatly troubled housekeeper that she was going to take Miss Annabella into the air, and when her great-aunt just stared at her, making no comment whatever, she knew she was saving all she had to say for later when the child was abed and she was off duty. She hurried back to the nursery, where Annabella was waiting for her dressed for outside in an alpaca coat and cream bonnet and carrying in her hand a small basket in which lay a napkin containing the food.

27

The journey to the field was made in silence, and when they reached it, there was no sign of the children, but Annabella, under the accusing eyes of Watford, laid the napkin under the hedge, and Watford, looking down at the hideyhole, said, "This is dreadful, awful. You don't know what you're doing, Miss Annabella, encouraging them, 'cause they're bad, that lot, idlers, nothin' but scum."

On the journey back to the house, her hand held firmly in Watford's, Annabella pondered the fact of how strange it was that her father, besides bathing a strange lady, could beat Constantine, who served him so faithfully, and hit Watford, who served her so faithfully, yet could still be considered a good man, but that the children who were so hungry they rammed the strawberries into their mouths with the stalks on, and were so poor that their clothes were in rags, were bad. It was all very puzzling; she wanted it explained to her. She wished, oh, how she wished she could talk to her mama about it.

2

From the moment Rosina Lagrange entered the house she knew that something had happened during her absence, although on the surface everything was as usual.

Before the coach had stopped, Faill was on the drive, and when the horses were brought to a standstill it was he who opened the door and let down the steps and then extended his hand to assist her, and with the usual quiet courtesy she used toward servants, she thanked him.

In the plant-lined conservatory, Harris, his portly figure encased in black as befitted his rank, bowed toward her, saying, "May I hope that you've had a pleasant journey, madam?"

"It was very agreeable, Harris, thank you," she replied; then turning to where an old woman was lumbering into the conservatory burdened by a long box, she said, "Relieve Miss Piecliff of that package, Harris, but be careful with it and see that it's taken up to the nursery." Whereupon Harris took from the old governess the long box which he guessed held a doll, then almost as if it burned his fingers, he passed it on to Armorer, the second lackey, who had been hovering in the background.

Three steps from the broad staircase, Mrs. Page was waiting. Her gray serge was impeccable; her goffered cap was set straight on top of her head, of which there wasn't a hair out of place, but the fingers which clasped each other in front of her waistband moved nervously over the chatelaine which was hanging there, and the lid of her right eye was twitching.

During years of saying little, and looking and listening much, Rosina had learned to observe such things.

"I hope that you've had an enjoyable day, madam, and that the journey hasn't been too much for you?"

"The journey was more pleasant than usual, Mrs. Page, thank you. Miss Annabella, she's quite well?"

There was the slightest pause before Mrs. Page answered, "Yes, madam. She's about to take her bath, and I'm sure she's anxious to see you."

Rosina inclined her head toward her housekeeper, then mounted the stairs, followed by Alice Amelia Piecliff.

Alice Piecliff was always addressed to her face by the staff as Miss Piecliff. Having, from governess, taken on the position of lady's maid to Rosina's mother, Mrs. Constance Conway-Redford, then devoted the same two services to Rosina herself, she was a person to be reckoned with in Redford Hall. She had power far above that of Harris, and as for the next in the hierarchy, Mrs. Page, she could flaw that formidable lady with a look.

Alice Piecliff was seventy years old; she was thin, and her face showed no wrinkles, only gray skin stretched over protruding bones. She wore, without variation, black silk, and when she went abroad she donned a black bead bonnet and matching cape that came well below her knees. She believed firmly in God and beheld Him each night from her knees as a gigantic figure in white flowing robes, and always He had His hand held high admonishing her to prepare herself for the life to come. She had two weaknesses which caused her often to explain to her forbidding God that they in no way detracted from her love and fear of Himself. The weaknesses stemmed from the same source: she adored milady, as she called Rosina's mother, and she loved Rosina with a love that she would have given to her own child had the creation of such a being not been denied her on account of its being connected with man and sin.

Her relationship with the mother and daughter to whom, one or the other, she had given all her working life was unique, for she was the confidante of both, and perhaps because she had brought them up, so to speak, she could talk to them in a fashion that was indeed privileged, for this was the age when most servants were considered just a grade higher than animals and, at best, could rise only to a position of authority over their own kind; this was the age when the desire to read made a man or woman suspect by his employer. Of the forty-five servants on the estate and farm, not one of them could read or write and no one showed any inclination to alter the situation because each knew his place in life and kept it. Anyway, why should they bother their heads about learning, it got you nowhere, only into trouble, as was proved by those who started the strikes in Rosier's Pit and in the Jarrow Shipyard.

All the employees at Redford Hall knew they were well in. The Redfords had looked after their people for as far back as three hundred years, and, although Edmund Lagrange was master now, there was still a Redford on the estate, a Redford who counted, a Mistress Constance Redford. But still, as some said, it wouldn't make all that difference when she was gone because Lagrange was a good master, free with his money—or her money, whose it was didn't matter; he spent, and there was always plenty for everybody, and always the opportunity to make a bit on the side. Live and let live, that was the motto that got you by, so why bother your brain by wanting to read or write? Do a modicum of work, have a full belly and silver in your pocket at the end of the year, this was life, and you'd have this life as long as you kept your place and had no fancy ideas. This policy of the staff was well known to Alice Piecliff, and because of it she considered them as much beneath her as did her mistress.

When they entered the dressing room, she ripped off her cape and bonnet and dropped them onto a chair; then, going to the assistance of her mistress, she helped her off with her gray silk dustcoat, then unpinned her large pale-blue straw hat which was trimmed with a single ribbon and had only one flower lying on its brim. Then flicking her fingers here and there, she pushed the hoops of her skirt into place so that she could sit down before the dressing table.

"Something's happened, Alice." Rosina looked into the mirror, waiting for a reply, but Alice took her time as was customary with her. First of all, she took a pad of cotton wool and liberally sprinkled it with eau de cologne; then standing behind her mistress, she dabbed at first one temple and then the other before saying, "Well, you've always had a nose for such things and it's never led you astray yet. Didn't you feel it—the tension?"

"Yes, I felt something. Mistress Page I saw was uneasy."

30

They now stared at each other in the mirror; then Rosina said softly, "She said the child was all right. I—I must go and see her."

"There's plenty of time. Rest yourself awhile, she won't run away."

It was as Alice finished speaking that the cry came from above and caused them both to look sharply upwards. Before it came a second time, Rosina was at the door. She did not run along the corridor to the stairs because she never ran, but her steps were so rapid that they left Alice far behind. Before she reached the nursery door she heard her daughter shouting as she had never shouted since she was a small child, having in the meantime learned to control her emotions, but now, when she entered the nursery, she was amazed to see her standing in her stays and bodice and using her hand in a smacking motion toward Watford.

"Annabella!"

"Oh, Mama." The child turned and flung herself against her mother's wide skirt. Her arms spread across it, she lifted her tear-stained face upwards, crying over and over again, "Oh, Mama! Oh, Mama!"

'What is this, Watford?'

"I—I don't know what's come over her, madam, I don't. She just won't have the blindfold on. She's never been like this afore."

"She won't have what on?"

"The blindfold, madam."

"The blindfold?" Rosina's hand became still on top of her thick auburn hair; her tone still even, she said, "What are you talking about? What blindfold?"

Now Watford, her mouth in an elongated gape, was looking from her mistress to her mistress's maid, and not until her mistress said, "Well, I'm waiting," did she close her mouth and mutter, "She's always blindfolded afore I take the last of her things off to get into the bath."

"She's always blindfolded?" Now Rosina's voice was spiraling. "You mean to say—Who gave this order?"

When Watford again looked toward Alice, Rosina turned her head slowly and met the gaze of the woman who was closer to her than her mother, or even her child; then after a moment she turned back toward the agitated nursemaid and, holding out her hand, said, "Give that to me."

When Watford handed her the blindfold, she stared at it before adding, "Never, never—do you hear?—do such a thing again." Then pressing the child from her, and attempting to

31

still the anger she was feeling, she said, "Have your bath now, my dear, and I will return and see you when you are in bed." She paused, looking down at the upturned face, then added with tenderness, "Dry your eyes, there's a good girl, dry your eyes."

In her room once again, she stood stiffly as she looked at the old woman, and her voice, her only real attraction, was now overlaid with incredulity and anger as she said, "How could you do such a thing, Alice?"

Alice stared back into the pale-skinned, long, plain face; then, her chin tilting, she walked to the window, and it said a great deal for the tenure of her position that she could do this before she answered, "I did it to keep her mind clean; she'll come to know sin soon enough."

Rosina was left speechless for a moment as she followed her maid's reasoning; then she said, "Hiding her body from her will only arouse curiosity in her mind."

"What the eye doesn't see the heart doesn't hanker after."

"Don't be foolish, Alice."

"All right, madam, I'm foolish." When Alice used the term "madam" in private, it meant she was upset.

After a moment Rosina sat down heavily on a chair, and joining her hands on her lap, she stared ahead as she said, "Imagine what would have happened had . . . the master found this out." And Alice's answer to this was, "It's a habit that some people could take up with advantage to their souls."

"Oh, Alice." The words were almost a deep groan and Rosina dropped her head onto her chest, and within a second Alice was by her side. Her shaking hands resting on Rosina's shoulder, she whispered, "I'm sorry, I'm sorry. I asked God to show me the way to keep her pure and it came to me; it just came to me like an answer."

At this moment the sound of a distant laugh brought them both taut and straight; then getting up from the chair, Rosina went to the dressing table and picked up a comb and began to pass it through her hair, while Alice, going to the huge wardrobe that almost took up the whole length of one wall, said in a voice that was still trembling, "What will you wear?" and as Rosina replied, "The blue taffeta," there came a tap on the door. Almost at the same time it was opened, and Edmund Lagrange entered the room.

Stopping for a moment, he looked toward his wife's back and said, "I didn't hear the carriage or I would have been down."

Rosina didn't look at her husband in the mirror—she didn't

look at him at all, but she turned her head to the side and in his direction as she said, "We have only been in a few moments."

"How did you stand the journey?" He was limping toward her, leaning heavily on his gold-headed stick.

"It was very agreeable, more so than usual."

"Oh, I'm glad, I'm glad. It's been a beautiful day."

"How is your leg, Edmund?"

"Much better, my dear, so much so that I've decided to go downstairs to supper this evening. I sent word to Harris. I'm sure you're ready for something."

"I'm not very hungry—we had a very good dinner—but I'll be down in a little while."

She looked in the mirror now and found his eyes waiting for her. There was a question in them and she could have answered it with a slight shake of her head but she did not wish him to erupt in front of Alice, not that that would be anything unusual, but she preferred the battles, the dreadful soul-searing battles, to be fought in private whenever possible. Yet she well knew there was little privacy in this house; every door had its listener, and she sometimes visualized the kitchen as an assembly of Parliament when the whole serving household got together and put forth their opinions as to the rights and wrongs of the running of the establishment, Mr. Palmeston being ably represented by Harris, for like him, her butler could move from one party to another as the circumstances warranted. Harris had been the devout supporter of her father's principles as long as her father was alive, but now that her husband was in charge, he as devoutly, seemingly, supported his principles, and there had never been two men so opposed in what they stood for.

She knew that she had inherited part of her father's strength, and his principles, but when she dared bring these traits to the fore, life became a living hell. Yet she would have endured this hell and eventually gained release from its perpetuation if it wasn't for one thing, the child. Nothing held her to this house, to this man, to this existence of mental torture but the child, and the child was Edmund's weapon, the only weapon he possessed against her. And should she not comply with his wishes, he could use the weapon like a knife at her throat.

"How long will you be?" His voice, soft and deep, would have given an outsider the impression that he was asking this question because he was eager for her company; and in a way he was eager for her company tonight, he was eager for her

33

news, because so much depended on what she had to say and its being favorable. But when she replied, "About fifteen minutes," he thought to himself derisively, fifteen minutes! Another woman in her place would have said an hour, or more, but his Rosina did not dress, she merely changed her frock; not for her the touching up of her eyes and lips, the powdering of her skin, the scenting of her armpits and nipples. No, she washed her face with soap and water, and instead of pomade on her hair, she used a brush covered with a piece of silk that made it look like a shining, wet-tarred cap.

In the mirror, Rosina watched him limping toward the door, and even at this stage of her life and knowledge of him, she could understand how women fell before his charms. With all his excesses his body had up till now remained thin; there was no flabbiness of neck or chin or cheek. Only in the yellowing white of his eyes could there be detected the reflection of his way of life. There were few people who knew him as a really evil man: her mother, Alice, her Uncle James and Aunt Emma. They knew of his ways, but then only to some extent; she and she alone knew that incorporated in Edmund Lagrange was an accumulation of many evils, some so subtle as to be unspeakable, untranslatable into speech. If there had been words to explain them, she would, before now, have surely unburdened herself to Alice, or her mother. But there are certain things forbidden through speech. Her mind, she felt, had created this barrier to save herself from madness.

"What will you do?" Alice was whispering the words as she hooked up the crinoline dress, and as softly Rosina answered, "I don't know. One thing's certain, he won't believe I tried, and I did, Alice, because begging from Uncle is preferable to begging from Mother."

Alice finished the last hook on the bodice, then patting the back of the embroidered collar, she came round and stood before her mistress and adjusted the points of the collar. Patting them into place, she said, "It's got to end somewhere; if you lose the factory it'll be the finish."

To this Rosina made no reply, but she thought to herself, I wish it were. But for one thing I wish it were.

As she made for the door she said over her shoulder, "I will say goodnight to Annabella before I go down"; then, turning her head, she added, "Don't wait up, you must be tired. Have your meal and go to bed. I can manage. I—I may be late."

34

Alice made no reply to this, and they both knew that she would not obey the order.

The meal was ending, the servants were departing; Edmund Lagrange, in spite of his impatience, had enjoyed his food; the stuffed mackerel had been delicious and he couldn't have bettered the curried lobster in any club in The Mall. The saddle of lamb had been rather ordinary, but the goslings had made up for it and the gooseberry pudding, as the saying went, melted in the mouth.

He had drunk a bottle of wine, and now, with a brandy in his hand, which he swirled expertly round to the very rim of his glass without allowing a drop to spill over, he looked at his wife at the other end of the table and thought, My God, she gets plainer every day. Even the candlelight that was kind to most people, and now was being enhanced by the deepening twilight, was not kind to her. He turned his gaze away and rose from his seat. He did not go and assist her from her chair; he knew that she would sit through what she had to tell him, good or bad, and it was characteristic of her that her face gave no indication of what news she had to impart. Her power to hide her thoughts had always irked him.

"Well! How did it go?"

She moved the solid silver dessert knife back and forward between her finger and thumb before she replied, "Uncle could not see his way clear to loan me the money." She did not say "us," or "you." She heard him swallowing but did not look at his face, and went on, "He reminded me that we are still ten thousand pounds in his debt."

"He picks up the bloody interest, doesn't he?"

It was beginning again. She sat up straighter in her chair and pressed her shoulders tightly against the back of it.

"Did you tell him we could lose the works?"

"I implied as much."

"Well then?"

"He reminded me that the five thousand you borrowed from him four years ago and the added mortgage you placed on the house did not save the candle factory, as the previous five thousand did nothing to help the pottery or the pipe factory."

He was standing at the end of the table again, gripping the back of the seat he had vacated and glaring at her. "The pottery was finished, you know it was. As for the pipe factory, it had been losing money for years, long before I came on the scene."

35

She raised her eyes and returned his infuriated gaze with a calm stare. "That isn't so. The pipe factory always paid its way; its profits did not fluctuate to heights as those of the glass works were apt to do, but its returns could be relied upon. Father—"

"Blast your father! Do you hear me? Blast your father!" His voice was low and thick and even his breath seemed to exude hate on the word "father." "Your father had as much foresight as a pig's arse, or he, instead of Swinburne, would have taken over Cookson's years ago."

She couldn't bear it. She was tired, exhausted, mentally and physically exhausted; she couldn't bear this tonight.

"When Cookson started his sheet-glass works in '37, did your father have the sense to copy him then? No, he was as blind as the buggers who thought that there'd never be a steel factory and that the Palmer brothers were mad. What your father couldn't see or wouldn't see was that sheet glass was the stuff of the future, that anything could be made with glass, ANYTHING. Doors, furniture; yes, furniture. And why not floors? Anything. No; he had to go on with niggling little shades, bottles, candelabra, and encourage them to make their piddling glass fiddles, windmills and spinning wheels so they could carry them in their processions, dressed up, aping their betters in swallow-tailed coats and top hats—Pah! your father!"

At this point he stretched his arm wide, and with his fingers stiff he flicked them against one of the eight arms extending from the candelabrum on the table. With a crack like the lock of a pistol closing, it snapped from its support, and when, with its lighted candle, it hit the table, the sound was as if the pistol had been fired.

She willed her hands to be still, she willed the muscles of her face not to twitch, but the rest of her body was trembling.

What he had said was right. Her father had refused to compete with Cookson's glass works, and he had been wise, for the Cooksons had been a dynasty in glass from the end of the seventeenth century, whereas the Conway-Redford works had been established in Shields for only fifty years. Nevertheless, her father had been an artist in glass, a man who loved glass. He had not, as her husband did, visited the factory once a week, if then, but had ridden daily from the Hall the six miles into Shields for at least forty weeks in the year. He had known all his men by name, and had looked after them, the drunkards and the temperate ones alike.

He had first taken her to the works when she was six years

old, and, fascinated, she had watched a man sitting in a wooden seat blowing down a pipe into some hot liquid that was hanging from the end of it, and a short while later she had seen a beautiful red bottle born. Her father always gave his men the best materials; his sand came from the sandstone dug out of the forests of Fontainebleau in France and from Alum Bay in the Isle of Wight; not for him the sand from Wales, Bedfordshire or Lancashire. On other visits she had watched fine sand being purified still further, washed in water, burned to rid it of impurities, then sieved to further purity until not a trace of iron, lime, alumina, chalk or magnesium was left. She had longed, in her early teens, to be a boy so that she could handle the tools of the glass factory. But because she couldn't make glass, it wasn't to say that she couldn't learn how to make it, and with the encouragement of her father she steeped herself in the books relating to glass-making down the centuries. She read of the Venetians, the Syrians, the French refugees who, flying from tyranny and taking refuge in this country, brought back to it the lost art of glassmaking. It seemed to her now cruelly ironic that it was through her knowledge of glass that she had first met Edmund Lagrange.

Her father had always spent two months of the year in London to give her mother "the season" and also in order that she herself should become accustomed to high society, for although the family of Conway-Redford bore no title, the Redfords, on their side, could go back three hundred years, whereas on her mother's side, the Conway family was dotted liberally with titles of lords and earls, ladies and countesses.

It was at the ball given for her eighteenth birthday in their London home that her father brought to her a tall, startlingly beautiful man and introduced him as Edmund Lagrange, someone else who was interested in glass.

Edmund Lagrange was the third son of a prosperous glass-maker in Surrey. He could discourse on glass most knowledgeably; she was entranced with his knowledge, his voice, his manner and his face; oh yes, his face. That he should need and seek her company appeared to her as something that put all the miracles in the Bible into a pale shade. She was plain and she knew it; she also knew that she was intelligent and men did not like women who used their minds, but Edmund Lagrange was different. When her father told her he had asked for her hand, she fainted.

When, after their London season, they returned home, Edmund Lagrange had followed, and from a friend's house thirty

37

miles distant in Cumberland, he courted her. He courted her for six months, and then they were married.

There were a number of the Lagrange family present at the wedding, all of them apparently extremely happy at Edmund's choice; "relief" would have been a better word to apply to the Lagrange family's reaction, but they called it "happiness." They were so happy that Edmund had settled down; they said it in dozens of different ways.

It wasn't until the honeymoon was well over that Rosina fully realized why the Lagrange family had been so happy that Edmund was settled, for she discovered quite by accident that he had been disinherited two years previously, that his father had made a public statement that he was not responsible for his third son's debts. Disillusionment followed quickly; she was soon to learn that she had married an inveterate gambler, a liar, and a man who was in debt to the amount of forty thousand pounds, but it was two years before she discovered that her husband consorted with low women, that he was a frequent visitor to a certain brothel house in Newcastle, and that he maintained a woman in an apartment in Shields. She came upon this knowledge quite by accident. It happened that she had informed her husband that, in company with her mother, she was going to visit the cottage, as they called the ten-room house on the edge of the estate, to see how the renovations were proceeding, but they had only walked a quarter of the distance when a thunderstorm burst and they hurried back to the house. Having taken a shortcut, they emerged on the south terrace and let themselves in through the French windows which adjoined her father's study. Their entry must have been drowned by a clap of thunder; it also shut out from them the voices in the next room, until Rosina, about to exclaim on the storm, heard her father's voice raised in anger, saying, "You are an utter waster!"

When she made a move toward the partly open door, her mother's grip on her arm stayed her, and in frozen silence she listened to her father's denouncement of her husband.

For months past she had tried to cover up her husband's misdemeanors, at least those known to her. One thing she knew she must keep from them was that her private fortune, even after this short time of marriage, was now almost non-existent. But even so, she forgave him his spendthrift habits; but she couldn't forgive this. This dreadful denouncement spelled the end of her marriage, as she knew marriage, the end of her life.

From that day the pattern of her existence changed. Her

permanent occupancy of another room brought no objection from her husband, and when her father died six months later and her mother moved into the cottage, he barely covered his jubilation.

Her father, after providing amply for her mother, had left the remainder of his fortune to her, but with a proviso: she could not touch either capital or interest until she was thirty-five years old. He also left to her the pottery, candle and pipe works, but to these, too, he put a provisio, profits over a certain sum made by these factories were to go to her mother. The glass works he left to her unconditionally because he knew that it would take all its profit to maintain the Hall and its commitments.

It had seemed at the time that her father had made sure that for quite a few years her husband would have to work to afford himself the pleasure of gambling and his other pursuits, but John Conway-Redford had underestimated the misplaced ability, the cunning, and above all the innate knowledge his son-in-law had of his wife's character.

So it was toward the end of the third year of their marriage, and a full year after being deprived of his wife's bed, that Edmund Lagrange brought home, late one night, a month-old baby.

For some time previous to this, he had been trying to get Rosina to sign a paper which would help to ease his present desperate financial situation. All he required of her was a signature to confirm the sale of the pottery works, but she had remained obdurate. Of course, he could have forced her hand; all she had was his legally, but further pressure on her would anger her mother, and he did not want another set of provisos when she died, which he thought might be soon if the rapidity of her breathing was anything to go by. But on this particular night, drunk and frustrated, he had defied caution, and, thinking up the greatest humiliation he could heap on his wife, he had brought to her a child which he knew was his. He had burst into her room at dead of night, awakening her from sleep, and almost flinging the bundle onto the bed, he had cried, "My daughter, Annabella Lagrange. I'm bringing her up in this house. What have you to say about that?"

The candlelight had danced wildly as he waved the heavy candlestick back and forward, and she had shrunk into her pillows away from him, away from the wriggling thing sunk deep into the eiderdown, and she had stayed like that until, roughly pulling the shawl from the child, he tipped it onto its face, smothering its cries as he did so. It was then her hands automatically went to right it, but stopped before they reached it, and she brought them together and held them joined under her chin as she stared at this fiend of a man. She stared at him, her eyes not flinching from his drunken, embittered gaze until the fact that the child was no longer crying drew her eyes to it again, and then her hands were flinging it over, lifting it, shaking it. She had never held a child in her arms in her life, but instinct led her to shake the breath back into this one, and when short, hiccoughing wails told her she had succeeded, she was further startled by her husband's dropping the candlestick onto the bed table, then throwing himself backwards across the foot of her bed and laughing as a madman might laugh. When he raised himself, he was still laughing, and between spluttering gasps he pointed his finger at her, crying, "You've got a daughter. What do you think about that? You, a virgin, have given birth to a child, because you still are a virgin, aren't you, Rosina? If you had ten men a night, you'd still be a virgin, because, you know something, you're not a woman, your father didn't beget a woman, he blew out a piece of glass. And now the glass has given birth; you're a mama, Rosina. YOU'RE A MA-MA! And now you've got a little glass virgin of your own."

He had gone reeling out of the room, leaving the child in her arms. She had still heard his laughter as he threaded his way along the gallery to the Old Hall, which he had refurnished and made his own.

And it was almost as he had said, she had given birth to a child, for from that night, try as she would, she couldn't get the child out of her mind. And she did try. For the next two months she left it solely in Alice's care, except for looking in on it at times, times when she thought she would not be observed.

Then one day he informed her that he was going to take the child back to its mother, and her reaction had been as automatic as her heartbeat. "You can't!" she said. "I want her to stay." And knowing that anything she wanted he would do his best to deprive her of, she had pleaded, "Please, please let her stay," and it was then that he knew that the object which he had used to inflict pain and humiliation on her would prove a weapon the like of which no calculated cunning of his could have devised.

As the years went on, he used his weapon to better and greater advantage. If at times she proved stubborn, he had only to put a pen before her and casually mention Annabella's name and all went smoothly.

40

But now, after seven years of signing her name, there were no more papers left to sign except those connected with the glass works, and if she ever signed the final papers on the works, Redford Hall would be no more.

He was as aware of this as she was, and from time to time he made an effort which took the form of visiting the works daily for a week or so, harassing those in charge with the instructions to harass in their turn those under them.

Left to itself and those who cared for it, the glass works went steadily on keeping up the same output each year, bringing in approximately the same income, which to a man of Edmund Lagrange's tastes was merely survival money, for he would like to have been known as another "Lambton of Durham," "jogging along" on seventy thousand pounds a year. But at this particular moment he was virtually penniless.

He now came to the table, and leaning over and toward her, he demanded, "Have you any idea of the expenses incurred this year?"

She swallowed deeply in her throat before she replied quietly, "As I haven't seen the books this year, or for the last four years, you wouldn't expect me to know the extent of the dues."

He remained in his bent position, staring at her, then growled, "Accounts, ledgers, they're not a woman's business."

"Then the expenditure is not my business either."

"Isn't it?" His voice ended on a soft high note of inquiry; then he went on mockingly, "Then I'm going to do you a favor, I'm going to let it be your business. Why do you think I need eight thousand pounds, and now? Simply because that is the amount needed to meet the creditors. And, let me tell you, it will merely pacify them, not pay them off. But if they're not pacified, and at once, they will restrain—Now, my dear Rosina, will you make it your business?"

Her hand went slowly to her throat. She had thought he wanted the money partly to erect a separate works about which he had talked for some years now. This was to be a glass works that melted down broken glass, remade it and sold it cheaply. Numbers of glass companies resorted to this practice although it was forbidden by law. It was also an offense to use the waste from crown glass, although this waste went a good way toward improving the quality of bottle glass.

The restrictions imposed on the glass industry had irked her father, especially when in his time the excise dues had been so high that to do good business meant bringing your

41

firm to ruin, but on her husband, although now free of the excise restrictions, they had a frustrating, almost maddening effect.

But eight thousand pounds! What had happened to the firm's profits? She drew her hand down over her flat breast until it came to rest on the silver buckle at her waist and she gripped this as if for support as she said, "The profits, what has become of them?"

"Oh, Jesus Christ!" He raised his eyes upwards but at the same time was aware that she had closed hers tight against his blasphemy, and at this point he warned himself to go easy with her. Yet he found it almost an impossibility to resist hurting her, taunting her, even when there was a big issue at stake, as now.

He took out a scented handkerchief from the cuff of his coat and mopped his brow; then, walking back to the head of the table, he lowered himself into his chair again, and, his voice sounding calm, he said, "Men have to be paid, and everything is dearer, labor, materials, everything. Kelp has gone up, even the dues for the boats that carry it have been raised. Everything, I tell you."

His voice trailed away and he leaned his elbow on the edge of the table and rested his chin in the palm of his hand and with a good imitation of resigned calmness, he said, "If I haven't the money by the end of the month, then I'm afraid it'll be the finish."

A silence fell upon the room; it seemed to still the air. The candlelight ceased to flicker; the only movement was the grease leaving the wick and spilling in tear drops into the silver linings of the glass holders.

He had his eyes deeply downcast, and he kept them like this, telling himself to have patience, to make no move, and he didn't until the rustle of her gown told him she was rising to her feet. And then he, too, rose, and with the courtesy that might have been expected of a man who had partaken of an agreeable meal in the company of his wife, he went before her to the door, and after opening it he stood aside and held it in his hand, as a lackey might have done, until she had passed through. He did not follow her, for he knew that she would be making straight for her room.

The door closed, he returned to the table and poured himself another large measure of brandy, which he drank in two gulps; then, sitting back in his chair, he pressed his lips tightly together and patted them with his fingertips.

It was as good as done and he hadn't had to dangle

Annabella in a noose before her eyes. If she had proved more obdurate, then he would have been forced to use pressure through the child; but today he'd had enough of Annabella—even the mention of her name tonight would have played on his nerves. That business this afternoon had shaken him. What if, inadvertently, she should let slip to Rosina what she had seen? No doubt Rosina would leave the house, even ask for a divorce, and he didn't want that because his wife was the pipeline to the only remaining well, her mother.

Rosina was well aware that he held gaming parties in his quarters, and if she suspected anything else she gave no sign, because she had no proof. He had been very circumspect, he considered, about that side of his life, always making sure she was miles away before he entertained any female. It never crossed his mind to think that one of his staff might betray him. You did not cut off the hand that supplied your meat and drink and did both generously. But this cynical philosophy did not extend to Alice, because she, given the chance, would cut his throat and smile while about it. It was fortunate that she always attended her mistress.

He went out of the dining room, across the hall and into the drawing room, and there, sitting at a little desk near the window, he made a few notes. On a piece of paper he wrote down: "Works, five thousand pounds." This, not eight thousand, was the sum he required to meet the outstanding debts of the business. But he had other debts equally important.

He next wrote: "G.B., a thousand guineas."

Boston would have to be content with that for the time being, the damned upstart. He either had the luck of ten devils or he was cheating. Yet what need had he to cheat, son of a dressed-up scissors manufacturer who had risen from the grindstone and was now lording it in a country mansion, aping the gentry, opening the doors of exclusive clubs with a millionaire's key.

The next entry on the paper read: "Leighton, three hundred guineas."

This entry brought a stir of excitement into his bowels because it was for the purchase of a new hunter. Leighton, damn him, wouldn't let the beast out of the stable unless the cash was in his hand, and for the past six months he had wanted this horse with an intensity equal to that of his desire for a woman.

The next entry read: "Tailor, a hundred pounds."

This sum would act merely as a sedative to the man who, he knew, didn't want his patronage but who nevertheless was

43

afraid to refuse it, knowing that a word from him would reduce his clientele considerably.

The next scribble on the page read: "Blunt, two hundred guineas."

Blunt was the name of his cook, and his cook's husband was his blacksmith, and his blacksmith was a man who used his fists. Edmund Lagrange had great respect for James Blunt. Over the years he had won him some tidy sums and in a fortnight's time he was to fight Bull Cragg from Shields. They were equally matched and they might go fifty rounds; but, fifteen or fifty, he was backing his man to win.

He made one more entry on the paper. Slowly he wrote the name "Jessie," and against it he placed the sum of one hundred pounds. Then, his head on one side, he smiled for a moment before he changed the sum to two hundred. He was always generous to his women; that was one of the reasons they fought for his favors.

After reckoning up the amount, he burned the paper in the flame of the candle; then, sitting back in his chair, he nodded to himself. He would be left with a clear thousand; he'd have to get by with that for the time being.

He felt as sure of the money as if it were in his hand; that is, until the thought of his daughter pricked his mind again.

Tomorrow morning he would rise early and take her birthday presents in, and he'd get her that pony whether Rosina liked it or not; it was high time she learned to ride. And he must make a point of seeing her more often and showing his affection for her. He would have to put himself out in some way to erase today's picture from her mind.

As he stared toward the window and the now dark garden, it came to him with not a little surprise that this afternoon's business had disturbed him; the thought of losing his daughter's love—he did not put the feeling under the heading of "respect"—caused a small tide of fear to rise in him, and it was a strange sensation, for he and fear had never yet become acquainted. The child had certain feelings for Rosina, he knew, but him she adored, and he wondered now, if what she had witnessed this afternoon should change her feelings toward him, how he would react. And when the answer came, he pooh-poohed it; yet he was startled by his self-knowledge because he knew that those who did not love him, or were no longer of use to him, he kicked out of his life and made sure that the kicking, whether aimed at the high and mighty or the lowly, had, in some way, a crippling effect.

3

Annabella was still at breakfast when her mama came into the room followed by Alice, who was followed by Cargill carrying a number of packages.

"Happy birthday, darling!"

"Oh, thank you, Mama."

"Happy birthday, Miss Annabella."

"Thank you, Alice."

The greetings over, she began to undo the packages. Child-like, she opened the big one first and was delighted with the beautifully dressed doll her Aunt Emma and Uncle James had sent her. She exclaimed, "It's beautiful, beautiful, Mama," yet at the same time knowing that she preferred the little Negro boy whose eyes blinked when you pulled a string. Her papa had come to her room before she was awake and brought her a musical box that played "Ring-a-ring of roses," and, "Here we go round the mulberry bush," and the Negro doll. The effect of seeing her father so early in the day had at first made her speechless, that is, until he made her laugh when he whispered to her, "I mustn't stay; it's time for the servants' rising and if they saw me at this hour, they'd all drop dead." He had pointed backwards toward the door. "If Watford comes out, she'll swoon right away." The picture of Watford swooning and all the servants dropping dead because they had seen her papa up early caused her to clap her hands over her mouth to suppress her gleeful laughter; and it was as her body shook with suppressed mirth that her papa had said a very odd thing. "That's it," he had said; "laugh long and loud at everything, don't give God a chance; be gay."

He had waved to her from the door and left her with mixed feelings, still wanting to laugh but wondering why she shouldn't give God a chance. But the feeling of laughter won and she played happily with her new doll and musical box until Watford came to dress her and give her her breakfast.

Now she opened her mama's presents. First, there were a half a dozen beautifully embroidered handkerchiefs—Rosina excelled in this art; next, a book of stories by Hans Christian Andersen. The third gift was a diary bound in red leather with a silver ornamental clasp and key.

".Oh, Mama!" She kissed Rosina. "They're lovely, beautiful."

Then Alice presented her present. It was a Bible. The strange defiant feeling that had been born in her before her bath yesterday prompted the naughty thought that, of course, Alice would give her a Bible, but she became afraid when she felt the inclination to laugh at this thought as she had laughed with Papa earlier.

From the background, Watford now stepped forward with her gift. It was a pen wiper made of red flannel and edged with fancy stitching, and not only did Annabella thank Watford most kindly but Rosina also thanked her. It was a most thoughtful present, she said, but it wouldn't be put to use today because it was a special day and a holiday, and first of all Annabella was to accompany her as far as Grandma's.

It was always as far as Grandma's. Annabella never went into Grandma's house; once they were within a short distance of the house, her mama beckoned to Watford and they would play games until her mama returned. Her mama said that Grandma was an old lady and not very well; yet she went to the chapel twice a week—she had heard Watford say so—but she wasn't there on a Sunday when all the household were present.

She had seen her grandma only twice in her life. She was a tall lady dressed in dark clothes and had a white face. Annabella had worked it out for herself that perhaps children weren't allowed to see their grandparents until they were of a certain age, perhaps ten years old.

At eleven o'clock she was dressed and ready for her journey across the park. The day was beautiful and warm, but she wore a cream coat over her plain blue silk dress, and on her head was a straw hat with a large brim so the sun wouldn't catch her face.

It was as she sat on the gold-upholstered chair in the drawing room, her toes just touching the ground and her hands folded one on top of the other on her lap waiting for her mama to come from her business room, which was the room where she consulted with the staff, that she thought again of the strawberry field and the poor children. Perhaps when her mama went into Grandma's it would be nice if she could go and see if the children were there and give them some pennies so that they could get some food from the cook. She wondered if she should go and consult Watford, who was waiting in the hall, and then she remembered that Watford had said that the children were bad, so she decided she'd wait for her mama to come in and ask her for some pennies.

And this is exactly what she did, and by this action set into motion the events that were to shape her life.

"There you are, my dear. I've been a long time, haven't I?"

"No, Mama. I didn't think it was a long time because I've been thinking."

"Oh! And what have you been thinking about?" Rosina was easing a white silk glove onto her long hand.

"About poor children, Mama."

"Poor children?" Rosina's head came forward inquiringly.

"Yes, the poor children who eat the strawberries because they are hungry. Mama, may I have some pennies?"

Rosina, about to button the glove, stopped and asked, "Why do you want pennies? Is there something you wish to buy?"

"No, Mama, they're for the poor children, because if they had pennies they could come to see cook and get some food."

"Come to see cook and get . . ." Rosina's voice trailed away, and slowly she sat down on the edge of the spindle-legged couch and, looking at Annabella, said, "Tell me about these poor children, my dear, and cook."

Now the situation was becoming difficult. It meant involving Watford, and she didn't want Mama to be angry with Watford so she began, "I was very naughty yesterday, Mama; I was in the gallery and I saw some children in the strawberry field and I ran out because I thought it would be nice to play with them, but they were frightened and very hungry and I told them to come to see cook and she'd give them something to eat, and they said they couldn't because they hadn't any pennies, cook only gave food to those who had pennies, and so I thought it would be nice on my birthday if I gave them some pennies . . ."

Now her voice trailed away; her mama was angry. She put out her hand and gently touched Rosina's knee, saying, "I'm very sorry, Mama; I'll never go out without Watford again."

Rosina gently took the small hand and patted it, saying, "It's all right, my dear. Don't worry, you'll have some pennies for the children, but wait just a little while longer. I'll be but a minute or so."

So this was it, this is what had happened yesterday. The child must have been missing for some time—they had all likely been searching for her. But the selling of food. How atrocious! How absolutely atrocious!

"Bring Mrs. Page to me." She was addressing Harris, who was standing ready at the door to see her out.

She had just seated herself at the desk in her business room again when Mrs. Page appeared at the doorway.

"Come in and close the door, Mrs. Page."

"Is—is something amiss, madam?"

"Very much amiss, I should say, Mrs. Page. Are you aware"—she paused here and stared at the housekeeper before going on—"and I want a truthful answer, Mrs. Page. Are you aware that the cook sells food, our food, to poor people?"

To answer this truthfully, Mrs. Page would have had to say, "Yes, madam; I know she does a bit on the side, but so does everybody else in the house, from Harris downwards. Surely you're aware of this. It's part of the workings of an establishment; without perquisites you'd find it difficult to run any staff." But what she said was, and stammering, "Se-selling food? Cook, madam? Never to my knowledge. No, madam."

"Then all I can say is that you, Mrs. Page, have been remiss in your duties, part of which is to know what the female staff is about. Cook, I must inform you, sells food by the pennyworth to the starving wretches who, from time to time, find themselves forced to live on the open fells."

"Oh, madam!" Mrs. Page, whose face was now stiff and gray, murmured, "I can't believe it. Somebody has been lying, I'm sure."

"My daughter doesn't lie, Mrs. Page."

"Miss Annabella?"

"Yes, Miss Annabella, who was left to run wild yesterday and who found some starving children in the strawberry field. So, therefore, you will understand, Mrs. Page, that you receive your information from the source itself. Fetch the woman here."

"C-cook, madam?"

"Yes, cook, Mrs. Page. No—better still, call Harris, and don't go, Mrs. Page, farther than the door."

When Harris appeared in the doorway, Rosina said, "Bring me cook, Harris, please."

Harris almost repeated what Mrs. Page had said, "What! Cook, madam?" But he refrained. Nevertheless, he looked indignant; for such a message Reeves, Faill, or Cargill should have been summoned. Nevertheless, he hurriedly departed and a few minutes later cook, evidently bemused, stood before her mistress.

"You sell food to the people from the fells, cook?"

The cook was dumbfounded. How did one meet such an attack? What had Mrs. Page said? She opened her wide,

48

slack mouth, closed it, then opened it again and managed to bring out, "Now and then, madam."

"What do you sell?"

"Just the scraps that would go into the pig bucket, madam."

"And for the scraps that would go into the pig bucket you charge these homeless people a penny a time?"

"Well, well, madam, if you didn't charge them—well, they'd come in by the droves."

"Indeed! And how do they get in in the first place? Does Horton let them in through the lodge?"

"No, madam; they come in by the east drive, the back way."

"Indeed! Well now, cook, go to your room, pack your things and be out of my house by noon. Mrs. Page will give you what is due to you."

"But—but, madam." It was the housekeeper who was daring to speak. "What—what about the dinner? Who—I mean at such short notice."

"You have a kitchen maid and a scullery maid, have you not, Mrs. Page? And they have both been in the kitchen for some years, I think; if they have learned nothing from cook in that time, then I think they should be dismissed, too. Riley is it not who is the kitchen maid? Then tell Riley that she has to cook the dinner. That'll be all."

Stunned, the two women departed, cook so forgetting herself as to walk out in front of Mrs. Page. And, what was more, neither of them had bent her knee.

Almost on their heels Rosina entered the hall, and saying to Watford, "Bring Miss Annabella," she moved with her accustomed slow step toward the door, and when she had passed through the conservatory and reached the front step, she waited until Watford came up to her holding Annabella by the hand.

Rosina now took hold of Annabella's hand and together they walked across the gravel drive and through the pagoda. Watford, walking at a distance of thirty paces behind, wondered uneasily what the row was about, and was greatly agitated by the thought that she was in some way connected with it. Of this she was given practical proof when the mistress stopped in the usual place and, beckoning to her, looked at her grimly and said, "I have given Miss Annabella three sixpences. She's to give them to the children she met yesterday." There was a long pause here, during which Watford's eyelids fluttered downwards and her throat became dry. Then her mistress went on, "See that she doesn't touch the children—

they may be verminous; let her put the sixpences on the ground. And I wish you to give them a message from me. Tell them that on Tuesdays and Saturdays they are to come to the west lodge, where they will be given food for which they will not be asked to pay. You understand that, Watford?"

"Yes, madam."

There was another pause, and Watford stood with her eyes downcast waiting to be dismissed. But Rosina said, "Do you know how many families are living on the fells, Watford?"

"About a dozen, madam, I think."

A dozen, and that likely meant dozens of children. She could quite easily give the order that all the children had to be fed as long as their parents were out of work, but that would mean that Mr. Rosier would come astriding over and likely as not accuse her of prolonging one of his numerous strikes, because it was only through starvation that the men were driven back into the mines. She detested the Rosiers, as her father had done before her; they were mine owners but they were poor class. She compromised slightly now by saying, "Tell the children that there'll be enough food for six of them. . . . And, Watford—"

"Yes, madam." The eyelids fluttered upwards.

"I will want to see you in my business room when I return."

When, almost two hours later, Rosina returned to the house she felt as worn out as if she had battled physically, as well as mentally, with her mother and she longed for a respite. But it was not granted her, for, notified of her return by Constantine, Lagrange sought her out immediately, and although her news meant that he was sure of the money, the conditions made him furious. Her mother, Rosina said, had agreed to advance the eight thousand necessary not as a loan, but in the form of shares.

Now the Conway-Redford glass works was a family company. John Redford never had any wish to supply quantity instead of quality, and he had lived by the maxim, as his father and grandfather had done before him, that if you were to preserve quality, then you had to give to the product personal supervision. And so Redford's works had remained small in comparison with firms like Cookson's, but it had also remained exclusive and superior in both its products and its management.

The shares of the firm were divided, at present, among Constance Redford, her brother James and Rosina, Rosina holding sixty percent. The suggested arrangement would now give Constance Redford control. Lagrange found the idea monstrous, and he said so, while Rosina sat, her back straight, and held her peace until he had finished; and then into the rage-filled silence she said evenly, "These are the only conditions under which you can have the money; moreover, Mama stated emphatically that it will be the last she will loan me."

He cursed her mother, and openly, then demanded, "What is the earliest I can have it?"

"I will arrange for Pollit to come tomorrow with the necessary papers. A week hence, I should say."

He left her. She had not for a moment expected thanks, so why should she feel like this, devastated. Somewhere within herself she was crying bitterly. She was twenty-eight years old and life was a great burden; the only comfort she had in it was that derived from the child. More often of late she felt that God had some special reason for making her suffer, and that one day it would be disclosed to her.

She was deep in her thinking when the door burst open and her husband startled her by reentering the room.

"What's this I'm hearing? You've dismissed cook?"

After a moment she said, "Yes, I've dismissed cook."

"What the hell for?" His face suffused with anger, he glared at her.

Now she got slowly to her feet and confronted him. Her chin high, she said, "Since you are aware that she's been dismissed, you'll likely also be aware of why she was dismissed."

"Selling a few bloody pig scraps to the rabble! You mean you dismissed the woman for that?"

"The rabble, as you call them, were your friend Rosier's workmen, the evicted ones, and my cook was selling my food to them. If they had a penny they could eat, if they hadn't they starved. And where do men on strike get pennies?"

"What Rosier does is no bloody business of yours."

"Will you kindly control your language when you're speaking to me, Edmund?"

"Control, be damned!" He advanced toward her until he was within a foot of her; then thrusting out his chin, he growled low, "Do you know what you've done? You've lost me two thousand pounds. Blunt is not a bond man, he's free to go, and he'll go now that his wife's dismissed, and likely over to Boston or Rosier. He's the best fighter in the county, and now because of a few bloody scraps you've lost him to

51

me. Even if he does stay and does fight, he won't have his heart in it; he'll get his own back by selling the game, I know Blunt."

She looked at him steadily before saying in a trembling voice, "You must have wagered a considerable sum if you expect the return of two thousand pounds and at a time when you tell me there is no money at all in the bank."

"I backed him over a year ago, long odds." His lying was so perfected that he could even make himself believe it. "And up to this morning the money was as good as in my hands. Look." His voice suddenly dropped to an almost soothing softness. "Reinstate her. Caution her—I'll do it for you—but have her back."

"No, Edmund; I'll do no such thing."

He stared at her, the gray eyes narrowing as the seconds passed. This morning she had saved him from sure bankruptcy and also saved his face among his gambling friends, but even so he could say to her now and in slow, soft tones that made his words more terrifying, "I was thinking of looking up the Continental firms in Germany, France and Belgium; I might learn a trick or two, and perhaps find markets in Spain or Portugal. They want good quality there and we can offer it. It's years since I was in Italy; I've always been intrigued by the Venetians, and Annabella would love Venice. I think that seven is old enough for her to travel and see something of the world. What do you think about it?"

His tone suggested that they were discussing the child's education amicably. He watched the blood drain from her face, he watched her hands tremble, he watched the dress at her flat breast suddenly heave. "I'll be in to supper," he added; "we'll discuss it further this evening." Then, bowing slightly to her, he turned and went from the room.

The only authority she had left was the running of the house, and now she was to lose that. That woman would have to be reinstated. In future she would merely be a figurehead in the eyes of her staff, an empty figurehead. From where did one get the strength to bear such humiliation? Only from God.

She locked the door of her room, then knelt by her bedside and, bowing her head, buried it deep into the bedcover.

But the events of that particular day weren't quite over. It happened that Annabella asked Alice the meaning of a word.

Annabella had found that the day hadn't been as happy as she anticipated. Her mother had stayed a long time in her grandmama's house, and Watford had acted very strangely on their way to the strawberry field. Once she had stopped, and, shaking her hand which she was gripping tightly, she had looked down on her and said, "You're a little—" Then she had stopped.

They had found the children in the strawberry field. They were gleaning among the leaves. When she approached them, they stood close together and very still. She would have gone nearer to them and dropped the sixpences at their feet but Watford stopped her. It was she who grabbed the sixpences out of her hand and threw them at the children, and they were so startled that they didn't scramble in the grass and pick them up. Then in a gruff voice Watford gave them the message from her mama and all the while they stood gaping at her.

It was very disappointing, Annabella thought; things would have been quite different if she had been on her own, and she would have felt much better if she could have put the sixpences in their hands. But, as her mama said, they were very dirty children and had an offensive smell about them, yet still she would have liked to talk to them.

After delivering the message, Watford had pulled her away and refused to play games. She felt peeved with Watford, yet at the same time she was sorry for her because Mama was going to speak to her in her office, and that meant Mama was angry with her.

Then there were the other servants. Mrs. Page had looked the other way when she saw her coming, and Pierce, the girl who was called Fanny and had a red, happy face and always said, "Hello, miss" when she saw her on her own, she too passed her, only looking at her slantwise. And Watford's friend Rawlings had stared at her hard as if she didn't like her. She couldn't understand it. Then Rawlings had come into the day nursery, and as usual she and Watford talked and as usual she herself listened. She didn't think it was wrong to listen, for the simple reason that she didn't repeat anything they said. They often talked about Faill and Cargill and they talked about the cook and Mrs. Page. When they talked about Faill and Cargill they laughed, but when they talked about the cook and Mrs. Page they didn't laugh. But this evening they were talking about her, and Watford kept saying the word that she had missed this morning. She kept saying. "The little barstard." What was a "bars-stard"?

She asked Alice. "What is a 'bars-stard,' Alice?"

Alice, not being of gentle birth, hadn't the privilege of

fainting; her reactions only went as far as covering her ears with her hands and gazing wide-eyed heavenwards. Then, her whole body working as if agitated by bellows, she whispered in awe-filled tones, "Child! Child! What are you saying?"

"I was only asking what is a—" Annabella was a little frightened at the reaction of her question on old Alice, and when Alice, with upraised hands, cried, "I know, I know what you're asking, but where did you hear such a word? Tell me, where did you hear it?" she remained silent.

She thought of Watford. Watford wasn't pleased with her so she mustn't get her into further trouble or tomorrow would be another day like today when Watford wouldn't play with her properly, and the servants wouldn't smile at her, and so she answered, "I don't know, Alice. Someone said it. They said I was a little—what I said."

"If they said that, child, then you must know who said it. Was it Watford?"

"No, no, Alice; it wasn't Watford. It wasn't Watford, really and truly." She knew she was protesting too strongly, so she stopped and stared into the taut-skinned face before her.

"Look, child, tell me at once. Who said that to you?"

"They didn't say it to me, Alice, I just heard it."

"Will you tell me?"

"No, Alice."

"Very well."

Alice marched out almost on the point of a jog trot and at the same speed she entered her mistress's room, then came to a dead stop at the unexpected sight of her master. For him to call on her mistress two nights running meant trouble. She was about to retreat when Rosina said, "What is it, Alice?"

"Nothing, madam, only when you have a minute, would you kindly come up to the nursery?"

Rosina, remembering last night and the blindfold, rose to her feet, asking anxiously, "Is something wrong?"

"Not exactly wrong, madam." She always gave her mistress her title in front of the master.

"Then what is it?"

Alice became flustered. "Just something I think you should know, madam, but it can wait."

"Is she sick in some way?" Now HE was walking toward her. She always thought of Edmund Lagrange as HE, for HE was an intruder in the house, an alien, an evil alien.

She said, "No, master, she's not sick."

"Then what ails her, woman, that you think her mistress should go to her immediately?"

She stared back at him unafraid. She was unafraid of devils because she had God on her side and this man was composed of a number of devils. She would tell him what the trouble was and find pleasure in the doing. Looking him straight back in the eye, no timidity in her manner or voice, she now said, "She asked me the meaning of 'bastard.' Someone has used the name on her."

She watched his brows gather into a cleft above his nose; she watched his cheeks move upwards and almost obliterate his eyes; she saw anger like a red flame sweep over him; and then he brushed her aside and rushed from the room.

"Oh, Alice! Alice!" Rosina was also rushing past her, but, stopping for a second, she looked at her and said, "Who? Have you any idea?"

"No, none whatever. She says it isn't Watford."

When they reached the nursery, it was to see Edmund Lagrange in a most unusual position. He was sitting on his hunkers. His fine striped trousers tight around his hips, he balanced on his toes as he held his daughter's hands and looked into her frightened face and demanded yet again, "Tell me at once, Annabella. Who called you that name?"

"I—I don't know, Papa." Annabella's fear-filled gaze now flicked past her father to where Watford was standing, her back and hands pressed tight against the frame of the intersecting door, and the combined actions of his daughter and the nursemaid were telling enough for him. In a springing movement he was on his feet and towering over the frightened girl. "You!" The spittle from his lips sprayed her face. "You called my daughter a bastard?"

The twitching face and shivering body were answer enough. He had pulled back his arm, his fist clenched, when Rosina's cry of "Edmund! No!" checked the blow but did not prevent him from knocking Watford sidewards and almost onto her back.

Rosina, now looking at the cowering girl, said the same words for the second time that day: "Go to your room and get your things. Mrs. Page will give you what is owing to you."

Watford did as she was bid. With shaking limbs she went to her room and then to the housekeeper's room, by which time she had regained enough of her natural courage to tell her aunt she could keep her reprimands to herself; she had said what she had said and it was the truth anyway, and she was glad she was leaving.

Then, the aggressiveness of her kind when roused rising in her, she made a final gesture. She didn't leave by the kitchen but went into the hall in order to tell Harris what she thought of him, and incidentally to get him to open a door for her—this once.

She hadn't reckoned on the master and the mistress descending the stairs at this time, but, undeterred, she went on toward the door, and calling to Harris in a loud voice as if he were at the far end of the room, she said, "Well, she is, isn't she, nothing but a little bars-stard?" Then in her black straw bonnet and faded red cloak and carrying her bundle of belongings, she went out into the driving rain to walk the five miles to Jarrow. She was never to forget the journey and the incident that happened on the way which she kept to herself for years until the memorable night when she found herself sharing a room with her one-time charge, and then she spat the details into her face.

The result of Watford's dismissal was that Rosina engaged a governess. This was not a little dictated by her husband's suggestion that the child's education under herself was meager.

Miss Christina Howard was a young woman in her early twenties. She was highly intelligent and if she had been born a hundred years later would no doubt have found a position in the diplomatic service. It didn't take her long to realize that her mistress wished her daughter to be well informed and charmingly mannered, but above all she desired that she be instilled with high principles, whereas her master wished his daughter to be amusing and gay, to have more than a cursory knowledge of languages and, strangely, that she should learn something about the glassmaking trade. Perhaps this was because his wife was knowledgeable on this subject.

She herself knew nothing about the glassmaking trade, but in the gallery there was a bookcase holding more than fifty books about the trade on which this particular family's fortunes were founded, so she had all the information necessary to teach the theoretical side of the business to her pupil.

And so it was that on Annabella's tenth birthday, when she paid her first visit to the family works, she could recognize and name and even explain all that she saw.

It was on this day, too, that her cousin Stephen kissed her for the first time, and she knew that she loved him. And it was on this day that she met the Spaniard who was known as Manuel Mendoza.

Book Two

MANUEL MENDOZA

1

There was great excitement on the drive, at least Annabella felt that everyone was excited, because her own body was bubbling with it. She was happy because of a number of things. First, because she was ten years old; and secondly, because her father was happy, and had been happy for days. Perhaps this was because Mr. Boston had been staying with them. Mr. Boston was quite a young man but he was her father's friend. Then there was the fact that her mama had kissed her a number of times and held her very close as she wished her a happy birthday. But above all, yes, above all, there was the joy of having her cousin Stephen's company for a whole week. Her papa had even been agreeable to Stephen's staying; at other times he had objected to anything other than her cousin's paying a short visit.

Her papa's dislike of Stephen was something she couldn't understand, and it troubled her. Sometimes she wondered if it was because her mama liked Stephen. Then there was another thing that had been troubling her of late: the disagreement that existed permanently between her parents.

But today everyone was happy because they were going to visit the glass works. For such a long time now she had wanted to visit the glass works, and her papa had promised to take her on her tenth birthday, when he had laughingly informed her and Miss Howard that she was to conduct the tour and explain all the mysteries of glassmaking to the party.

In the open landau Annabella sat between her mother and her cousin, a fair-haired youth of sixteen. Opposite sat George Boston, a plump, already florid-faced young man of twenty-three. When Edmund Lagrange entered the carriage, Harris closed the door, then gave a signal to the coachman, and they were off.

Such was her excitement that Annabella almost forgot to wave to Miss Howard, who was standing at an upper window. She wished Miss Howard could have accompanied them because she was very fond of Miss Howard, but her mama had not agreed to it.

Rosina glanced at the glowing face of her daughter and her heart contracted, as it always did, when she thought of how quickly the years were slipping away; she looked upon each birthday of Annabella's as a step nearer parting, because she could be married at sixteen, or seventeen at the latest. Then what would become of herself? There was one glimmer of hope in the fast approaching empty future; Stephen, she knew, was very fond of his small cousin and Annabella was in a childish way greatly attracted to him, but should this feeling ripen with the years, then she would not lose her daughter, for Stephen had a regard for herself, and for a boy so young he already showed a deep understanding.

Stephen, too, was looking at his cousin. He thought she looked very pretty today and much older than ten, twelve at least, but that was, he supposed, because she was tall for her age. He was glad he had been invited to stay for a week, but he must not run afoul of his Uncle Edmund. He now looked at his uncle across the narrow space. He did not look like a bad man, he thought; but how did you tell a bad man? From his looks? His uncle he considered most handsome and attractive in manner. He had once voiced this opinion to his Great-Aunt Emma, and her reply was that there had never been a handsome man yet that was not possessed of the devil. This, he thought, was a pity because he hoped that he himself would grow into a presentable person. He might never be so tall as his uncle, or so thin, but he hoped that he might become as comely.

Edmund Lagrange, too, was considering his daughter. She was ten years old today. Was it ten years since the night he had brought her from Crane Street? She was showing signs of real beauty. Did you ever see a pair of eyes so deeply green? Not hazel or bluey-green, but a summer sun-splashed green, warm and clear; and to her looks add her fresh, affectionate charm. It was odd, he thought at this point, that she in no way resembled her mother. Her mother. He chuckled deeply inside himself. What would she think when she saw her daughter for the first time? He was exceedingly glad the day was fine and they had been able to use the open carriage; otherwise it would have meant her hovering in the vicinity of the glass works and watching them alight from the coach and then she would only have caught a glimpse of the child, whereas today she'd be able to walk down the full length of the street and beyond and look her fill.

He wondered what Boston would say about the situation if

60

he knew the ins and outs of it. Likely raise his blasted plebeian eyebrows. It was funny: the lower the gutter they came from, the higher they wanted to fly, and the more finicky they were about morals. For instance, he didn't like openly visiting Crane Street, which, after all, was just as well, he supposed. When finally he had persuaded him that the thing to do was to set up a mistress in a small establishment, he had chosen a house on the outskirts of Newcastle. His principles, set against his urges, put a great strain on his horse's legs.

Edmund Lagrange would have been somewhat surprised if he could have read his friend's mind at this moment, for Boston's thoughts were traveling along almost the same channels as his own, because George Boston, remembering incidents from the previous night, was thinking, He's got the taste of a pig-swiller; and he wondered how much the stiff-faced madam sitting opposite knew of her husband's life outside the Hall. He wondered if the fortune that was coming to her in four years' time was as vast as Lagrange made it out to be. He certainly hoped so, else he could say good-bye to his loans. He had wiped a number of slates clean in return for Lagrange's taking him under his wing and introducing him into select sporting circles, but he'd been thinking of late he'd been paying a lot for damned little. But still, Lagrange wasn't a man to cross, or drop. In spite of his notorious name, he still had entry to a number of good houses, perhaps not in the Percy or Redhead class, but families of substance, from whom he himself hoped to choose a wife.

His father had said, "Get yerself away from around this quarter where the women not only want brass but a refined twang. Go into Cumberland or Durham; set up there, an' kill two birds wi' one stone: Find tha self a wife; she needn't have a shift but see she's got a bit class, an' at the same time keep tha eyes skinned for small firms hard-pushed for cash. Buy up as many as you can; make George Boston and Son, manufacturers of needles, scissors and knives, not forgetting pins, a firm to be reckoned with."

His father had met Lagrange once and thought him a man of breeding. He would have spat on him if he'd really known what he was like.

Breeding! He snorted inwardly and the snort covered the whole family, including the white-faced boy. The boy was looking at him as if summing him up. He said to him in a manner he imagined was superior, "And what school are you goin' to?"

"Eton, sir."

"Eton!" His chin went up, there was derision in the action. "And what are you going to do when you leave Eton?"

"I hope to go to Oxford, sir."

Now he repeated the word, "Oxford!" his chin again making an upward movement. "And from there, what? Prime Minister?" He laughed now jovially, but the boy was straight-faced as he answered coolly, "I don't aspire to that, sir, merely to becoming a barrister."

He had the urge to take his hand and smack the young snot across the ear. Eton, Oxford, and then a barrister.

"Have you a glass works, sir?"

"What?" The question had come from Annabella, and for a moment he was taken aback, and in the pause before he answered, Edmund Lagrange put in on a high laugh, "No, my dear; he hasn't a glass works, but he has every other type of works. You name them, George Boston has them."

The two men smiled at each other.

The carriage turned out of the drive and onto the rutted road; the bumping disturbed Rosina but delighted Annabella. She looked first to one side and then the other, and everywhere the land rolled away in open fells, showing great sweeps of purple, brown and green. Then of a sudden, into her view came a huddle of makeshift shelters constructed from what looked like pieces of furniture, and scattered about them were a number of children who, on the approach of the carriage, ran toward the road.

"Oh, Mama, look! the poor children."

"Sit back, dear," said Rosina calmly.

Annabella sat back but she could still see the children running along the high bank keeping apace of the carriage. They were all barefoot, and, like the three distant children in her memory, they were dirty and gaunt and none of them was laughing.

Edmund Lagrange now shouted to his coachman, "Speed her up there!" Then in an undertone to Boston he said, "Rosier's rabble; another strike. It took the militia to get that lot out; he's filled the village with Irish. There'll be serious trouble one day, mark my words. He can't handle the men, never could, neither he nor his father." He spoke as one who could handle men.

Two miles farther on they passed through Rosier's village. The dust flew up from the horses' hooves and smothered the women standing at the doors of the row of cottages.

There were children here, too, standing at the side of the

road, and some of them waved and shouted, and Annabella had the desire to wave back, but she knew she mustn't.

Another two miles farther on, they entered Jarrow, and Annabella was again sitting on the edge of the seat.

In the past ten years Jarrow had emerged from a pit village and a small boat-building community into a bustling, over-crowded town in the making. Two men out of every three had an Irish brogue; fighting and drinking were the order of the day; and the reason for the prosperity that enabled working men to drink frequently was the birth of Palmer's ship-yard.

In 1850 there had been between two hundred and fifty and three hundred houses in Jarrow; now, in 1859, there were three thousand and builders were working like mad grabbing at the green fields to erect row on top of row of flat-faced, single brick dwellings.

The carriage tour was to take in Palmer's shipyard, so they emerged into Ellison Street, so named after a man who owned a great deal of the land thereabouts. And the horses going at a spanking pace along the street brought women from the communal taps at the corner ends, customers out of shops, and even turned men's heads from their beer drinking to crowd at the public-house windows and ask, "Is it Palmer?" and hear the reply, "No. Bloody gentry; bloody bloodsuckers."

When they reached the gate of the steelworks, Edmund Lagrange called a halt to the coachman; then, standing by the side of the carriage door, he pointed out the great smok-ing chimneys, the mass of towering iron that was the gantries and cranes, the ships in the river hugging the wharves, and, of all things, a big, black-looking boat sailing down the river with the smoke pouring out of a funnel in the middle of her as if the whole erection were on fire.

The wonder of it all struck Annabella dumb, but not pleas-ingly so. In her ten years the only place she had visited outside the perimeter of the grounds was Durham, and Dur-ham was different from this Jarrow, for it had a wonderful cathedral standing on a rock towering over the river and it was very imposing and everything looked clean, except some of the men who were usually covered in coal dust and who, she understood, were miners. But this Jarrow, this was a different world; the great ships, the noise, the men scurrying about like ants, and the crowds in the streets all dressed in dark, drab clothes. She had noticed a dreadful thing outside one of the inns; she had actually seen a woman lying in the gutter. The sight had made her speechless for a moment and when she went to remark on it, her mama began speaking to Mr. Boston, so of course she couldn't interrupt.

When Lagrange got back in the carriage, he leaned toward her and said, "Would you like to see how they make steel in the great furnaces?" and when she replied, "I don't know, Papa; it's all so big and rather frightening," he put his head back and laughed; then, looking toward Rosina, he asked her politely, "Shall I make arrangements with Palmer to visit? Would you like that?"

"Yes, thank you; it would be very interesting."

Her answer and the way in which it was delivered made George Boston think, She talks to him as if he were a mere acquaintance. She hates him. Aye! I think she hates him. But she loves that girl. Fancy a woman like her, as plain as a pikestaff, giving out something as pretty as that. He stared at the girl. She was pretty, unusually so; in a few years' time when she thickened she'd be a sight to look at.

The carriage had turned round and once more the horses were galloping down Ellison Street with children running on each side of the carriage now, shouting in what sounded like a foreign language.

"Hoy a ha'penny oot!"

When no money was forthcoming, the words, still unintelligible, took on a derisive, offensive tone.

"Gan on, ya big gob skites!"

"Aal dressed up like farthin' dolls."

"Sittin' up' a height like bloody stuffed dummies."

When Armorer's whip licked along one side of the carriage, the children shied away, except one who yelled up at him, "Go on, ya fatarsed lackey. Come doon offa that an' Aa'll rattle your cannister for ya. Go on, ya stink." The boy hung onto the door of the carriage now and yelled at the company, "Ya all stink; ya rift up me belly like a bad dinner."

All this while Edmund Lagrange had been talking to George Boston as if the carriage were running through open deserted country, and Rosina sat straight-backed, her eyes directed toward the coachman; but Annabella and Stephen stared at the children, Stephen with an amused smile on his lips, and Annabella straight-faced and troubled, especially when Armorer kept using his whip.

The carriage now passed the expanse of land where disused salt pans lined the banks of the River Don; it passed the church where St. Bede had preached and taught; it crossed the river by a stone bridge, then on past the Jarrow Slacks, and down the long country road with farms and fields on one side and the River Tyne on the other, and so into Tyne Dock, where on the third of March in that very year the new docks had been opened.

Edmund Lagrange pointed derisively at the huge gates as they passed and remarked to George Boston, "A white elephant if ever there was one; a new dock and the river's so silted up you can walk across to North Shields at low tide! It's ludicrous, don't you think? Then they grumble about Newcastle getting all the shipping. Ten years they've been making that dock; you would have thought the '54 business would have deterred them, but no, somebody got an idea and they must carry it through."

Rosina looked at her husband as he talked. Anyone who didn't know him would think that he had the town and its affairs at heart. His reference to '54 which Mr. Boston likely knew nothing about, was the terrible day when sixty-three ships which were seeking refuge in the river were wrecked and many lives lost, and all in sight of people standing on the shore. But Edmund didn't really care if the town sank or swam; he talked to impress Mr. Boston, and there could be only one reason why he wanted to impress this young man, for Mr. Boston was a common man and ungainly in both manner and speech. She wondered to what extent her husband was in this young man's debt and what hope Mr. Boston held out of being repaid.

Her eyes widened a little when her husband now directed the coachman away from the main road which led into South Shields and along by the river and through what she knew to be a most disreputable area which led to The Gut and finally to the Market Place. When he gave further instructions that Armorer should walk the horses, she felt a protest rising in her but checked it before it escaped her lips. Annabella, she felt, had seen enough of sordid living for one day, but what she had witnessed in Jarrow would be nothing to what she would see if they went through Temple Town, which was obviously where Edmund was directing the carriage.

Armorer, too, was obviously surprised at his master's orders, for he repeated, "Through Temple Town, sir?"

"Yes, yes; we'll see more of the river that way, and the ships." He turned to Annabella. "You'd like to see the ships, wouldn't you?"

"Yes, Papa."

But she didn't see the ships for some time. What she saw were roughlooking people, poor people, and lots of children, and mostly barefooted. The towns seemed full of poor children, the whole world seemed full of barefoot children. Of course, the weather was warm; perhaps that was why they were without shoes or stockings.

Sometimes she herself longed to take her shoes and stockings off and run in the grass with her feet bare, that is, when it was warm; but perhaps these children had no shoes and stockings on when it was cold, wet, snowing. She said to no one in particular, "They have no shoes or stockings on," and her papa answered, "They don't need them, my dear; the soles of their feet are like leather."

"Really!" She moved her head from side to side and smiled slightly at her father. His answer was very reassuring.

But the farther the carriage went into the old town, the more she became aware of the drabness, the dirt, the stench. All the people were odd-looking. Perhaps, she surmised, they were from foreign lands. Then an awful thing happened; she saw a lady empty a chamber pot from an upstairs window and Armorer had to jerk the horses into a gallop to avoid the contents. She was amazed that the lady had aimed the filth at them and that she continued to laugh aloud.

Looking at her mama after this incident, she saw that her face was very white and her mouth tight, as when she was angry. Her father swore, but Mr. Boston laughed, and when she looked at Stephen, she was surprised that he, too, was almost laughing.

They now entered a street named Crane Street. It was facing the river and she didn't know whether to look at the ships or toward the pavement, for a lady was walking in step with the carriage. She was different from all the other ladies she had seen because she was wearing gay-colored clothes. The lady was looking at her, staring at her, and when they were some way down the street, the lady smiled, and she smiled back at her; then her gaze was diverted from the lady to a high window where there were a lot of ladies, and they were hanging over the sill and shouting. All their faces looked merry and happy and she saw her papa look up at them and smile slightly, and so did Mr. Boston. But her mama was looking at the lady who was walking by the carriage; but the lady wasn't looking at her mama, she was looking at her. She had never seen a lady before with such a colorful face; her eyes were very dark and her lips and her cheeks, very red.

Rosina's heart was beating as if it were trying to escape from her body. He couldn't! No! No! He wouldn't be as vile as this. Yet this wanton walking by the carriage with her painted face under that frightful, befeathered hat, and her bare breasts almost pushing out of her gown—but no! it wasn't possible. Yet stripped of the paint the resemblance could be there. She was tall and had a heart-shaped face, the bones good. But again, no! no! He wouldn't subject her to this, surely not.

When her glance flickered toward her husband's face, she saw that his eyes were on the woman and she knew he had subjected her to this. . . . And those hussies at the window, they hadn't been there by chance, they had been waiting. Dear God! Dear God! Why? Why? What had she done that she must suffer such humiliation, such insult?

Of a sudden she caught Annabella's hand, and, pulling it onto her lap, she gripped it tightly. Now the woman was looking at her, and her husband was looking at her, and quickly her glance flashed from one to the other, and only years of training in self-control prevented her from screaming at them.

Edmund Lagrange now gave the coachman a sharp order and the horses went into a trot. The woman tried to keep up with them for some way farther, then she was left behind. The carriage went down the hill, into the Market Place, across it, down King Street and up another hill, toward the glass works.

Annabella was always to remember her first sight of the glass works and she almost exclaimed aloud in her disappointment. What she saw was an open space containing one long, low building with a large cone-shaped chimney attached to the end, and three similar buildings of smaller size. At one side of the main building was a great mound of small coal; at the other side and near the last building, a stack of wood set so as to form an arch.

There was no bustle or activity like that she had witnessed at Palmer's shipyard, no noise of machinery; in fact, the place seemed deserted except for one man who was carrying timber from a pile near the gate and laying it against the wooden arch.

She had for the past two years, under Miss Howard's guidance, read numbers of books dealing with the making of glass, and when Miss Howard questioned her, she answered, parrot fashion, what she had learned. Glass was composed of silicate, soda, potash, lime or chalk; there were various kinds of glass, such as crown, bottle, sheet, plate and flint glass. She also knew that glass could be blown or thrown. She knew, too, that mostly Frenchmen were employed in glassmaking in England and that there had been great trouble between them and their English masters because they would not share the secrets of their trade. The Italians, too, were fine artists in glass, but they, also, guarded their secrets. She learned that the ingredients that went to make glass were universally known, but the secret lay in how they were used. Altogether, she felt she had read a lot of books about something that was very simple. After all, you took some sand and some of these other ingredients and you mixed them up, then put them in a pot inside a furnace, and when they were melted together and forming a liquid, you shaped them, either flat or round or indeed any shape you liked. And if you wanted colored glass, you just added copper for red and green glass and iron if you wanted blue.

She had been longing for this moment when she'd show her papa how knowledgeable she was about their family business, and now she was standing inside the main glass house and she was struck dumb. She was looking across a large room toward a dome-shaped structure with holes in its side. At some distance from it were troughs holding water. There were three men standing in front of the troughs blowing through long tubes and making great bubbles with glass. Other men were sitting in chairlike structures, spinning small quantities of glass on the ends of rods. The place was singularly quiet except for a slight hissing and grinding noise.

A man, detaching himself from a group of men at the far side of the house, came quickly toward them, and Lagrange said airily, "Oh, there you are, Bignall. Everything in order?"

"Yes, sir." The man touched his forehead.

"Mr. Atkinson about?"

"Yes, sir; he's in the office."

"Kindly tell him we've arrived, will you?"

"Yes, sir."

As the man went to pass the company he looked at Rosina, and, touching his forehead again, he said, "Good-day, madam," and she answered, "Good-day, Bignall. How are you?"

"Very well, madam."

"And your wife and family?"

"Doing nicely, thank you, madam."

She inclined her head toward him and smiled, and he smiled back at her before hurrying out.

Lagrange looked at her, his eyebrows raised as he said, "I forgot you knew Bignall."

She could have answered him, "I knew Bignall before I knew you," but all she did was incline her head again.

The manager came hurrying in, full of apologies, and the tour began.

Edmund Lagrange knew this business, the business of glass-making, and if he had applied himself to it wholeheartedly, he could have expanded and made it competitive, at least with the works in the town owned by the Cooksons. Although the Cooksons were a formidable name in glass, having been established in 1730—fifty years before John Conway-Redford had begun his business with one small glass house—they had in 1833 owned ten of the thirty-eight glass houses in New-castle. So, although it would have been foolish to think that the Redford glass works could have competed with the Cook-son dynasty of glassmakers, with attentive supervision it could have held its own locally.

The making of glass needed strict supervision; each house needed a manager to oversee the blowers, founders, gatherers and flatteners, and the managers had to be ever watchful, not only concerning the quality of the sand, but of the figures in the ledgers.

At this particular time France and Belgium were transport-ing glass to Britain, and it was of a better color than the English glass, also cheaper and duty-free. The foreigners could do this because they paid lower wages to their men and less for the materials they used, whereas the British glassmakers were prohibited from selling in France and were charged a high duty on their sales in Belgium. Many manufacturers had in the past to resort to fraud to avoid the excise duty. Those who gave the government the tax they demanded often found themselves without a business. In short, the glass trade needed hard work and constant supervision, as well as expert sales-men; they had to be especially expert when they tried to sell the dregs of the industry in Ireland; but above all, in order to survive, it needed men with—the touch.

Out of dozens of young boys employed by any one firm, the number that would eventually become expert blowers could be counted on one hand. It was nothing for a firm to entice blowers from another firm with the offer of bonuses and higher wages. Men had been offered as much as three pounds a week as blowers and thirty shillings a week as gatherers, while the usual rate for these expert craftsmen was twenty-eight shillings for blowers and twenty shillings for gatherers.

Besides Annabella's and Stephen's, it was also George Bos-ton's first sight of the interior of a glass works and he listened eagerly to all Lagrange had to say, but he barely covered his impatience when his host deferred to his daughter so that she could show off her learning. He didn't want to listen to the child prattling her schoolroom facts, and when she bowed her head in front of the workmen and remained silent, he thought it became her better than her jabbering would have done. He guessed rather than knew that a lot of the process here was rather old-fashioned. He understood that coal was now used for most furnaces, but this particular house was still getting its heat from wood.

Lagrange was asking his daughter what the man was doing who was puddling clay with his bare feet inside a lead-lined bin, and again she hung her head until her mother spoke her name. "Annabella," she said; and then the child, still with head bowed, said, "He's making pots, Papa."

"And what will he do with the pots when they're finished?" asked Lagrange.

Her head came up a little as she answered, "He will put them into the pot arch, Papa, and bake them."

"Yes, yes." He nodded at her rather impatiently. "And then what happens? What goes into them?"

"Glass, Papa. I mean the ingredients for glass. They—they dry sand and add lead to it, red lead and saltpeter and"— she paused again, then looked up toward the domed ceiling before adding quickly—"if they want to make flint glass, they add arsenic and . . ."

"Yes, one more thing." He prompted her with a nod of his head.

"Borax, Papa."

"And something else for flint glass."

"Glass, broken glass, Papa."

She took in a deep breath and let it out slowly as Lagrange said, "There, what do you think of that?" He looked around the company, which included four workmen and the man in the puddling bin, and the men smiled and jerked their heads and said, "Aye, aye; she's a clever miss," and Lagrange, smiling at his daughter, said, "Indeed, indeed, she is a clever miss." Then, taking her hand, he proudly led the party from the shop and into the next one.

In this house they were just in time to see pots being opened. From a safe distance they watched the blower, or footmaker, as he was called, gathering the glass onto his blowing iron. The man twisted the molten glass round on the end of the iron, much as a housewife would treat treacle on the end of a spoon. Again and yet again he pushed the iron back into the furnace pot, gathering yet more molten glass onto it; then going to his chair he sat down, put the end of the pipe in his mouth and began to blow, and his catch of glass took on the elongated shape of a large bottle, the creation of which excited Annabella.

They now turned their attention to a second footmaker, who was drawing from another pot in the same circle. This man lifted his catch of molten glass onto a polished steel slab, and when he began to roll the metal along it, Edmund Lagrange, again looking at Annabella, said, "And now, my little expert, do you know what they call this process, eh?"

Without hesitation she replied, "Marvering, Papa."

Stephen, bending down to her, laughed now and said in a teasing fashion, "Aren't we clever!" and as she laughed back at him and tapped his sleeve with her hand, Lagrange, turning almost angrily on the boy, said, "Could you answer any questions on glass, young man?"

Slightly taken aback, Stephen stared at his uncle, then said frankly and, what was more annoying to Lagrange, fearlessly, "Not one, sir."

"Well then, it beholds you not to deride those who can, doesn't it?"

Rosina turned away at this point and beckoned to Stephen to accompany her out.

As they made their way to the next shop, a young man passed them carrying three long lengths of wood on his shoulder and Rosina's glance was drawn to him because he was unusually tall, well over six feet, whereas all the men in the shops, both workers and clerks, were of small stature, the tallest being no more than five feet six. It was evident that the man was a foreigner; the glass trade more than any other was supported by a mixture of nationalities.

The third shop was a very special shop where they were making sheet glass and they stayed quite a while in here as Mr. Boston asked many questions. It was as they came out that Annabella saw the cat. It was an extremely large tortoiseshell cat and it was sauntering leisurely across the yard and she exclaimed, "Oh! look at the pussy, Mama. Isn't it beautiful?" As she made to go toward it, Rosina caught at her hand, saying, "We're leaving now."

"But can't I stroke it, Mama?"

"It—it might scratch you." She didn't add that it might be verminous.

"It's a big one," Stephen remarked, looking at the cat. "It's likely a ratter. We've got one at school; it catches rats as big as itself."

On this information Rosina chided her nephew, saying, "Oh, Stephen!" and he laughed at her as he replied, "It does, Aunt; it does really."

She looked fondly at him now as she said, "Have you enjoyed your visit?"

"Extremely. Yes, extremely."

Her glance remained on his open, frank face. He meant what he said. In spite of Edmund's manner toward him, he hadn't taken offense. He was a dear boy, Stephen, such a dear boy; she hoped with all her heart that things would go the way she wished in the future, and they could, for he was already very fond of Annabella and he was just the suitable number of years older than she.

As they got into the carriage, the foreign-looking young man passed with another pile of wood on his shoulder. He turned his head toward them and looked at them, one after the other, then looked away again and continued toward the stack that he was making.

It was just when Reeves put the horses in motion that the dog came through the open gate, saw the cat and raced toward it. The cat, which had been sitting down and about to wash itself, was startled into erratic flight and scampered straight across the horses' path, with the dog only inches behind it. One horse whose forefoot had been flicked by the dog's tail neighed loudly and reared upwards, and this affected its companion. Reeves was bellowing now and pulling on the reins, but without the slightest calming effect on the animals, and the next minute they were galloping wildly out of step toward the open gates.

The animals themselves might have got safely through the gates but the carriage, rocking from side to side as it was, would surely have been dashed against the brickwork if the horses hadn't been drawn to a sliding, slithering halt only yards from the gate itself.

Tumbled together and gasping, the occupants of the carriage righted themselves and stared toward the figure spread-eagled between the two animals. The man's arms were extended to their utmost, with the black, dirt-grimed hands gripping the bridles; for a full minute they stared and for a full minute they listened to him talking in a language no one of them could understand because the sounds he was making weren't actually words, but a mixture of pleasant, deep grunts and sounds like long drawn-out notes picked haphazardly from a scale. His arms slackening, he brought his hands down the

72

face of each sweating animal and they became still; then looking at the people who were all staring at him, he stepped to the side and the spell was broken.

Edmund Lagrange got hastily down from the carriage, followed by George Boston. Lagrange looked at the horses; they were more calm than they had been a few minutes ago when they had been pawing the ground impatient to be off. Then he looked at the olive-skinned young fellow and said with sincerity, "Thank you. That was a very brave thing you did."

The young man stared back at him saying nothing.

"You"—Lagrange now glanced at the horses—"you understand horses, apparently?"

"I like horses."

Lagrange's eyes were brought quickly to the young man again for the simple reason that he had omitted the "sir."

"Have you dealt with them before?"

"Most of me life."

"You're not from these parts—you're Irish, aren't you?"

"I was brought up in Ireland, but I'm a Spaniard." The tone, a deep soft burr, was even, conversational, not that of a workman answering the master.

"What is your name?"

"Manuel Mendoza."

Lagrange narrowed his eyes at the man. "How long have you been here?"

"In the glass house?" He jerked his head backwards. "Five weeks. In England, three months."

"And you're settled, you like it?"

"Not very much. I don't think I'll ever make a glass man, not cut out for it."

Lagrange's feeling of gratitude was quickly turning to one of irritation. He did not like the fellow's manner; it put him, strangely, at a disadvantage, and that of course was wrong. He thrust his hands into his breeches pocket, and, drawing out a soft kid purse, he extracted three sovereigns from it and, handing them toward the young man, said, "For your pains."

Manuel Mendoza did not lift his hands from his sides, but he looked at the money in the palm before him; then looking at the giver, he said, "Thank you all the same, but I don't need payin' for that, it was a sort of exercise; I was grateful for the chance." He now turned and looked toward the faces in the carriage and he smiled at them, and his eyes glinted darkly and his teeth showed white and even. Then, with a

73

small downward movement of his head to the two men before him, he turned away and walked toward the glass-house door, which was now crowded with workmen.

Lagrange looked after him for a moment; then thrusting the money back into his purse, he looked at George Boston and remarked under his breath, "Odd customer," and George Boston replied, in a tone tinged with awe, "I've never seen anything like it; I mean the way he stopped them. For all his thinness he must be as strong as an ox." Then turning and looking toward the door through which the foreigner had disappeared with his workmates, he asked more of himself than of Lagrange, "I wonder if he can use his fists?" and to this Lagrange replied somewhat tartly, "He happens to be my man."

"Ah, yes. But remember, he said he was no glass man," and on this Boston laughed at his scowling host and got up into the carriage.

Her birthday was almost over. It had been a most exciting day. That wonderful ride through the towns of Jarrow and Shields, the children running by the carriage, and that pretty lady smiling at her. Then the tour of the glass works. She wouldn't admit to herself that she had been disappointed in the works, but the visit had been made exciting by that brave man who had saved all their lives. The carriage would surely have been dashed between the walls of the gates and they would all have been seriously injured, her mama had told Alice, and she had also said he was a most unusual young man because he had refused money, and so few people refused money.

Then there had been that wonderful dinner awaiting them, and for the very first time she had sat at a full meal in the dining room with both her parents and guests present. Later, when the elders were resting, she and Stephen and Miss Howard had gone into the park and played hide-and-seek and catch ball. In the early evening tea had been served in the drawing room and Harris had brought in the most beautiful cake, with her name and age written in colored candy flowers on the top. Her mama said she must go personally and thank cook, and after the tea she did this.

The cook was new; she had been with them only a few months. She was pleasant and kindly-looking, not like Blunt, who never smiled at her. All the servants in the kitchen had smiled at her today and wished her a very happy birthday.

And now she was in bed and not the least tired. It was

very warm, but Miss Howard had insisted on tucking her in. She kicked down the bedclothes until her feet were showing, then lay looking at them as she wriggled her toes. Next year she would be eleven, and the following year twelve; then thirteen, fourteen, fifteen, then joy of joys sixteen, and by the time she was that great age, she'd be able to dance correctly, and sing, and play the pianoforte, and have all the accomplishments that were required of a lady; but what was more important, she'd be the age to go to London and attend balls and wear beautiful gowns and dance the quadrille.

Her papa had said there were great regattas in London on the Thames between London Bridge and Hammersmith, and paddle steamers, on which brass bands played, went up and down the river and people picnicked on the riverbanks, and at Putney there was a great fair where she would see fat ladies and performing pigs and giants and dwarfs, and everywhere people enjoying themselves. Sometimes she felt she couldn't wait, she'd die with impatience before the time came when she could go to London and see all these wonders.

Her mama never made any reference to her going to London, and because of the certain feeling that existed between her mama and papa, she was wise enough never to tell one what the other said.

Still full of energy, she now jumped out of bed and ran to the window in the hope that she might see a carriage coming or going, but to her disappointment the drive was deserted; then she felt a wave of excitement when from out of the pagoda to the side of the drive she saw Stephen appear. His face was straight and he looked rather lonely.

Her window was shut tight to prevent the night air entering, and it was much too heavy for her to attempt to open, so she rapped hard on it with her knuckles, and when Stephen looked up, she waved at him and he waved back. Then he came and stood under the window, and when she beckoned him up with a curl of her finger, he laughed and nodded, then disappeared into the conservatory.

Now she scrambled to the wardrobe, and, taking down a housegown, she put it on over her nightgown, and when a few minutes later she heard Stephen come in through the nursery door, she ran to meet him, asking, "What were you doing in the garden? I mean, why are you not with the gentlemen?"

Smiling at her, he said, "Uncle and Mr. Boston and the other two gentlemen are along in the Hall." He nodded his head to the side.

"Oh," she said understandingly. Then laughing, she added,

"I can't sleep, I'm not tired; come and sit on the sill." She ran back into the bedroom, and he followed her at a distance, saying, "Where is Miss Howard?"

She pointed toward the communicating door which led into Miss Howard's room. "She'll be back shortly, she's having supper."

So they sat on the deep windowsill, he with his legs dangling to the floor, she with hers curled under her, and she prattled on about the events of the day, although she had been over them several times before; and he found he was happy to sit there and listen to her and look at her, for she was extraordinarily pretty. He saw very few girls, at least pretty ones. The maids at school were anything but pretty; most of them had very heavy buttocks and very thick ankles, and when he was home for the holidays his Uncle James and Aunt Emma never entertained anyone young. That was the reason, he supposed, why he liked coming to his Aunt Rosina's, because even as a small child Annabella had been entertaining. Also, of course, he was very fond of his Aunt Rosina, so much so that he often wished she had been his mother. Even now, at this age, he missed not having parents; aunts and uncles were different somehow, they didn't quite fit into the empty parts inside you. When he went to stay with his friend Roger Bollard, the difference became very apparent. Parents, he felt, were necessary to happiness; and yet, was there any happiness in this house between his Uncle Edmund and Aunt Rosina? None at all, he would say; yet both, in their own ways, made Annabella's life happy.

As he stared at her, it came to him with a kind of surprise that she was like neither parent, and he became lost in the process of comparing each of her features with those of his aunt and uncle, so when she grabbed his hand and shook it, he was slightly startled.

"What are you staring at? You're miles away. What are you thinking about? About the brave man? He was wonderful, wasn't he? Oh, it's been a wonderful, wonderful day. You know what I was thinking, Stephen, just before I saw you?" She didn't wait for his reply but went on, "I was thinking of when I'll be sixteen because on that day I'll be in London, and I'll be wearing a beautiful gown and I'll go to a ball and I'll see all the great sights, and the Queen. Papa says I'll be presented to the Queen. Just imagine, Stephen, being presented to the Queen." She leaned her head back on her shoulders and gazed up at the big brass rings on the curtains as she said quite solemnly, "I do hope I don't grow up ugly, Stephen."

His burst of laughter brought her head forward and she shook his hand again, saying, "What are you laughing at?"

"You growing up ugly, and the way you said it. You know fine well you won't grow up ugly, you're a little minx." He was leaning forward looking into her eyes now. "Every year you'll grow more beautiful and by the time you're sixteen and you go to London, you'll be so ravishing that all the gentlemen will ride out to accompany you into Town, and the band will play and flags will wave and everyone will forget about the Queen and they'll say, 'Who wants to look at that plain-looking thing when there's the beautiful Miss Annabella Lagrange?' "

Her head was back, her mouth was wide and her laughter high and gurgling, not at all as her mama had taught her to laugh. And Stephen was laughing with her, but when she, of a sudden, threw her arms around his neck and kissed him on the mouth, he fell back against the stanchion of the window and to save her and himself falling off the sill, he put his arms about her. And that was how Edmund Lagrange saw them when, attracted by their laughter, he came through the open door of the nursery and into the bedroom.

Stephen had never been afraid of his uncle. He was aware that his uncle did not like him very much, but this he put down to the fact that he himself was related to the Conway-Redford side of the family. From as far back as he could remember he had heard rumors of his uncle's exploits and for over a year now he had known that his uncle, besides being an inveterate gambler, was a womanizer; yet even with this knowledge and all the warnings his Great-Uncle James had given him regarding the man, he still had a sneaking regard for him, for when in a good humor he found his uncle very entertaining.

But now, with his uncle's hands around his throat and his breath almost leaving his body, he kicked and punched at the man until he found himself floating away to the accompaniment of Annabella's screams.

When he regained consciousness, he was lying in his room and his Aunt Rosina was pressing a wet cloth to his throat. He tried to speak, but Rosina said softly, "It's all right, it's all right." However, he must speak. His mind was very clear, startlingly so; he knew why his uncle had attacked him. His aunt must know the truth. He raised himself on his elbow

77

and began, "I—I didn't do anything wrong, Aunt Rosina. We —we were laughing, just laughing, and I said she was pretty and she—" He moved his head in a wide sweep, feeling that it wasn't gallant to say Annabella had kissed him, but Rosina helped him out. "It's quite all right, dear," she said softly; "Annabella is impulsive, it would be she who kissed you. I understand."

"Thank you, Aunt Rosina." He lay back on the pillow and drew in a long, shuddering breath. Then looking at her again, he said, "She's just a child, Aunt Rosina, only ten. How could Uncle—?"

"Don't trouble yourself anymore about it, Stephen."

"Will—will I have to return home?"

She lowered her eyes as she said, "Yes, I'm afraid so; but don't worry, you may come again shortly."

Once more he was shaking his head. "I'm so sorry, Aunt Rosina. It had been such a wonderful day for her, and I spoiled it."

"You mustn't blame yourself in any way, Stephen. As you say, Annabella is but a child and she acted like a child. She's very fond of you, Stephen."

"And I, too, Aunt Rosina, I'm very fond of Annabella, very fond; she's been like a sister to me."

He was looking up at his Aunt Rosina and she was looking down at him, and now she said a very strange thing. She said, "But she's not your sister, Stephen, and there's no need for you to go on thinking of her as your sister—you understand?"

No, he didn't, not quite, in fact not at all. He was sixteen but rather young for his age, yet if anyone else had said these words, he would have put on them a certain construction, a construction that he was sure his aunt never intended, so therefore he didn't quite understand her.

She said now, "I will tell Faill to come and attend you and I'll see you in the morning before you leave. I will give you a letter for Aunt Emma explaining everything. Now don't worry." She touched his brow lightly with her fingers, then went out and along the corridor, and she wasn't surprised when Alice, standing some distance from her bedroom door, signaled to her that her husband awaited her within.

She paused a moment while she stared at Alice, then she opened the door and went into the room to see him standing in the middle of it, his face still white, his hair still disheveled. She saw at once that his rage had not diminished.

"Huh!" He jerked his head up as he made the sound and

went immediately into a tirade. "The name of Lagrange stinks in your nostrils, doesn't it? It spells for you lechering, whoring, gambling, chicancery, anything but what's decent, whereas the name of Redford is synonymous with the pure, the chaste, the godlike, and a sixteen-year-old Redford wouldn't dream of practicing on a ten-year-old, now would he? But he did—ripe for bed, he picked a ten-year-old."

"Be quiet! Be quiet, do you hear me?" She hissed at him as she bent forward from the waist, her long-sustained anger forcing itself through the armor of her facade. "Whatever was done, whatever you saw was prompted by Annabella."

"You're a liar! She's still a child, as innocent as when I first threw her on that bed." He flung his arm backwards.

"There you make a mistake, for it would be impossible for her to be wholly innocent having sprung from you. But one thing she hasn't learned from you yet, and that is to lie and cheat and torture." She paused, her breath catching in her throat, while they glared at each other; then she went on, "She's admitted to me quite frankly that it was she who put her arms around him and kissed him. It was her way of thanking him for helping to make her birthday happy. But your jaundiced eye saw nothing but evil, because you live by evil, you ooze evil, you have not one decent human trait in you." She swallowed deeply and moved her tongue inside her mouth. Then she made herself voice something that she had told herself all day must be ignored and placed in the dark chamber of her mind, where lay all the other things he had imagined had hoodwinked her. "That woman, you arranged for her to be there, taking the carriage down that notorious street, those creatures at the window, but her, brazenly staring, staring. . . ."

When she couldn't go on speaking with her lips but only with her eyes, he glared back at her and, with his mouth almost square depicting his feelings of scorn, he sent words like icicles through her flesh. "And why not?" he said. "I don't consider it a sin that a mother should look at her daughter once in a while. You look down your long, aristocratic nose at her and her like, don't you? But she produced what your barren belly could never do, she produced a child, and the irony of it is, that child is your life now and"—his words slowed and became weighted with threat—"I have the power to cut off that life and it would pay you to remember that, my dear, pure Rosina. And while I'm at it, I may as well tell you what I've been considering for a long time. Her education is going to be changed, there's going to be less God

79

and quite a bit more Mammon in it. She's going to be got ready for marriage, and I, my dear Rosina—will pick the man."

The hate between them rose like a mist and blurred her vision, and when Rosina next saw him he was at the door looking toward her, and as if through his last words he had read her own desire with regard to her daughter's future, he ended, "And don't let me catch your precious, mealy-mouthed nephew in this house again, because if I do, I swear I'll take a horsewhip to him."

He pulled the door behind him with a resounding bang, marched across the landing, down the main staircase, through the hall and the conservatory, and Cargill, the third footman, not being agile enough to get to the doors before him, he wrenched them open, banging one back into the man's face.

When he reached the stables there was no one about, but his bellowing soon brought the coachman and the stableboys rushing from the room above the coach house.

"Get me Fairisle saddled."

"Yes, sir. Yes, sir." The stableboys ran into the stable on the double—they saw that their master was in a mood and it would behold them to watch out. But Armorer, the coachman, who directed the saddling, was a little peeved. He'd had a long day. And then there was that business at the glass house; that had shaken him more than he cared to admit openly. And now, almost nine o'clock, here was the master demanding a horse to be saddled. There was only one good thing about it, Fairisle wasn't tired; she'd had no exercise for two days. She was fresh and rearing to go; the time of day didn't matter to her.

The horse saddled and brought into the yard, Lagrange mounted, then set the animal off almost immediately into a gallop down the west drive, which was unusual, and as Armorer said to Heron, somebody would have to go along the whole length and level that out in the morning.

The lodge-keeper, too, was surprised when he was called upon to open the gates, and when, with the privilege of long service dating from the mistress's grandfather, he dared to speak first and say, "I hope, master, there's nothing wrong, no trouble at the house?" for answer he got a dark, ferocious look which told him that the only trouble at the house was his master's being in a mood.

Off the road and out on the open fells, Lagrange gave the horse its head, and as it galloped over heather-covered flats, hillocks and loose scree hills, his anger gradually seeped from him.

The long twilight was deepening as he passed through Rosier's village; the men squatting on their hunkers outside their houses in the dry mud street, the women sitting on their steps, their blouses open to let the cool air to their sweating bodies, the youths on the open ground playing quoits, all looked at him with interest. He knew he was known to them as Lagrange the gambler, the man who would bet on anything from a frog to a Frenchman, and the title didn't displease him.

Farther on he passed the mine, and when, in a narrow lane, he came on a group of miners who had just come off from their shift and who showed no intention of making way for his horse, he had the urge to gallop into their midst. But at the present moment he was deep in Rosier's debt for coal supplied to the works and the House, and were he to injure one of his workmen, animal-like individuals though they were, Rosier would perhaps turn nasty. So, not waiting until they came to the end of the lane and letting them think they'd got the better of him, as was their intention, he set the horse at a steep bank and turned in the direction of home again.

He was going at a trot through a copse when he saw to the right of him a number of milling figures, and not until he had drawn the horse to a halt did he discern that they were fighting. This he found interesting, so he guided the horse gently over the leaf-strewn ground toward them, and as he drew nearer he noticed, through the deepening twilight, that two men were already laid out on the grass apparently senseless, but others were still battling it out. It looked as if four men were attacking one.

He guessed by their dress and their small stature that they were miners, likely Rosier's savages, and he was about to leave them to their dispute when a foot came upwards and kicked one of the men in the stomach and sent him reeling, then a hand was thrust from the melee and gripped the hair of another assailant. As this man's head was brought downwards, Lagrange saw for a fleeting second the face of the victim of the attack straining upwards. It was that of the Spaniard, one of his men.

When he rode his horse at the group, his whip lashing downwards, they scattered like rabbits into the undergrowth leaving their two mates and the long figure of the Spaniard on the ground.

By the time Lagrange had dismounted, the Spaniard had raised himself onto his elbow. But he looked the worse for wear; blood was running freely from a slit in his temple, his coat sleeve was half ripped off and blood was oozing through his shirt.

"Can you get to your feet?"

"Yes. Yes, I'm all right."

Lagrange put one hand under his armpit and helped him up. When erect, the young fellow leaned against a tree and closed his eyes tightly for a moment. Then, giving a single shake to his head, he looked at Lagrange and said, "Thanks. It's lucky for me you were passin'."

"You're a long way from your place of work, aren't you?"

"Aye, but I like to get into the open; I take a stroll in the evenin'."

The man was his workman but he wasn't giving him the appendage of "sir" and again the omission irritated him. He said curtly now, "How did you manage to run afoul of that mob?"

"I just asked them the way. All I said was, 'Can you tell me where Mr. George Boston lives?' and not one of them answered me, they just walked on. Then about five minutes later, when I came through the wood, here they were waiting. If they'd come two at a time I'd have managed them, but they came in a bunch." He wiped the blood from his mouth and cheek with the side of his hand.

Lagrange stared at him. He was looking for George Boston. Why? "Why were you looking for Mr. Boston?" he asked.

"Because he has horses, breeds them. One of the glass men told me. I'd like to work with horses again, dearly I would." He moved his head to one side while still looking at Lagrange and ended, his tone half apologetic, "I'm not cut out for glassmakin', as I told you earlier on. The wage is good and it's the first job I was ever given drink money in. I like a drink, but they're sodden with the beer most of the time. Then there's their Society; you've got to join. I'm against being pressed. Too much like slavery. No; give me horses."

Lagrange continued to look at him. Boston would snap up this fellow, not only for his horses, but also because of the man's fists. That's what he had said as they left the yard: "I wonder if he can use his fists." Good boxers were hard to come by, as were men who could really handle horses. He said abruptly, "You're miles away from Mr. Boston's place—

he's across the county. Look, I think you'd better come back with me and have that eye attended to."

"Oh, that's all right, thanks all the same, but—but I'd better be makin' me way back to the town, I don't know the roads hereabouts and, who knows, I might run into another bunch."

"That's not unlikely." Lagrange turned toward his horse as if about to mount, saying as he did so, "You want to work with horses?"

"Indeed I do."

"I need a groom, particularly someone who can teach my young daughter to ride and handle a horse. She's afraid of horses."

"Is she, now? Well, I could learn her. And thank you for the offer. Thank you, thank you, indeed." He was still wiping the blood with the side of his hand from his cheek and one eye was swelling, but his face looked darkly bright and alert as he ended, "An' I'll take you up on your kind offer and come along with you." Then looking toward the still prone figures on the ground, he said, "What'll I do about them?"

"Nothing. As soon as we're gone, their mates will return." When Lagrange saw him hesitate, he said abruptly, "Don't bother, I tell you, come along." And with that he mounted his horse and moved off.

Manuel Mendoza walked by the side of his new master, who was also his old master, and he laughed gently and said, "This is like a miracle. I'm very grateful an' I can promise you that your daughter'll lose her fear of the animal." He put out his hand now and touched the horse's coat with gentle fingers.

Edmund Lagrange had followed hunches all his life. When he followed them faithfully, he made money; when he was dilatory in following them, he lost money. He now had a hunch that he was onto a good thing with this young fellow; yet at the same time he was irritated by him. Looking down at him now, he asked, "Have you ever done any boxing?"

"Boxing?" The arched black eyebrows moved upward. "No."

"But you are very strong, you've got unusually strong hands."

"Aye, yes, I have that." There was no arrogance in the admission; it was merely a statement. "But I keep them for the animals. I have no desire to bash a man's face in."

"No? But you want to protect yourself; look what happened tonight."

"I didn't do so bad all told. I had the first two on their backs in seconds and if they'd come in pairs, as I said, I'd have managed them."

"If you had learned the art of fisticuffs, you would have been able to deal with the lot of them and at one go, I'm sure."

"Very likely."

The reply was conversational and the manner not that to which Edmund Lagrange was used when dealing with his employees. The fellow's attitude showed no sign of his awareness of class and the distinctions therein. He was addressing him as an equal, as he himself might address one of his own acquaintances, and his bearing, strangely irritating in an inferior, had a haughtiness about it. Dressed differently, he would likely have passed for something other than he was, that is, if he didn't open his mouth, for although he had the attractive burr of the Southern Irish that distinguished him from the coarse, guttural twang and almost unintelligible jargon of the Tynesider, his speech was that of the common man. He was a common man, and if he was to be in his service, he must be made to realize this, and from the beginning. So looking down on to the blood-streaked face, he brought it sharply round in his direction by saying, "It is usual for my servants to address me as 'sir.' "

Their eyes held in silence. Lagrange's body swayed with the movement of the horse. Manuel Mendoza's shoulders hardly moved with his walking, for unconsciously he carried himself from his hips.

The horse had taken eight paces and the man hadn't answered. Lagrange's jaws were tightening, his face darkening, when the fellow said, "Very good." Yet he still did not add the required vocative. For a moment he thought of him as an unbroken horse that needed taming, yet the eyes looking back into his were those of no colt, rather those of an experienced stallion. He was puzzled by the fellow, intrigued, yet all the while irritated, but he warned himself he must not show this, for he may this night have acquired a very remunerative sideline, a very necessary sideline to his strained finances.

2

It was just getting light the following morning when Manuel Mendoza sat up on his pallet bed in the attic space above

84

the hayloft and bumped his head against the roof. This did not cause him to put his hand to the top of his head but to the side of his cheek, which under the bandage was throbbing painfully. When he moved his left arm, it was only slightly stiff, and on this he drew in a deep breath. The knife had only seared the skin. But what matter a few scratches? He stretched his arms outwards, clenched his fists and, putting his head back on his shoulders, tensed his neck muscles; then, getting to his knees, he looked out of the window.

He had fallen into heaven. It was right, then, what Margee had told him. He could hear her voice as if she were speaking this minute as she had read his palm, an unusual thing for her to do, for she didn't waste her talents unless there was money in it. "You'll end up in a big house, lad, with servants spillin' all over the place. And," she had said, "many strange things'll happen you, some bitter, some sweet, an' some terrible. But where e'er you be, you'll never have to call any man master."

Well—the look in his deep brown eyes was skeptical—he had landed in a big house, all right. She was right there. But the thing she had emphasized most was wrong, because he'd had to call a man master. "Call me 'sir,'" he'd said. But what odds—he had landed in heaven and he'd call him "God" if he so demanded. He looked down to the yard below, and the sight of the stables and the knowledge of what was in them made him tremble with excitement.

He had been sleeping naked and now he hastily pulled on his torn shirt and trousers, and, his feet bare, he walked softly across the floor and let himself down through the trapdoor into the hayloft. Then, groping his way between the bales, because it was dark on this floor and he hadn't his bearings yet, he came to the open trapdoor, went down the short ladder to the ground floor, then into the yard.

He already knew that the harness room was next door, for that was where they had fixed him up last night and brought him that fine meal. He now went slowly toward it, and opening first the top half and then the bottom, he entered before standing in awe looking at the things that appeared like jewels to him. The wood-lined room was dotted with pegs and hooks from which hung halters, snaffles, pieces of harness, bits, and brasswork. Then over against the far wall was a line of saddletrees holding the saddle pads. The smell of harness was perfume to his nostrils and the gleam of the leather warmed his soul.

Slowly he walked round the room, touching one thing after

85

the other as if they were sacred relics, and he stood for a moment with his two hands on the warm boiler, looking at the banked-down fire in the rough stone fireplace to the side of it. Then he went out and into the stables.

A bay mare was lying in its stall and it turned its head and looked at him; then in two movements it rocked itself to its feet and, head up, stared at the strange intruder, snorting its disapproval.

Manuel, standing perfectly still, made a sound in his throat, then another, which he repeated at least half a dozen times before he began to move slowly forward. Now, hand extended, he touched the long, silk muzzle, he just touched it, no movement of the fingers at first, then slowly he began to stroke the cheek, his throat continuing to send forth the strange sounds.

He was aware that someone had been standing in the doorway for quite a while before moving, and then he didn't turn his head until the voice said, "Eeh, God sakes! Him lettin' ya do that."

"Mornin'." Manuel turned and looked at the blear-eyed stableboy. It was the one called Danny Dinning. Danny did not give him a good morning in return, but said, "He's wild, that one. Mr. Armorer, he's the only one can handle him. Kicks hell out of everything at times; breaks up his box, the lot. Sakes alive! You know horses, mister. I forgot your name."

"Manuel. Manuel Mendoza."

"What's this?"

Now they both turned toward the door and were confronted by Armorer, who looked from one to the other; then, his eyes coming to rest on Manuel, he added, not unkindly, "I should have warned you, I'll see to him. Best to keep your distance from him."

"He's all right."

"That's all you know." The coachman turned on Dinning, crying harshly, "Well! what you standin' there for? Fifteen past five and not one of them watered yet. Do you want my boot in your arse afore you start?"

The boy scurried away, and Manuel said, in a voice that held much more deference than when he had been speaking to Lagrange, "I'd be obliged if you'd put me to work."

"The master said nothin' about you startin' right away, you're in a mess. How do you feel?"

"Oh, stiff, that's all. An hour or so strapping at them"—

he jerked his head back at the horses—"will soon put that right."

"You're used to horses, then? Not just Irish donkeys?"

Manuel's face became straight, the look almost aggressive, as he answered, "Not just Irish donkeys."

"Oh, well"—Armorer jerked his chin up—"the Irish that come over here, they talk about horses but what they mean by horses are little snotty-nosed donkeys. But then, after yesterday"—he nodded his head slowly at Manuel now—"you couldn't have stopped that pair if you hadn't have known what you were about. Well—" He turned abruptly and walked along the stables, continuing, "Dinning and Heron muck out the stalls first thing, then they bring the water from the river. There's a well, but the water's too cold for them. Everything's weighed—chopped straw, bruised oats, barley dust, salt, the lot. I'll show you later. Fairisle, Beauty and Sandy there" —he pointed to the three boxes one after the other—"they're exercised between six and seven; after they get back, they're brushed and strapped, that's after they've been washed if they're mucky. . . . Do with another hand here, I'm tellin' you; you haven't come afore time. Six horses, two carriages, we're goin' at it from Monday mornin' till Sunday night. The master, he's particular, finicky I'd say, where the animals are concerned; not above flinging the dandy brush at you and knockin' hell out of the whole place if the turnout isn't right, whether it's Fairisle or the coach. That's Fairisle; but you saw him last night. This other one's Chester; you won't recognize him but it was him and Sandy you pulled down yesterday. Then the one you were comin' to terms with along there, the holy terror, he's called Dizzy."

And so Manuel followed George Armorer over his whole establishment, listening intently to every word he said, taking in everything he saw. Nothing escaped him with regard to the horses or their surroundings.

And nothing escaped him, either, when at nine o'clock he went into the kitchen for his first meal.

All eyes were on him, especially those of the women. The cook sat at the head of the table, and down one side, on her left, were the female staff, seven in all. The kitchen and scullery maids waited on the table, eating after the others were finished. Down her right side sat the seven menservants, the two stableboys coming at the bottom of the table, and between them and George Armorer an empty space had been left, and when Manuel came late into the kitchen, because he had been washing himself under the pump, Armorer beckoned him to the vacant seat.

No one spoke to him, but the women, down to Fanny Pierce, the youngest, flicked their glances at him between giggles until brought to silence by the cook. The men, on the other hand, talked among themselves, yet everyone at the table was curious about the big, foreign-looking young fellow whom the master had brought in out of the night all bleeding and messed up and said he was to be the new groom.

When, having finished his meal, Manuel rose immediately to his feet, excusing himself, but to no one in particular, by saying, "I'll away then," they all looked at his departing figure in amazement; it was usual to sit after the meal, if only for five minutes, and discuss the business of the house and any little titbit that would arouse interest, and in the case of a newcomer this would be the time they asked him questions about his last place of service, the conditions and so on.

Reeves, the first footman, was a man of position when in the kitchen and he was annoyed; the fellow acted already as if he were somebody, as if he had authority. Well, it was up to himself to show him just what his position was in this household. Thrusting his face forward and looking down the table toward Armorer, he said, "You'd better let him know how things stand; if you don't, I will," and to this Armorer replied coolly, for in his own sphere he felt equal to Reeves if not above him, "He'll learn in his own good time. An' what I'd better remind you of afore you try on anythin' is that he's the master's choice, private like. An' something else you didn't know, he's one of his glass-works men." And with slow emphasis, he now ended, "An' if anybody'll be tellin' him anythin', it'll be me." And on this he, too, left the table, and the company looked at one another and the women said, almost in one voice, "Fancy that!" And the men talked together and they were all agreed that the fellow wouldn't fit in. Master's choice or no master's choice, he wasn't right somehow.

It was ten-thirty the same morning when Lagrange brought Annabella into the stable yard. Manuel was in the act of leading Dizzy, ready saddled, from the stable, and Lagrange looked at him appreciatively before calling, "Come here!" The tone was imperious, and although Manuel stopped the animal from moving on, he did not leave it and come forward, but said, "I'd better take him back—" There was a split second before he added, "sir."

88

As Manuel went to turn the animal round, Lagrange, after a moment's consideration, called in the same tone, "No, bring him forward." It would have been much simpler for him to have gone up to the horse and the new groom, but that would never have done, and in this case it was important that the fellow realized he had to bend the knee, metaphorically speaking, by touching his forelock. He, like the horse he was attending, had to be broken in if he was going to be of any use to him; yet he warned himself to go gently—there was no contract or bond between them as yet to hold him; he'd have to see to that as soon as possible.

A feeling of impatience, akin to anger, assailed him as he watched the fellow coax the animal forward, speaking to it in some gibberish. When it was within two yards' distance, he pulled it up but kept his knuckles moving slightly against the beast's gullet while holding the reins short.

"This is my daughter. I wish her to ride and ride well."

Lagrange looked down at Annabella, and Annabella, her face white, her lips trembling slightly, looked at the new groom. He looked a very dark man, and he had been hurt, but the eye that wasn't swollen was smiling kindly at her.

"You'll take her every day, rain or shine, until she can ride. Put her on Chestnut to start with. I—I would see to her training myself but I haven't the time." He did not say that he had taken her out but twice. The first time she had fainted and fallen off the animal, and he had blamed Rosina for putting her up to that refined trick; the second time she had wept openly and been sick over the animal's mane. That had nauseated him and he had wanted to take his hand and knock her flying. With anyone else he wouldn't have hesitated, and it was only the fear of what he might be driven to do that had prevented him from taking her out again. He had tried getting Armorer to teach her, but the man had said she couldn't sit a horse and had dared to add he doubted if she ever would.

"For how long each day, sir?"

"What? Oh, whatever you think necessary. An hour, two if you like." He wanted to warn him that there might be faintings and falls, but he'd let him find out that for himself.

Manuel again looked at the child, and now with interest. He had heard she was but ten. She was very tall for her age, and much too thin to his mind, but what came over to him most forcibly now was her fear. He could actually smell it, and the animal could smell it, too; he felt it in the quiver passing down its neck.

Lagrange was saying, "You don't know your way about yet. One of them will show you the meadow, it's off the east drive. There's hurdles there, all that is necessary, but"—his lips took on a twisted smile—"I don't suppose she'll be needing hurdles for at least a week."

The fellow did not grin at his joke and again he felt a strong feeling of exasperation. He said abruptly, "About boxing. There's a bout being held at Marsden, outside Shields, on Saturday, six o'clock. You should go and see it."

Manuel looked at his new master and only stopped himself in time from saying, "Aw, it's of no interest to me," but he had been quick to realize that fisticuffs meant a lot to this man, and the stableboys' prattle had borne that out already. Very likely he would have left him to get on with it last night if it hadn't been for his interest in the game, for if he had learned anything about men, this man and his type did nothing for nothing: there was always a purpose in their every action. But this man had horses, and if he himself wanted to stay with horses—and aw begod he did, for without the animals life was empty for him—then he would have to take an interest in boxing. But that's all he would take. He wasn't going to have his face battered flat to please this fellow or anybody else. But he'd let his new master come to this knowledge quietly. And so he parried now by saying, "If I can get leave, sir."

"Oh, that. I'll see to it."

"Thank you."

"Well, now." Lagrange looked down at Annabella. "What am I going to hear after this first lesson?"

Annabella swallowed deeply, then murmured, "I'll try, Papa; truly I'll try."

"That's a good girl." He straightened her hat with the tips of his fingers, then looked down at the green cord habit that he had ordered to be made for her last year. The skirt was a little short now, indecent, the old hag Alice had said.

He was standing with his back to the house but he knew without turning that his wife was stationed at one of the windows. Her first protest had been that the child's lessons would be interrupted; that was until she had learned he was sending her out with a new servant, then her protest had taken energy. What! a man they knew nothing about except that he had worked for a few weeks in the glass works and had been prompt to stop the runaway horses yesterday? Moreover, he looked foreign. It was preposterous. When he had informed her that he was a good judge of men and that he could rely on his own judgment, she had answered that if the company he kept was the result of his judgment, then no decent man would take it as a reference. He had thought, and often of late, if it weren't for the trump card he held in the child, he'd have a much more difficult time with her than he had already.

Ten minutes later, Rosina watched her daughter walking by the side of the dark-visaged groom who was leading two horses. There was something about the man, she told herself, that she didn't like. She was suspicious of him. True, he had saved them from a bad accident yesterday, but he had also refused money, which was very odd in one of his class. Moreover, if he knew so much about horses, why had he been working in a glass factory? Why not at an ostler's or a brewery? She knew they were making for the east drive and the meadow, and hastily she went to her room and decided to take a walk in the grounds.

Manuel didn't speak to the child until they were halfway down the drive, and then, not looking at her but casting his eyes from one side to the other, he said, "It's a beautiful garden you have here, miss."

"Yes, yes, it is."

"You've a lot of beautiful flowers; I've never seen the like in Ireland and I've traveled over most of it."

"Oh."

"Do you know something?"

"What? What did you say? I—I don't know your name."

"Manuel. And I was sayin', do you know something, an' you won't believe it, but over there in Ireland I knew a little girl the same size as yourself an' practically the spit of you, an' you couldn't get her near a horse either, she was scared out of her wits of them, just like yourself."

"Really! Did—did she never learn?"

"Oh aye. Oh aye, she learned, but it took some time. Once she knew what the animal was thinking, she got on like a house on fire."

"What the animal was thinking?"

"Yes. You see all animals, particularly horses, they want to like folks, they're very affectionate, and if you don't like them, well they sort of know, sense it like, and decide to keep their distance. They're almost like people, horses, and you know yourself, if you don't like somebody, they're not goin' to like you in return."

She was staring up at him, and he was staring down at her. She was thinking he was the strangest servant she had

91

ever met, the strangest man. She had never heard anyone talk like this; he didn't use her name, and he wasn't—well, he wasn't deferential, yet he was kind. She sensed his kindness; it was in the story about this other girl. She didn't know whether to believe him or not, but she wanted to believe him because she was so unhappy. She had caused Stephen to be sent home. She hadn't meant to do anything bad, really she hadn't, but she knew now she should never have kissed Stephen. Her papa's anger had terrified her and she had been sick all over the bedroom floor.

They had now reached the gate of the meadow. Her eyes were wide and her hands trembling when he thrust the horses' reins into them and said, "This must be the field. Just hang on to those for a minute while I open the gate." And when he had opened the gate, he called to her, "Come on, bring them in." Just like that—"Come on, bring them in": no "miss" or "Miss Annabella." And he was assuming that she could lead horses.

She did not look at the horses before she started to walk; if she did, she knew she would drop the reins; but she kept her eyes on the strange man's face. Then she was through the gate, and he closed it and stood looking about him. Pointing toward the broad trunk of a fallen tree, he walked away from her, saying, "Fetch them this way; we'll have a sit down for a minute."

As someone mesmerized, she followed him, her arm extended to its fullest extent, and the horses docilely followed her.

When she reached the trunk, he took the reins from her hand and led the animals toward another tree, where he secured them loosely, then patted their muzzles.

He now started to turn away from them and toward her, but as if they had spoken to him, he looked back at them, and with one eye still on her, he put his ear down to the muzzle of first one horse and then the other, and nodded at them, after which he walked toward her and, with his black eyebrows raised, he said, "Do you know what they tell me?"

She shook her head.

"They like you."

She laughed. She opened her mouth wide and she laughed as she had done last night before she had kissed Stephen. She had thought this morning that she would be sad for the rest of her life, but here she was laughing again, and this strange groom was laughing with her. He was a funny man, so very amusing. Never, never had she met anyone like him, and when he indicated that she sit on the log and he sat beside her, the breach in propriety was not lost on her but she could do nothing about it. She didn't want to do anything about it. She said to him, "Did you have horses in Ireland?"

"Horses? Oh, yes, we had horses. Princes they were, every one."

"You were a groom there?"

He moved his head twice before he said, "No; I couldn't say I was a groom. You see, the people I stayed as from a child, they trained horses, broke them in, made them into racers or carriage horses or whatever they were suited for."

"You did not live with your parents?" she asked.

He jerked his chin upwards before saying on a little laugh, "No, I didn't live with my parents, but I was brought up by a grand couple, John and Margee McLaughlin. He was the trainer for Mr. Fielding and he taught me all I know about horses. And Margee, she was a great woman, she had second sight. Do you know that? She had second sight." He turned and nodded to her, and she asked him now, in a voice scarcely above a whisper, "What is second sight?"

"Oh." His black brows now went up to the black shock of hair lying on his forehead, and he said, "It's the power to tell the future, it's the power to tell another human being what's going to happen to him. Do you know something?" He leaned toward her. "She told me I'd land in this very house. She did, she did that."

His face looked serious, but she had a great desire to laugh again. He was indeed the most amusing person she had ever met, ever dreamed of meeting. She made her face remain straight as she asked politely, "Where are they now?"

"Margee is dead, and John, well, he's traveling the roads in Ireland. I went with him for a while, but a tinker's life wasn't in my line."

"You became a tinker?" She knew what a tinker was, a man who went round the towns grinding scissors and such like on a wheel. "Why did you become a tinker and leave the horses?"

"Oh, Mr. Fielding, he met hard times. He had houses in both England and Ireland and it was very expensive, so he closed up the Irish establishment and that was that, and when I found the road wasn't for me, I thought I would come to this country and see what it was like."

She said now politely, "A lot of Irish people come to this country; Mr. Rosier has a lot of Irish people in his village."

"Has he now? But I'm not Irish."

"You're not?"

"No, no, I'm not Irish, I'm Spanish. Doesn't my name tell you I'm Spanish, Manuel Mendoza?"

"Oh, I'm sorry, I didn't know." She almost said, "Mr. Mendoza."

"Well, how were you to know? We've hardly but met." Now it was he who had to stop himself from adding something, for he had almost said, "But I've got an idea that we're going to be firm friends," for who knew but that the little miss might carry every word he was saying back to her ma and da. They were a funny lot in this country; some were too stiff with you and others took liberties. He liked neither way.

He said to her now, "By the way, do you know what a horse likes?" and when she shook her head, he went on, "It likes to feel a child, say of your build, sittin' quietly on its back, just sittin', neither the child nor it moving, just like you're sittin' there, just sittin' at your ease sort of."

"Really!"

"Yes, come on. Come on and I'll show you."

She hesitated for a moment before she got to her feet, and then she followed him as he moved away, and when they reached the horses, a most surprising thing happened. The dark-faced, amusing groom put his hands under her armpits and with an "Up you go!" lifted her right onto the saddle. It was usual for the groom to cup his hands so that she could put her foot into the palms and this helped her to scramble up onto the animal's back, a process she always found frightening and disheveling. But here she was now sitting on the horse's back, and it wasn't going to move because it was tied to the tree.

"Does that feel comfortable?"

"Yes, thank you."

"Push yourself a little farther back. There, that's it. Now lift your knee a little bit. Ah, now you've got it and you look very elegant, very elegant indeed. Now take your hand and hold the reins, so, and with your other hand stroke his neck. Go on, stroke his neck and have a word with him. Say, 'Hello, Chester,' 'cause this is Chester. Yes, an' that one's Sandy. I hardly know them meself yet. Go on now, talk to them."

When she lowered her head and made a sound very like an unladylike giggle, he put his head to one side and looked up into her face and said, "Don't be shy—ask him what he had for breakfast. Say to him, 'Did you have a good bellyful, Chester?'—Oh, I'm sorry, I'm sorry." He shook his head at her. "You would never say that. A lady would never say that; she would say, 'Did you have a nice meal, Chester?' "

She was laughing again, her mouth so wide now she had to put her hand over it.

For half an hour longer she sat on the horse while the new, strange and entertaining groom talked to her; then once again she was leading the horses, but out of the field now, and again they were walking along the drive in the same way as they had come. But just before they came within sight of the house, Manuel stopped and, looking at her, said, "Would you do me a great favor"—and now he did add her title—"miss?" and she said, "Yes, Manuel, if you tell me what it is."

"Well, you know how you sat back there on top of Chester?"

"Yes."

"Well, would you do it again? You see, if we walk back into the stable yard, your father will think I'm not earnin' me way, you understand? I'm being paid to make you ride and it's ten to one he'll want to kick me from here to—" He omitted hell and substituted, "Shields, if he sees us walking in."

"Oh, I understand, Manuel. Yes, yes, I'll sit on Chester." She didn't term it riding him—riding was being bounced up and down, riding was seeing the ground from a great distance away and knowing you're going to fall on it.

When he again hoisted her up into position, she smiled at him and said softly, and with deep sincerity, "Thank you, Manuel," for it had come to her suddenly that it wasn't his position he was worried about; he was thinking of her and how her father would react toward her if he felt she hadn't made any progress at all.

Of late she wished more than ever to please her father because of late she had become a little afraid of him.

Manuel, looking up into the green eyes, thought, Poor wee thing, there's joy in her, but it's been clamped down somewhat. He'd have to see what he could do by way of letting it escape now and again.

So, for the first time, Annabella returned to the stable yard on a horse feeling neither sick nor faint, and after once more thanking Manuel, she ran into the house to find her mama, and when she was told her mama was walking on the grounds, she dashed out again and kept running until she saw her at the far end of the pagoda.

Rosina saw at once that the child was happy and excited,

95

and she let her go on prattling about the kindness of the new groom. She had not thought it unseemly that they should sit together in the field on a tree trunk. She had observed them from the cover of the wood. She had also observed the man lifting the child onto the horse in the most unorthodox fashion and kept her sitting there for an unusually long time, making no effort to train her; yet apparently she had ridden the horse back into the stable yard. The young man's methods may have been prompted by the fear he saw in the child, but to her mind, even from a distance, his manner openly expressed familiarity, so now, taking Annabella's hand, she told her that she was happy she had enjoyed her first lesson under the new groom, but she reminded her gently that, no matter how kind or sympathetic servants might be, they remained servants and therefore had to be kept in their place, and that place could only be made clear to them through the manner of their superiors. Did Annabella understand?

Yes, Annabella understood.

Rosina couldn't tell her that in the future she must not sit on a log with a servant because that would put herself in a position of having spied, but she felt she had made the point quite clear, and she had. But this did not stop Annabella from thinking that something nice and surprising had come into her life. Manuel, she considered, was more like a young person, someone like Stephen, even younger, although he must be all of twenty years old. No one had made her laugh as he had, and he was so kind, kind and gentle.

And she thought this way until a fortnight later when, entering the stable yard with her father, she came upon the most surprising scene.

Manuel felt he had been at Redford not only for two weeks or two months, but for two years. He was not only doing the work he loved, he was being well fed and well quartered. No longer was he sleeping under the rafters; he now had a room to himself above the end stable. It was only a small room; some would consider it bare, but he preferred bareness, after sleeping six to a room in that rat warren in Shields, knowing that as soon as you jumped out of your bed another jumped in. What was more, he was getting the amazing sum of thirty pounds a year and livery with all necessities. The livery suited him. It was of a warm, tan color matching his skin, and giving him a fine set up look.

There was only one fly in the ointment. This was what he termed to himself as "them ignorant galoots in there." They

96

didn't like the way he had jumped into his position and they weren't past showing it. The womenfolk were all right, but then womenfolk were always all right toward him, too all right for comfort at times; they were out to hook a man and most of them were sluts at bottom. He was particular about the woman he was going to have permanently in his bed; about the others who came and went, well, you hadn't much choice. When nature piped, you had to dance and take whatever partner was available at such times.

He had known for a few days now that things were coming to a head. They were skitting at him from behind their hands during mealtimes, talking about people sucking up to the master, foreigners an' that. His stomach couldn't stand such jibes, for he sucked up to no man, he had no need; deep inside he was his own man and always would be.

On this morning he entered the kitchen late for his meal. It had been a busy morning; they had been going at it hell for leather since five o'clock because the master was riding into the works at half-past nine, and Fairisle had to be got ready. Also, the mistress was taking the coach to Durham around the same time; and then the young miss was for her lesson. He had worked like two men polishing and strapping.

Armorer was going with the coach, taking John Heron with him, and as they both had to get spruced up, he had said to Armorer, "Leave it to me and Danny, and away and get your meal and changed. The coach will be glinting like a tiara, never fear." Armorer had laughed and thumped him on the back and said, "You're a good bloke, Manuel; I bless those fellows who knocked you about," and they both had laughed. Armorer knew he had respect for him because he was a horseman and he returned it.

So now he entered the kitchen almost at the end of the meal, and when Dorrie, the kitchen maid, smilingly placed a large bowl of porridge before him, he smiled his thanks at her and she hunched up her shoulders and giggled.

He was halfway through the porridge when his spoon halted in midair for a second before continuing its journey to his mouth. Faill and Cargill were talking in undertones, but they were undertones that were meant to carry. He heard the name of the governess mentioned, then Faill saying, "Up in the world. I wonder if he puts his hand on her backside to hoist her?" The porridge stuck in his throat. He knew they were skitting about the new order of things. Having taken the child out but once on his own, they were thereafter accompanied by the governess. She'd had her orders, too, that she

97

must learn to ride, but she was more scared of the animals than was the child, and so she was content to sit on the tree trunk while he took the child round the meadow. He was not averse to the governess's being present; she was a comely-looking young woman, older than himself by six years or more he'd say, but very pleasant, if a little stiff; however, he meant to do his best to soften that stiffness, for she seemed a part of Margee's prophecy. He saw her as a means to an end. He had another great desire in his life besides a desire to work with animals, and that was to be able to read and write, and who better to teach him than a governess?

When Faill and Cargill rose from the table, they were still laughing, but they didn't speak until they reached the door that led into the yard; then Faill's voice came to him, saying, "Put the devil on horseback and he'll ride to hell, so they say, but put an Irish Mick on horseback and where does he go? I'll tell you—"

Faill never finished the sentence. He was so startled by the attack that even if he had been any match for Manuel, he wouldn't have put up a fight. He found himself lifted from the ground and pinned against the wall by a steel hand at his throat and another gripping his shoulder, and he hung suspended there for seconds like a rag doll until Manuel let him drop to the ground but still holding him as he growled, "What did you call me? Say it! What did you call me?"

Faill was unable to speak for the pressure on his throat, and when Cargill came to his assistance, he was knocked onto his back by a side kick like that from a horse.

Manuel now took his hand from Faill's throat and gripped his other shoulder with it, then he repeated the question, "What did you call me?"

"Aa . . . Aa . . . Aa . . ." Faill was gulping, drawing in great drafts of air. "Aa only said . . ."

"Aye, go on." Manuel waited, but Faill just moved his head from side to side while he stared into the eyes that looked like blazing black coals.

"You called me an Irish Mick. Well, let me tell you, I'm no Irish Mick. My name is Manuel Mendoza. What is me name?"

There was a pause before Faill muttered, "M-Manuel Mendoza."

Manuel slowly took his hands from the shivering shoulders; then, straightening his own back, he looked about him. The kitchen door and window were crowded with servants; Cargill was lifting himself from the stones of the yard and holding his hip; and surveying the scene from the entrance to the yard were the master and young mistress.

"What's this, brawling?" Lagrange came slowly forward. He kept his voice stern and his face straight, but he wasn't displeased. The fellow had lifted Faill up as if he were a child; he had amazing strength, yet he had shown not the slightest interest in the match last week. In fact he had been slightly scornful as he had watched the two best fighters in the county. He had no praise for the forty-five rounds they had gone; he had been amused that they had been so stupid as to get their faces flattened, as he put it; yet he could use his fists, that was evident, and he couldn't see any local man standing up to them for forty-five rounds.

As he confronted the fellow, he saw that he was still angry and noted to himself that he was a handsome individual, much more so when his face was ablaze. He demanded of him now, "What do you think you're up to? Trying to kill someone?"

"I am no Irish Mick—sir." Again the pause that irritated Lagrange. "And I won't be named as such. Me name is Manuel Mendoza."

"We're aware of that, but the term 'Irish Mick' is the common term applied to Irishmen around here."

"I don't want it applied to me, sir, and what's more, I'll see it isn't."

Lagrange was aware of the stretched, staring faces about him. They were amazed at the way the fellow was answering him. What he should do was to raise his crop at him and then send him packing, but Boston was waiting for just such a move. He had come in the yard yesterday and talked to the fellow. Quite openly he had asked him how he was getting on. Did he like his new job? Such attention from his betters was giving the man a bloated opinion of himself. He should be taken down a peg; yet if he were to do it, ten to one that would be the end, and what he needed at present, and very badly, was a new interest, an interest that would be lucrative.

He swung about, wielding his crop, shouting, "Get about your business, all of you, and let me hear or see no more of this!"

And like rats scurrying into holes they all dispersed, all except Manuel. He, too, went about his business, but his step was measured and his back was straight because the voice inside of him was crying loudly, "Margee and her tales! Get out of this. Animals or no animals, you'll never be your own man here. There's something on the place. Go when the going's good."

99

3

Miss Howard had a toothache; Mrs. Page and Alice had tried all the known cures but without avail. Alice had held the offending molar between a piece of zinc and a silver sixpence, a sure cure, but the dying nerve in Miss Howard's tooth refused to be electrified. They had tried tincture of myrrh on cotton wool, creosote on cotton wool, but now, as a last resort, the poor young woman was sucking camphor.

Being in such a state, Rosina knew that the governess could not accompany her charge during her riding lesson; she was all for canceling the lesson, but the child was ready and would be greatly disappointed should she be deprived of it. What was more, Edmund had insisted that she should continue with her practice until she could gallop, so for the past two months, for five mornings a week, except when the weather was inclement, her daughter had gone riding with the groom, but, after that first morning, always accompanied by Howard.

The groom had seemingly done what others before him couldn't; he had eliminated the child's fear of horses and brought her to the state where she could trot comfortably. She seemed to have great confidence in the man; she herself wasn't sure whether she liked the man or not. Of course, that didn't matter one way or the other as long as he carried out his duties, which apparently he did exceptionally well. She had noticed a slight difference in him from the other servants. She had wondered at the difference at first until she had realized that he was less subservient than the others, yet his manner could not call forth reprimand; a stiffening of one's manner toward him, perhaps, but not reprimand.

Annabella was looking at her expectantly, and so she said to her, "Go along, then."

"Oh, thank you, Mama." Annabella reached up and kissed the pale cheek, then turned away on the point of a run; but, remembering that ladies never run, she brought her step to a walk, and, holding the loop of her skirt over one wrist and her riding crop in the other hand, she walked sedately from her mama's boudoir all the way to the stable yard, where Manuel was waiting for her.

Manuel was very sorry to hear that Miss Howard had a toothache and he said the only sure cure for toothache was to tie a piece of string round the tooth and attach a smoothing iron to the other end of the string and get somebody to throw it against the wall. The remedy caused her to hunch her shoulders upwards but at the same time made her want to laugh because she knew that Manuel was making a joke. He was very amusing, was Manuel; she had never met anyone like him in all of her life. But he was only amusing, she had found, when they were alone together, walking or trotting round the fields. He never said amusing things in front of Miss Howard; he acted very properly in front of Miss Howard, and her governess seemed to think highly of him.

This morning, when they reached the gate, Manuel did not dismount and open it, but sat looking at it for a moment before saying, "There's no real room in that field; the animals are tired of it. Like people, they want a change. Would you like to go out on to the fells?"

"Out on to the fells, Manuèl?" Her eyes had sprung wide in surprise. Her mama and papa had never said she could ride out on to the fells. In fact, she never went outside the gates unless it was in the carriage. But if Manuel thought it was all right, then it must be all right.

Manuel himself knew that if he had asked leave to take her out on to the fells, it would have been refused, by the mistress anyway, but, as it was, no one had said he shouldn't take her out into the open country. He, like the horses, was feeling hemmed in. He wasn't grumbling at the job; it was all right, at least for the time being, but in a way it was restricting. There were days when he wanted to pick up his bundle and go; it was only the thought of the animals that kept him. Unlike the rest of the staff, he didn't take his half day a week or use his one day a month. Harris had been dumbfounded when he had asked if he could save his leave and have it all together. He had given no reason for the strange request, for he couldn't say that at the end of a month he would have three full days in which to drink and ease his body. What could a man do with a half a day which didn't begin until two o'clock in the afternoon and with five miles to walk into the town? He could drink or leave it alone, but when he drank, he did it as he did other things, thoroughly, and sometimes he didn't come to himself for three days. Harris had hemmed and hawed until Manuel had said, "Well, if you can't decide I'll ask himself," but, fearing to have his authority diluted, Harris had himself granted the request. It was another thing that added to Manuel's strangeness in the eyes of the staff.

"Come on," he said, "we'll be little divils, miss, eh?"

Manuel said the strangest things.

They went on through the wood, then along the field path where the men were working, and they all touched their forelocks to her and she inclined her head and smiled at them; then they rode until they came to the dry-stone wall that marked the boundary of the estate, and to a part where the wall was crumbling, and they went over this and on to the fells.

Sitting straight, she looked about her and there came to her a most odd thought. The air on this side of the wall seemed to be different, sharper, and there was a wind that lifted her hair back from her neck and attempted to blow her hat off.

Manuel, looking at her, thought, "It's now or never," and so, quickly, he said, "See that tree over there. I'll race you to it. Remember what I told you now, sit tight. Up, Sandy! Up, Chester!"

She had no time for apprehension; the horse was away and she with it. Like lightning flickering before her eyes, fear passed through her, and then it was gone, and she knew a great ecstatic feeling of exhilaration, not only because she was galloping but because she was ahead of Manuel. When she shouted, she couldn't believe it was her voice; ladies didn't shout. She reached the tree first and when Manuel came abreast and pulled Chester to a halt, she leaned forward onto Sandy's neck and laughed and laughed. Then, seeming to remember who she was, and whom she was with, she straightened her body, and, looking at Manuel, who was sitting smiling broadly at her, she said, "You—you didn't let me win, did you, Manuel?"

"Let you win, miss? Good gracious! It took me all me time to keep on his tail. Let you win? Not on me life. How did you like it?"

"Oh—oh, Manuel, it was wonderful. And—and you know something? I'm not afraid anymore; I'll never be afraid of horses again."

"Well, this is a day to remember, 'tis indeed."

"Shall we have another one?"

"No, not yet. I'd walk them a bit. Let's go down by the river. They could do with a drink."

Even the river looked different. It rushed along quicker here than it did in the park; it tumbled over the rocks and curved and twisted as if it were having a game at evading you.

After the horses had drunk, they continued along the bank; then, passing an outcrop of rock, they turned into a grassy, marshy dell, at the far side of which a woman was stooping over some long stalks. She lifted her head and looked toward them, and when they came up to her, Manuel said, "Hello, there," and she replied, "Hello." She looked from one to the other, then said, "I would mind where you're goin', there's a bit of bog over there. I'd keep close to the bank for a while."

"Thanks." He nodded at her. Then, bending from the horse, he said on a high note, "Don't tell me that's flax you're picking?"

"Flax? Lint we call it; I'm after the seeds."

"I had the idea it never grew outside Ireland."

"Well, that's as may be, but this bit comes up year after year, never more, never less. It's sheltered here and damp, perhaps that's why."

"There's not enough, surely, to make any linen?"

"No, perhaps not," she said on a laugh; "but then, I wasn't wantin' it for linen. I use the seeds for medicine, for poultices. Can't be beaten for poultices." She looked again from him to the young girl, then added, "You're out of your way."

"Not so far," he replied; "we're from the Hall, back yonder, Redford."

"Oh, aye. Aye. Why, yes." Her voice spiraled. "And this is the young miss?" She nodded her head at Annabella, but didn't dip her knee.

Annabella looked back at her and smiled. She was an old woman, but not so old as Alice. Her face was very wrinkled, but kind looking. When she said to her now, "It's a rare and a beautiful day, we only get days like this in September," she answered politely, "Yes, it is a beautiful day."

As Manuel asked, "You live hereabouts?" Annabella had the idea that he wanted to stay and talk with the woman. He had obviously never met her before, yet he spoke like one would to an acquaintance, if not a friend.

"Just along the bank there and through the copse. It's warm. Would you like a drink? I've got some herb beer; it's nice and sharp, been standing for four days or so."

"That's kind of you." He now turned and glanced at Annabella, saying, "You'd like a drink, wouldn't you?"

She stared at him for a moment. Yes, she'd like a drink, but her mama wouldn't be at all pleased if she knew she'd accepted a drink from this old lady, and what was more, she'd be very displeased that Manuel had allowed such a thing to happen. But her mama lived within the walls, whereas she was outside the walls and in another world. She smiled at him and said quickly, "Yes, please."

Without further ado, the old woman went before them along the riverbank, through a small copse, then up a broad grass path in a garden that apparently had no boundary, and to a flat, roughly paved piece of ground with a small stone house in its middle.

"If you'd like to step down and rest your bones, you can be seated there." The woman pointed to a wooden bench against the stone wall, and Manuel said, "Thanks, Mother."

The use of the word "mother" to this strange person brought Annabella's eyes wide; then Manuel was lifting her from the saddle. He hadn't lifted her like this since the first morning they had ridden together.

When they were seated on the wooden bench, he looked at her and said, "Now, isn't this grand?" and she answered, "Yes, Manuel." And in a way it was grand, grand and exciting; nothing like this had ever happened to her before.

When the old woman came out of the cottage with two frothing mugs of liquid and handed her one, she thanked her, then sipped at her beer and just prevented her face from wrinkling in distaste. It was sharp and bitter.

"It's good, isn't it?" Manuel had half-emptied his mug in one go, and she gulped and smiled as she lied, "Yes, it's very nice."

The woman was now looking at Manuel. "You're not from these parts?"

"No, Mother; I'm from Ireland, across the water, you know, but I'm Spanish by birth."

"Yes, I would have said so."

Manuel smiled in evident pleasure, and the old woman smiled back at him. "Can I fill that again for you?"

"Do, and thanks." He handed her the mug, and then the woman, looking at Annabella with her head on one side, asked, "And you, missie?"

"No. No, thank you; I have sufficient. It's—it's very nice."

"I'm glad you like it."

After Manuel had finished his second mug, he rose to his feet, saying, "I'm much obliged to you, Mother," and nodded slowly down at her, and she replied, "Oh, that's all right; you're welcome any time. . . . What do they call you?"

"Manuel—Manuel Mendoza."

"Ho-ho! that sounds Spanish enough, if you like. Me husband was a seagoing man. Dead this ten years. He used to talk to me about foreign places. I got the feel of the words."

"And your name, Mother?"

"Amy Stretford."

As he continued to look at her, she said, "Don't be a stranger; if you're passin' this way anytime, drop in. I can always wet your whistle with something."

"I'll keep you to that, see if I don't."

Annabella gazed at them in some bewilderment. Their conversation was very intriguing; it was like listening to characters coming alive from a book. In a way, the old woman was like Manuel in that she was different. Manuel was like no servant in the house; he neither talked nor acted like them, and, of course, he didn't talk or act like a gentleman, like her father, or Uncle James, or Mr. Rosier, or Mr. Boston—or Stephen. These were the sum total of her male acquaintances, and her mind touching on Stephen, she thought, Oh, I wish he were here; he would have enjoyed it so. She knew that Stephen liked odd situations because he would relate to her what happened on his journeys to and from school.

The old lady, she noticed, did not extend the invitation to her; but of course she wouldn't; being a sensible old lady, she would know her place. And yet she felt a sort of regret that she hadn't been included in the invitation. She thanked her once more for the drink; then Manuel mounted her again and they went down the broad, grassy drive to the riverbank, and from there Manuel turned and waved to the old woman as if he knew she would be standing watching them. And she herself succumbing, as her mama would have said, to an impulse, also waved her hand at the old woman, not only once or twice, but a third time.

"You enjoyed that?" Manuel spoke to her over his shoulder as they went through the copse, and she replied quite loudly, "Oh, yes. Yes, Manuel." And then she added, "I'll have something to tell Stephen when I see him."

He stopped and waited until she came abreast; then, his face straight, he said, "It'll be wiser if you don't tell Mr. Stephen, if you don't tell anybody, because we won't be able to do this very often with Miss Howard coming along—you understand?"

Yes, she understood. She understood that this was an adventure; she had known from the minute they had come through the gate it was an adventure and that no one must know about it, not even Stephen. But Stephen would never carry tales; she said so. "I really could tell Stephen, Manuel," she said, "because we have secrets." She nodded twice with her head to give emphasis to this statement, and he nodded back at her, saying, "Oh, well, perhaps then, perhaps."

She sat looking at him. He had very black eyes, and his mouth was nice, at least when he was smiling. He was, she supposed, a very handsome man, but of course he wasn't so beautiful as Stephen. But then he was older. She said to him, "I won't tell Stephen, Manuel; I won't tell anyone."

"Good for you."

She noticed once again that he rarely gave her her title when they were alone. She should inform her mama of this, but of course she wouldn't; she would never do anything to cause trouble for Manuel, because he was so nice. No one among the servants had been so kind to her as Manuel. He could really be her friend, yes, he could really be her friend. She would have loved to say to him, "You can be my friend, Manuel," but of course she must never do that. But she could tell him her secrets just as if he were her friend openly. She leaned from the saddle now and said to him, "Do you think Stephen is pretty, Manuel?"

She watched a spasm pass over his face. His eyes stretched wide, his lips came firmly together, but he did not smile as he said, "Indeed, I do; he's the most pretty young man I've ever seen." He had only seen the boy once; that was when they had driven to Durham.

"You really think so, Manuel?"

"I've said it, I do."

"I'm going to tell you a secret, Manuel."

"Well, it'll be safe with me."

"Manuel." She paused for a number of seconds. "Mr. Stephen and I are going to be married."

He sat up straight in the saddle. His eyebrows now came down into a frown, his lips stretched wide showing his even, blunt white teeth; then, composing his features again, he asked quietly, "Does—does Mr. Stephen know of this?"

She shook her head. "Not yet. Well, at least we don't talk about it; he may know inside, you know what I mean?"

"Indeed, indeed I do." His voice held the most solemn tones. "When is this going to happen?" he asked.

"Oh!" She wagged her head just the slightest and gathered the reins into her hands. "When I'm sixteen, perhaps seventeen. Yes, seventeen." She nodded sharply now. "Seventeen at the latest."

He, too, nodded his head as he said, "Well, I wish you both every happiness and the largest family in the county, ten children, no less, because children make for happiness."

106

"Thank you, Manuel."

They rode on side by side in silence now until, pulling her horse abruptly to a stop, she turned her face toward him and firmly said, "I wasn't going to say this, Manuel, but I feel I must. I think you are my friend and I would like to be yours."

There was no laughter in his eyes, no amusement lurking on his lips. He put out his hand and after a moment she placed hers in it, and he said gallantly and quite sincerely, "I've never been knighted by a king, but what need have I of that after receiving such an honor? Thank you, Miss Annabella; I'm yours for life."

As she smiled back into his face, there came a most unladylike lump in her throat and a smarting in the back of her eyes. Dear, dear; she mustn't cry.

He rode silently by her side. Never before could he remember being so touched by anything that had happened to him, but his thoughts nevertheless were aggressive. Of all the people in that bloody establishment, there was no one she could be herself with, there was no one she could be a child with. She wasn't a child; they had smothered the child and were foisting on her the manners of their kind, their stiff, proper, adult kind. At ten years old she should be running, scampering, getting mucked up, playing kiss-in-the-ring, with children of her own age. And what was before her? Marriage to the young gentleman? Well, not if the opinion below stairs was anything to go by. He had heard from Armorer about the whole setup. Everybody on the estate knew except the child herself. A nursemaid had been dismissed on the spot not long ago for putting a name to her little mistress. How old would she be before the truth was given her? And when she did know, what effect would it have on her? The love of that stiff, soulless woman, her supposed mama, wouldn't be able to compensate for the stigma, if he was any judge of it. As for her marrying Master Stephen, what would that young pip have to say when he knew that his sweet cousin was nothing but the fly-blow of a Shields whore.

It was strange that this child, who followed her mother's dictates and tried her best to keep him in his place, should be, like himself, a bastard. In this moment he prayed that the knowledge of her heritage would never come to her, for then she would feel as he did at times; and there were some pains that were too hard to be borne even by a man.

Book Three

THE HERITAGE

1

The year was 1866. Since the beginning of the '40's when the railways had come into existence the North had known a growing prosperity; villages, like Jarrow, through its steel works, had mushroomed into towns. Middlesbrough, only a few miles away, had in 1830 been a hamlet housing just over a hundred people, but by the year 1853 it was a thriving port with nearly twenty thousand inhabitants. Names had become synonymous with places. Henry Bolckow of Middlesbrough who was actually a German by birth; Stephenson of Newcastle; the Lehmans of Sheffield; and not forgetting John Brown, who, from an apprentice in a cutlery firm, rose to be the owner of a large steel works; Vicars, Armstrong, and Ramsden were names that spelled steel, names on which thousands upon thousands of men depended for their livelihood; names that were carved in stone at the base of statues and busts, representing the gratitude of thriving towns to the benefactors who had erected gigantic municipal buildings or who had donated a public bath or perhaps a library.

The North at this period was an empire, an empire of coal mines, steel works, and railways, not forgetting glass works. It was a time when a few outstanding men rose from muck to millions and, having done so, housed their families in palatial establishments. A percentage of lesser men made a good deal of money, and they too lived well. And then there was the gentry, and they, as they had always done, lived high.

But quite suddenly on a May day in 1866 the empire of the North shuddered and collapsed as if struck by an earthquake, and small men, middle men and those in high places felt the tremors.

There was panic in the City of London. Banks failed; railways went out of business; steel companies had to join forces in order to survive; businesses that had been held jealously within families were either bankrupt or merged with companies that had been fortunate enough to escape the earthquake.

This one and that were blamed for the disaster, but the fault seemed to be with the company of Overand and Gurney, who financed a great deal of the Northern industries at the time and were overspent by many millions; and so the flame of panic spread from the banking houses in London and swept the North.

The catastrophe afforded Edmund Lagrange a protective screen. He could, and did, put the failure of the glass works down to the slump, whereas every employee in the works and the owners of all other glass works from Shields to Birmingham knew that the firm was finished.

Edmund Lagrange was now forty-seven years old. Until he was forty his body had stood up to the pace of his life, but over the last few years it had grown tired of resisting excess, so that now he looked like any overindulged man of his age. He had a paunch, his neck was thick, his face florid; but to many he still presented a fine figure of a man, and there was no apparent slackening of his vitality, for he rode as hard as ever, drank even more than ever, ate all too well, gambled indiscriminately and was consistent in his main amusement.

But these pastimes had become merely an armor behind which he hid himself, for he had had many personal defeats during the past seven years. One that rankled most had happened just a year ago and it concerned the mother of his daughter.

Whatever faults Lagrange had, meanness wasn't one of them, and where he loved or liked, he was overgenerous. What matter if his presents were bought with the money squeezed out of his wife, which process was becoming more difficult each time he attempted it. Or what matter if the money was borrowed, for he worked as hard at borrowing as other men did at earning. The man to whom he was most in debt was his friend Boston, and it was this selfsame friend who had brought his pride low, for he had taken his mistress.

Jessie Connolly had been fifteen when Lagrange first took her, and she was a virgin, which fact pleased him because it was unusual, at least in the quarter from which she came. He had become greatly enamored of the girl because, besides being very pretty, she was vivacious and gay and had a kindly way with her, and she was out to please a man. So, on the condition that she remain solely his, he took rooms

112

for her in Crane Street, and it was in this street that his young mistress got the idea that she would like to own an establishment. He had been highly amused by her idea, and, being flush with money at the time, he bought her a house and she was in business.

Jessie, he would have sworn on oath, had remained faithful to him over the years, one of the reasons being, he imagined, that, once having had him, she could not resort to the type of customers she supplied for her girls.

The apartment at the top of the house, which was kept especially for him and which was approached by a back entrance, had over the years become a kind of refuge, and although it was long since he had ceased to have any affection for her, she was still kind and attentive, and pleased him at times.

He had been very drunk on the night he introduced Boston to the private apartment. He had done it out of bravado and had regretted the impulse the next day, but it never dawned on him for one moment not to trust his mistress, until one night, feeling the need for comfort, he had gone to the house. It wasn't his usual time for visiting; he had his set times and had been with her the previous evening. But on his arrival in the street he had been surprised to see Boston's coach and man discreetly hidden up a side turning. Riding on past the house, he had waited, and presently Boston had emerged through the back door.

His feelings on that particular night had been of murderous rage and frustration. Boston must be laughing up his sleeve at him, yet he was powerless to say a word to him because he was so much in the man's debt. But there was a stronger reason why he couldn't expose him; it was because ultimately he intended that Boston should marry his daughter. The alliance would be his only hope of ever ridding himself of the debts he owed him and finding security for the future, for Boston had his finger in every pie in the county. He didn't see any obstacle to the union except from one source, Rosina. Boston himself had been very attentive to Annabella over the past year, so he wouldn't need much pushing. As for Annabella, she'd obey him. The only obstacle was Rosina; but then in the long run, what could she do?

The effect of the financial explosion in the North had, in a way, brought Rosina's life also to a climax. The fact of closing the family business was like an operation that had been put off for years. The final act of closure was excruciating, but, like the aftermath of an operation, there was relief attached to it.

The money she had inherited had been swallowed up and the process of begging from her mother had begun again, but now that was over, too.

They could no longer maintain the House and all its commitments. This, in a way, did not worry her, for she would find a home in the cottage with her mother and, in making the transfer, would be free at last, free from the slights and the shame, free from the pretense that she had to keep up before the community.

Where her husband would live was of no concern to her; the only concern left in her mind was with regard to Annabella's future. Yet, in a very short while, this would be settled. In two days' time Stephen was returning from London and he would speak then.

For years now he had given Annabella his attention and sweet consideration. Because of her husband's manner toward him, he no longer visited the Hall, but over the past two years she had made it her business frequently to visit Durham when he was home from the university. When last year they had spent two months in London, he had paid regular attendance on Annabella and had been her constant escort when her father wasn't present.

Stephen had grown into a handsome man and was very popular with the ladies, but she knew, as she had always known, where his deep affection lay. She'd had a letter from him two days ago and one line had brought comfort to her heart, for it said, "I shall be home for Annabella's birthday. Please bring her to Weirbank for I have something to tell her, and you also, dear Aunt. You have been so good to me all my life that I want you to share my happiness."

Only one highly disagreeable task lay before her now, the interview with her husband which would deal with the closing of the House and Hall; the servants must be given notice as soon as possible. Alice, of course, would go with her to the cottage, and perhaps Harris, but that would be all.

She rose from her desk, and as she passed the window she saw in the distance Annabella walking through the pagoda with Mr. Boston, and she remained still, watching them. It always gave her a sense of pleasure not unmixed with personal achievement to watch Annabella walking, for she held herself so well, and her manners were impeccable. The only fault with her decorum was that she was inclined to be a

114

little too gay at times, and her laughter too loud, but marriage and responsibility would through nature itself subdue such exuberance.

Mr. Boston had been visiting a lot of late. She didn't like that man. In spite of his expensive attire and his elaborate establishment, he still remained a coarse individual. Part of her was surprised that some of Edmund's polish had not rubbed off on his friend, for they had been close associates for years now, but the man appeared to her as gauche an individual as on the first day she had met him almost eight years before.

Annabella shared her mama's feelings with regard to Mr. Boston. She, too, thought he was a gauche individual and she was forever comparing him with Stephen. Yet it was strange that she saw more of this man and talked with him more frequently than with any other male person of her acquaintance.

Mr. Boston could be an amusing companion and sometimes made her laugh—he had a cynical turn of wit—yet his whole person, his face, his manner, and his voice were objectionable to her.

Four times during the past year she had been to dinner in his home, and once to a ball he gave. She had enjoyed the ball because she loved dancing, but she never enjoyed the dinners, nor did she care for his house. He lacked taste, she thought. Her papa had said that what the house needed was a mistress, for there were twice as many servants as they had, ten gardeners at least. She wondered why Mr. Boston had not married. He was, she understood, thirty years old.

Sometimes she thought she was imagining that his manner had changed toward her during the last year. Up till she was sixteen he had been, in his own way, very polite. There was even a certain deference in his manner toward her, but during the past months he had taken to teasing her when they were alone, and was, she considered, much too free in his conversation. Of course, Stephen could have acted in a similar way and she would have loved it, and laughed and been gay and teased him in return, but Stephen was different: Stephen was the man she was going to marry.

Her pulse quickened and a soft smile spread over her face at the thought that in exactly two days' time she would see Stephen, and on that day he would ask her for her hand. Her mama had shown her the letter he had sent. Her mama had talked to her for a long while last evening. That the House was to be closed came as a shock to her, for she loved the House, every bit of it; she even liked the Hall. She'd had access to the Hall over the last two years. Her father had said to her quite suddenly one day, "Why don't you come and see my pictures?" He had said it in an accusing voice as if he were blaming her for not having used his part of the house. Since that day the oak door had been left open, except in the evenings, when he was gaming.

Her mama, she knew, had been relieved when she showed no excessive interest in visiting the Hall. She'd made her happy by telling her she much preferred the pictures in the House to those in the Hall, and it was quite true: she did prefer the pictures in the House, because they were of people she knew, pictures of her grandmama and grandpapa at various stages of their lives, and of her great-grandmama and great-grandpapa, and their mama and papa.

Her excessive interest in her grandparents stemmed, she thought, from the fact that she had never once, in all her seventeen years, spoken to her grandmother. Of late this unusual fact had troubled her and she wanted an explanation, but some nicety of feeling prevented her from asking her mama pointedly why she was never taken to see her grandmama. Yet she had discussed the matter quite openly with Stephen, and Stephen's opinion had been very comforting. He said that Grandma Conway-Redford had always been a very austere, elusive kind of person; he himself had only seen her twice since his father had died. He had the idea that she didn't like children. . . .

George Boston was saying, "I'm extending the stables. You must come over and see them."

"You are getting more horses?"

"Yes, another half dozen."

He spoke of buying horses by the half dozen when the majority of people in the county and the next were selling their carriages and horses. Was he thinking of buying her papa's stable? Although he was a friend, that would be dreadful.

In this moment her sympathy was with her father rather than with her mother, although she knew, and had known for some years now, that her father was not a good man. He had gained her sympathy even more at times than Rosina had, because her mother, she sensed, had the steellike power of integrity of character to support her, whereas she recognized that Lagrange was a man who lived by his charm and his wits and by a facet of his character which she hated to name as intimidation. In growing awareness over the years she knew that he showed one side of his character to her and another to her mother. This had become very evident when at fifteen she was allowed to move her bedroom from the nursery on the first floor to a room opposite her mother's boudoir. Sometimes when her father visited her mother the murmurings were low; at other times his voice was filled with rage and his language so startling that she would put her hands over her ears to shut it out. Yet within a short space of time following such occasions he would cup her chin and exclaim in a velvet-toned voice, "How is my beauty?" or "What about a race over the fells?"

More and more of late he claimed her company when riding. She thought that if he had to sell the stable he would go mad; horses were his life.

"It's a great pity about the works having to go."

"These things happen." She brought her attention back to Boston; she had the idea that he didn't think it was a pity at all that the works had closed but rather that he was gloating.

"What are you going to do with yourself?"

"Oh"—she turned her head slightly and smiled at him—"I shall find plenty to do." She was thinking of the journey to Durham on her birthday. She ended, "We're not going to be evicted onto the fells, you know, Mr. Boston; we have plans."

He laughed heartily at this, his mouth so wide that she could see the white fur on his tongue, and her nose wrinkled slightly with distaste.

His laughter suddenly cutting off but his face still holding an amused smile, he repeated, "You have plans?"

She turned her head toward him, and the action was slightly coquettish, as she replied with emphasis drawn from the secret she shared with her mama, "Yes, I have plans, Mr. Boston."

"Ha-ha, I smell a mystery. Is it any use my asking what your plans are? I assure you I would bury your confidence deep in my heart. Come, what are these secret plans?"

His gallant joviality conveyed to her that she was being too free with him. Her mama was always warning her about her easiness of manner, which was not to be confused with ease of manner; it was, her mama said, apt to slip into a freedom that could give the observer the wrong impression. She said now with studied stiffness, "My secrets, if I harbored any, Mr. Boston, would be of no interest to you, for I'm sure you'd consider them childish and immature."

"Not in the least, not in the least. Seventeen on the twenty-first, you could hardly be termed childish and immature. Dear, dear! I've known you for many years, Annabella, and even as a child I never considered you immature; indeed, you used to frighten me with your wisdom and knowledge. I've never forgotten the day we visited the glass works for the first time. You staggered me."

"You are laughing at me, Mr. Boston."

Whatever remark he was about to make was interrupted by Faill's appearing and addressing Annabella. "The mistress would like a word with you, Miss Annabella."

"Thank you, Faill. Will you excuse me, Mr. Boston?"

"Of course." He was still laughing at her. "But I'll walk back to the house with you; I want to have a word with Manuel. Fine fellow, that, with animals, isn't he?"

"Yes, he's a very good horseman."

"Your father's hardly had need of a vet since he's been on the place. That's the kind of a staff to have, the kind that will save you money."

As he talked he smiled, and his last remark made her think, He's enjoying the whole situation. He'll take Manuel—he's always wanted him. On this thought there entered into her an emptiness. There had never been a servant like Manuel. He was the only one of the household staff she would regret losing. Why couldn't her mama keep Manuel instead of Harris? She'd put the suggestion to her. But then her papa might decide to take Manuel with him. Yet where would he take him? Where would her papa live if not in the Hall? And how would he live without the glass works and her mama? This question she had asked herself more than once since last night.

On the drive she parted from Boston and went into the House, where Harris met her and told her that madam was in the little drawing room.

The little drawing room was at the end of a long passage on the east side of the house. It held a piano on which Annabella practiced. It was a small room compared to the others, and less formal and, because of its position, more private than the main rooms, and it was for this reason that Rosina chose it for the interview with her husband.

She knew that he was going into Town with Mr. Boston and when he went into Town he sometimes didn't return for two or three days. She understood he stayed at his club; where he stayed was of no interest to her at all now, but in the circumstances, and the circumstances were that no money was coming in from outside and that she herself was now utterly dependent on her mother's charity, she must talk with him about the state of their affairs.

When the works were closed, he should have been the one to come to her and discuss the situation, but as ever he would not face up to facts. He always imagined that there would be some gullible person to loan him money, or he would win some, but now he'd have to win a great deal—in fact, a small gold mine in order to sustain his way of living. No, this was the end of a long, reckless road for him and he had ridden over so many people on the way that she doubted if there was a friend left who would help him; except, of course, Mr. Boston. Their relationship, she considered, was very strange, for he acted as if Mr. Boston were in his debt and not he in Mr. Boston's.

Now their last talk, their last discussion about money would be over in a few minutes. She had asked him to wait on her here. She had also called Annabella to the meeting because, she told herself, this concerned her as much as anyone. But the real reason why she wanted Annabella with her at this interview, and which she scarcely hid from herself, was that she hoped her presence would temper her husband's rage, for she was tired, deep inside she was tired.

Annabella and Lagrange met almost outside the door of the small drawing room, she coming from the House and he coming from the Hall.

"Hello," he said. "What's this?"

"Mama wishes to see me."

He pulled a long face at her, then said mockingly, "And Mama wishes to see me, too; let us not waste time." He took her hand and led her into the room as if onto a dance floor; then looking toward his wife, who was seated by the window, he exclaimed, "Here we are, madam. Here we are." Although his manner was frivolous, there was no sign of jocularity on his face; his countenance looked strained, his skin blotched, and his eyes had a glint in them that told Rosina he was in no good temper.

She said gently, "Come and sit down."

Annabella obeyed her, but Lagrange just stood looking at her. The request, to say the least, was surprising. He stared at her waiting for her to begin, and when she did, he noticed that her voice trembled slightly and also that she used his name as a prefix, which was more surprising still. "Edmund," she said, "I would like to get the matter of the House and servants settled."

He brought his head forward just the slightest. His chin drawn in, he repeated, "House and servants? What matter?"

"Their disposal, at least the servants. The matter of the estate can wait awhile, but you must know that we cannot go on keeping this large staff now that we no longer have any income from the works."

He moved a step forward and sat down on the edge of a chair and slowly leaning toward her, his elbow on his knee, he surveyed her for a moment before he said, "You sit there and calmly tell me that we're to dismiss the servants. Not just cut down the staff as I expected you to say, but dismiss them, lock, stock and barrel?"

"Yes, Edmund, that's what I said. Unless you have some source from which you can feed, clothe and pay them."

He waved his hand slowly at her now, saying, "We'll come to that in a minute." His voice, too, was slow as he went on, "Tell me, Rosina. The servants all gone, the house empty, where did you propose we should live?"

Rosina lowered her eyes for a moment and her teeth almost imperceptibly bit at her lower lip before she could bring herself to answer, "I'm going to the cottage with Mother; I'm taking Harris with me."

"Christ Almighty!" He was on his feet; his chair spinning away from him across the polished floor gathered into a heap an animal-skin rug in its flight. "You can sit there, woman, and coolly tell me you are dismembering the House and going to live with your mother—who by the way you should never have left—and where in all your planning have you arranged for me to live? On the fells?"

He had used the same phrase as Annabella had earlier.

"I imagined you would live at your club; you—you spend a good deal of your time there; it should make very little difference to you."

His next reaction brought an exclamation of fear from Annabella, for, bending his body almost double, he gripped his hair in his fists and raised it from his scalp, while his face became so contorted almost to be unrecognizable.

Rosina sat rigid, her face deadly pale, and Annabella sat gripping the arms of her chair, staring at her father's performance, her mind telling her that this show of rage was an example of what her mother had had to endure for years.

Now Lagrange was looking at Annabella, pointing at her, speaking to her. "And to where are you going to be allocated? Not the cottage, that's certain, because dear Grandmama has never been able to stand the sight of you."

"Edmund!" Rosina's voice was sharp and he turned toward her, saying mockingly, "Yes, Rosina dear, have I said something I shouldn't? But tell me, because you've got it all planned out, where is she going? Oh"—he held his arms wide as if about to embrace her—"don't say that you are going to leave her in my care. Is that what you intend to do? And without a fight? Come, come. Let me hear you say it."

The muscles of Rosina's face were twitching as she said, "Annabella's future is—is taken care of, or will be very shortly."

"No! Her future taken care of? Well now, this is very interesting." His voice had dropped deep in his throat and his eyes were stretched in genuine surprise. "Go on, tell me more."

"I can tell you nothing further until Friday."

"Friday? Why Friday? Oh yes, it's her birthday." He swung himself round toward Annabella; then, bending over her and looking down into her face, he said, "What's going to happen on Friday that makes your future secure? Come along, my dear, you can tell me."

Annabella now put her hand to her throat. She dragged her eyes from her father's penetrating gaze and looked at her mother, but she received no signal from her, neither an acquiescent bow of the head that would indicate she could tell her father, nor a slight shake which would mean that she had to remain silent, and so, forcing herself to look back at Lagrange, she said, "I'm hoping to marry Stephen, Papa."

A long heavy silence followed this statement, during which not even a muscle of Lagrange's face moved, and he kept in the same position, half-bent over her. He stayed like this for seconds that seemed countless to Annabella, and then he startled her, and his actions now she likened to those of a madman, for he began to laugh. It was a high, raucous, jarring sound, a terrifying sound, and all the while he flapped his arms from side to side as if he were aiming to leave the ground and fly. Finally, he threw himself over the table, his whole body convulsed with his mirth.

Rosina had risen to her feet and she stood white and shaking, staring at him. His actions and the sound of his laughter recalled the night he had come into her room and thrown Annabella onto her bed.

His laughter slowly subsiding, he levered himself up and, again pointing at Rosina, he said, "You fool! You blind, senseless fool! You've planned this for years, haven't you? And now you think the time is ripe, eh, you think the time is ripe for their mating? How nice for you, Rosina. You're telling yourself you've saved something out of the chaos of your life, aren't you? Tell me, just as a point of interest, what makes you think that he'll pop the question on Friday? Tell me, I'm listening."

Through dry lips she said, "He wrote and told me so."

"WHAT! Woman, you're crazy, you're stark, staring mad. That young pip would do lots of things, but he would never write and tell you he was going to offer his hand and heart to my dear Annabella. You're making it up, aren't you? Wishful thinking?"

"It is not wishful thinking; I have his letter and he asked us to go on Friday."

She watched him lower his chin onto his chest, then, with the palm of his hand, thump his forehead, before dashing to the door and yelling, "Reeves! Faill!"

When Faill came running down the corridor, he cried at him, "Go up to the Hall. In my office you'll see some newssheets on the desk. Fetch them, and quick. Quick, do you hear?"

When he turned, Annabella was standing close to Rosina, and slowly he walked to the middle of the room and looked at them. Then, his eyes focusing on Rosina, he growled low, "You know what you want, woman, you want horsewhipping. All these years you've led her to believe that he meant something and that something was marriage."

"Papa!" Annabella's voice was trembling. "Stephen loves me and I love him."

He moved now until he was standing in front of her, and then he asked her a question.

"Has he ever said it? Has he ever put it into words?"

Her eyes flickered away from him and across the room. No, Stephen had never said, "I love you," but his every action had told her of his feelings, and she knew that he would have declared his love openly before now, but he had to put all his mind to passing his examinations both in Oxford and in London. But there were the words he had written in her mother's letter. Didn't they speak plainly enough? She returned her gaze to her father, and he, flinging his head up and to the side, exclaimed, loudly, "Huh! God!" at which moment there was a knock at the door, and Faill entered bearing three slim newspapers. Lagrange grabbed them from the man and, selecting one, he turned over the double sheet, saying, "This is Monday's *London News*. I got

122

it yesterday. I intended to bring the little announcement to your notice this morning but under the pressure of other business it slipped my mind. But wait, wait." His finger moved down the paper, and then he exclaimed, "Ah! here it is." He now folded the paper and held it some distance from him, and, looking first at Rosina and then at Annabella and back to Rosina again, he read, "Mr. Stephen Conway-Redford and Miss Kathleen Wainheart. The engagement is announced between Stephen Conway-Redford of Lincolns Inn and Weirbank House, Durham, only son of Stephen Michael Conway-Redford, deceased, and Kate Mary Conway-Redford, also deceased, and Kathleen Wainheart, eldest daughter of Colonel James Wainheart, and Lady Amelia Wainheart of The Dolphins, Ascot, Berkshire."

He looked at them. They were standing shoulder to shoulder like a pair of petrified deer, and he said, "There can be no mistake, can there? Stephen Conway-Redford of Lincolns Inn and Weirbank House, and you'll both remember Miss Kathleen Wainheart from your visit to London. If I'm right, she attended all the balls you attended. She had blonde hair, blue eyes and a china-doll complexion. Perhaps you've forgotten her?" He was looking straight at Annabella now.

There was a great stone weight on her chest, there was a great stone weight on her mind; it was trying to prevent her from crying aloud, "Oh, Stephen! Stephen! No, no, Stephen!" Stephen loved her. He kissed her and teased her, they shared jokes. He had chased her round the garden at Weirbank, and when he had caught her, he had put his arm around her waist. If these actions did not speak of love, then what did they speak of? What advances had a man to make before you could think that he loved you, that you were always in his thoughts? Her father was speaking again; his voice level and cold now, he was saying, "Even if he hadn't become attached to this girl, and even if he had wanted to marry you, I wouldn't have let it happen in a thousand years. Do you hear me? Not in a thousand years." Now turning on Rosina again, he cried, "Your plan has gone awry, hasn't it? But my plan won't. I told you years ago that I'd pick the man for her and you should have known, even then, that when I say a thing I mean it." He spoke now as if Annabella weren't there, adding, "She will marry Boston and she'll be secure for life."

"WHAT!" They both said the word together as they stepped back from him, but it was Annabella who, now detaching

123

herself from Rosina, cried, "Marry Mr. Boston! That man? Never! I'll never marry Mr. Boston, Papa! How can—how can you be so cruel?"

"Don't talk nonsense, girl. Boston is a man of wealth. He is not too old and not too young for you, he is just right; and the important thing is your future will be secure."

"And yours." The words were a bitter whisper squeezed through Rosina's lips. "That's why you don't want the servants dismissed. You've given her to this Boston man at a price, and the price is not only her future security but your own. Well, I'd rather see her dead first. Do you hear?" Now she was bending toward him. "Married to that man, she'd have a life similar to that which I've known with you. You're two of a kind."

"Be quiet, woman!"

"I shall not be quiet; you'll not have your way in this."

"Don't drive me too far. Remember, don't drive me too far."

As Rosina began to shake as with an ague, Annabella went to her side and, putting her arm around her shoulder, said brokenly, "Don't worry, Mama, don't worry, nothing on earth would induce me to marry that man, nothing." And looking with pain-filled eyes at her father, she added, "Do you hear, Papa? Nothing you can do will make me marry Mr. Boston."

Lagrange, too, was shaking, but with suppressed rage, because he saw that this being whom he had used as a pawn since she was four weeks old was no longer under his control, and he also saw clearly that he himself wouldn't be able to induce her to marry Boston. But Rosina would, ah yes, Rosina would.

He now turned his infuriated gaze on his wife and said slowly, "What about it, Rosina? You can make our dear daughter see sense, can't you? You can tell her that after all it is the sensible thing to do if she wishes to continue to live in the style in which you've brought her up."

The trembling of Rosina's body passed through Annabella, and her mother's evident distress caused her to forget her own heartache for the moment and, again confronting her father, she said, "It's no use intimidating her; nothing she can say will make me consider Mr. Boston for a moment. I'd rather beg my bread than marry that man." She had no idea of what the cliché entailed, but at this moment she meant it.

"Oh!" He gave a short mirthless laugh. "You'll never have

124

to beg your bread, my dear. There's ways of earning it, especially looking as you do. What do you say, Rosina?"

Rosina turned her head slowly and looked into the face of the only person on earth she loved. If she persuaded her to marry Mr. Boston, which she doubted she could do, she would be lost to her, and she would have before her, as she had said, a life of humiliation. If she refused to cooperate for the last time with her husband, then he would make plain to her child—and she felt that Annabella was her child in every sense of the word—he would make plain to her her early beginnings.

Annabella returned her look with tenderness, and her voice catching in her throat, she said, "Don't worry, Mama, you could never persuade me to marry Mr. Boston. If—if I cannot come to Grandmama's and live with you, then I—I will find someplace else."

Lagrange, seeing his plans melting away before his eyes, seeing his future outside of this house barren of all comforts, no Hall to himself, no servants, no stable, NO STABLE, there erupted in him a force that burst with a yell and brought their shoulders hunched up against the sound. And now he was screaming at Annabella, "You thankless bastard! Get out of my sight, get back to where you sprang from! Do you hear? Get back to where you sprang from, Crane Street. Remember—remember the nice lady who ran by the carriage and wanted to look at you, remember? Well, she's a whore and she runs a house of whores and she—she, my dear Annabella, is YOUR MOTHER! Do you hear me?" His voice rose to a thin scream. "Jessie Connolly is her name and she's your mother!" He now flung his arms wide in Rosina's direction. "This is simply my wife, a barren woman. I brought you to her when you were four weeks old, and I threw you at her, and her starved, cold body clawed at you and sucked warmth from you. But she's not your—dear mama; she's no more to you than a nursemaid. That's what she's been to you, a nursemaid."

The saliva was running over his bottom lip onto his chin and down onto the broadcloth of his coat. Annabella watched the drips; from a great distance she watched the drips fall. It was as if she had sprung aside out of herself and was looking at the girl who was looking at her papa. The girl looked stunned and shrunken, bent over, beaten down like corn in a summer hailstorm.

This woman standing gazing at her with the tortured look

on her face wasn't her mama, this beloved creature wasn't her mama, this woman who had taught her all she knew, who had guided her learning, who had dressed her in beautiful clothes, who herself had combed her hair and piled it in a crown on the top of her head, who kissed her and held her in her arms and frequently murmured over her, this was not her mama. He had said that her mama was that woman who had run by the carriage, who had often run by the carriage up till about a year ago—the woman she had come to think of, not as the nice lady of her childish imagination, but as that creature with the dissolute face.

NO! No, it couldn't be. Something was happening to her; she was having a bad dream, a nightmare. As a child, she had frequently had nightmares, especially after she had heard her papa shouting. She was having a nightmare now, she was dreaming that Stephen didn't love her and that he was going to marry Miss Wainheart. She had met Miss Wainheart. She had been a very agreeable girl, pretty and lively. She and Stephen and herself had laughed together. They had visited the Tower of London together and the galleries; she had liked Kathleen Wainheart; but Stephen couldn't be going to marry Kathleen because Stephen loved her. He must love her, he must, he must, especially now. He must!

She was watching herself again from a distance. She saw herself crouching in the corner of the big chair and watching her mama going toward her papa. She saw her grip the edge of the table until the knuckles of her hands showed up like the bones of a skeleton. She watched her leaning right across the table and saying dreadful things. She was calling on God to wreak vengeance on her papa; she was saying she hoped he died in torture and alone without a friend near him. She said things that were very unlike her mama—but then, she wasn't her mama.

She wished, oh she wished she could wake up out of this nightmare; but she couldn't. She rose from the chair and walked down the room while her papa and mama continued to face each other across the table, and, like people in a dream, they took no notice of her as she passed them. She went out into the corridor and up the main staircase and into her room and locked the door. Then she sat down by the window and put her head in her hands and tried to shake herself awake, but she remained deep in the nightmare. At one time she thought she wasn't having a nightmare at all and this was reality, but then she felt her face and she wasn't crying, and if this was reality, surely she would be in a paroxysm of tears. So she told herself to sit quietly and it would pass and she would wake up.

When, ten minutes later, Lagrange went through the conservatory and down the steps, he was staggering slightly, but it wasn't from the tumbler of brandy he had just thrown off but from the emotions that were still tearing through him. Damn her! Blast her! If only she had responded as she had always done; she could have persuaded Annabella. . . . Annabella. He stopped on the drive. He had lost Annabella; yes, he had lost Annabella. Part of his anger seeped away on a wave of remorse. He loved the girl, in his own way he loved her, but now she'd be seeing him as the devil himself. If only that cold-blooded stone of a woman had, for the last time, used her influence.

As he kicked viciously at a shingle, he saw Boston coming out of the stable yard leading his horse. He saw him stop and look toward him, then turn away again. When he reached him, Boston was adjusting the animal's girth, and with his head lowered he said, "By the way, would you mind giving Annabella a message for me?"

His whole attention seemed taken up with what he was doing, and Lagrange, looking at the bent head, said dully, "A message? Yes; what is it?"

"Just tell her that I never had any intention of asking her to marry me." He now turned his head, and Lagrange, whose face was a deep purple, spluttered, "Now, look. Look, George; she's talking like a young girl, they always go on . . ."

"Be quiet!"

"What did you say?"

"You heard what I said."

"Well, don't use that tone to me, I'm warning you."

"I'm in a position to use whatever tone I like to you."

Evading the insult, Lagrange swallowed deeply, then growled, "I hope you enjoyed your eavesdropping."

"I wasn't eavesdropping, I was walking toward your study looking for you. But your whole establishment could give word for word what was said in that room. You were squealing like a stuck pig, and your womenfolk were good seconds. I shouldn't imagine there's any need to eavesdrop when you're all at it. Talk about side shows."

"Get out!"

"I'm going, but only for the time being. I'll be back for the stable." He started to mount.

"You'll what!"

"Have I to repeat everything? You heard what I said. You owe me money to the right side of twenty thousand pounds; your horses after all won't lessen it very much, but I'm taking them, and Manuel—I told you I'd get him one day. And by the way, I wouldn't try to palm the poor girl off on to any decent family around here because it's well known that she's Jessie's. You're going to have a hard time fixing her bed and board in a respectable—"

He didn't finish the sentence before Lagrange sprang at him, causing them both to fall against the horse's flank and send it off at a gallop down the drive. Then, locked together, they lost their balance and rolled on the ground and fought like the men they usually backed, but with more viciousness.

It took Manuel, Armorer and Heron to separate them, and Manuel had to hold Lagrange against the balustrade at the bottom of the steps while Armorer dusted Boston down, then helped him toward the horse which Heron was now leading back up the drive.

Not until Boston was safely down the drive did Manuel loosen his hold on Lagrange's writhing body, but once he did, he had to put his hands swiftly back to support him again, for he almost toppled over; it was as if he were drunk.

Straightening himself with an effort, Lagrange walked up the steps and into the House, where he fended off Harris's attempt to assist him. Going slowly up the staircase and through the long gallery, he entered the Hall, and, calling Constantine to him, he ordered him to prepare a bath, after which he sat down before the standing mirror and stared at his reflection.

2

Annabella arrived at the entrance to Temple Town at four o'clock. She had done the five miles from the House in just over one and a half hours. The first mile she had run all the way—she could run now that she was no longer a lady. The new, strange self told her to pick up her skirts and run, as she had seen Rowlands and Pierce doing.

When she had reached Primrose, she stopped by the stream for a moment and, kneeling down, had splashed water on her sweating face. It was then it began to rain, not a gentle summer rain but stinging and pinging drops that hurt her skin. Over her gray fine cotton dress that was embroidered on collar, bodice and cuffs with silk rosebuds, the handiwork of Rosina, she wore her garden cloak, a long dark blue cape with a hood which she donned when she walked in the garden in inclement weather. On her feet she had soft black leather shoes with silver buckles.

Within fifteen minutes of leaving the stream at Simonside the buckles were covered with wet mud. The narrow road before her was a deceptive stretch of puddles, some a foot deep, into which she sank from time to time.

The first shelter she found was under the new arches that spanned the road adjacent to the Tyne Dock wall, over which rumbled wagons laden with iron ore from the ships lying at the wharves.

There were others sheltering under the arches and her presence caused no comment because they were mud-bespattered, too. The hood around her face was sodden with water and covered the top part of her features, so no one saw the look in the girl's eyes that might have caused them concern.

The rain lessened and she moved from under the arches, went on past the dock gates, and so into Temple Town. She knew the street, she knew the house. Up to a year ago the carriage had passed that way whenever she was paying a visit to the glass works. Her papa had been very proud of her knowledge of the glass industry and from time to time would take her and Miss Howard to the works. Proud of her knowledge! That she could have been so deceived all these years seemed impossible. But her papa was a clever man, a wicked, clever man, and had she been deceived! Hadn't she thought more than once that there was some connection between him and the woman who always seemed to be waiting on that particular street?

When she entered the street she stopped. There was the river on one side, and a big sailing boat with sails flapping was going toward the piers; another was coming from them. She kept looking at the ships, her head turned from the houses, until she was in the middle of the street, and then, as if a hand had pulled her roughly around, her head jerked sideways and there was the house. It had been newly painted a buff color, and it had a brass knob on the door and a bell to the side of it.

She found she couldn't touch the bell, and she leaned against the wall, her two hands gripping the neck of her sodden cloak. It was then that a man about to pass stopped and smiled at her. He wore a cap, and his face was running with rain and his teeth were broken and black. Pressing her back tight against the wall, she moved one step along it and into the shelter of the door, and when her hand touched the bell, the man moved on; still smiling, he jerked his head at her as if saying *au revoir*.

When the door opened, she was standing sideways to it, her back still tight against the wall. Her eyes moved upwards and took in the figure of the man looking down at her. He was a very big man, a huge man. His face was flattish and there was something wrong with his nose—it was askew. As she pressed her head back in fear, the hood slid from her hair and she watched the man's mouth and eyes open wide; then he was putting his hand behind him, flapping it. He did it a number of times before he spoke, and then he said, in a voice that seemed very small in comparison with his size, "Mary Ann. Mary Ann."

Now a young woman was standing by his side looking at her. She was wearing a loose overall kind of garment, very low at the neck, and after a moment she said, "God Almighty!"

It was she who put her hand out and, tentatively taking hold of Annabella's arm, as if she expected her to disintegrate or disappear, drew her into the hallway; then she looked at the man and said, "I'd better tell her," and he replied, "Aye, aye," but never once did he take his eyes from Annabella's face.

"Look, take her in here." The young woman drew her across the narrow hall, then let go of her hand, and he opened a door and waited for Annabella to enter the room, but she didn't move. It was the young woman who again took hold of her arm and, leading her past the man, set her down on a red plush chair.

Sitting bolt upright, Annabella stared at the man as he continued to stare at her. Once she sniffed slightly, for there was an aroma in the room that was very like that which emanated from the billiard room in the Hall; it was a mixture of cigar smoke, wines and ales. Not an unpleasant smell.

She turned her head slightly as the door burst open and there stood the woman, with the other woman behind her. Then she was standing in front of her, her mouth opening and shutting.

"In the name of God, what you doin' here?"

There was no paint on the woman's face today and she looked very ordinary, not unlike Cogg, the housemaid, except Cogg wore a smart uniform, while this woman, like the first one, was dressed in a loose garment.

"Answer me, what you doin' here? What's happened?"

"My papa sent me."

"What! Lall!"

Now the three people looked at each other before they looked at her again.

"Are you my mother?"

"OO-H GORD!"

She watched the woman put both hands up to her head and hold it, very like her papa had done earlier in the day, although she wasn't showing rage.

"The bastard!" The woman turned quickly from her and walked toward the fireplace and then back again; and now, her hands joined in front of her and her body bent forward, she said softly, "Tell us. Somethin's happened—tell us what it is."

Annabella considered for a moment. She had to sort the words out in her mind because her thoughts were confused—all except the question she had asked. That was quite clear; it was standing out right before her eyes in great letters, and she read it and asked again, "Are you my mother?"

The woman straightened her body. She pressed her lips tight together, then she put her arms around her waist as if hugging herself; and again she glanced at the big man and at the other woman before she spoke, and then dully she answered, "Yes, I'm your mother."

It had been said. It was true then, not just her papa's spite to hurt her mama, who wasn't her mama. It was the truth; this woman was her mother.

"Don't worry about it." The woman was bending over her, patting her hand now. "I'll explain it all later."

"I—I can't stay, please tell me now." The request was polite and the manner in which it was asked caused the woman to hold her head again. Then sitting down on the extreme edge of a couch and some distance away, she said, "I wanted to do the best for you. He—he hadn't any kids, I mean she didn't give him any, so I saw it as a good thing an'—an' I couldn't keep you here. Well, what I mean, I knew I couldn't as you grew up. It was done for the best. Not that it was easy, mind. I'm tellin' you it wasn't easy 'cause I knew I wouldn't have another, not if I knew anythin' about it. But tell us." Her voice was low now. "What's brought it on? He couldn't have done it for spite against me, 'cause if that was the case, it would have happened a year since." Her glance flickered once more toward the other two as if they could perhaps offer some explanation.

"I—I wouldn't marry Mr. Boston."

"WHAT!"

"I wouldn't marry Mr. Boston."

" 'Cause of that? He told you just 'cause of that?—Well!" The words seemed to eject her from the seat and once more she was pacing the room, yelling now, shouting, using language that seared Annabella's ears. "The bloody, dirty bugger! The spiteful swine! I can see it. He thought he was on a good thing; he owes George a mint and he's been holdin' her as an I.O.U. and he thought it was going to pay off, an' it didn't, so the spiteful sod's done this. By God! but he'll not get off with it! Mary Ann!" She pushed her face out toward the young woman, her teeth clenched and her lips squaring away from them, she ended, "I'll get even with that bugger, you see if I don't."

"Don't blame you." Mary Ann nodded back at her mistress. "What'll you do?"

"I know what I'll do. If I know anythin' about my Lall, I know that once his mad rage is over he'll come lookin' for her"—she nodded toward Annabella—" 'cause at bottom he's crazy about her. Used to strut like a peacock when he spoke of her. God, I'll take the struttin' out of him, I'll put a stop to his gallop if it's the last thing I do. What do you say, Jimmy?"

The big man moved his head slowly from side to side; then in a ludicrously small voice, he said, "Ah, Jessie, I'd be careful like, there's the chance she'll not like it."

"Like it? She's had to like the other, gettin' me bein' her mother slapped in her face, hasn't she? Well, she's not goin' to get half the truth." She sprung round now and, gripping the wooden ends of the high chair, bent her face close to Annabella, and she said, "You've stood so much the day, a bit more can't do you any harm. I'm goin' to tell you somethin', lass. It might make you feel better or worse, I don't know, but anyhow, I'm goin' to tell you. Now, listen to what I'm sayin' and it's the truth. Lagrange, the vindictive sod, is no more your dad than the mayor of Shields is. He's your dad—him." She lifted one hand and thumbed over her shoulder toward the big man. "And afore you turn your nose up, he didn't always look like that; he was handsome, was Jimmy, in his day. It was the boxin' that did that, and he went into boxin' just to get money for me. I knew Jimmy long afore I knew Lagrange. In fact, we were both brought up together, next door to each other—an', lass, you're his. Though mind, I didn't go with him until after I met Lagrange

132

and he had set me up. He was away for two months or more in London—it was then that Jimmy and I got together. An' when I fell, I knew I'd have to say it was Lagrange's, else I'd been out on me neck an' Jimmy'd be back in the ring, more battered than he is now. So there it is; you have it, the truth, an' it'll make no difference 'cause he can't do anythin' to me now, I'm set fair. I bet he wishes he had my little pile the night." She bent forward again. "Don't you worry, lass, I'll think of somethin'. You won't go down in the gutter to please him or no other bugger like him. . . . Look." She put out her hand and for the first time she touched her daughter's face and became silent for a moment; then she said softly, "Look, are you listenin' to me?" Then quickly she added over her shoulder, "Bring somethin', a cup of tea with a dash of hard in it, quick." But even before she had finished speaking, Annabella had slid sideways into a dead faint, and as she went she knew she was laughing; like any common person she was laughing loudly.

It was half-past eight the same evening when Rosina stood in the same room and faced the woman, the trollop, the wanton, as she had named her hundreds of times over the past years. In her mind's eye she always saw the creature with a smile on her painted face, a superior, all-knowing smile. But the woman who confronted her now was an agitated creature who aroused neither her jealousy nor her scorn; but neither did she arouse compassionate concern. She was gabbling, "Mary Ann, one of my—women, she had left her only a few minutes. Jimmy, he was out in the back, and I was upstairs gettin' into me clothes, I live up top. And then Mary Ann comes runnin' up to say she can't find her. She had vanished like into thin air. The front door's heavy but none of them heard it open or shut, and Katie and Lena were knockin' about, they were—" She bowed her head at this point, then shook it from side to side, adding, "What odds. What odds; she's gone, and God knows where, an' it gettin' dark. And around this quarter!" She now stared at the tall, stately, plain-looking woman before her and added meaningfully, "She could be eaten up. You understand that? She could be eaten up." She bounced her head forward on the last word, and Rosina, finding herself hardly able to speak, murmured, "Have—have you sent anyone out looking for her?"

"Aye, yes, of course. Jimmy's been runnin' hell for leather along the entire quay right to The Gut, and into the Market;

133

the lasses have been out an' all. I tell you it's a bloody, dirty trick he did, and that's swearin' to it, an' I don't care if me words offend your ears, ma'am." The title was not spoken in a deferential sense at all, and she went on, "You know what he is, he's a bloody, spiteful bugger. But I've no need to tell you that 'cause he's put you through the mill if I've known anythin'. Mind, it wasn't my idea that he should bring the coach down this way all those years gone; she was being well brought up and that was enough for me, but he kept sayin' that I should see her. Not that I didn't want to see her, I was dyin' to see her, but I was afraid that once I saw her I'd want her back. An' I did the first time I clapped eyes on her. But then I knew it was no use, not for her it wasn't. She'd had ten years set in your ways, she was your kid; she still is. When she comes back to her senses, she'll know that. Me, I'm just somethin' that has almost turned her brain, somethin' to be deeply ashamed of— oh, aye, I know—an' I've got that big-headed bugger to thank for it. But I've fixed him. Oh aye, I've fixed him. As I told her, he'll come crawlin' back and wantin' her once he gets over his mad bout, but I've paid him back where she's concerned. And"—she considered Rosina for a moment— "it'll be news to you an' all, but you might as well know now. I've told her, you see, he's not her father, never was. I led him on to think so 'cause it suited me. Her father's Jimmy, who let you in. He acts as me houseman an' chucker-out, when things get rough, an'—" She stopped as Rosina exclaimed below her breath, "What did you say?" Her head was bent forward, her eyes wide, her nostrils moving quickly in and out as if accompanying her heartbeats.

"I said your man's not me girl's father. He set me up, Lagrange did I mean, and then he went off sportin' in London and when he came back, well, I'd fallen an' I told him it was his 'cause I wanted security. I'd the taste of a bed that wasn't flea-ridden and I meant to keep it."

"You're saying that my husband isn't Annabella's father?"

"Aye, that's what I'm sayin'. Look, do you want to sit down?" She pushed a chair forward, but Rosina waved it aside with a slight movement of her hand, and at that moment the door opened and the big man entered; and the woman turned to him quickly and said, "Well?" and he shook his head and answered, "Not a sign of her, and nobody seems to have clapped eyes on her."

The man was staring at Rosina and she at him, and the woman said, "This is Jimmy. This is her dad—father."

134

Rosina looked at the enormous man, at the big, bruised face. This man Annabella's father? There arose in her the most odd feeling; it was a triumphant feeling, a feeling of elation, a feeling that urged her to laugh, which at this moment and in the circumstances would have been most unseemly. Her daughter—and Annabella would always be her daughter—was lost. Her mind unhinged by the shock, she was alone in this low quarter of the town, and night coming on. This was no time for laughter, this was no time for elation—that would come later. Ah yes, she would give it full rein later. This was one emotion she would not bury; this was one emotion she'd enjoy to the full.

She now brought her eyes back to the woman and said, "If you find her, will you send word to the Hall and I will come immediately."

"Aye, I'll do that."

"Will you please see that the message is delivered to me and to no one else? You—you understand?"

"I understand all right." Now they each made a movement with their heads: one was a nod, the other a slight inclining; and they stared at each other, not enemies, never friends, but two women connected with the one man. One who had been used by him and one who had used him, they were both in this moment hating him equally.

Rosina now turned away from the woman, then went on past the man who was gaping at her, and out of the room. There was another woman standing by the front door and she opened it while keeping her eyes riveted on the visitor all the while.

As Rosina stepped into the carriage, the door of which Manuel held open for her, she said under her breath, "She's not there. Please drive around the town, and quickly, before the light goes."

Over the last seven years Manuel had got to know Shields very well, especially this quarter of the town, during his monthly leave. So now he drove the carriage furiously up narrow street after narrow street, but always returning to the waterfront; he even tied the horses to alley posts and dived up the alleys, disturbing drunks and whores at their business. He ran here and there and questioned people, but always when he returned to the carriage he looked at the face peering at him and shook his head.

It was almost dark when he drove into the Market Place; he stopped the horses and lit the lamp, and going to the carriage window he said, "We can do no more here the night, madam, and I was thinking she might have made her way back home."

"You think so?" Rosina looked into the groom's face. Next to herself and Howard, this man had had more to do with Annabella than anyone else. Years ago she had been stupid enough to be jealous of him. Telling herself that it was quite beneath her to be jealous of a servant brought no ease to her feelings, for Annabella could not restrain her pleasure when she knew that she was riding out with Manuel, or when Manuel was up on the box.

She used to think, at first, that there was something odd about the dark-visaged young man, some power that wasn't quite normal. She had broached the subject to Howard, diplomatically of course, and Howard had at first said that he had an enchanting way of telling Irish tales and that he was a most unusual man, quite superior to the ordinary run of servant. Then something happened that changed Howard's opinion of the groom, for from showing eagerness to accompany Annabella when she was having her riding lessons, she had begun to make excuses, such as having a painful instep, or a sprained wrist, always something that would prevent her riding. It was Alice who told Rosina the real cause of the change in the governess. Apparently she had not been adverse to the attentions of a groom, which in her position she should have considered beneath her, until she found that his attentions were not being bestowed because of her attraction but only in order that she could teach him to read and write.

She herself had been even more suspicious of the man after this. A groom desiring to read and write, a groom who cut himself off from the rest of the staff, except from Armorer and the stableboys, and a groom who disappeared during his accumulated leave they knew not where. For Alice had said that Mrs. Page had said that Harris had said that no one, not even Armorer, knew where he spent his time; only one thing they could be certain of—it wasn't in a monastery.

And yet here he was now searching for her daughter, and the only one besides herself, she was sure, who was really and truly concerned. Howard was no longer with them, and her own mother would say, without hesitation, good riddance. And those in Weirside? Would they care, really care?

She had returned from Durham earlier in the day after a disastrous, dreadful, shame-filled visit in which her Uncle James had told her that he had informed Stephen many years ago about the condition of Annabella's birth, and that Stephen's attention to her had been affected by his compassion for her. He had always tried to show her that she was a sister to him. Sister indeed!

Then, when she had reached home, there they were all waiting to tell her that Annabella had gone. They said they had searched the house and the grounds and there was no sign of her, and her whereabouts was a mystery until the carrier had called and remarked that he thought he had seen Miss Annabella on the road to Shields. But then, he said, he must have been mistaken.

She had stood for a moment and looked from Harris to the group of servants at the top of the steps, and then she had turned and looked at Manuel, and he, without waiting for an order, had mounted the coach again and she had entered it, and he had raced the two tired horses without stop to the town.

She said to him now, "But if she hasn't returned home, Manuel, what are we going to do?" and he replied promptly, "First of all, I'll take you back, madam, and then I'll ride down again. I'll be able to get round better on me own, you understand?"

She moved her head slowly twice, then sat back in the carriage, and he mounted the box and turned the horses for home.

The house was a blaze of light when he drew up before the door. Harris and Reeves were immediately in attendance and they answered Rosina's question with, "No, madam, Miss Annabella has not returned."

After moving one lip tightly over the other, she asked of Reeves, "Is the master in?"

"No, madam; he hasn't returned, either."

She now looked at Manuel, who was standing at the horses' heads, and he said, "I'll change and go right back, madam."

"Thank you."

As she went up the steps and into the house, Manuel, handing the horses to Armorer, said quickly, "Saddle Dizzy, will you? And get me something to eat, anything. I must get out of these"—he patted his wet cape. "I'm drenched to the skin, but I'll be no more than five minutes. You'll see to it?"

"Aye. No sight of her?"

"No."

"Where did the mistress go?"

Manuel looked first to one side, then the other, then muttered under his breath, "Crane Street."

137

"Name of God!"

"Aye, name of God; I've heard of houses fallen, but man alive you can hear the crunch of this one go right through your head."

Armorer, leading the coach horses into the stable yard, said dolefully, "I hear we've all got the axe, all except Harris," and Manuel called back to him, "The world's wide." Then, running up through the loft to his room, he changed into dry things and fifteen minutes later he was galloping down the drive again and into Shields.

3

It was nine o'clock the following morning when Rosina watched the groom ride up the drive. When a few minutes later he stood before her, she looked at him without question, and he made no verbal answer, only shook his head. After a moment she said, "Go and rest and I will send Armorer in to inform the police."

He said now, "I talked to one or two, unofficial; they could tell me nothing."

When she made no comment on this, he turned away, his head bowed, and he had reached the door when she said, "Do you think she would throw herself in the river, Manuel?"

He remained with his back to her, his head still bowed. She had voiced the thought that had ridden with him all night as he had traveled the waterfront back and forward from Tyne Dock to the piers. The question now acted like a punch in his stomach, bringing an actual pain and causing his muscles to tighten into knots. But she had to have an answer, and he couldn't tell her what was in his mind, and so, turning, he asked her a question, "Is there anyone at all she could go to, madam?"

Rosina hadn't to think before she shook her head slowly, for whom could she have gone to? Whom did she know outside these gates except the family in Durham, and they were the last people she would go to. She had been as isolated most of her life as if she had lived in a convent, and Rosina knew there was no one to blame for that but herself. She had hedged the child in with proprieties; she had kept her from associating with families in the county that would gladly have accepted her, since most of them had young male members, because she had been determined to keep her for Stephen—

and herself. No. No, there wasn't a soul outside these gates that she could turn to—except that one person who had given her birth.

If only she herself hadn't gone rushing off yesterday to Durham. But even seeing the announcement in black and white she could not believe it was anything but a great mistake. Stephen, she would have sworn, was the soul of honor, and would not have played fast and loose with Annabella's affections; and she found that he hadn't.

All the way home she had told herself that she wasn't of this world, of this time; she must be living in some bygone age of knights and their honorable intentions. What label did a man tie to affectionate actions so that they could be distinguished as brotherly?

She was alone some minutes before she realized that Manuel had gone. Alice came to her now and said, "You must eat something; you've never had a bite or a sup since yesterday. I've just come from across the park and the mistress would like to see you as soon as possible."

Rosina didn't answer Alice for a moment, but went and sat by the window, and looking out onto the drive once more she said, "I'm not moving out of the house, Alice, until I have news of her. Take that message to Mother."

Alice stared at her mistress, her mouth slightly open. It was the first time she had known this daughter to disobey a request from her mother, a request that was always an order.

For most of the day Rosina sat by the window, only leaving it at the sight of the policemen riding up the drive. They hadn't come to bring her news, only to ask for particulars, and the chief officer could only marvel at the white-faced woman who asked him coolly if he thought that her daughter could have drowned herself. He was at a loss for a moment before replying, "Well, if she did, ma'am, she would likely go out with the night tide, the four-o'clock one."

It was forty-eight hours later when Lagrange returned home. Alice woke Rosina from a doze to give her the information. Sitting up in a chair in which she had slept during the past two nights, she said thickly, "A wet cloth, Alice."

Alice brought a bowl of cold water and she wrung out a cloth, sprinkled some eau de cologne on it, then held it to her mistress's face. As she did so, she said in a trembling voice, "Now, go careful; you're in no fit state to confront him. You've never eaten for days. Look, let me get you something first."

139

"There'll be plenty of time for that later, Alice."

"Well, let me change your dress."

"No, Alice; once this is over I will lie down and rest." She sighed on the last word and, taking a towel, dried her face, while Alice drew a comb through the top of the straight hair and tucked a strand in here and there.

Getting slowly to her feet, Rosina said, "He should have my message by now. He may be here at any minute. You'd better go."

Reluctantly Alice left the room. If there was one time she would have dearly loved to stay with her mistress, it was now, because if anything would bring the devil low, it would be what she said to him in the next few minutes.

But it was a full half-hour later when Lagrange entered his wife's room. When he saw her standing silhouetted against the light of the window, the change in her was immediately apparent to him. Her face was still white, still plain, but her eyes seemed to be on fire and her whole attitude was different. She was no longer controlled by that calmness that always maddened him. He couldn't put a name to either her manner or her expression; he only knew that he had never seen her like this before.

He himself felt dreadful. He had been drinking hard for two days and two nights and had only partly slept it off, but he was sober enough now to hate himself for having revealed Annabella's identity. Not that he was worried by the effect on his wife, but what did affect him was the breach that would surely open between himself and his daughter.

His mind was brought alert by Rosina's saying in a voice that was little above a croak, "Have you seen the newssheet? It should be in today. They said her body could have gone out with the tide."

"What are you talking about, woman? Whose body?" Even as he said the last two words a fear gripped him and had the effect of almost closing his windpipe.

"Whose body? Whose body would I be talking about but Annabella's, of course?"

He stared at her as he felt the blood draining from his face; then, his voice like a rapier, he demanded, "What's happened?"

"You don't know? Of course you wouldn't. You've been about your business, your entertaining business." She held out her forearms, her palms upward. "Well, you may remember you told Annabella to go to her mother, didn't you? And she did just that. She went to her mother, to the house in

140

Crane Street. Now that shouldn't surprise you, but what should surprise you is that I also went to see her mother in that house in Crane Street." She paused now as she watched the blood sweep back into his face, turning it almost purple; then she went on, "But I was too late to catch Annabella. She met her mother, and she also met someone else."

She now moved from the window and actually walked toward him until she could have touched him with her bent arm, and from this distance she looked into his face and asked, "Now, whom do you think she'd meet there besides her mother? But why am I asking you? Because you wouldn't guess in a thousand years, Edmund. You, the virile, child-producing man would be the last to guess, so I'll tell you, shall I? She met her father."

The word came soft, thick and husky. It brought Lagrange's eyes into narrow slits. He surveyed his wife. She had gone mad, she had lost her reason. But she was speaking again and now his eyes sprang wide open, for, reading his thoughts, she said, "No, Edmund, I haven't gone mad, I'm perfectly sane. Listen. I'll say it again. Annabella met HER FATHER in that house. He is the big, stupid creature. But your mistress has a regard for him. She told me quite a lot of things because apparently she was annoyed that at this stage of her daughter's life you should disclose her parentage."

He was still staring at her as if fascinated and powerless to speak, and after a moment she went on, "I recollect, it was early in our marriage, when you stayed in London for some ten weeks on business. I remember being hurt by your absence and rather lonely, and apparently your mistress was, too, because she took to her bed the man called Jimmy. I understand they had been brought up together, and, as I said, they had a regard for one another. But she was ambitious and she saw in you a means of furthering her ambitions. She would make you father of her child and then she'd have a hold on you—"

"Shut up!" He was towering over her, his teeth clenched and every muscle of his body knotted. "She's lying! She's a lying bitch."

His attitude hadn't the slightest intimidating effect on her now, and she cried at him, "No, she wasn't lying! And if I had doubted she was lying, the man would have proved me wrong because, strangely, Annabella resembled him. Your mistress said the man had been good-looking in his time before his face had become brutalized, but he still has green eyes, just like Annabella's; and his mouth, too, was Annabella's.

141

It's a wonder you've never noticed the resemblance. If only I'd had the advantage of meeting your mistress years ago, and the man, I'm sure I would have guessed and——" The mocking tone leaving her voice now and bitterness weighing heavy on each word, she cried, "I would have saved myself years of hell, years of humiliation. You, you dared to blame me for not bearing a child. If I had married any other man, I would likely have been the mother of a large family today, but no, I've been tortured for being barren while you have black-mailed me with what you imagined was the proof of your virility, while all the time you were being hoodwinked by a wanton, a whore——"

His fist came out and struck her full across the mouth and sent her reeling back against the desk, which saved her from falling; and now, her hands sprawled back on the desk to support herself, she glared at him. Her mouth was bleeding but she wasn't aware of it; she was aware of nothing but the face before her, the face she saw as a devil's. And when her fingers slid over the polished leather of the desk and touched the heavy glass inkwell, she didn't stop to consider but threw it full at him. Her action had been so quick and unexpected that he couldn't avoid it; the inkwell hit him in the neck and the ink splashed up over his face and down his clothes.

Now he had to put up his arm to avoid the heavy silver paperweight; then she was picking up a vase from the window-sill, and as it missed him and crashed against the wall, Alice came rushing into the room. After pausing a second, she flew to her mistress and, putting her arms tightly about her, cried, "There, there! Give over now! There, there!" Turning her head toward her master, she dared at last to shout at him, "Get out! Get out!" After a moment, while he glared at them as if about to kill them both, he turned and staggered from the room.

Half an hour later, Rosina, assisted by Alice on one side and Reeves on the other, walked slowly across the park to her mother's house, and having reached it she collapsed. Reeves, running for the first time in years, returned to the stables and ordered Manuel to ride into the town as quickly as possible and bring the doctor.

Following the habits of a lifetime, Reeves and Mrs. Page kept the household working and as if still under the direction of a master and mistress; true, they were visited each day by Alice, who in her way was more formidable than the mistress or even the master. To their queries as to how the mis-

142

tress was faring, they received the same answer day after day: she was still poorly. Alice would not say that her mistress had lost the will to live and that she lay scarcely speaking and that if she didn't eat, and soon, she'd surely die.

When the least of the servants stopped her and asked after their mistress's health, Alice thought cynically of the staff's change of attitude. Her mistress hadn't gained their full respect until she had started to throw things. Her self-control over the years had not evoked their admiration, but she asked herself bitterly, What did they know about self-control?—shutting her eyes to the fact that both she and they had had to study this facet of character from the moment they entered service, and that they had seen in their mistress's retaliation their own release from subservience. She herself had forgotten the moment of glee that she had experienced at the sight of her master bespattered with ink and the room strewn with the remnants of the Ming vase and other articles.

The servants as a whole did little work. What was the use? they said. Everything was being covered up and they had three weeks in which to work out their notice and find another situation. But there was the rub, find another situation, when houses all over the North were cutting down, so, as they said to cook practically in one voice, Eat while the going's good. The cellars and the larders were still full and what would happen to the food, anyway, when the house was empty? They'd never get through all this stuff down at the cottage. Half of it would go bad. None of the staff could get to know from Alice if the estate was to be disposed of altogether, or just part of it including the House, and leaving the cottage for the old mistress, because Alice didn't know herself.

There was only one among them who was certain of a job besides Harris. This was Manuel, because they all knew that Mr. Boston had had his eye on him for years, and now all he had to do was to pick up his traps and walk across the county into a stable ten times better, it was said, than this one, with anything from fifteen to twenty horses in it—Mr. Boston hadn't been hit by the slump.

Then the household was amazed by the news that Manuel was not going to Boston's. It was in its own way as big a surprise as the unprecedented ructions the other day. But, they said, didn't that prove what they had always said about him was true, he was odd? But this was the latest, the fellow must be balmy. Folks fighting tooth and nail for any kind of work at this time and he turning down a heaven-sent job like that. He was completely nuts, said every one of the male staff, except Armorer.

Manuel, too, thought that he must be a little crazy not to take the situation that Boston was holding out to him, that of head man over his stables. He knew he might live to be a hundred and never have the same chance offered again, but there it was—he didn't like the man, and he knew it would never work out. Not that he had been all that enamored of his present master. There were times over the past years when he had almost snatched up his bundle and gone. Yet, in a way, he felt there was something about Lagrange he understood. Perhaps it was his love for the animals. But understanding apart, he was getting away from this house as soon as possible. He had a feeling on him that told him to be gone.

This was the morning of the fifth day since Annabella's disappearance and the thought of her had never left his mind for one minute. She even dominated his fitful sleep. He hoped to God, and very sincerely, that she had gone in the river; if not, he wouldn't let himself think where she'd be and what would be happening to her at this very moment, for he knew only too well that a girl of any kind couldn't be abroad at night in that quarter of Shields and not have a man's hands on her.

He had been up since four and tramping through the park, but the dawn was now breaking and it was time for him to get back. He stopped for a moment when he got to the gap in the stone wall and he recalled the day he had taken her through it for the first time. He went now and leaned on the broken masonry and looked in the direction of the river, which was blotted out in early ground mist.

It was as he stared that he saw the disembodied head bobbing above the rim of the floating vapor. The sight startled him and brought him taut, the hairs on his neck rising until he saw the head become attached to a trunk, and he let out a long breath as he recognized the bulk of Amy Stretford. Taking a side leap, he was over the wall and going toward her, and from a distance he called, "Hello there, Amy!" And she stopped for a moment before hurrying to him, saying, "Oh, Manuel. Manuel."

When they met, she gripped his hands with her own ice-cold ones, then said, "I must have wished you up out of bed. I was coming to try and find you."

"What is it? Are you in trouble?"

"It depends how you look at it, lad. Come back this way with me."

144

"But, Amy, it'll soon be five, and I'm due with the animals."

"They can wait. Let everything wait; come on back with me." She now took him by the arm and they had gone a few steps before he said again, "But what is it, what's happened?"

She peered up at him through the lifting light and said under her breath, "It's your miss, I've got her in the house."

"Miss Annabella?" He gripped her arms until she winced and then he said quickly, "Oh, sorry, sorry, Amy, but when?"

He was hurrying forward now, almost carrying her along, and she said between catches in her breath, "I've had her with me two days but I've been frightened to leave her in case of what she might get up to, she's been raving. I was frightened of the river, but I've been as far as this a half dozen times in the hope that I might see you, but never a glimpse, so when a half an hour ago she fell into a dead sleep, I thought I'd chance it. But, Manuel, I'd better warn you, if she comes round, don't mention taking her back to the House because she'll start her screaming again. I set her off twice by saying I'd go and fetch somebody. The first time she flayed and struggled to get out as if she was behind prison bars, and the next time she did get out and made straight for the river. She's demented."

They were going up the path when he said, "How did you find her?"

"I didn't, she found me. There was a thud against the door as I was making for bed, and there was this huddled shape lying on the step. Oh, you never saw anything like the state she was in; she was caked mud from her hair to her toes and she was soaked to the very skin of her, and her body was burning up."

They were in her kitchen now and she said under her breath, "Come in here," and went toward a door in the corner. "I couldn't get her up the stairs so I made a shakey-down in the front room. I've kept the fire going night and day. It's enough to bake you, but it'll help to sweat the fever out of her."

Manuel went into the small front room and stopped just within the door and looked at the figure lying on a biscuit mattress a few inches from the floor. The face was white as plaster of Paris, and as stiff as a cast made of the same. The brown hair was strewn on the pillow on both sides of her as if she were afloat on water.

Dropping to his knees, he tenderly picked up the boneless-looking hand from the top of the blanket and held it firmly

145

clasped between his own for a moment while his throat contracted and he gulped at his spittle.

Amy, from his side, whispered, "Why do you think she made for here? She hasn't been here not a half dozen times in as many years."

He did not take his eyes from Annabella as he said, "If we ever came out alone, she always suggested we call; she couldn't when he or the others were with her. She liked coming here, Amy." He said now, "She's in a high fever," and she answered, "It should be down by this evenin'."

"Do you think she should have a doctor?" He glanced up at her and she shook her head. "He could do nothin' more than I'm doing for her. I've given her a stiff dose. It's a brew I have for fevers, made up of potash and sweet spirits of niter and a few herbs and things. It's running into the third day and reached its peak so she should be cooled down by this evenin'; if not, then we'll talk of the doctor again. I'd leave her now."

Slowly he got to his feet and followed her into the kitchen, and there he said, "I'd better get back and let them know."

Amy now shook her head slowly at him. "If you want my opinion, I wouldn't, for every time I mentioned gettin' help, which meant going across there, she went on like somebody insane, I told you. Once or twice she became clear in the head and she said to me, pathetic-like, 'Let me stay, Amy, let me stay quietly for a little while; I'll go as soon as I'm rested,' and I said to her, 'Where are you thinking of going, child?' and she answered, 'I have plans.' And I said to her, 'Well, what about your mother, she'll be worried?' and she answered to that, quite sanely, 'She's not my mother, Amy.' Well, of course, I knew that; there wasn't anybody around the countryside that didn't. But there was something I didn't know, and if it's true, then God help her, because I said to her, 'Well, shall I tell your father?' and she laughed at that, a weird, funny, painful laugh, and I thought she was going off her head again, but she said, 'He isn't my father, either, Amy. Now, would you believe that? She isn't my mother and he isn't my father. My parents both live in Crane Street.' Then she asked me if I knew Crane Street and did I know this house in Crane Street. . . ."

Manuel screwed up his face. "He's not her father?"

"That's what she said, he's not her father, either."

"God sake, this is worse." He rubbed his hand slowly up and down one side of his face; then he walked to the door and stood looking out. It was a beautiful morning now;

146

the light had dispersed the mist. A morning like this always brought peace to his turbulent spirit. Yet a morning such as this always made him think regretfully that if he could write he would put this morning down on paper; a newborn morning such as this always made him glad he was alive, even if he knew the day before him was going to be irksome.

But this morning he was filled with a sadness he had never experienced before. A girl who had been brought up as a lady. For seventeen years she had been coached to be just that, a lady. And now she had all the mannerisms of a lady; her mind worked along ladylike channels, and, being a lady, she had come to consider the niceties of life her due; from her station she saw life filled with equals and inferiors. She had been brought up to think she would marry an equal—an equal, Mr. Stephen. What about Mr. Stephen? He turned to Amy quickly and said under his breath, "I know where she could go, Durham, Mr. Stephen. There's something betwixt them. She's always had her heart set in that direction. I'll—"

"Save your breath, Manuel; that avenue's closed an' all as far as I can gather, because in her ravings she was on about him marrying someone called Kathleen. Her father had read it from the paper."

He stared at her for a while, then he bowed his head deeply on his chest and, walking away from her, said, "I'll be back as soon as I can."

She called to him softly, "I wouldn't say anything until you know what she wants to do."

He did not turn toward her but nodded his head in agreement, then went down the path and along the riverbank, and as he went there came back into his mind the thought of Margee. He hadn't thought of her for years now, but her prophecy seemed to be coming true, for trouble had fallen on this house. Yet, in a way, the house had no connection with himself, so it wasn't his trouble, except that he was sorry to the very heart of him, to the very core of him, for Annabella—for *Miss* Annabella, he prompted himself harshly. It didn't mean that because she had been thrown over by the rest of them, she was to lose her title. He wasn't given to titles, no begod; deep in him he hated calling a man "sir," or "master," but this was different. This was one title he'd speak and always speak with deference, Miss Annabella.

It was late in the afternoon when he again leaped the broken wall. He had never known a day like it in all his time in the stables. The master was going mad, he thought, for he hardly left the stable yard. He had ordered three horses down to the forge to be shod and them not needing it. He had gone over all the bridles, girths and saddles like a housewife over her kitchen pots. He had said the carriages looked dingy and ordered Danny to make up a new polish. He had stood over him while he melted the yellow wax and pounded up the litharge with the water, and he had come back at him before he had had time to put in the ivory black, and he had said the coach was in the state it was because they had forgotten to put the turpentine in the last lot, as if a man making up a polish would forget to put the turpentine in. Then he had been on Manuel, saying that he was giving the animals too little exercise and too much food; and once he had turned on Manuel and yelled, "You won't get your own way in Boston's like you have done here," and just in an effort to soothe him he had replied, "I have no intention of going to Mr. Boston's, sir." And on this Lagrange had come to him and patted his arm, and smiled at him and said, "Good. Good, Manuel." And then he had added, "He'll never get one of them as long as we stand together, eh?" He hadn't understood him but he had nodded. Then he had watched him go round examining the locks on all the doors; it was as if he expected a raid on the stables. And just five minutes since he had gone riding out hell for leather on Dizzy. He didn't often ride Dizzy, for he didn't like her, nor she him. He had never been able to break her spirit; she still bucked and reared on the slightest provocation, and the very last time he was out on her she had thrown him.

When Manuel reached the cottage, Amy was bending over the fire stirring something in a pan. She turned her head and straightened her back and said, "You've been long in coming."

"I couldn't get away—he's on the rampage. How is she?"

"She's herself, in her mind that is, but she's far from well."

"Can I go in?"

"Aye, of course. I told her you had been an' it didn't distress her."

The heat of the room met him as he opened the door. It was a heat that would bring the blood to the surface, but the face on the pillow still had the plaster look about it. He slowly lowered himself onto his hunkers by her side and looked into the eyes that were like wells of sorrow.

"Manuel."

148

He nodded his head at her a number of times before he could speak, and then, because he couldn't think of anything to say at the moment, he asked, "How are you feeling?"

"Better, Manuel. I—I'll be quite well soon. Amy is—very kind." Her speech was halting; she seemed to have to drag each word up from the depths of her and force it out.

He said, "We've been worried."

"That's—that's kind of you, Manuel."

"Oh, not me alone." He smiled at her. "Everybody. The mistress has been—"

His mention of the mistress acted like a blind being dropped over her eyes. She was still looking at him but as if she weren't seeing him, and she began to cough now. It was a harsh, racking sound and her whole body shook with its force so that, when it ended, she was gasping. Then half-apologetically she said, "I'm sorry, I've—I've caught a little chill. What day is it, Manuel?"

"Monday, Miss Annabella."

"How long have I been here?"

"I think you came on Friday night."

"Friday?" she repeated, her mind groping back at the past events.

He said now under his breath, "Where did you get to? I searched that waterfront for two days and nights."

She was looking at him again. "That was kind of you, Manuel; I'm sorry I put you to so much trouble."

"Oh, tish," he said; "it was nothing. It was only that—I was worried." He did not say "we," now.

She was silent for some time, her head turned away from him, looking in the direction of the window, and then she said, "Do you know that little cave you once showed me on the side of the green tor? Well, I woke up in there and the sun was shining on me. I can't remember when I left the town, but"—she nodded once—"I knew I was making for here. It's strange, isn't it, that I should make for Amy's?"

He shook his head slowly and smiled softly at her as he said, "Not strange at all; Amy's a fine woman, a good woman."

She moved her head again and said, "Yes, she is, but one thing worries me."

"And what's that?"

"I have no money to pay her."

His voice was loud. "Pay Amy? Don't be silly, she'll want no payment." He now leaned over her and smiled and said,

"You're a godsend to her, do you know that? She's been dying to have someone to practice her herbs on for years. You never liked her ginger beer, did you?"

The question brought not a vestige of a smile to her face and she replied, "I am sorry. It's very good beer but not to my taste."

The smile left his own face and he stared at her and thought, Always the polite, ladylike reply. God, but she's going to find it rough. She'd have to build up a number of skins on herself if she was going to survive. He got slowly to his feet, saying now, "Just rest, I'll be in later. If not, I'll be across first thing in the morning."

"Thank you, Manuel."

He made for the door; but there he stopped when again she spoke his name, "Manuel!"

"Yes, Miss Annabella."

"You won't tell them."

He paused before he said, "It would be the best thing because you'll have to go back in the long run."

"No! No!" She was resting on her elbow now. "I won't have to, never. You—you don't know what's happened, Manuel. I—I can't go back."

"Now, now." He came toward her again. "Don't trouble yourself, rest now. Don't worry, I won't say a word till you get on your feet and then we can talk about it again."

"I—I won't change my mind, Manuel, when I'm better. I can never go back there. You don't understand, I don't belong—"

"Now, now." He lifted his hand and patted the air above her head as if he were touching her, saying soothingly, "I understand, I understand right enough. What you don't understand is that you are in a very low state at the moment. You rest for a few days longer and then we'll see what's to be done."

She started to cough again and he said, "There, see. Amy will give it to me for upsettin' you. Now rest easy. I'll say nothing until I have your leave, how's that?"

She was gasping when she said, "Thank you, Manuel."

As he went out of the room, he thought, What's to become of her if she doesn't go back? And he voiced this to Amy where she stood pouring some gruel into a basin, and her answer was, "Leave it. Leave it. God has a way of working things out, slow but sure. We'll take one thing at a time. But she'll be lucky if she gets over this with nothing more than a cough; lying soaking on the fells for two nights would

150

kill a horse." She added now, "I saw himself go galloping up the road a few minutes ago and I thought how strange it was, them searching the countryside for her and her not a kick in a backside, so to speak, from their own back door."

"Lagrange went past—on the main road?"

"Aye. Aye, in the direction of the lodge."

"Well, wherever he's been, it's been short and sweet," he said. "It means I'd better be back, and soon, or else the mood he's in he'll try for my scalp. I'll be over around dawn again, Amy."

"All right," she said.

He paused before going out, and putting his hand on her shoulder he added, "You're a good woman, Amy," and she gave a hic of a laugh as she replied, "I am as God made me; I'm good to those I like and I curse those I don't, and I do both well."

They laughed together understandingly; then, bending forward, he kissed her hastily on the cheek and went out, leaving her red in the face as if she were a young lass.

4

Most of the servants were gone; there were in the house now only Harris and Mrs. Page and outside only Armorer and Manuel. All that remained of the farm staff was the blacksmith, because the stock had been sold. The only place that wasn't changed on the estate was the stable yard; it still housed all the horses, and Lagrange, seeming to become stranger every day, haunted the place.

When Armorer had pointed out to his master that it would be nigh impossible for him to see to all the animals after the morrow when Manuel left, the reply he got was, "Manuel isn't going, he's staying; he'll stay as long as I want him."

When Armorer had conveyed this to him, Manuel had looked at the older man and said quietly, "I'm not staying, George. I'd give me life for the animals, you know that, but I've got a feeling I must get out of this, just a feeling. Somehow I think he means me no good. Can you understand this?"

Armorer had shaken his head. He couldn't, not really, because the master had always shown leniency toward the young fellow. Even after he had refused to box for him and told him so to his face, he hadn't sent him packing with a horsewhip around his shoulders as he would have done any other of them. He just champed on his bit and flew at everyone around him, but strangely not at the one who had aroused his ire.

Lagrange had told no one what his arrangements were, but it was plain to those left in the house that he intended to stay in the Hall, because he had sent most of the staff scampering a fortnight before their time was up. He had paid them full money, but, as he had said to Reeves, they weren't going to sit on their backsides eating the cellars bare, and thereupon he had ordered most of the food from the House cellars into those of the Hall.

But now this was the last day of the month and all of them would be gone tomorrow, except Harris and Armorer, because Armorer had said, Pay or no pay, he couldn't go until the horses were disposed of.

Manuel had been working from dawn all through the hot day with a dead weight on his heart because everything he did he knew he was doing for the last time, and the horses seemed to sense this, too, for one after the other they nudged him with their heads and played for his attention; even Dizzy pushed her muzzle into his hand without his having to placate her first.

He knew he was deserting a sinking ship and that in principle he should stay on with Armorer if only for the sake of the animals; yet some stronger force countermanded his sympathy and told him to be gone.

However, the weight inside of him was not created alone by the situation in the stables, but by the more dire situation in Amy's house. He couldn't get Annabella out of his mind. It was worse than when he thought she was lost forever, for then there had been no future to think of. The plan she had in her mind, and about which she had spoken to Amy, was to turn governess, until cool reason told her that mistresses didn't take strangers into their homes to look after their children without references. He himself had suggested to her that she should write one out herself, and this had shocked her, and he had thought she was going to get bigger shocks than that before she was much older, that is, if she was thrown onto the world by herself.

He had kept his promise to her and not mentioned her presence to a soul, but tomorrow he'd be on the road going God knows where, and he couldn't take with him the thought of her being adrift, for of all things she had now got it into her mind to make her way to London, there to get a position of waiting on in one of the dress establishments she had visited as a customer.

Amy had said to him on the quiet, "She doesn't know what she's talking about; the staff of those places live like rats underneath those shops, and they're fed scarcely better. I had a cousin who was a seamstress and came home to die, and the tale that she told me was almost unbelievable. But for her being a God-fearing girl, I'd have taken her story as ravings."

At last it was Annabella's determination to make for London that decided him that, promise or no promise, he was going to tell the mistress where to find her daughter, for he imagined the woman would always think of Annabella as her daughter. The best thing to do, he thought, was to bring them face to face, surprise her like, and that being accomplished, there was no doubt but that something would be worked out. And that done, he'd leave easy in his mind.

In his room, he bundled up his few belongings so that he'd be ready in the morning. There was an extra pair of trousers, an old coat, two shirts, a pair of boots, some small clothes, stockings, and odd cooking utensils. Having put them into a bag that he had made from two sheepskins with loops at the ends to go over each shoulder and make it easier for carrying, he looked around the room, then rubbed his hand around his middle, where in a flannel belt he kept his money, then went down the steep stairs into the yard. He was crossing toward the pagoda walk when Lagrange's voice came at him, saying, "Where you going?"

He turned and looked over the distance at the bloated face and bleary eyes and answered quietly, "Just for a stroll, sir."

"What's this I hear about you leaving tomorrow? Sneaking off, eh? Well, you're not going, do you hear? I'll break your neck if you go outside those gates without my leave, understand?"

He remained quiet. He didn't want to argue with the man; all he wanted was to put distance between them; it wouldn't be long until tomorrow morning. He had been paid, with the rest, a week ago. There was no possible chance of getting the remainder that was owing to him, but that didn't matter; all he desired was to get away. It was unreasonable, he told himself, but that's how he felt.

"You heard what I said?"

"Yes, sir."

"Well, pay heed."

Lagrange turned away, and Manuel turned away but kept his step even all the way through the park just in case Lagrange had taken it into his head to follow him, and when he came to the broken wall he leaned on it for a moment as if enjoying the warm evening. He listened for telling sounds in the undergrowth of the copse to the right of him, but there was nothing, only the chattering of the birds, and so he went on toward the cottage.

As he went up the broad, grassy path he saw Annabella sitting on the wooden seat outside. Her face had lost its chalky pallor, but her features still retained the stiffness of hardened plaster. She looked as if she had never smiled, or would not know how to. The eyes were still lying deep in sadness and the voice was listless when she said, "Hello, Manuel."

"Hello, Miss Annabella. Hasn't it been a lovely day?"

"Yes, Manuel, it has."

Yes, she supposed it had been a lovely day, yet it was only at this moment that she had become aware of it; for all day her thoughts had clouded her vision. Tomorrow Manuel would be gone; she would never see him again. What was she to do? She couldn't stay on indefinitely with Amy, although that kind woman had said she'd be happy for her to stay as long as she wished, and today she wished she could go on living here forever, for it was so peaceful and no demands of any kind were being made on her. She didn't know what was going to happen to her; she couldn't think clearly. Only one thing was prominent in her mind at present: tomorrow Manuel would be gone.

But now, looking at him, she told herself, as Rosina would have done, that she must take herself in hand and not rely upon this kind servant. Yet Manuel was no longer a servant, not to her. He still addressed her as "Miss Annabella," in fact, he had called her "Miss Annabella" more times these last two weeks than he had done since the day of their first acquaintance, that day seven years ago when he had stopped the horses from running away. It was on that day, too, that she had first kissed Stephen. Her head jerked, as if she had acquired a tic. She must not think of Stephen. She must not even recall his name. If she did, she knew that the pain in her body would dissolve into tears. She could cry in the night when there was no one to see, but to give way to her emotions before these two very dear people would be unthinkable.

In one breath she would tell herself that she was different,

154

she was no longer Miss Annabella Lagrange, she was just an ordinary girl who would now in some way have to earn her living; yet in the next she would be acting and thinking in accordance with her training of seventeen years, showing consideration which was nevertheless threaded with condescension.

As she stared up at Manuel, a feeling of panic attacked her every nerve and she realized in this moment that without him she would be adrift; she wouldn't know to whom to turn. There would be only one thing left for her to do—go back and throw herself on the charity of the woman she called "Mama," the woman who in her hour of greatest need had left her alone. Had she on that awful day insisted on seeing her and offering her comfort, she doubted whether she would have made that journey to Crane Street; but after tapping on her door and merely asking to speak to her, she had left her alone, and she had sat there in silence for hours and no one had come near her, not even Alice or the servants. A bitterness had entered into her when Rosina's continued absence forced her to the conclusion that her adoring mama had found the exposure too much to bear. She could look upon her as her "darling child" only as long as the dark shameful secret of her birth remained a dark secret. Her mind, she realized, had been slightly deranged on that day, but even now, when it had returned to normal, the bitterness still remained against her mama's defection.

She could not prevent herself from saying now, "Must you go tomorrow, Manuel?"

Before answering, he bowed his head. "I'm afraid so, Miss Annabella; I want to look around and get myself fixed for the winter. Then, come the spring, I've got an idea I'll go and see Spain." He lifted his eyes to hers, and she looked into the dark, warm depth and said quietly, "That will be very nice for you, Manuel. It'll be nice to see the country of your ancestors."

He put his head back now and laughed, saying jocularly, "Ah, Miss Annabella, thereby hangs another tale." But his laughter did not bring forth even a vestige of a smile to her face, and he turned from her, saying, "Is Amy about?"

"She's up in the attic, I think."

He went into the main room, then looked up the ladder and through the hole in the floor, saying, "Are you there?" and when her face appeared above him, she said, "Aye, come on up."

He couldn't stand upright under the eaves so he crouched

on his hunkers watching her taking clothes out of an old wooden box.

"There's a piece of stuff in the bottom," she said; "it's good serge. Harry brought it back from sea to make me a dress, but it was really too good, the material, so I thought she could make herself a skirt, because, wash as I might, I wasn't able to get the mud stains out of her clothes. . . . You're about ready, then?" She didn't look at him as she asked the question, and he answered, "Yes, Amy; me bundle is fixed for the road."

"What am I going to do with her?" She now turned her head slowly toward him and he blinked once or twice before shaking his head and saying, "There's only the one thing. As I said in the beginning, I must tell them where she is. It's unthinkable that she should be left on her own."

"She doesn't want that, she's dead against it."

"She doesn't know what she wants; she's still in a state, Amy. She's acting like men do after a battle. They don't think it's over, they still think it's on. On me way back, I'm going to the old lady's place to see if I can have a word with the mistress and tell her. I'll let you know what happens. I may not get over afore dark if he's still on the rampage. He's going off his head, I think; he's turned the stables into a fortress and he thinks I'm one of the garrison, but I'm not. Do you know something, Amy? I won't breathe easy until I'm on the road and miles away from that place tomorrow."

Amy now closed the lid of the box, and, holding the piece of blue serge material to her breast, she looked at him and said, "I'm going to miss you, lad."

"And me you, Mother."

On the term of endearment he sometimes used, she bowed her head and the tears rolled down her cheeks, and he bent toward her and drew her into his arms and stroked her hair as he said, "I'll be back. One of these days I'll be back, and that's a promise I'll make to you on the cross." He marked out a cross with his finger on the top of her gray hair and after a moment she pulled herself away from him, and, her head still bowed, she said, "Go on, get back and get it over."

He went down the ladder and out into the sunshine again, and standing before Annabella he said thickly, "I'll see you in the mornin' afore I go on me way." He now bent slightly above her and said softly, "Don't worry. Everything will pan out, you'll see," and she answered dully, "Yes, Manuel."

Ten minutes later he went through the gap and into the grounds, but this time he didn't take the path toward the

156

stables. Instead, turning left, he made for the cottage. It had always amused him that a house of this size should be called a "cottage."

When he approached the front door, he saw it was open and crossing the hall was the familiar figure of Alice. She turned her head quickly at the sight of him; then, coming toward him, she said, "Yes, what is it?"

"I—I would like to speak with the mistress."

"You can't do that, she's very poorly. She's still in bed. She sees no one."

"This is important, Miss Piecliff. I've got to see her. It's about Miss Annabella."

"They—they've found her?" She brought her thin face closer to his, and he said, "No, they didn't find her, but I know where she is."

"Dear Lord, dear Lord. I don't know. I don't know." She held one hand against her ear now and rocked herself, then said, "I'd better tell the mistress—I mean Mistress Constance. Stay there a minute."

He stayed where he was for five minutes before Alice returned and then she said under her breath, "Come this way," and he followed her across the hall and into a long, narrow room where, at the far end, stood a figure dressed in black.

He had caught sight of the old lady at intervals over the years, sometimes walking in the park, and once or twice in the early days he had seen her going into the chapel, but she always went in before the household and took her seat behind the partition that screened her from prying eyes, and she never left until the place was empty. Now, for the first time, he was looking at her face and was really surprised to see the remnants of a beautiful woman. She bore no resemblance at all to her daughter, except perhaps in the steely dead blankness of her expression.

A big book, which he took to be a Bible, lay open on the table, and above the fireplace hung a large ebony cross.

Her approach was abrupt: "Yes, what have you got to say?"

"I would like to speak to the mistress, madam."

"My daughter is too ill to be disturbed; whatever news you have you can tell me."

He hesitated a moment, then said, "Miss Annabella is staying at Mrs. Stretford's cottage"—he jerked his head backwards—"along the riverbank. She's been ill. She made her way there and collapsed about—about three days after she left here."

The gray eyes were looking straight into his and her voice sounded emotionless as she said, "Well, wherever the girl is, is no concern of ours."

"But the mistress, she was concerned?"

"She's no longer concerned. My daughter has been very ill; the doctor has given strict orders she's not to be disturbed in any way. My daughter is at last free—" She checked herself; the features had tensed, her lips were straight and tight. Manuel watched the whole body of the woman give a shudder before she continued, "For years my daughter has suffered torment because of that girl. Now it is over. The girl, I understand, has a home to go to; the quicker she adapts herself to it, the better. You can convey that message to her."

He stared at her unbelieving. "Do you know what kind of home she's got to go to, madam? It's a house of prostitution." His voice was loud, harsh, and Alice put in quickly, "Manuel! Manuel! Remember whom you're talking to."

He looked at her and said, "I know who I'm talking to an' I won't forget in a hurry." He now looked back at the old lady and continued with hardly any change in his voice. "You say she's to adapt herself. What do you think is going to happen to a girl like her who's been brought up to think she belongs here? She talks like a lady, she thinks like a lady, because the mistress made her that way."

"Manuel, be quiet. You're forgetting yourself," Alice put in again.

He almost answered, "Forgettin' meself be damned!" but the old lady was speaking. "Then she should be grateful for the advantages she has had over the last seventeen years. It doesn't fall to the lot of everyone born as she was to be so fortunate."

He glared at her hardly able to believe his ears. Then almost flatly he asked her, "Have you thought that they might meet? What if Miss Annabella stays around here? They could easily bump into each other."

The old lady did not answer for some seconds. Then she said, "It would make no difference. My daughter would not recognize her; she has lost her mind."

Alice turned her head swiftly and looked at her mistress as she ended, "You can inform the girl of this too. That will be all."

He did not leave her presence immediately but continued to stare at her. The coldness of these women, the inhumanity of them. God give him the women in Crane Street any day.

He turned and stamped out of the house and made his way back to the stables, there to be confronted by Lagrange, who, finding no one to take care of his horse, was in a frenzied rage. He stood now within the stable door, his feet apart and pulling his riding crop through first one clenched fist, then the other, and what he said was, "You're asking for trouble, Manuel, aren't you?"

"I want no trouble, sir." Although his feelings were enraged with the whole lot of them, he tried to keep his voice even.

"Where have you been?"

"I went for a stroll, sir."

"You're not paid to go for strolls."

"My time is up tonight, sir."

"Your bloody time is up, man, when I say it is and not before. Understand? You attempt to walk out of here and I'll be after you and skin you alive."

Manuel's answer to this was to walk forward, take the horse and lead it into the stable.

A moment later Lagrange was yelling at Armorer, who had been in the house having a meal which he had had to prepare for himself.

When the coachman came into the stables, his face was gray, and under pretense of examining the horse's hoof, he said in a low undertone, "He's beside himself. I've never seen him as bad as this. Do you know what Harris has just been telling me? He says Constantine told him that the nights the master's been riding out, when he thought he was in Newcastle at the tables, he's been raking the whole of Shields. He still thinks she's somewhere there. In a way I'm sorry for him; he'll go off his head with one thing and another."

"Armorer."

"Yes, Manuel?"

Manuel now went swiftly toward the stable door and looked into the yard; then coming back, he said hastily, "I'm leaving tonight. My time's up tonight, so I'm going."

Armorer was standing straight, his face anxious, as he said, "But in the dark? Where will you get to in the dark?"

"Oh, it won't be the first time I've tramped the roads in the dark. I'll be all right, never fear. But I've got to get away when the going's good. He's not accountable for his actions and I wouldn't be accountable for mine should he raise his hand to me. You know how it is."

"Aye, Manuel, aye, I understand. But I'm tellin' you this."

159

He held out his hand. "I'll be sorry to see you go. I've never worked with anybody that understood the animals like you; I'm heart sorry to see you go, man."

As Manuel gripped the outstretched hand, he said firmly, "And me, too. But I won't lose sight of you, George. You'll be staying on here and one day I'll be around this way again; I've promised meself that."

Armorer turned away quickly now, saying, "I'll try to get some grub from the kitchen to put into your sack. What time will you be off?"

"Late twilight I should say, because, if he does take it into his head to follow me, he'll have a job picking me up in the dark."

And the twilight was deep when Manuel again shook hands with Armorer and set out, the skin bag on his shoulders. He went by way of the middens and came to the broken wall by way of the orchards and the strawberry field. As he walked along the riverbank, he peered over the distance of the fells in the direction of the main road where he thought he heard the sound of a horse galloping. The road was sunken from the actual rise of the fells and he could see no one, but he stopped and listened. There was no sound of a horse's hooves, only the bark of a fox dog.

When he came up the path, Amy was sitting by the door and she said in some surprise, "You're going now, then?" and he answered, "Aye, it's better so." He lowered his voice when he asked, "Where is she?"

For answer Amy jerked her head backwards toward the inner room, then asked, "Did you tell them?"

"Aye, I did, Amy, I told them, at least the one I saw, the old one."

"And what happened?"

"Nothing." He dropped the pack off his back as he said, "There's some bitter, hardhearted swine in the world; you learn more about them every day." He drew her away from the door now and onto the stone slabs forming the rough terrace, and there he added, "They'll have none of her. 'Let her go back to Crane Street,' she said."

"Never!"

"I'm tellin' you, Amy, that's what she said to me. 'She's got a home to go to,' she said. 'Let her go back to Crane Street.' "

"I can't believe it."

"Oh, you can believe it. Do you know something? I

160

wanted to knock her down. Never before have I felt that way toward a woman. . . . They're a strange lot back there, Amy, they're heartless, all of them. I'm glad I'm goin'. The only thing I'm sorry for is that I don't know what's to happen to her, for what in the name of God will she do?"

"Manuel."

"Yes, Amy?"

"Take her with you."

Such was the effect of her suggestion that his body made a movement as if he were going to spring from the ground. He did step back, with his trunk and head pushing away from her, and his eyes narrowed as if to get her into focus in the fading light. "You mad, Amy?" he muttered.

"No, Manuel, I'm not mad, an' it isn't today or yesterday I've thought about it. I say again, take her with you; they don't want her, nobody apparently wants her. I'm a stranger to her compared with you. You've known her since she was a child. Take her along."

His mouth open, his head shaking wildly on his shoulders, he was about to exclaim, "In the name of God! what would I do with her on the road?" when a movement in the shadow of the doorway turned them both sharply about, and there she stood, her face like a ghost's, the eyes lost in their sockets. She walked over the threshold and onto the terrace until, standing before Manuel, she stared up into his face, and whispered, "Please, Manuel, please do as Amy says and take me with you."

He couldn't speak. He could only work his tongue in his mouth to bring the saliva running again; his throat was dry, his mind in a whirl. Part of him wanted to laugh. He was going on the road; he would be sleeping wherever a shelter afforded, a barn, a hayrick, under a bridge in a town. He had done it all before, and even he himself wasn't looking forward to doing it again after years of having a roof over him and a good bed. And here was she, the daughter of the house, asking to come along with him. It was insanity of the first order, and he said so.

"No, Miss Annabella." He moved his head slowly and emphatically with the words. "This is one thing I cannot do for you. You don't know what you're askin'. You stay here along with Amy and something will turn up. Write to one of your friends. The world isn't filled with people like them back there." He jerked his head again.

"Manuel." She now actually caught hold of his hands with her thin fingers. "You know I have no friends who would

161

take me. I can't go back there, you've just said so yourself. I heard what you said, every word; they don't want me, and —and I don't want them any longer. Also, there are reasons why I can't go to—" Her chin made a downward movement before she added, "Durham. I have no one to turn to."

He was gripping her hands now close to his breast but almost unaware of what he was doing, for his head was swinging in a wide half circle, his eyes were closed and his mouth was open to say emphatically, "It's impossible, impossible," when a sound brought his eyes springing open and his head jerking round toward the end of the terrace.

They were all looking toward the end of the terrace half expecting to see an animal, for the sound of the low growl was that of an animal, but out of the dusk walked Lagrange. His body was arched, his left arm held out at an angle as if to balance himself, while his right fist, gripping his riding crop, was moving slowly back and forward along his thigh. His lips were parted, his eyes wide and staring, and his whole face looked in the evening light as if it were running in blood, so red was it.

"You! You little bastard." His mad gaze was fixed on Annabella. He took two steps forward, then stopped again, and, his neck now craned outwards, he spluttered a mouthful of profanities all punctuated with "You! You! You!" Then his left hand thumped his breast and he cried loudly, "Searching the docks, the whorehouses, night after night, and all the time you nesting within a stone's throw. You, you bloody little—"

"Be quiet!"

Manuel was still holding one of Annabella's hands, and now he thrust her behind him as he said, "It can be explained."

Lagrange gaped at Manuel, his mouth and eyes even wider, as if he were reading another explanation written on the air between them, for, his voice rising in a spiral from deep within him and finishing almost in a scream, he yelled, "You dirty whoremaster you! You've been laughing up your sleeve, haven't you? All these weeks playing the meek one, you bloody, foreign-looking pimp! I'll finish you for this. I've always intended to finish you, do you hear?" His last words seemed to lift him from the ground and the next minute he was flaying Manuel with his crop.

Manuel, putting up one forearm to shield his head and face, tried to get a grip on the infuriated man's shoulder with his other hand, but Lagrange was a man possessed, and he flayed the crop backwards and forwards over Manuel's head, until, becoming incensed by the rage of his assailant, Manuel shot out a fist and caught Lagrange on the side of the jaw, and the blow sent a shudder through his own body. Gasping, he saw Lagrange stagger back for some steps, then stand perfectly still for a moment before falling heavily to the ground.

Amy, who had been holding Annabella, released her now and came and stood by Manuel's side as she whispered hoarsely, "Are you hurt, lad?"

Yes, he was hurt. You couldn't have a flaying like that and not be hurt. His head was throbbing as if it had been hit by a hammer; the side of his throat was burning where the whip had licked round it more than once.

Annabella moved from the wall, then slid along by the seat until she was close to Manuel's side again, and the three of them standing in a row looked down at the twisted figure lying on the stones. There was no movement from him and Amy whispered, "You've knocked him cold. You'd better get going before he comes round."

Slowly Manuel walked forward now and stood by the head of Lagrange; then, dropping to his hunkers, he stared into the still face and there came over him a feeling as if death itself had touched him, and he cried loudly within his head, "No, no! Oh, God, no!" Slowly now he put his hand inside the waistcoat. The silk of the shirt caught at his rough fingers as he pressed them over Lagrange's heart. Then with a quick movement his head was on Lagrange's breast, his ears to his ribs, and like that he turned and peered up at Annabella; and then slowly he rose to his feet.

Annabella looked down at the still face of the man she had always called "Papa," of the man she had loved for years; even when she knew he was a bad man she had still loved him because he had loved her. Up till that morning in the drawing room when he had doled out to her the same treatment that he had doled out to his wife for years, he had loved her; but not from then, because she had dared to cross him; and now he was— Oh, no! No! Because if he were, if he were dead, it would mean that Manuel— She looked at Manuel. Even in this dim light his dark skin looked pale. She looked from him to Amy. Amy was kneeling by the figure now, lifting its eyelids. When she got to her feet she stood with her head bowed and her body visibly trembling.

Annabella felt a faintness sweeping over her but she closed her eyes tight and shook her head against it. The prerogative of ladies was no longer her due; her papa—she'd always think of him as her papa—was dead. Manuel had killed him; with one blow Manuel had killed him. What would they do to him?

Manuel was thinking the same thing. What would they do to him? He knew what they'd do to him; he knew the penalty for a man killing another, and when you were a servant, the verdict was a foregone conclusion. They still talked in these parts of the gibbeting of William Joblin, a miner, who together with his friend had done just what he had done, hit a man, and the man had fallen to the ground and died. They had hanged him one August day and the rope had slipped and his death had been long and horrible. Then they had covered his body with pitch and gibbeted it on a post in Jarrow Slakes, and the body, on its way to the gibbet, had had to be surrounded by a big force of the military. At times, at the long table in the kitchen, they had spoken of this, for some of them, both men and women, had been present at the hanging. The awful thing, they said, was that the man had not been guilty; it was his companion who had struck the blow.

In his own case there was only himself to take the consequences of his action. He felt his stomach heave. He closed his lips tightly to stop himself from retching; then, moving two steps back, he leaned against the wall and Margee's voice come to him from the past, "Good things will happen to you, an' terrible things." She had been right, all along she had been right. He should have followed the instinct that had told him to get away from here months ago, for then it had been strong. Now it was too late.

"Manuel! Manuel!" Amy was shaking his arm. "Listen to me."

He looked down at her but didn't speak, as she said, "His horse must be around here somewhere. Now look, do you hear what I'm sayin'? Come to, man, and heed me, or else you'll be in dire trouble."

"I've killed him, Amy."

"It was either you or him. He meant to do for you; it was in his eyes."

"But why? Why?" His voice was slow, the words deeply questioning. "You know I didn't really dislike him; there were things about him—"

"Be quiet and stop your babblin'. I don't want two of you on me hands with light heads. She's standing there as if she's been knocked into a stupor, so you come out of it and

164

listen. Go round about and see if you can find his horse—
go on, now." She pushed him along the stones. Then, coming
back to Annabella, she grabbed her arm and drew her into
the house, saying, "Get into your cloak and bundle up the
skirt you were sewing. You can finish it on the way. And
look. Take these boots." She darted to the corner of the
room and picked up a pair of rough boots. "They'll be a bit
big, but you're going to need them, for those light things
you've got on your feet will be through afore you go a mile
or two. Make a carrier out of this piece of burlap here."

"But he won't—"

"Yes, he will. You be ready when this is over and he will,
he's got to."

"Amy."

"Yes, what is it?"

"I—I feel slightly ill. I fear I'm going to be sick."

"Well, that's not surprisin'. Get your head over the bowl
there." She pointed to the side of the kitchen. "I'll be back
in a minute."

She ran out of the door and along to the end of the terrace, and there was Manuel coming over the rough grass
leading the horse. "Where was he?"

"Tethered just off the road." He spoke as if out of a dream.

"Well now"—she wagged her hand in his face—"the
ground's as hard as flint here—he'll leave no tracks—but
down near the marsh where the flax is, he'll show imprints.
Now, look." She flung her arm back toward the figure on
the stones. "Lift him, and hoist him over the saddle."

"Amy. . . ."

"Never mind Amy, do as I bid you. Give me the horse
here an' you go and get him."

Manuel stood over the figure of the man whom he had
deprived of life and he, too, wanted desperately to be sick.
As his hands went under the armpits and the head lolled
back, his stomach reared as if it were going to erupt through
his throat.

When he reached the horse and laid the body over the
saddle, the animal bucked, and he had to go quickly to its
head and calm it. The beast knew there was death on him;
it was a thing with animals, they could always smell death.

Amy said, "Lead him down the drive toward the river,
that way." He obeyed her, keeping his eyes ahead not only
to peer through the deepening gloom but so as not to turn
round and see the dangling legs of the rider.

Once they had reached the patch of marsh, Amy ordered

165

him to stop. Groping her way forward knowledgeably, she fingered some flat stones, then whispered to Manuel, "Bring him here."

When Manuel laid Lagrange beside her, she turned the dead man's face to the side, and, peering at his chin, she said, "There's hardly a mark. Help turn him over and rest his face on this stone."

When this was done she asked softly, "What will that beast do if he's turned loose?"

"There's no knowin' with him; he might go straight back to the stable, or he might start cropping or wandering round—oh, Christ alive!"

"Never mind Christ alive. It's you who's got to keep alive, so look, tie him up there, just for the time being. I'll set him free in a while after I've walked him round to cover up our footprints. But come on an' don't stand there lookin'. I tell you, that won't help. And keep it in your head—it was either you or him, an' by all accounts he's best gone and won't be missed."

He didn't speak until they had almost reached the grass drive again and then he said softly, as if to himself, "He was always wantin' me to use me fists. At times he was tempted to strike me because I wouldn't use me fists. He wanted to bet on me, but I wouldn't have it. I've always been in fear of using me fists, and God, I had right to be."

"Forget it, forget it. Just remember that you left his service an hour ago and you know nothin' more of him. By the way, you did tell them you were goin', didn't you? I mean the ones that are left back there?"

"Yes, I said good-bye to Harris and Mrs. Page."

"Well, that's all right, then. Now, it's like this. If the horse goes straight back and they start searchin', there's only the two of them, as you tell me, and they're not going to get very far in the dark, and if they haven't found him when daylight is well up, I'll be takin' a stroll and I'll find the body."

When they reached the terrace, a dark figure emerged from the doorway, and Manuel didn't take in immediately that Annabella was dressed for the road. He didn't take it in until Amy said, "There now, get yourselves away and God speed you."

And then, his voice more natural than it had been since he had argued against the same thing a short while ago, he said, "Amy, no! I tell you no. Begod no!"

"She's got to go"—Amy's voice was insistent—"whether she goes with you or by herself, because if they come round

166

here lookin', somebody's bound to spot her. And you know something? I'll get into trouble. Have you thought of that? I'll get into trouble for harborin' her when I knew the whole countryside was looking for her. They'll want to know why, and it won't be much use me protesting that she wouldn't let me tell them, me with a pair of legs on me and a voice."

Annabella came close to him now and like a child she said, "I'll be no trouble, Manuel, I promise. I'll—I'll do everything you say, and I'll learn to look after myself."

"In the name of God!" He turned to the wall and, leaning his forearm on it, dropped his head against his wrist, but Amy, pulling at his shoulder, said, "Look there's no time for that; the greater distance you put between yourself and this place tonight, the better it'll be for you. Here, let me help you up with this." When she bent down to lift the heavy pack, he came from the wall and slowly hoisted the skin bag onto his shoulders; then he and Amy stood looking at each other and simultaneously their arms came out and they held tightly together for a moment. Then she pushed him away with one hand and Annabella with the other, and she kept her hands on each until they reached the end of the grass drive, and here, turning to Annabella, she took hold of her face and kissed her on the cheek, saying, "God speed you, lass, and don't worry. Everything will turn out all right, you'll see."

"Thank—thank you, Amy. Oh, thank you. Some day I may—"

"Never mind about that now. Go on. Go on." And with a final push at each of them, she sent them into the night and into another life.

Book Four

THE HIRINGS

1

It was forty-eight hours later, but to Annabella it was like forty-eight years. She felt she was in another nightmare, very like the one that had taken her into Shields, only this one was bringing her physical pain. She ached in every limb and for the first time in her life she was experiencing blistered heels.

Determined not to be a drag on Manuel, she had kept up with him without murmur or complaint during the six-mile walk to Newcastle. They had skirted the town and reached Denton Burn about two o'clock in the morning; the moon was high and the night as yet was warm, too warm, for she was perspiring freely.

At the stream Manuel had stopped and, kneeling on the bank, had sucked up the water, then splashed his face and neck, and turning to her he spoke for the first time since they had left Amy. His voice rough-sounding to her, he said, "You'd better cool yourself." And she knelt down and awkwardly scooped some water into her hands and drank it; then she, too, cooled her face by dabbing her wet handkerchief around it, while at the same time longing to put her burning feet into the water.

After a while he walked away from her and she rose hastily from her knees to follow him, but he, stopping in his walk, his back to her, his head turned to the side, said, "Stay where you are a minute."

When he disappeared into the bushes a few yards ahead, she turned quickly and looked down into the stream. Her head was bowed in confusion, yet at the same time she was telling herself that she, too, should make a journey into the bushes. But she couldn't. How could she, in the open, even if it was night? Then a voice that seemed a mixture of the woman's from Crane Street, Amy's, and those of all the servants she had known, said, "Don't be stupid; you've chosen your road and you've got to learn how to walk it."

A few minutes later, when she came from behind some high undergrowth, she saw Manuel lifting the pack onto his shoulders. He did not look at her nor she at him; and then they started to walk again.

The dawn was well up when they reached a place called Walbottle. Here they skirted a big house and came to farmland. In one of the fields some distance from the farm was a broken hayrick, and having climbed over the low stone wall, Manuel said, "Sit on the top and swing your legs over." This was only the second time he had spoken to her.

Swing her legs over when she was scarcely able to lift one foot above the other!

She almost rolled over the top of the wall on her side; then, stumbling to the hay, she dropped onto it and lay back staring upwards, hoping that she might die, because if this was to be her life, then she couldn't live it. She had made a mistake. Manuel was right, she should never have come. She had a longing, greater than any desire in her life before, to be back in the House under any conditions. Her spirit, she felt, would be able to withstand humiliation as long as her body could experience a little comfort. The pains in both her heels were so excruciating that she wanted to turn on her face and cry, but this would have taken effort. The only thing that could be said for the agony she was enduring was that it had blotted out from her mind the dead face of Lagrange.

"Here, drink this." Manuel was bending over her with a little china mug in his hand.

She lifted her eyelids slowly, then raised herself to her elbow and gulped at Amy's ginger beer, and it tasted like wine to her.

He was now handing her a thick slice of bread and a piece of cheese and she shook her head, saying, "Thank you, but I'm not hungry."

"You'd better eat, you'll need it." His voice was still harsh, his face stiff, and he bore no resemblance to the Manuel she knew.

He was sitting within a yard of her, munching slowly and staring ahead, when he said, "We've got to get our relationship right; we'd better talk it out."

Her tired eyes widened slightly and she stared at him. Then he looked at her and added, "If we're travelin' together, they'll want to know who we are."

She drew in a deep breath, then said, "Yes. Oh, yes." And with an air that was natural to her and suggested, in spite of the circumstances and her utter weariness, that she was bestowing an honor on him, she said, "You could say I'm your sister."

"Huh!" His head went back, but he wasn't laughing, and he looked at her again as he said, "Talkin' and actin' like you do, and me being meself, it would be evident to the dumbest that we didn't spring from the same branch."

"Oh, Manuel." She bowed her head. "I'm sorry. I'll—I'll try to be different. I must."

"We can't change what we are." He jerked his chin upwards as he now said, "You could be me dead sister's child brought up in a convent, or some such place."

She bowed her head again and shook it from side to side, saying softly, "That's worse; I could never call you 'uncle,' could I?"

"Why not?" His voice was aggressive now, and she added quickly and soothingly, "Because—because you don't look old enough."

He got abruptly to his feet and stood staring over the land while he growled, "This idea's madness, Miss Annabella, and you know it. There's bound to be a house round about that would take you in."

Minutes ago she had longed to go back, longed for comfort no matter from where it came, but now she said dully, "I—I don't want to be taken in, Manuel, and the only way I'd get into a house in this district is through the servants' entrance; my background will be common knowledge from one end of the country to the other and beyond; I'd be an embarrassment to those I was in the habit of meeting. One thing I've learned during the past few weeks is that people can't stand disgrace. I've learned it from my own experience, for I couldn't bear the thought of facing anyone who knew me before." She paused. "Except you. It's strange, but I don't mind what you know about me, Manuel."

She had meant her words to soften him, to bring him back to the Manuel she was used to, but their effect was to cause him to mutter something under his breath before turning away and walking toward the stone wall. And when he disappeared from her view, she hung her head deep on her chest, then put her fingers tightly on her eyeballs to suppress the wave of tears she felt welling in her. She mustn't give way to tears, she must think and plan. She'd find work of some kind, even menial work that would give her the money to pay the coach fare to London. Once there, she would find employment. She was sure she would. In the meantime, she must try not to upset Manuel. If only she weren't so tired, if only her heels didn't hurt so. She now eased off one shoe after the other, and, looking up to see that Manuel wasn't in view, she quickly lifted her skirt and pulled down her garters, peeled off her stocking until it came to the heel, and then found that the blister had burst and the stocking was sticking to the raw flesh. When she went to ease it off, the pain was so great that she curled her body and turned on her side; and she lay like that for a few minutes before straightening up again to find Manuel looking down at her foot.

"I—I've got blisters on my heels."

He knelt down on the hay, and turning one foot over he gripped her ankle, saying, "Hold hard," at the same time pulling the stocking from the flesh.

"O-oh!" For a moment she thought she was going to faint.

"You have a petticoat on?"

"A—a petticoat? Yes, Manuel."

"Well, you'll have to tear a strip or two off it to bandage them up." He nodded toward her feet and she said, "Oh. Oh, yes."

He went to his pack, keeping his back to her while she tore the lace off the bottom of her top petticoat and then a three-inch strip of fine lawn, and when she said, "I've done it," he came to her and, cutting the strip in two, smeared a piece of Amy's dripping on one end, then wound the bandage round her foot as he would have done around a horse's fetlock.

When he had finished the second one, he said, "Put on the boots. You'll never get the shoes over that lot."

A few minutes later she stood up and looked at her feet encased in Amy's boots. They looked big and ungainly, and when she attempted to walk, it was as if she had iron weights attached to her feet.

"You'll get used to them."

She doubted it, but she said, "Yes, yes, Manuel; and thank you, they feel so much better."

They were sitting on the hay again when he said, "We'll have to rest; then we'll make our way to Corbridge, then to Hexham. There's orchards round there—there should be work." And on this he lay down and turned onto his side.

After a time she, too, lay down; but now she was feeling extremely embarrassed, too embarrassed to sleep. She couldn't sleep by Manuel's side.

She woke with the sun directly overhead, and when she tried to move and found it impossible, she thought she was pinned in some way to the ground. She turned her eyes about until they focused on Manuel. He was sitting paring his fingernails with a penknife. He looked as if he were waiting patiently. But he didn't look the same Manuel that she knew; he looked years older and his face had lost the glowing tan color and now appeared mottled, except where the red weals stood out around his chin and neck.

With an effort she pulled herself upwards, saying, "You should have woken me; I've slept a long time."

"The day's young." He glanced at her and said curtly, "You feel better?"

"I'm—I'm very stiff."

"That'll wear off." He rose to his feet. "We'd better find a village where we can buy some food and stock up a bit. But it'll be difficult, it being Sunday." He now lifted his pack onto his shoulders, and adding, "Ready?" he moved off.

She wasn't ready; she was still half asleep and her body felt as if it had been stretched on a rack. Again she had the desperate longing to be back in the comfort of the House. It was twelve o'clock in the day, the time when in the summer they had cool drinks and in the winter hot chocolate. Dragging herself to her feet, she picked up the bundle and staggered after him.

She wasn't alone in wishing she were back in the House. What, in the name of God, Manuel was asking himself, was he going to do with her? What? She'd never be able to stand this life, and at this moment he had enough on his mind without the responsibility of her. All night he had walked beside a dead man. Wherever he had looked the moonlight had shown him Lagrange's face, suddenly white after being red, still after being agitated with fury; and it was his hand that had killed him. He had always been afraid of the strength of his hands. Margee used to say, "You will be a horse breaker because you've got wrists like steel." And there were times when she would hold his hands and look into the palms and say, "They're fine hands. You could be anything with those hands, Manuel, anything. They're not made for labor, Manuel, not ordinary labor." Aw, Margee. Margee and her trashy talk. Yet she had foretold what had happened, and she had warned him never to use his hands against any man; that was after he had thrashed Peter for belting into her. Peter was three times his age and twice his bulk, but he had knocked him cold and he was only fifteen at the time. And

175

just before she died, she had said to him, "You'll come to wealth, lad. You'll come to wealth." Wealth? Huh! He didn't want wealth, he only wanted work and a shelter for the winter; and then he'd be off to find the sun in that far country that had always beckoned him. But now wherever he went, and however long he lived, he'd remember he had killed a man.

They had gone almost a mile before he spoke, and then he said abruptly, "You'll pass without comment except when you speak. Do you think you can say 'Ta,' instead of 'Thank you'?"

" 'Ta'?" She turned her head to one side and looked up at him.

"Yes, 'Ta.' The less you talk like yourself, the less comment will be made."

"Oh, yes, I see. I'll try to remember, Manuel."

"And try sayin' 'Aye,' instead of 'Yes.' "

"Very well."

Another mile; and then another, and another and in silence. The country they were walking through was beautiful. They passed little hamlets with stone cottages, whitewashed and shining in the sun. They passed medium-sized houses standing in precisionally neat gardens. People here and there looked at them but made no comment. Men sitting outside their doors, some in Sunday gray, some still in working smocks, gave them a salute, for they were just a couple on the road looking for work; and there were many such these days. Two years ago the sight would have been rare except for tinkers, or traveling gypsies, or an odd beggar or two, but now, since the big houses were turning out their staffs, it was no uncommon sight to see couples walking the roads.

By four o'clock in the afternoon they had only got as far as Ovingham because by now Annabella was limping badly. Manuel had kept the banks of the river Tyne in sight, and when he saw that it would be impossible for her to go any farther that day, he scouted around until he found a low bank where she could sit and dangle her feet in the water near an outcrop of rock, with one section overhanging which would afford them some shelter in the night, for, wet or fine, they would have to stay where they were.

After taking off his coat and neckerchief, he lay flat on the bank and ducked his head two or three times under the water, for the weals on his neck now felt like red-hot laces attached to the skin. After he had dried his face and hair on a rough piece of sacking, he put his things on again. Then,

176

taking a can from his pack, he said, "I'll have to go lookin' for a shop of sorts."

She looked up at him with eyes like those of a frightened doe, and, his manner less brusque, he added, "I won't be long; you'll be all right here. You're well away from the road, and should anyone happen along, say I'm just over there." He thumbed over his shoulder in the direction of a copse.

She didn't speak and he turned from her and walked along the bank, his step steady and even, as if he had just started walking.

He had to walk more than two miles before he came to a hamlet with a shop open, and in the shop he learned how fast money can fly when you had to buy food. "How much is an ounce of tea?" he asked the old woman behind the counter, and when she surveyed him for a moment before saying, "It's Sunday an' sevenpence," he knew she was sticking on a copper or two because of the day, but he didn't argue. "And a pound of sugar?" he asked.

"Ninepence."

"Give me half," he told her.

"And what's your cheese?" He pointed to a lump of Cheddar reposing within a finger's breadth of a bundle of tallow candles.

"That one's tenpence a pound."

He stared at her before he spoke again. "I'll have three-penn'orth," he said.

"You want bread?" she now asked him, and when he nodded she said, "It's ninepence quarter stone."

"I'll take that," he answered. "And that bacon." He pointed toward the knuckle end of a ham.

"Oh, that's the best, it's tenpence." She stared at him.

"I'll have half." Now pointing to a sack that stood to his side filled with oatmeal, he added, "And two penn'orth of that."

"Do you want milk?" She looked at his can. "I can fill it for a penny."

"Is it fresh?"

"As fresh as the cow could give at eleven."

He stared down at the rim of the pail with the hooked can dangling from it, both covered with flies.

When she had filled the can, he said, "I paid five pence ha'penny for an ounce and a half packet of 'baccy in the town. What you chargin'?"

"Oh." She grinned. "I'm cheaper than them. Five pence farthin'."

177

"And a clay pipe?"

"That'll be another ha'penny." She added up the things now and said, "That'll be three and a penny farthin'."

As he left the shop he thought in future he'd have to buy at a different rate from this or there would soon be a hole in his hoard. He had sixteen sovereigns and five half sovereigns in his belt. He had saved this amount during the years he had been at the Hall, and this in spite of his indulgence during his accumulated holidays.

Even without working, he had enough to keep himself for a year, but not two of them, and not if he had to afford her shelter in an inn, for she would never be able to tolerate his kind of lodgings; and she couldn't keep sleeping out in the open. . . . But what the hell! He'd sort that out when he knew where he stood. She might yet have to see to herself. If Amy's plan went wrong, anything could happen. He must get to Hexham and get hold of a newssheet. She'd be able to read it. He could think of nothing clearly until he knew where he stood, and it might be under a gallows tree. Dear God! Why had it come about like this? He wished to hurt no man, but he had to go and kill one, and that one a gentleman, and a man, be what he may, who had, in the first place, taken him on trust and given him a job.

She was sitting under the shelter of the rock out of the sun when he reached her.

"I haven't been so long, have I?"

She shook her head. He had been gone hours, days, years. It had come to her as she sat here alone that she had never lived one hour of her life up till the day she went to Crane Street without people near her, in the house, in the garden, out driving, always someone had been near her. For the past hour she had sat gazing across the river, across the open fields rising to the sun-drenched hills, and the loneliness had terrified her. She felt as if she had been dropped onto another planet. At one point she had found herself crying in her mind with longing, "Oh, Mama! Oh, Papa!" and she had chastised herself, she must stop calling them that; but as yet she couldn't stop thinking about them and she couldn't stop mourning because he was dead. She couldn't quite believe he was dead because he had died so quickly: one blow from Manuel's fist and he breathed no more. She still couldn't believe that Manuel had killed him. She looked at Manuel now. He was making a fire. He looked grim and troubled, and he had a right to be. What if they should discover the truth and take him away? Oh, no! No! That would be unthinkable.

178

She watched him putting bacon into a round black iron pan, and when it started to sizzle the aroma pricked her nostrils, and a few minutes later, when he handed her the tin plate with the hot bacon and a thick slice of bread on it, she was surprised when she found herself eating the rough food and almost enjoying it. But the tea he brewed had a bitter tang to it. Nevertheless, she managed to drink a mugful.

The meal over, Manuel took the clay pipe and, having filled it with tobacco, lit it with a spill from the fire, then sat with his back against the rock and drew deeply at the stem.

Annabella had never seen him smoke before, and somehow the clay pipe offended her. It was the utensil used by the farmhands and the lower servants. But she was always forgetting Manuel was a servant. The clay pipe brought home to her the fact that her thinking, too, would have to change. She must not only forget to say "Yes" and "Thank you," but she must remember that she herself was, as it were, now below stairs. The thought rushed on her that she would never come to think this way, for the conditions necessary to bring about such a change would surely drive her insane. She could never become a menial; all her instincts were against it.

After a while Manuel rose to his feet, and taking up the piece of coarse sacking that had been drying on the grass, he walked away without a word and went along the riverbank and round the bend and out of her sight.

She sat and watched the shadows lengthening and guessed that it must be about seven o'clock. Manuel had been gone half an hour or more now, and once again she began to feel uneasy. Gently, she eased her boots on and walked slowly and painfully along by the river. If he was sitting around the bend, she told herself, she wouldn't disturb him, yet she hoped that she wouldn't see him sitting by himself, for it would mean that he couldn't bear her company.

As she rounded the bend, the sun was full in her eyes. The river stretched straight for a long distance from this point, its bed broken here and there by boulders over which the water frothed and gurgled. She brought her eyes from the far distance to some flat shelves of rock not more than a hundred feet from her, and there, lying submerged in the lee of the current, she saw him. He was lying as if in a bath, the water flowing over him. Her hand came up and across her mouth, and, flinging herself around, she hobbled as quickly as her painful heels would allow back the way she had come.

When she reached the outcrop of rock and sat down, her

179

back was straight and stiff. She could have been Rosina, so deep was her indignation. Bathing in the river like that! He should have warned her. Had he seen her? Oh, no! She cupped one cheek with her hand and the heat of her skin told her that her face must be flushed.

If only she could go back home. If only she hadn't heard Manuel repeating what her grandmother—no, what Mrs Conway-Redford—had said, she knew now she would subsequently have returned.

Another half hour elapsed before Manuel appeared. He looked cool and fresh and his black hair was lying flat on his head. He looked at her in surprise, saying, "You haven't been down to the river?"

"No." The monosyllable was stiff.

He continued to stare at her for a moment, then gave a slight shrug with one shoulder—before he asked, "Would you like the remainder of the milk? It will be sour by mornin'."

"No, thank you."

He stared at her again. Her tone was like the mistress's when she was giving an order or dismissing a servant. He now pulled his pack well under the shelter of the rock; then, taking the blanket out of it, he handed it to her, saying, "I would cover up. There'll likely be a lot of dew in the night. An' I'd get what sleep you can now because we'll be on the road early. I want to make Hexham tomorrow."

When she didn't answer, he scrutinized her through narrowed lids. He knew her well enough to detect that she was on her high horse about something, but what? Well, anyway, if she felt like that, it might augur for good; she would go back and leave him to his own road.

He lay down, conscious that she was still sitting up, her back as straight as a ramrod. What had got into her? What had upset her? He hadn't done anything. He had hardly opened his mouth except when it was necessary. Something had happened since he had gone into the river—He brought his lips into a silent whistle. Ah, that must be it. She had seen him bare in the river. God sakes! that must be it, her dignity was offended. Even after all she had gone through, her mind could still give her time to be offended at his nakedness. Well, all he could say was that if that could straighten her back she was going to see things in the future, if she stayed with him, that would bend it over double.

He put his hands behind his head and stared up into the clear blue sky, and a mischievous thought, edging its way into the deeply troubled morass of his mind, said, If the boot had been on the other foot, it wouldn't have put him on his high horse, rather got him out of the saddle as if he'd been tossed. Then, turning quickly on his side and facing the rock wall, he chided himself for his levity. She was still Miss Annabella and he'd better not forget it, and he wouldn't so long as he remained solid and sober.

It was three o'clock in the afternoon when, after traveling miles through dripping-wet orchards, they entered the town of Hexham.

Manuel had been here a number of times over the years and he led her straight to the Market Square and to a low, deep arch under a high building that looked like a peel tower, and from there he pointed across the square, saying, "That sweetie shop over there, it deals in newssheets. Would you go and get the latest one?"

She wiped the rain from around her face with her fingertips, then nodded and took from his hand a sixpence.

Within a few minutes she was back with the *Hexham Courant* and not until she went to hand it to him and he didn't take it from her did she remember that he could neither read nor write.

"Will you look and see if it says anything?" His voice was rough, and she opened the paper and scanned the small printed headlines. He watched her eyes going up and down the columns. Then she turned a page, and after a moment her gaze became still and he saw her lips tremble slightly, and he knew that she had found it. He bent close to her, asking under his breath, "What does it say?"

She moved her head slightly twice but didn't answer him. She was reading to the end of the report, and he was biting tightly on his lower lip when finally she looked up at him and said in stiff, stilted tones, "The horse arrived home riderless and Amy—Mrs. Stretford, a cottager, found the body and reported it to the House. Death, they say, must have been instantaneous. Mrs.—Mrs. Lagrange is prostrate—the funeral is to be on Thursday."

The wave of relief that swept over him brought the sweat running out of the pores of his head and it mingled with the rain and ran off the end of his chin. The noose had dropped from around his neck, and so heady was the reprieve that he didn't consider what effect the report might be having on her, but said now brightly, "We'll go and have something to eat; there's a place in Fore Street, she serves up a good dinner. Come on." He walked away through the arch and she followed him, her eyes unblinking, her thoughts like an anchor dragging her back to the House where the body of her papa lay.

When they entered Mrs. Paterson's establishment, the serving maid looked them up and down and said, "You can't take that kit in there, leave it over yonder." And when he hesitated, she said roughly, "Go on, there's nobody gona pinch that."

The dinner was good, and for one and six they ate their fill, but all the while Annabella chided herself for eating at all. She didn't know how she could. In some way it seemed, if not actually improper, then callous. Also, she reminded herself she was eating at Manuel's expense. But in spite of all her worthy feelings, she ate.

Out in the street again, Manuel said, "We'll have to have a place for the night," and then he stood pondering as to where he would find a place that would be suitable for her. As for himself, if he had been on his own, he would have gone round to the Battle Hill district. He had slept in that quarter before, but it was no place for her. He remembered seeing a small inn up one of the side streets off the Market Place and he now led the way to it. There was a courtyard fronting it open to the road, and a coach and pair and three horses were tethered to the stand posts.

As they went to enter, she touched his arm and brought him to a stop and said under her breath, "I'm—I'm in a very muddy state." She looked down at her boots and the bottom of her dress then added, "They mightn't—"

He didn't let her get any further. With a twisted smile he said, "They'll not refuse money—mud, packs, and bundles, they'll not refuse money."

But there he was mistaken. As they entered the main door of the inn, a man in a black waistcoat hurried across the room and, taking them in at one glance, said, "Round the back with you."

Manuel remained standing perfectly still. "We would like a room for the night." He did not say "rooms" and the man, again looking them up and down, said, "I'm sorry, we're full up. If you want a drink, you can get it in the bar round the corner." He thumbed to the side of him. Then turning quickly to a patron leaving the room, he bowed and said, "Good-day, sir. Good-day."

"I have money and I would like a room for this lady."

The man stared at Annabella. Anyone looking less like a lady would be hard for him to imagine and his eyes said this,

182

and his insolent look gave Annabella the courage to speak. Holding herself as she would have done if she had just stepped out of the carriage, she said, in a manner of which Rosina would have approved, "It's perfectly all right; we'll find accommodation elsewhere. Thank you." She inclined her head toward the man, whose eyes and mouth had simultaneously stretched to the utmost. Then adding, "Would you kindly open the door," she waited until the astonished porter had done her bidding, and she sailed out, Manuel following her, and they went the full length of the street before they stopped.

It was his jerky, strangled laugh that stopped them. He leaned his pack against the wall, and, his head falling back onto it, he let the fear and the worry flow from him in deep, spasmodic, tension-releasing laughter which brought passers-by to a standstill to stare at him, a foreigner who was evidently amused at something. Then they went on their way smiling.

Yet his laughter didn't cause Annabella to smile, because for a moment she was back in her class and feeling its power, the power it held through the speaking voice and the subservience in others that good diction could evoke.

As they walked on again, he said, "There are other inns and they'd better mind their p's and q's, hadn't they?" He cast a slanting glance down at her, but she was looking straight ahead and she kept her gaze steadily forward as she said. "We must choose some place——" She paused. She didn't want to say "common" or "cheap," for he might imagine that she was putting a stamp on him, but he said it for her, "Well, I know a place. I've slept there meself, but it's not for you. The beds are clean but that's all that can be said for them."

"I don't mind as long as we have shelter." She was looking at him now, and he returned her gaze, then jerked his chin upwards, saying, "Well, all right, we'll try it."

They had to stand aside at this point to allow a great herd of cattle to pass down the street, and the sight of them caused him to say, "It's market day tomorrow, Tuesday; I think we'd better get round there and claim a bed or else we'll be unlucky this time an' all."

They went through the Battle Hill district until they came to a quarter that could have been a miniature Temple Town, except there was no river. The houses were higgledy-piggledy, the streets narrow, little more than alleyways, and up one she followed Manuel, then through a door of a tall, three-storied building, and into a dark passageway.

"Wait here a minute." He put his hand back and stayed her before going forward down the passage to a door at the end. Knocking, he called, "Anybody there?"

Annabella saw a small man emerging wearing a leather apron, and he peered up at Manuel in the dim light, then exclaimed, "Aw, it's you. Hello there. Never seen you for a time."

"Hello, Reuben," said Manuel. "Have you got a couple of beds going?"

"Beds? A couple? No, lad." The man cast his eye down the passage toward Annabella, then said, "A couple did you say?"

"Aye, I said a couple."

"Well, I'm sorry, but you're unlucky this time; it's market day the morrow, you know, and the drovers are in; there's only one bed left and it's in the main room."

Manuel's head drooped forward, and the man said, "I would send you along to Taggart but he's full an' all. He sent me some of his'un earlier on, but there's that one left."

Manuel looked up and stated, "But it's in the main room?"

"Aye, but it's different. I've had partitions put up; it's quite private like. Might get a bit noisy later on, but if you're in your own place, you'll take no notice of that."

"Just a minute." Manuel went down the passage and looked at Annabella for a few seconds before he said, "Well, you heard him, didn't you?"

She stared back at him, her eyes unblinking.

"It's either that or under a hedge."

Slowly her eyes lowered, and when she didn't speak, he said under his breath, "You've had enough warnin'. I told you; look, there's still time, you could take the train back." He shook his head vigorously. "Don't worry about the money, I can see to that; or, if you'd rather, the coach."

When she made no movement, he said grimly, "If you're worryin' about anything else, you needn't. You'll be safe enough. I'm used to sleeping on the floor."

He thought he heard her murmur, "Oh, Manuel," as her head drooped onto her chest; then he turned from her and went toward the man again, saying, "Well, let's have a look at it, Reuben. . . . Can I dump this till later?" He motioned to the pack lying against the wall of the corridor, and the man said, "Aye, if you're stayin' you can leave it in me room until the mornin'."

Annabella followed them up two flights of stairs and at each step the smell which she was beginning to associate with humanity stung her nostrils. Then they entered a room on the second floor and she stood looking aghast at the four mattresses that took up most of the floor space, divided from each other by small wooden partitions and leaving no space on either side.

"There, you see, it's more private like. Good as a single room and not half the price. Shilling a bed and the blankets clean. It's the same price for one, two or three. It's a sort of family room."

"I'm—I'm afraid it's a bit too cramped, Reuben."

"Well!" Reuben's tone implied total indifference. "It's up to you. I was only wantin' to oblige; it'll be gone within the next half hour if I know anythin', an' two dozen more if I had them."

"Thanks all—"

"We'll take it. Thank you."

The man stared at Annabella, his face showing as much surprise as had the porter's in the inn.

Annabella now turned and walked out of the room and down the stairs, the men not immediately following her, and she had reached the bottom step when she heard the man's low whisper, "Is she your woman? She's a bit different from your usual, isn't she?" She waited, her hand gripping the rail of the greasy banister, for Manuel's reply. And what he said was, "Aye, she's a bit different. Me taste's gettin' finicky as I get older."

The man's laugh now came to her and his whisper, "You always were an odd customer. You thinkin' of gettin' bottled the night?"

Manuel's tone was flat and slightly ironic now as he replied, "No, I don't think so, Reuben; I've got an idea she wouldn't like it."

Then the man's laugh again and him saying, "Well, that's somethin' to be thankful for, anyway; we won't have any hell raisin'."

Manuel and drink ... Manuel and women ... Manuel and —hell raising. She had never thought of him in these categories. Manuel had always appeared to her as a sober, reliable, highly respectable, even superior young man; and now here she had learned that he was known to this low lodging housekeeper in connection with both women and drink, and the outcome of the latter. She felt slightly sick and needed air.

She was standing outside the door when he joined her. He made no reference to her decision to sleep in the place,

185

but said, "The rain's stopped; we could have a walk round the town. Would you like that?"

Would she like walking round the town? She had walked for days, weeks, months; her feet felt like raw pulp. What she wanted to do was to lie flat on her back, on a soft bed between clean linen sheets, cool clean linen sheets; and, of course, she would have bathed first. "Walk?" he said. "And to see what?" She had seen all the places that had to be seen in Hexham. Only last year Miss Howard, and her mama, had taken a trip by train and visited the Abbey, and Miss Howard, partly for her instruction but more to show off her own knowledge to her employer, had drawn their attention to the remains of the Saxon Cathedral in the exterior of the west front of the building. She also pointed out the tombstone of the Roman standard bearer, and the fifteenth-century stalls. Her mama, she knew, had been very amused by Miss Howard because she herself could have taken the governess on a conducted tour.

The carriage had met them in the Market Place, for her mama had arranged to visit a Mr. and Mrs. Ferguson, who lived beyond Chesters and within a stone's throw of Hadrian's Wall. She remembered she had sat through a lengthy afternoon's tea listening to Mr. Ferguson and his plans for the benefit of Hexham. They were going to build a new town hall and corn exchange which would cost over six thousand three hundred pounds. She also learned that Mr. Ferguson was a member of the Haydon Bridge Cricket Club, a member of the Haydon Hunt Club; he also enjoyed rifle shooting. Mr. Ferguson did so many things outside his work of running a lead mine that she thought he was a little like her papa— he made time for all things but his business. Mrs. Ferguson seemed to have as many side pursuits as her husband, yet hers were of a less personal nature. She was very interested in the workhouse and seemed to take great pleasure in relating that it held a hundred and thirty inmates; she was working hard to start a soup kitchen for the poor; she talked a great deal about the public library, which held over three hundred books.

To anyone not acquainted with the time, labor and money entailed in these private and public charities, Mrs. Ferguson would have given the impression that she had accomplished them all singlehanded.

She hadn't liked either Mr. or Mrs. Ferguson and she couldn't understand what her mama had in common with them, but altogether she had remembered that it had been a pleasant day. Would she ever know a pleasant day again?

The sun was shining once more and the steam was rising from the cobbles, and when the street suddenly became flooded with people, she wondered for a moment if the sun had brought them out. At one point, when she was knocked into the gutter, Manuel's hand grabbed her arm, then trailing her behind him he went on, pushing his way through a crowd of laughing, jabbering women until, finding a deep doorway, they took cover.

"What is it?" she asked him, bewildered.

"It's the factories coming out."

Yes, of course, the factories. The glove factories, the hat factories, the tanneries. Hexham had them all.

One buxom young woman, pausing opposite the doorway and pulling her companion to a halt, laughed up at Manuel, saying, "What you hidin' for, frightened of gettin' dunched into?" Then, digging her companion in the ribs with her elbow, she added, "Isn't he pretty, now?"

Annabella looked from the girl to Manuel. His eyes were bright and there was a twisted smile on his face, and when he said, "Go on with you, unless you want your backside smacked," she knew that he was enjoying this little encounter. She was discovering things about Manuel that were distasteful and annoying.

"Like to try it on?"

"Shut up, Em!" Her companion was giggling loudly now. "Can't ya see; he's got his lass wi' him."

"Aw, so he has." The girl looked at Annabella as if she had just realized her presence; and Annabella stared back at her, the will strong in her to put her in her place. In case she should be tempted, she drooped her head, and Manuel said again, his voice changed now, "Go on, get on your way," and the girl, throwing her head back and crying, "Huh! Huh! he's feared he'll get it in the neck," went on her way.

Within a few minutes the street was back to normal. They went through Priestpopple and looked at the shops, some with antique furniture, grocers with delectable food on display in the windows, butchers, pastry cooks, milliners, haberdashery. At one point, a coach passing down the street went through a series of puddles and bespattered them both. A few yards ahead it drew to a halt and the coachman jumped down from his box and assisted a voluptuous-skirted lady onto the cobbles, and at the sight of her Annabella turned swiftly round and walked away from Manuel. She had been thinking of Mrs. Ferguson only a short while previous and now she had come almost face to face with her.

She was halfway down the street when Manuel caught up with her, and continuing to walk on he said, "You knew her?"

"Yes."

"Well, I doubt if she would have recognized you even if she had looked under your hood—your face is all mud."

She put her hand up to her cheek and rubbed it, and he said, "Your clothes. You look no different than the girls"—he jerked his head back—"the factory girls."

It was on the point of her tongue to say, "Thank you!" She said stiffly, "Can we leave the town—I mean for a little while, perhaps walk on the outskirts?"

"All right."

But his choice of a walk was unfortunate. Of all the places he could have chosen, he had to pick Skinner's Burn, and instead of the orchards that surrounded the town and the great stretches of gooseberry fields, here was the unpleasant sight of huge rubbish dumps lining the stream's banks, and the smell of sewage lost nothing in the warm evening air.

"Come on." He turned her about and they retraced their steps, crossed a stile and another stream and came to an open field, and there, pointing to a blasted tree, he said, "Come and sit down."

When they were seated, he was quiet for a moment because the position of the field and the fallen tree was almost an exact replica of the riding field back at the House, and he recalled the first morning he had taken her into the field and they had sat on such a log and he had talked to her.

He leaned forward and, dropping his elbows on his knees, said, "We can't go on like this; you can see the whole idea's impossible."

Yes, she knew that, none better; but what was before her? If she returned, it wouldn't be to the Hall; the only place from which she could claim any hospitality would be the house in Crane Street, and the very thought of the place and the people in it, her people, the people who had bred her, overran her body with nausea. Before she would even consider that, she would take to the river.

She said stiffly, "Where would I go except to the place in Crane Street? Would you like me to return there?"

His head drooped farther toward his knees, and when he remained silent, she said, "I'm a burden to you, but it

188

will only be for a short while. I'll—I'll find work of some kind. I'm educated—"

"Yes, that's the trouble." He had swung round and was facing her. "You're educated, an' what work is that going to provide you with, except as a governess, and you know what you said about that. The work that lies before you, if you stick with me, won't need any brains. What it'll need is brawn, endurance and humility. And how could you stick knuckling under, cleaning or waiting on people?"

Instead of his words sending her into the stiff, solemn silence that he expected, there came a lightness to her eyes and she exclaimed with something akin to excitement, "You've just said something, Manuel. That's what I could do, I could wait on people. I—I know all about the setting of tables and the serving of meals. Yes"—she nodded—"that's what I could do."

"A-aw!" The exclamation sounded like a groan, and he ran his fingers through his damp hair, forming it into ridges. Then getting abruptly to his feet, he said, "Let's get back. Better get settled in and snatch a few hours afore the others come in, because it might be impossible after." He walked a few steps from her, then stopped, and looking back to where she was rising from the log, he asked flatly, "Do you know what you've let yourself in for tonight, Miss Annabella?"

There was no deference in the title; she even sensed sarcasm, and it straightened her back and brought her chin tilting upwards as she replied, "No; but I shall know by morning, shan't I?"

They stood staring at each other, he looking into the mud-smeared beauty of her face, all the while telling himself that she was little more than a child, she into the deep brown eyes of the man to whom she had once offered her childish friendship, and of whom she was now becoming a little afraid.

The room was already occupied when they reached it. They heard one of the occupants long before they opened the door, and when they entered the room, the cough came at them hard and rattling. A woman was sitting propped up against a pack on the mattress to the left of the door, a man was holding a piece of rag to her mouth and he turned and looked at the newcomers, and his expression was apologetic. Having taken his attention away from the woman, the cloth slipped and showed the large red patch, which he now quickly doubled over, and, getting to his feet, he looked

189

first at Manuel and then at Annabella and said, "Hello there."
It was Manuel who answered, "Hello."

"It's the rain an' the cold; it brings it on." He glanced back
at the woman on the mattress, and Manuel said, "Ah yes, I
see." And he did see. The woman had the consumption and,
if he was any judge, she wasn't far from her end, poor soul.
He glanced at Annabella. She was standing at the foot of
their mattress. Her eyes, stretched wide, were fixed on the
woman, and there was fear in them.

He stood between her and the woman now, and looking
at her boots he said, "You'd better take them off afore you
get on the bed."

There was no space to walk up between the partitions at
either side of the mattress, so she sat down on it and took
off her boots and laid them at the foot, only to see Manuel
pick them up and toss them toward the head as he said under
his breath, "You don't want to go barefoot tomorrow, do
you?"

Hitching herself back over the prickly straw-filled tick, she
rested against the wall, her head touching the bottom of the
low windowsill, and, her eyes still stretched wide, she watched
Manuel take off his boots. Then he, too, was sitting with his
back against the wall and within inches of her.

"Don't worry." His voice was a low murmur. "You won't
catch anything. I'll push the window open to give you air."

She wished she could turn on him and say, "I'm not
afraid of catching anything," but she couldn't because she
was deadly afraid. She remembered her mama's warning her
never to go near people who "were in decline." She remembered two years ago one of the maids had started to cough
and she was sent from the house in a matter of days. "If
you are forced to be near anyone with a cough, suck a
lozenger," her mama had said, "and keep the greatest distance between you and them, and never, never on any account touch them, or anything belonging to them."

The man now came and stood at the foot of the bed. He
was a short man, wiry-looking. He said to Manuel, "Where you
makin' for?"

"Oh." Manuel hesitated. "Manchester, that way."

"Manchester. Got anybody there?"

"No."

"Oh by, then you're going to find it hard; they're pushing
out the rats, they say, to make room in the cellars. Plenty
of work, at least there was until last year, but no place
to bide. We were there two years ago and then the wife

got this." He thumbed his chest. "They said get her into the country, it was her only chance, so I did. Country? I'd say it was country, Plenmeller Common. God-forsaken place, if ever there was. Do you know it?"

"No," said Manuel; "I haven't been that far."

"There's a farm near there, Skillen's. They can't get nobody to stay. The summers are bad enough but the winters are hell, at least that's what I'm told. We didn't stay long enough—he wouldn't let us. He got scared about my missus." He jerked his head back. "There's a kid there. I was for gettin' work at the lead mine near but Bridget"— he again jerked his head—"she wouldn't have it. She didn't mind me being down the pit; I was down for ten years; you stand a chance with coal. But lead, God it's 'Bring out your dead!' every day. What's your missus do?" He now looked at Annabella, and Manuel said quickly, "Oh. Oh, she cooks."

"Oh, does she?" He nodded at Annabella. "Funny, my wife was a cook an' all until she got the cough; then that put an end to it 'cause some people get particular."

The woman started a bad bout of coughing again and the man shook his head as if to say, "Oh, dear me!" then, before he turned away, he said, "She'll settle down in a little while; she won't keep you awake long, and we'll be off in the mornin'. We're making our way to Blyth, that's where she was born. If she gets her native air, it'll pull her to again."

Annabella turned and looked at Manuel and he at her, and he shook his head slowly. Then, tugging the blanket from underneath him, he said softly, "Wrap yourself in it," and when she made no move to do as he suggested, he said still low but harshly, "Do as I say, wrap yourself in it."

So she wrapped herself in the blanket and lay down, and he knelt up and opened the window, then he lay down on the end of the mattress.

Again as in the haystack she was covered with shame and confusion, but more so, oh much more so, and she knew she would never sleep.

But she did sleep; she was so weary that she slept through the woman's coughing and the noise of late revelers coming from the street outside, and she didn't wake up till midnight, when the occupants of the other beds made their entry and terrified her for a moment with their singing and language and noise, and personal sounds which shocked and nauseated her. But this, too, died down after a while and there was

191

only the woman's intermittent coughing and the heavy snores; and again, in spite of them, she went to sleep.

It must have been around three o'clock in the morning when she woke up. Half the cubicle was filled with moonlight. She felt warm and snug and relaxed and she lay in this state for a few moments until she realized how it had come about. Then, only the fact that the reason for the snugness was sound asleep and breathing heavily stopped her from springing up.

She was lying with her back to Manuel, her body sunk into the curves of his. One of his arms was across her waist; the other arm was above his head lying on the straw pillow, and the fingers of his hand were entwined in her hair close to her scalp.

Wide awake now, and as Rosina would have done, she brought reason to the situation. Manuel had not done this consciously; he had in his sleep turned toward her. Likely it was the position he took up when he was with—her mind skipped a mental paragraph. And it also skipped back from Manuel and down the years, and she saw again her father chasing the naked woman round his bedroom. She saw him pushing the strawberries into her mouth; the fruit still looked soft and luscious. She saw him bathing the woman; then finally there appeared before her the contorted figures on the bed. This was always the end of the nightmare that wasn't a nightmare. But why was she thinking of this now, why?

Manuel stirred in his sleep; his fingers moved in her hair; he sighed deeply and rested more heavily against her, and life as she knew it was suspended for the moment. She was floating in a sea of comfort, of restfulness, even joy; then, as if the sea had been sucked away, she fell onto the rock of Crane Street, into the house in Crane Street, where the women wore loose clothing and girls laughed in the passages, and her mother, yes, her own mother, took money for their services.

The reason why she was enjoying the close proximity of Manuel's body was because she was the daughter of her mother. She wished she were dead, she wished she had the courage to die. But she knew herself to be a coward; if she weren't, she would have ended her life when she came out of that house that night and walked on the sands by the sea.

She began to wonder now what would happen should he awake and find himself in this position. If that should come about, then she must pretend to be sound asleep. Yes, that's what she must do, she must pretend to be asleep. But she had no intention of going to sleep again.

She didn't remember at what time she fell asleep and she didn't know whether she dreamed that Manuel's hand moved from her waist and cupped the bowl of her stomach, or that it actually happened at all, but when she next felt his hand on her shoulder, she started upright in the bed, staring at him as if he were the devil.

"It's all right. It's all right." He was handing to her a mug of black tea. "Drink this," he said; "it'll wake you up. We'd better be on our way."

She took the cup from his hand as she still stared at him. He was fully dressed; he looked clean and fresh. He said, "There's a pump in the yard and a bucket; you can have a wash down. And there's a dry scrubbing brush on the window-sill; use it to get the mud off your things. Look." He held his arms out and indicated his coat and trousers. "I'm like a new pin."

He seemed different this morning, happy, like the Manuel she had once known. The tea was sweet and hot and it brought her awake, and a few minutes later she tiptoed from the room, carrying her boots in her hand and keeping her eyes directly ahead and away from the huddled figures on the mattresses.

She found it difficult to wash without soap, and the coarse toweling hurt her skin. The early morning air was chilly and the water was cold, but after she had done what she could in the way of washing herself and brushing her clothes, she felt strangely refreshed. Her heels were hardly hurting and she was hungry, and the thought now wasn't where they would eat but when they would eat, and so she was somewhat deflated when Manuel, joining her in the passage, said, "We'll stock up with some food and get out of the town and make a meal."

Although it had just turned six in the morning, a number of shops were open, and after buying bread and steak and pigs' fat, they walked out of the town, cut across open fields and past orchards until they came to a clear stream, and on the bank he built a fire. He fried all the steak and the remainder of the bacon, and packed half of it away for later in the day, then divided the rest between them. After she had cleared everything on her plate, he asked her, "Can I cut you another piece of bread?" and, when she said, "If you please," he smiled at her as he remarked, "You were hungry."

"Yes, yes, I was."

"That's a good sign."

"Is it?" She didn't ask of what, and she didn't punctuate everything she said with his name now, either. This latter fact wasn't lost on him and he stared at her. She, too, looked different this morning. It wasn't that she was on her high horse or playing the lady; she was just different, more ordinary like. It must be the good night's rest. He'd had a good night's rest. He didn't know when he'd had a better; he'd woken up feeling a new man, and if he could keep Lagrange's face out of his mind, he'd remain so.

They kept to the South Tyne until they reached Bellingham, and there Manuel inquired the way to Plenmeller Common and Skillen's Farm. After being told to follow the river as far as Melkridge, he was to cut off south in the direction of Whitfield and halfway between he'd come to the farm.

His inquiry was the first indication to Annabella that he was making for any particular destination and she said to him, "Why are we going to this farm?" And he replied, "You heard what the fellow said last night. He had worked there and got the push. I'm sorry for him, but it's work I want and, by the sound of the place, it's off the beaten track, and there won't be many as yet know that there's a job goin'."

To this she had said with the fear in the back of her eyes again, "But—but if you get work, what will I do?"

And he had smiled and replied, "Well, I don't suppose his wife sat down all day; there'll likely be a job for a woman an' all, that's if you're still of the same mind. It's up to you."

She had not answered anything to this, and they had gone on. He had said that the place was off the beaten track and she wanted to find some place to hide, some place where she wouldn't run the risk of meeting people like Mrs. Ferguson, though, as Manuel had said, she doubted if Mrs. Ferguson would have recognized her, and she thought, with some slight bitterness, clothes maketh the man, and certainly the woman. Also, that when you were foot weary and mortally tired, you did not appreciate beautiful scenery.

They had passed through some wonderful country; they had climbed hills as high as mountains; they had walked through wooded valleys; they had, in the heat of the day, sat in the mouth of a tunnel that led to a disused ore mine, where they could hear the water dripping in the black depths behind them, and Manuel had picked up a handful of blue copper-sulphate crystals, and some of a beautiful violet color, and she had marveled at them.

Now they were standing on the top of a scree cliff, and Manuel, pointing into the distance to a gray flat stretch of land, said, "That must be the Common, but there's no sight of a farm."

She let herself slowly down onto the shale as she said heavily, "Didn't the man say it lay between the Common and Whitfield? It's more likely to be over there, toward the Dale of Allen." She lifted a heavy arm.

"You know this part?" He was still gazing ahead.

She shook her head. "I know the lay of the county from my geography."

His brows moved slightly upwards. He looked down on her hair. The hood had fallen back and the auburn mass, which was no longer combed and banded into neatness, shone in luxuriant disorder. He saw the weariness of her and he said, "Would you like to stay put until I go and look round?" Whereupon she pulled herself to her feet, answering briefly, "No."

Slipping and sliding, they went down the cliffside to the valley again; they rounded the foot of it and were walking along what looked like an animal track when quite suddenly they came upon the end of a rough quarry stone road. The road was definitely in the process of being made and Manuel turned to her and smiled as he said, "I think we've hit it."

Following the road, they passed a dense thicket, then came surprisingly into open pasture land with large numbers of cows grazing on one side, while the other was taken up with small walled fields, some holding vegetables and potatoes, but the greater proportion of them were filled with gooseberry bushes now stripped of their fruit.

The road bent sharply around a clump of trees, and in a field right in front of them there was a man driving two horses and a plow. He reached the end of the field as they came up, and Manuel, his hands on the dry stone wall, said, "Is the farmer hereabout?" and the man, coming toward the wall, said, "I'm the farmer. What is it?"

"Oh, good-day to you."

The man didn't answer but waited, and Manuel said, "I hear you're lookin' for a hand."

"Who told you that?"

"Makes no matter, is it true?"

195

"Aye, I'm lookin' for a hand. What can you do?"

"Anything with animals." Manuel smiled while he thought of horses alone.

The man said, "Where you from?"

"The Tyne."

"What did you do there?"

"Worked for a Mr. Lagrange for six years."

"And why aren't you working for him now?"

"Bad business hit him. It's hit all the houses—all the staff was dismissed." For a moment as he spoke he saw Lagrange's white face lying on the stones, and, as remorse was about to overwhelm him again, he thrust it aside. He was alive, he had to eat, he had to work.

The man now said, "I've eighty cows."

"Oh!"

Something about the exclamation made the man say, "Well, you can milk?"

"Truth is, I've never milked, but what will take one man a day to learn, I can do in half the time. I've dealt mostly with horses." He looked toward the animals, poor specimens in his eyes.

The man surveyed him up and down, then said, "I'll give you a try. Four shillings a week, your cottage, dinner an' what milk you need. . . . Your woman"—he nodded at Annabella without looking at her—"will work indoors, a shilling a week." He waited.

They were both staring at him, Manuel thinking, God, four shillings. Those Tolpuddle men had suffered in vain. What good had their union done them? Thirty years and more gone by and still only four shillings a week. And Annabella was telling herself that the man was surely jesting. The lowest creature in their establishment, the scullery maid, had received two shillings a week and her uniform and her allowance of beer, or tea and sugar, and Manuel, he had been receiving at least ten shillings a week, together with excellent food and splendid livery.

"We'll try it."

The man then said, "I'll give you a month to see, then I'll bond you. Go on down to the house." He pointed.

Manuel turned away without further words, and when they were out of earshot, Annabella said under her breath, "But Manuel, only four shillings a week!" She did not add, "And only a shilling for me." And, his gaze directed straight ahead, he replied, "It'll give us a roof and breathing space; what's more, it'll give you an insight into what's afore you."

He did not know how true his words were to prove.

It looked to them as if the farmhouse and outbuildings were resting in an island of mud. The yard facing the cow stables was a morass, hoof-patterned and ankle-deep in slush, and this went right up to the farmhouse door, and the only evidence that it wasn't welcomed indoors was a boot scraper set into a niche in the gray stone wall.

A girl answered the door. She was about the same age as Annabella. She had a thin, white face, a thin body but bulging breasts. She was wearing a coarse apron over a blue print dress, and her sleeves were rolled up above her elbows.

It was Manuel who spoke. He had said to Annabella a few minutes earlier, "Leave the talking to me and remember what I said a while back, about 'ta' and 'aye.'" He said now, "Your master sent us; we're hired on."

The girl stared from one to the other. Then putting her head back on her shoulders, she looked at someone and said, "Mistress, there's a couple here."

The mistress came to the door. She, too, was thin but it was a bonyhard thinness, and the hardness was reflected in the depth of her eyes, which gave no indication of what she thought of the new employees, but she said without any preamble, "He's hired you on then?"

"Yes, ma'am."

"Your cottage is round the corner." She pointed. "I'll be with you in a minute."

"Thank you."

They turned away, went round the corner and saw the cottage. It looked little more than an enlarged hut. The door was low and there was one tiny window on each side of it. Manuel had to stoop to enter. Then they were in a room ten feet by eight with an open spit fire and a bread oven taking up one wall. A table and two chairs stood against the other. The wall facing them held shelves on which was an assortment of old crockery and pans. Next to it was a door leading into the other room. They both stood in the doorway and looked at the bed. It was merely a straw palliasse on a rough wooden frame. At the bottom of the bed were folded two patchwork quilts. Annabella turned away, her head not bent but thrust forward on her shoulders as if on the point of a run. Manuel continued looking at the bed for some minutes, and when he turned he saw her standing leaning over the table, her hands flat on it, and he said roughly, "I'll make a ticking with the skins." He kicked the pack where he had dropped it on the floor, then added, "Filled with straw, I bet it'll be more comfortable than that."

She turned to him now and said in a breathless sort of way, "But—but that woman, she's been sleeping in there and—and she had consumption."

In less time than it had taken her to speak, his face was suffused with anger. His eyes narrowed, his tone grim, he said, "All right, don't sleep on it, you can have this." He flapped his hand toward the floor. "The trouble with you is you're afraid of the death you'll never die. You're more likely to go from exposure than you are from consumption."

"That may be so, but I would prefer it that way." Her voice was stiff, haughty.

"Oh, my God!" He turned from her and what he was about to say next was checked by the outer door's opening and the woman's entering. She stared at them both hard for a moment before saying, "He told you you'd have your dinner?"

When Manuel didn't answer the woman, Annabella nodded her head and said, "Ye-aye," and the woman fixed her gaze on her as she went on, "It's a good oven; it gives plenty of heat in the winter and there's wood for the chopping. Now about your work. You'll start at four o'clock—"

"F—four?"

"Yes, that's what I said. You're not hard of hearing, are you?" She waited. "You'll weigh the milk an' help get the cans onto the road for the town. After, you'll scour all the coolers and the cans ready for the next lot. Breakfast at seven, you get half an hour for that; after, you'll help in the house. There's always plenty of washing and scrubbing in there. Dinner's at three. Then you bring the cows in from the meadows and you're finished at six. That gives you plenty of time to see to this." She nodded her head three times; then, looking at Manuel, she added, "The master will see to you. Milking and plowing you're for." Her eyes went back to Annabella again and she said, "Don't forget, four o'clock it is; I don't put up with lazybones."

When the door was closed, Annabella looked at Manuel; then, like the child who had once appealed to him, she said, "Oh, Manuel, what am I going to do?"

He didn't look at her as he answered, "I told you, didn't I? But still"—he paused for a moment—"it sounds a lot but it's all routine. The hardest part is gettin' up at that hour. Anyway, we've got a roof over us. But now, to get back to the bed. What's your choice?"

She looked into his face before she said quietly, "I'd rather

198

sleep in here." Then she watched his white teeth bite hard down on to his lower lip, and she actually jumped as he shouted at her, "You won't then, you'll take the bed. I'll put the things out in the air and shake them. Have some sense. If you've got to die of the consumption, then you'll die of the consumption. What's important is we'll want our rest, an' I won't welcome you screaming in the night because cockroaches, field mice, or rats are visiting you, so it's the bed." And on this he marched out, saying, "Now, if I can get that damn fire started, we might have a sup tea."

She sat down heavily on a chair. She had the feeling that someone had suddenly taken her by the shoulders and shaken her. She would never have believed that Manuel would have spoken to her like that, acted like that without any consideration for her fears of such a dreadful disease as consumption. And that woman had said she must rise at four o'clock in the morning. Would she ever be able to do all the things required of her? Well, she was here and she must, if only to show Manuel that she could. After all, she was intelligent and educated, as she had already pointed out to him, and these attributes should enable her to equal him in learning things, as he had boasted, in half the time. Servants as a rule were slow because they were without education, and of low intelligence; she would show him what she could do. She must look upon the whole thing as an experiment. Yes, that's what she must do, look upon the whole thing as an experiment.

2

The experiment nearly killed her. It brought the wrath of her mistress on her nearly every hour of the day, and if it hadn't been that the farmer was greatly taken with Manuel and his capacity for work, then Annabella would surely have found herself, and her bundle, on the road before the first day was over.

For five weeks the sun had shone most of the time, bringing with it a drought, and the mud in the yard had caked into hard ridges, except along each side of the sewage drain that ran in front of the cow sheds past the corner of the farmhouse and down to the stream, from which came the only supply of water when the well dried up, which happened, Mary Jane told Annabella, pretty often in the summer, and not only now when the land was parched.

Mary Jane was a kindly girl, and without her covert help, Annabella's total ignorance of kitchen and dairy would have brought not only her mistress's wrath down on her, but pertinent questions.

Mary Jane had taken to Annabella. The new help was different. She couldn't quite explain it to herself; she only knew that Annabella was like no one else she had encountered in her life.

Nor had Annabella encountered anyone like Mary Jane. She was filled with horror when the girl related that she, together with Andy, the deaf mute, who was the only other hand on the farm and who communicated in grunts and through wide, pain-filled eyes, had been taken from the Hexham Workhouse five years ago when she was eleven and he twelve. They had both got sixpence a week for the first two years, then Andy had got a shilling, but she had only come to get a shilling, she said, when the child was born.

The child lay in a wicker basket in the corner of the open spit fireplace, being moved only for feeding and when the meat was being hooked. It was enveloped in clothes up to its chin. Its face was always red with the heat, and it rarely cried. It was changed once a day and it smelled continuously.

Annabella had thought at first the baby belonged to Mrs. Skillen, but Mary Jane informed her on the quiet that it was hers, and that—HE—had given it her. HE was not Andy, as Annabella had first surmised, but Mr. Skillen.

This knowledge had made Annabella physically sick. Since this nightmare life had engulfed her, she had, she thought, encountered nothing but depravity. Strangely, she never set Lagrange's lapses under this heading or owned that it was he who had first made her aware of the—unmentionable thing.

It was ten minutes to six on this particular sun-drenched day and she felt ill with fatigue. Four o'clock this morning she had struggled out of bed and for two hours she had ladled milk from the small cans into churns, then she had helped Andy to roll them into the yard where Manuel pushed them up the ramp and onto the flat cart and drove them over the rough road to the point where the carrier would pick them up and take them to the town.

At first Annabella had been afraid of Andy, for he would spend minutes gazing at her as if in a trance, but she had come to know he was quite harmless. Evoking her compassion, she talked to him, safe in the knowledge that he could make no comment on her speech. Not like Mrs. Skillen, who,

200

coming upon her talking to Mary Jane, had demanded, "Where'd you learn to talk high 'n' mighty?" and she had been quick to reply, "I was brought up in a convent." "You a Catholic?" Mrs. Skillen had then asked with deep suspicion in her face and voice, and when she received a flat "No," she had nodded vigorously, saying, "An' you'd better not be or you won't remain here long. Mr. Skillen, he can't abide Catholics. Lyin', drinkin' lot!"

As she wrung out the last dish cloth, the clock on the mantelpiece told her there were still seven minutes to go before it would chime six. She had dared to leave at quarter to six one evening but she had hardly entered the cottage door before Mrs. Skillen had burst in on her, crying, "Get back over there! You're not going to start this."

As she turned from the bench, she saw Mary Jane stoop and pick the child from the basket, then, sitting down, bare her breast to it. This sight, too, had at first repulsed her, but now she found she could look at it without even feeling embarrassment. She lowered herself heavily onto the wooden bench that was placed at right angles to the black ovens at the end of the room and slowly her body concertinaed into a restful slump. But only for a minute, for she almost upset the bench when the voice from the doorway said, "This is it, is it, soon as me back's turned? You've got a good five minutes, and get that table sanded."

Annabella, outwardly scurrying, inwardly coldly raging against this awful woman, was going toward the cupboard where the sand was kept when Mary Jane's voice checked her, for she was saying to Mrs. Skillen in a tone that held authority, "She's been on her feet all day long. What if she should tell her man how you keep on and he goes? The master won't like that, will he, 'cause he's taken with him. He says he's the best worker he's had in many a year, willin' like. I'd go careful if I was you. That I would."

Annabella looked from the young girl, with the baby pulling hungrily at her full breast, to the thin, grim woman staring down at her. Her face suffused with hate, she looked like an animal about to spring, yet knowing that she couldn't because of the chains holding her. And now Mary Jane said, "He told me last night that Manuel would have that road meetin' the main one in less than a month, and then he was gona start him brickin' the yard. He's had four fellows on that road, you know, in the last year, and he said if he'd put me on I'd have done better than them."

201

Annabella realized that Mary Jane wasn't only talking about Manuel and the road, she was telling Mrs. Skillen something else.

Mrs. Skillen now hunched her shoulders up around her neck as she said through clenched teeth, "You've got a surprise coming to you, me girl; his fancy soon fades, and then God help you. If I'm alive, God help you."

"He will an' all. He always has."

Annabella watched the woman she had to call "mistress" hurry from the room; then she looked at Mary Jane. The girl was smiling placidly and nodding at her. "Get yersel' off," she said; "he'll be wantin' his tea."

"Yes. Thank you, Mary Jane." As if she were taking an order from a superior, Annabella turned about and left the kitchen. At this moment she loved Mary Jane. She supposed that by certain standards she was a wicked girl, and how she could possibly tolerate that repulsive little man, she didn't know, but she knew she loved her because she had dared to stand up to that woman.

She entered the cottage with a sense of elation. Now that Mary Jane had showed herself to be the favorite, life promised to be a little easier; yet the elation evaporated at the sight the room presented. The floor was dirty with caked mud, the utensils that were used for breakfast were still on the table, and she was so tired, so very tired. She thought, as she had done numerous times of late, that never again would she feel the bodily wonder of being rested.

The fire was low, it had to be blown; the dishes had to be washed, that is, after she had been down to the river to get the water to wash them with; and she had to wash herself, but again only after she had brought the water up from the river; and all she wanted to do was to sleep. Sitting down at the table, she pushed the dishes aside, and, folding her arms, she laid her head upon them.

A touch on the shoulder brought her out of a dream in which she had been eating her breakfast in bed, and she stared up at Manuel for a moment as if she didn't recognize him, and then shaking her head she said, "I'm sorry, I—" She always seemed to be saying the same words to him, "I'm sorry," always apologizing.

"It's all right." He swung a chair round and sat at the table facing her, and abruptly he said, "Do you think you could stick this another two months?"

"Two months!"

When she continued to stare at him, he said, "It's hellish I know, but it's like this. If you can stick it out, there's the hirings in Hexham on the eleventh of November and we could go there, and with the experience we've had here pick up a good job." He smiled wryly, then wiped the sweat off each side of his face with the back of his hand before adding, "It would have to be bad to be worse than this, wouldn't it?"

She made no answer, just continued to stare at him. It would be bad to be worse than this, yes, indeed it would. But she had thought that they were to be here for the entire winter, at the end of which time she felt she would be unrecognizable, even to herself. Her hands were red and swollen, the nails broken, and the skin of her face, which had not felt a cream or lotion since the day she left the House, and which before then had rarely been touched by the sun, was now almost as brown as his.

"I've got something to ask you."

"Yes?"

His eyes dropped away from hers, and putting his hand on top of a dirty mug, he began moving it backwards and forwards across the table before he spoke again. "It's like this." The movement of the mug stopped; his eyes were looking straight into hers. "If I get a better job, I'll likely be bonded, properly bonded—I've told him I won't bond us here, do what he likes. Well, I, I want to be able to sign me name. I want to learn to write, read and write."

She remembered vaguely hearing of his wanting to read and write before this, something connected with Miss Howard.

"Will you, I mean, learn me?"

Seconds passed before she said, "Yes, Manuel, I'll—I'll teach you to read and write."

She had laid slight stress on the word "teach" and he recognized he had gone wrong somewhere, and again he wiped the sweat from the sides of his face with the back of his hand. There was more he needed to learn than just reading and writing, but he would come by it, aye begod! he would come by it. She might never be of use to him in any other way, but she would in this. He said now, "There's plenty of slate on the hillside; I'll get a big bit tomorrow and chip down a piece to write with, like the school kids have."

She was staring at him, and of a sudden she wanted to cry. She didn't know really why; all she knew was she wanted to cry—while leaning her head against him.

"Thanks." His voice was soft, and he returned her gaze for a moment longer, then he rose from the table, adding, "Let's get some tea and the place cleaned up."

It was an hour and a half later when he said to her, "I've brought you some water up to wash; I'll away down to the river." He had half-turned from her when he swung around again and his eyes narrowed as he asked, "Why don't you come down and wash in the river?"

"What! Oh, no. No, thank you." It was Miss Annabella speaking and he smiled wryly at her and said slowly, as if he were explaining something to a child, "Look, there's nobody going to see you, and it'll be deep twilight by the time we get along to the place where I go. There's only one way down and the little pool's sheltered under a lee of rocks; it's off the mainstream and the water will just be coolish. It's a wonderful place. Come on." He held out his hand to her, but she still stood stiffly, and when he bent toward her bringing his head level with hers, she bowed her head as he went on, "I promise you no one will see you, only God. Those things must be sticking to you." He flicked his finger at her serge skirt, no longer blue, but stained now with overall patches of green and black.

"Aw, come on." She felt herself jerked forward and out of the door; then just as quickly jerked back into the room again as he said laughingly, "You will want this," and reaching out to the iron rod that hung above the bread oven, he pulled off a coarse towel, then grabbed at a piece of blue mottled soap from out of a dish standing on a bench, and, swinging her round and outside again, he ran her from the back of the house down the field path to the river and along its bank until, gasping, she cried, "Please! Oh, please, Manuel, stop."

When he did, she stood panting and holding her side. "I've got a stitch. . . . How far is it?"

"About ten minutes more."

She looked up at the sky. The twilight this evening seemed slow in merging into night.

At one point they were walking through a thicket with no sign of the river when he stopped her with a touch on the arm and, pointing to an almost imperceptible opening in the hedge to the left of them, said, "This way. Come in sideways and mind your hair doesn't get caught up."

She felt the broken branches of the thicket tearing at her clothes, but only for a minute, because the next two steps brought her into a clearing which was bordered by thick

204

shrub. She followed him through an opening at the side, then onto a grassy slope that had a rim of boulders, and there below was the river flowing fast over submerged rocks, and some yards away to the right, as he had said, in the lee of the mainstream was a little pool. The only way to it was over the boulders and downwards and pointing, he said, "When you get down there, you'll find a crevasse to the right, it's nice and dry, where you can put your clothes. Stay as long as you like. I'll be up above."

She did not ask, "When are you going to bathe?" The situation was too embarrassing; speech would only make it worse. She walked away from him and carefully let herself down from one steep boulder to the next until she was on the shore of the little pool. As he said, there was the crevasse like a stone-walled dressing room. Before she went into it she looked back, but there was no sight of him.

Slowly she began to undress, but when she reached her chemise, she found she couldn't take it off and walk the dozen steps to the water's edge.

Seconds passed into minutes before, clutching the soap and rough towel, she edged her way from the shelter and toward the water. When she reached the edge of the pool, she glanced apprehensively back toward the boulders, but she could hardly make them out, for the twilight was speeding into night now, and it was only the thought that Manuel would want to come down after she was out that spurred her to the last effort.

When she slipped into the water, the chill of it brought her gasping and clutching at the bank. It was deeper than she had imagined and came well over her waist, but the bottom was hard and firm, and after a moment she walked forward; then, standing quite still in the middle of the pool, she peered about her. It was beautiful; it was the most beautiful spot she had seen in her life. If only Manuel had brought her before; if only she had been able to come here over the hot, sticky nights during these past weeks. Of a sudden she found herself flapping at the water with her hands, splashing it over her shoulders and face. It was wonderful, wonderful. She walked to the bank again and, picking up the soap, began to lather herself. She had never felt so clean in her life, never, never. She was young again, alive. Oh, the wonder of it. The exquisite wonder of it. It was like the first time she had sat in the bath without wearing the blindfold. She shied away from the thought.

As she dried herself on the burlap towel which tonight did

not seem to scratch her skin, there returned to her the memory of their first day together when she had seen him lying in the river and her indignation at the sight. She had changed since then, oh yes, yes, indeed she had.

Dressed again, she made her way over the boulders, up the slope and into the clearing, but there was no sign of Manuel. She called softly, "Manuel! Manuel!" and when she received no answer, she became uneasy, for it was almost dark. Pushing quickly through the narrow passage, she reached the pathway, and again she called his name. Louder this time. Where was he? Where had he gone? It would soon be black dark. "Manuel!"

"Yes. Here I am." He came out of the shadows and along the path toward her. His hair was wet, and his shirt neck open to the waist. He had been in the water. She let out a long breath, then said, "You've—you've bathed, then?"

"Yes." He nodded at her. "I knew once you got in there you wouldn't come out in a hurry."

"I—I'm sorry."

"Don't be sorry." He was laughing at her. "Did you enjoy it?"

"Oh, it was wonderful, wonderful." She closed her eyes. "I've never enjoyed anything so much in all my life, really I haven't." When she looked at him again, he was peering down at her, his expression soft as she remembered it from years past, and he said now, "You're smiling. Do you know that, you're smiling."

And she was. She felt her cheeks were in an unusual position. Her face felt different, and not only her face, her whole body. She said solemnly, "I never thought I'd smile again, Manuel," and he replied, "Never is a long time."

They walked in silence for some way and slowly, as if enjoying the meandering, and it was dark before they reached the field below the cottage, and there she said to him, "You must buy a bundle of candles when next you're in town, because we'll go through one a night with your lessons."

"Yes, yes, I'll do that."

"We have two candles left; we could start tonight."

He slowed his step still more and half-turned toward her. "But you've got to rise early: you want your sleep."

"I don't feel tired now. In fact, I've got the feeling that I'll never feel tired again." She did not laugh, but made a little sound in her throat.

"How long do you think it'll take me to learn, I mean to be able to read?"

"Oh." Her voice was light. "Not all that long, because you know, as you said, you can accomplish things in half the time it takes other men."

His sudden laugh startled the hedge sparrows and sent them swarming over the field; then walking on, briskly now, he said, "That doesn't apply to everything." And on this a thought sprang at him and he only just prevented it coming out of his mouth in words, for it would have said, "I wish to God it did." Yet the words in themselves mightn't have conveyed anything to her. It would have been the regret in his tone that would have set off a train of questions and answers, and when, like most fuses, it eventually reached the gunpowder, their association would have been shattered into fragments.

3

It was half-past three on an ice-cold morning on the eleventh of November, 1866, and it was the day of the hirings.

The sheepskins had once more been made into a bag, which was already tied up on the table. Annabella's bundle lay by its side and it was slightly bigger than when she last carried it, for Mary Jane had, last night, given her three candles and some packages of food cribbed from the larder. There had been tears on both sides at the parting, but of the two, Mary Jane's prospects looked the brighter, for she had informed Annabella that the master wanted a son but she was holding out until he put something in writing so that she and the children would be provided for—and not with workhouse fare, either—if anything happened to him, and she knew he'd come round because he had a strong, daft fancy for her; and once she was all right, she'd see that Andy was an' all.

Annabella admired Mary Jane because she was so full of common sense and so practical. But the thought of her association with Mr. Skillen still made her feel sick.

Manuel now put the pack on his back and she lifted up the bundle and they went out, without a backward glance, into the bitter morning. Skillen had refused them a lift, saying there were too many cattle going in on the cart. He was mad at their leaving but couldn't hold them, as Manuel had remained firm in refusing to sign the bond, saying they'd be paid monthly or they'd go.

There was a carrier cart passed the toll road at six o'clock and if they kept going steadily, they hoped to pick it up.

They did not talk as they trudged through the dark, saving their breath for the long trek ahead. Anyway, there was no need for words at present; they had planned it all out last night what they intended to do when they got into Hexham and what they intended to say to their new employer, with regard not only to their working experience but to their relationship.

It was nine o'clock when the carrier cart put them down in Hexham, and for a moment Annabella imagined they had been brought into the wrong town. Gone was the quiet, lazy air; everywhere you looked there were people, all merry, laughing, pushing people, families who evidently knew the town and were here for a day of merry-making; peddlers out to make money on this God-sent day, thrusting their wares into your face; others grinning while looking slightly lost, being jostled here and there as they gazed up at the fine facades of the buildings.

Manuel paid the carter his sixpence charge and nodded knowingly when the man advised, "Look out for your pocket, lad, and your breeches, or you might find yourself the night hidin' in the bushes."

"There is no fear of that." Manuel smiled as his hips unconsciously shifted the belt lying round his waist; then he asked, "What time will they start, I mean signing on?" and the man replied, "Anytime. I would stick around until you get fixed."

"Thanks. Good-bye." He nodded to the carrier. Then, taking hold of Annabella's arm, he thrust himself and his pack sideways through the crowded street, pulling her after him. When they passed an inn, the smell of the ale wafted toward him and he licked his lips widely with his tongue. If he had been on his own, he would have pushed in there and downed a few mugs, if not for his thirst's sake then in order to celebrate his freedom, for although he might be bonded within the next few hours, he had the sense of being his own man strong on him now; and again, if it wasn't for her, he doubted if he would tie himself to any man, winter or no winter.

When they came to another inn where they were passing mugs of beer over the heads of the customers, Annabella, jerking his arm to draw attention, said, "If you want a drink of ale, Manuel, I'll—I'll wait."

He glanced toward the crowded pavement outside the inn, then at her, and replied, "It's no time to stop for ale. We'll think about that when we get fixed. . . . You dry?"

208

"Yes, yes, a little; but I think it's better to do as you say and—and get fixed."

The shops were all doing a roaring trade and there was the sound of a band playing in the distance. Manuel wondered how they would ever get into the Market Place if the crowds were as thick as this, yet when he eventually reached the Market Square he found there was some kind of order amid the chaos. Stopping a man, he asked, "Can you tell me where they're doing the hirings?" and the man, pointing, said, "Yonder, that side over there. Just take your stand and they'll come to you."

It wasn't until they had taken their stand against a wall and at the end of a broken row of men and women, some standing alone, some standing together, that Annabella began to feel sick, sick with fear of being recognized, perhaps by a prospective employer, but more sick with humiliation, for she was now viewing the whole scene as a modern slave market.

As she glanced about her, she saw the same look in the eyes of all those waiting. The look was apprehensive, and, what was worse, some faces showed the long stamp of resignation. These were the older faces, lined, weatherbeaten, gray faces over which hope hung like a thin veil and despair a heavy cloak. The anxiety showed up these couples because these were the ones who pushed the peddlers away, who refused to look at the trays of gaudy trinkets, who weren't amused by the toy monkeys on sticks, nor the live monkey that was now prancing on top of the organ grinder's barrow around which a crowd of children had gathered.

It was an hour later when the first employer showed up, by which time the line had trebled itself, and whereas they had appeared to be in the front row, now they were at the back. This in a way lessened the tension in Annabella, while she thought that it wouldn't spoil their chances because Manuel stood head and shoulders above most of the men present. She wasn't to know that his dark, foreign-looking appearance went against him among the conservative farmers.

Another hour passed and no man had stopped in front of them to question them, and Manuel said, more to himself than to her, "If we don't get picked we're not going back there. There's factories in the town; I'll get hired on somewhere. . . . Look, there he is coming this way with a grin on his face."

When Mr. Skillen pushed his way toward them and, casting his narrowed glance over Manuel, said, "No luck yet,

209

then? Be taking you back with me after all likely?" Manuel said stiffly, "That you won't, not if I know it."

"Ah, we'll see, we'll see. It's going to be a hard winter, and if you want to come through it, you'll be glad of any pickin's."

Manuel watched him walk away; he watched him stop before one couple after another, and it gave him some satisfaction to see the heads always shaking, never nodding.

A man standing within arm's length of them turned and asked, "You worked for old Skillen?" and Manuel answered briefly, "For a time."

"Bloody old skinflint that, never gives more than six shillings and wants your blood."

Six shillings, thought Manuel bitterly, and I did what I did for four.

Another hour gone. Annabella was leaning heavily against the wall. Her feet were numb to the ankles; she didn't know whether she had any fingers on her or not. The crowd of employees had almost disappeared; you could always tell when a couple passed you whether they had been hired because they would be talking and laughing. Some of the younger ones were even running, making for the fairground to push in a bit of enjoyment, something to remember in the long, dark months of labor ahead.

There were now not more than six couples left in the corner of the square, and two single women and four single men.

Manuel had been stamping his feet to keep warm, but now he was standing quite still, his eyes on the man threading his way from the far pavement. He was a big man, burly, and looked the typical pattern of a farmer. He wore a high black hat on a big head and his shoulders thrust their way forward, and when he came closer, Manuel saw that his attire was good: highly polished leather gaiters up to the knee, fine stout boots, thick cords and a three-quarter-length ribbed coat; although you could never go by looks, he told himself, this man was the most prosperous-looking farmer he had seen this morning. He watched the man's eyes roam over the rest of the remaining employees. He saw him walk toward a couple and talk to them; the conversation ended without a nodding or shaking of heads. Then the man was moving forward looking over the remaining people as he would over a pen of cattle; and now he was standing before Manuel and it was Manuel who spoke first. "Good-day, sir," he said.

The bold face moved into a smile, the round blue eyes

stared at him, then the man said, "And good-day to you." And then he asked, "What are you? I'm looking for a cowman and general hand and a woman for the house."

Manuel, looking back into the blue eyes, thought, I can give this man the truth, and so he told him, "Six years as a groom, four months with cows."

"Pity it isn't the other way round," said the man. "Where did you work last?"

"Mr. Skillen's farm."

"Oh, my God!" The man laughed a deep, rumbling laugh now. "There's one thing you will have learned there and that's what work means. What did he pay you?"

"Four shillings a week. I was hard put, else I wouldn't have taken it."

"You must have been at that. Well now, your woman here." He turned his glance to Annabella, then added, "Show us your face, girl."

When Annabella pushed her hood back, the man said, "Ah, you're pretty. The missus likes something pleasant around her, but not as an ornament. What can you do? Cook?"

"No, sir, but—but I can clean, do housework, and in the dairy."

"She doesn't want help in kitchen or dairy, she's got that; it's for housework she's needing a body. My daughter's getting married in a short while—she's seen to it up till now. Well, now." He looked at Manuel again. "I'm willing if you are. I'll bond you for six months. Nine shillings a week to start with. If you're worth ten, you'll get it at the end of the first month, and your missus two and six."

"We'll—we'll be very pleased to accept, sir, but there's a point I'll have to make clear. She's—she's not my wife, she's my cousin."

"Oh, cousin, eh. Well now, that's a bit of an obstacle." He scratched his chin. "Cottage goes with the job, but being cousins, well, you couldn't sleep there, could you?" He poked his big head toward Annabella, bringing the color to her frozen cheeks. Then, his brows gathering, he mused for a minute before saying, "Betty's in the attic, but it's big enough for two. Yes, one more palliasse will make no difference. Aye now, I think we can say that'll be all right. What's your name?" He was looking at Manuel.

"Manuel Mendoza, sir."

"Foreign-sounding; but then you are foreign, aren't you? What? Italian?"

"No, sir, partly Spanish."

"And what's the other part?"

"Irish."

"Oh, Irish." They were smiling at each other now, as if at a joke.

"And your name, girl?"

"Annabella—Connolly."

"All right then, Manuel and Annabella, do you know where the Phoenix Inn is?" and when Manuel answered, "Yes, sir," he said, "Well, be outside there at two o'clock sharp; we've got a long ride afore us. Oh." His head went up and he laughed again. "I forgot to tell you where we're going. It's between East Allen Dale and Devil's Water Glen, not as far as Blanchland. Lovely spot in the summer, never a finer, but a frozen prison in the winter. Better tell you."

"I'll chance it, sir." Manuel smiled, and the man, jerking his head at him, said, "Good. Good," then moved away.

Now they were looking at each other, both smiling. Manuel said, "There goes a man after me own heart," and Annabella said, "He seems honest and straightforward. I—I hope I'm going to like his wife."

"A man like that wouldn't pick a bad 'un. Come on, let's try and get something to eat, though that's going to be easier said than done. But if we manage it in time, we may be able to pop into the fair." His smile widened and his voice was teasing as he asked, "Would you like to go on the shuggies?"

"The shuggies?"

"Yes, the shuggy boats, you know, the little boats that swing back and forward that the kids love."

"Oh!" Her head nodded as she comprehended the meaning of "shuggies" and her own smile widened as she said, "I don't think so, Manuel, thank you. But I wouldn't mind seeing the fair; I've never seen a fair."

"Never?"

"No."

"Come on."

It was only the heavy pack that stopped him from running as some of the young people had done earlier. The clock chimed the half hour past twelve as they left the Market and it was well past one o'clock when they found some place to eat, and then only standing up and wedged tight in the corner of a packed room.

When they had finished a plate of hot pies and peas, Manuel left her for a moment, saying, "Stand on the pack and don't let anybody take it unless they take you." His voice ended in a deep, throaty laugh as he hoisted her up onto the skins; then he added, "Don't sit down on it whatever you do or you're likely to be trampled underfoot."

He hadn't been gone a minute when two young fellows, turning round and seeing her alone, edged their way toward her, and, grinning at her, one of them said, "Hello, me pretty."

When she made no reply, the other one nudged his companion, saying, "She be tongueless, a pretty one like her and tongueless. Now, ain't that a shame? Do you think she'll be tickleless an' all, Sam?"

"Why don't you try and see, Robbie?"

"Should I, Sam?"

"Aye, do, Robbie. You try and see."

They were both rocking with their jocular exchange now and when the taller edged himself to her side, and, his shoulder almost level with her waist, he went to put his arm around it, he received a hefty clout from a bundle on the top of his head.

Annabella could not believe that she had hit the man with her bundle, but then she was so frightened it would have been all the same if she'd had a knife in her hand, she would have used it.

"One to her!" the other young fellow shouted, and brought all the faces in the room turned toward her, all laughing.

Where was Manuel? Her heart was pounding with a mixture of fear and indignation.

"Queen of the castle, she is. Go on, Robbie, storm the walls." Egged on by a number of voices now, the young fellow, adopting a sparring attitude, put out his arms again toward her, but when she went to use the bundle this time, it was grabbed in midair, and the youth tossed it to his companion, and in doing so he turned his face from her for a moment and her hand came out and slapped his cheek so resoundingly that once again he staggered backwards. But now he was no longer smiling. His lips pushed outwards, his eyes screwed into deep sockets, he cried, "Want it rough, eh? Want it rough? All right, then, you'll have it rough," but before he could demonstrate what action his roughness was to take, he felt himself suddenly hauled upwards and balancing on the tips of his toes, and there dangling opposite to him was his pal Sam. Then as his head came in sharp, sickening contact with his friend's, he saw nothing but the proverbial stars for a few minutes.

Manuel dropped the two youths to their feet again amid a dead silence. Even the munching of pies and the slopping of peas had stopped and a pathway suddenly opened to the door. After retrieving her bundle and hitching the pack to one shoulder, he pushed her before him and out into the street.

They had walked some steps before she stammered, "I-t was—n't my fault."

"Who's sayin' it was?"

She felt a surge of relief as she saw he was grinning at her, and when he said softly, "That was one right ladylike clout you gave him," she drooped her head in confusion for a second before lifting it sharply and exclaiming, "You saw! You were there?"

"Not all the time. I came in as you were wielding the bundle at him."

She was looking down again as she said, "It is the first time I have lifted my hand to anyone. I never imagined I could."

He said soberly now, "The need for self-protection makes weaklings into warriors."

Outside the Phoenix there were groups of people standing, mostly men. They took up a position some distance from the door and waited. On one side of them there was a heated debate going on about the scandalous price being asked for Irish cattle, nine pounds ten a head. Scandalous. Scandalous, the voices said. On the other side a group were discussing the prices of the railway fares from Hexham to Blaydon just outside Newcastle. The disparity between the first class and second class was too great: two shillings for the first-class journey and only a shilling for the second class. Either bring the first class down or put the second class up. And if the speaker had anything to do with it he was going to create a rumpus until the gap between the two classes was lessened. This brought a guffaw and a quip from another member of the group. Laughing loudly, he cried, "Be careful what you be saying, Cranbrook, and how you go about it. You suggestin' that you want the upper class to come down and the working class to come up and meet in the middle? Lor' sucks! you're after startin' a revolution. You want to be careful, lad, or afore you can turn round you'll have Hetty Black's brood hammering on the doors of Mrs. Charlotte Bendle's Young Ladies' Academy, saying they've a right to be let in."

"Don't be so daft, man. It's prices I'm talking about going up and down, not people."

More laughter now as the loud voice cried, "People start with prices; change the prices, you change the people."

While Manuel's eyes were fixed on the inn, his mind on the man he was waiting for, Annabella's ears were picking up the scraps of conversation around her. She hadn't realized that ordinary farmers talked like this and discussed things. But then she had only met Mr. Skillen. Their voices might be rough and their laughter loud, but the substance of their speech indicated thinking and doing. She had never thought the common people capable of thinking. It came to her at this moment that although she had a great deal for which to thank Rosina, she also had a great deal to blame her for. She had brought her up to believe that there were only two classes in the world, those with education and those without. The people without were to be treated kindly, but kept in their place, in fact like domestic animals.

"There they are."

Hitching his pack upwards, he moved forward and she followed him.

"Ah! You've come, then." Mr. Fairbairn's voice was thick and jovial. "Missus." He turned to the woman at his side, whose head just came up to his shoulder and who, in her hooped dress and short cape, appeared like a small decorated barrel.

"This is the pair. There you are, what do you think I've picked?"

Mrs. Fairbairn looked first at Manuel. Starting with his head, her keen brown eyes swept over his body, seeming to pause where the muscles lay, then with a nod and a smile she said, "He looks as if he'll do." And now she turned her attention to Annabella. "Lift your hood, girl."

Annabella pushed the hood back from her head and for a fleeting second she again visualized the slave market, but her future mistress was nodding at her in the most pleasant manner. It was strange, Annabella thought, that the little woman had a face not unlike her husband's, and her manner was certainly similar to his, brisk but quite kind.

"You're a pretty piece, I'll say that for a start. But looks don't whiten no linens, so I can't say further till I've seen you work, can I, girl?"

"No, madam."

The little woman's eyebrows shot up. It was evident that she wasn't displeased with the title, in fact slightly flattered, but nevertheless she said, " 'Missus' is my title, not 'madam'; it's a farmhouse you're coming to."

"I'm sorry."

"No need to be for that. Well, let's get going, Mr. Fairbairn." Thus addressing her husband, she turned away and he, nodding at them, indicated that they should follow.

Their conveyance was awaiting them at the ostler. It was a twohorse wagon. It had been converted to suit all purposes: the driving seat had a wooden rain screen over it and the back was covered with sail canvas supported on a ridgepole like a tent, and this part was already more than half full with boxes and brown paper-wrapped packages, which indicated that the missus had been doing quite a lot of shopping.

"Up you get!" said Mr. Fairbairn, and on this Manuel helped Annabella up and under the canvas. Then, pushing in his pack, he hoisted himself onto the footboard, and sat with his legs hanging over the end of it.

As the cart began its rollicking way over the cobbles, he turned his head and looked at Annabella and smiled, and when, tentatively, she smiled back at him, he leaned backwards and whispered, "I've an idea we've fallen on our feet."

As the journey lengthened, the going became rougher, and time and time again they found themselves in a huddle against one or the other side of the cart. Before darkness descended Mr. Fairbairn stopped and lit the lamps and called to them, "Won't be long now, under an hour."

That hour seemed like ten to Annabella. Her body felt bruised all over; she was cold to the bone and so hungry—she couldn't remember feeling so hungry. When the cart finally stopped amid the barking of dogs and high voices, Mr. Fairbairn boomed, "Well, here you are. Get you down." Manuel lifted her from the back of the cart; she would have fallen onto her face if he hadn't steadied her with his hands.

"I've—I've got cramp."

"Stamp your feet." His voice was an undertoned hiss, for he was looking toward the lighted door of the house, and as she drunkenly stamped her feet and brought the circulation back into her legs, she too looked toward the lighted doorway, from which there seemed to be a crowd of people surging forward, hampered by the prancing dogs. When they reached the cart, they all talked at once.

"Hello, Ma."

"Hello, Ma."

"How did it go, Da?"

"Oh, you've got them."

"Well, come on, don't let's stand here, it's enough to chill your liver. Hold the lantern higher."

"Here you, Sep!" This was Mr. Fairbairn's voice. "See to the animals; they've had a hard pull and a long day. But wait, let's get these things out of the back. Down with you, Duke. You'd think we'd been away a year. And you two" —he was shouting at them now—"go on, get inside, you'll want a belly warmer after that ride."

Annabella went through the sea of shadow-splashed faces toward the stone-flagged porch, four steps across it and into a room, and all she took in at the moment of entry was that it was extremely large, so very warm, and held the wonderful smell of roasting food.

She stood just inside the door, Manuel by her side, his cap in his hand, and there flooded past them back into the house two big young men, replicas of the farmer, and a tall young woman of like size and coloring to her brothers, and they gathered round the little woman, taking her cape, her bonnet, her gloves, all the while talking, asking questions.

"What did you get, Ma?"

"Did you get my dress length and the thread?"

"I hope you didn't forget me 'baccy."

"You and your 'baccy, our Michael."

"Did you get that thing I asked you for Sarah, Ma?"

"Will you be quiet, all of you, and let me get me breath. You're touching nothing, you're getting nothing, until I get something to eat, until we all get something to eat. Come here, girl." She turned toward Annabella, then, nodding toward Manuel, added, "And you."

And when they moved forward and into the radius of one of the two lamps standing on a long table running down the center of the room, on which was laid a meal, she addressed Annabella, saying, "Well now, take off your cloak and let's have a good look at you."

Annabella's stiff fingers undid the hook of her hood and then the buttons of her cloak, and when she removed it, Manuel took it from her hand and laid it over his arm, and he stared at her, his expression slightly apprehensive now. But he need not have worried. Whatever she was feeling, she didn't show it, and he breathed deeply and looked at the two stalwart young men who were staring at Annabella, as was their mother. But not the daughter: the daughter was looking at him. She had a straightforward look, like that of her father. He didn't take the liberty of staring back at her, he just looked at her. She was a comely-looking girl. His attention was brought back to the little woman, who was saying, "You're as thin as a rake. You want feeding, me girl.

217

You can't work if you don't get your food. Now sit yourself down, both of you"—she pointed to one of the settles that ran at right angles to the big open fire—"and we'll all have a bowl of broth to melt our innards, and then we can talk. This is my eldest son, Willy." She went straight on as she pointed to the taller of the two men, and Willy inclined his head toward Annabella but said nothing. "And this is Michael, my second son." Michael also inclined his head toward Annabella, his eyes unblinking. "Sep, he's the youngest; he'll be in shortly. And this, my daughter, Agnes. And it's because she's going off and getting married that you're here. But more explanations later. Now that broth, Agnes."

"It's all ready, Ma."

Agnes now ran down the room and to another fire, which had baking ovens on each side and a big double-handled stew pot resting on the hob. Swinging it up expertly, she brought it to the table and having set it on a wooden stand she ladled thick broth into bowls, then swiftly handed them round, smiling all the while.

Annabella had never tasted soup like this before. They had had all kinds of soup in the House, Hessian soup, hare soup, partridge soup, pheasant soup, soup *à la reine,* but none of them had ever tasted like this.

"Would you like some more?" Agnes was bending down to her.

"If you please, it's delicious."

The farmer's daughter stared at the new help, and she just prevented herself from laughing outright, for it sounded as if the girl were mimicking a lady, like one you would get up at Falcon House across the moor.

"She won't have any more of that"—it was Mrs. Fairbairn speaking—"else she'll have no room for her dinner. By the way, girl, where did you learn to speak?"

Annabella did not glance toward Manuel, although she knew he was looking at her, before she said, "I was brought up in a convent."

"Ah! Ah! That's it, then." Her mistress was nodding knowingly at her.

"In a convent?" Agnes's voice was high and she went on to say what was in all their minds. "Then why, what I mean to say is, that if you were brought up in a convent, why are you—?"

It was Manuel's voice that cut her off, his tone even. "Her parents died and she had no one else, so—so she came over

218

to my people. We were distant relations, different to what she had been used to, but it was a home."

They were all looking at him, and then the two young men nodded as if to say, "Well, you did the right thing taking her in."

Mrs. Fairbairn said, "Pity, pity. But there, 'tis life. Come on you, Agnes, and get that dinner dished. Oh, here we are." She turned toward the door where her husband and younger son were entering, and she called to them, "Have your broth quick now, 'cause dinner's going on the table. She speaks well." The little woman, still looking at her husband, nodded toward Annabella. "She was telling us why." She now related the tale that Manuel had just told, briefly and almost word for word, and Mr. Fairbairn, looking at Annabella, nodded his head, and Sep, gazing at them, nodded, too.

"Now then, come and sit yourselves up. You, Manuel. That's a mouthful of a name, never heard one like it. Anyway, you'll sit there." She pointed to a seat at the bottom right-hand corner of the table. "That's your place." Then, pointing to one opposite, she said, "And that's yours, girl. And from now on you'll eat with us and be as one of the family. If you stay with us as long as Jack and Ruth that were here afore you did, then you'll be here well nigh eleven years. They only went 'cause he had a bit of land left him in the South. It was natural he would want to go. Now this seat next to you"—she pointed this time to the side of Annabella —"that's Betty's seat. Betty, she be gone to bury her mother. We took her in with us this morning and put her on the train for Blaydon. Likely be gone five, six days. However long it takes, that's her place. Betty's a good girl. She helps me in the kitchen and the dairy; yours is the house. Agnes will show you the ropes tomorrow and by the time her weddin' day comes you should be well in the swing of it."

"Yes, ma'am." Annabella's voice was low but Mrs. Fairbairn's was high as she cried, "No 'madam' or 'ma'am' I told you; 'missus' you call me. That's all, 'missus.' That's what I am and will be till I die."

All this while Agnes Fairbairn had been putting big covered dishes along the length of the table, and now finally she carried a huge delft platter on which was resting a roast leg of pork surrounded by bursting baked apples.

At one point during the meal Annabella wondered if she were dreaming, for when she felt she couldn't swallow another bite, Agnes brought onto the table an enormous fruit roly-poly and a great jug of hot syrup.

She looked across at Manuel. His eyes seemed to be waiting for hers, and as he smiled at her, she thought, He's happy, and I'll be happy here, too. But it all seems too good to be true.

The meal finally finished, the men rose and went toward the settles. Mr. Fairbairn said over his shoulder to Manuel, "Like a pipe?"

"Yes, sir."

"Well, come and put it on."

Manuel pushed his chair back and, after exchanging glances at Annabella, as much as to say, I told you we had fallen on our feet, he joined the men by the fire.

Annabella would like to have sat in the corner of the settle and held her feet out toward the blaze, but she was learning fast and so, getting up, she began to gather the dishes together at the bottom of the table, and her mistress said to her, "That's it, girl; the quicker they're done, the quicker you'll sit down. Agnes will give you a hand, and as she wants to see what's in those parcels"—she jerked her head toward her daughter—"I bet you ten to one these dishes won't know what's hit them afore they're on the racks."

There was a high laugh from Agnes and she began clearing her end of the table with a speed that bewildered Annabella, but she said to herself, This is what I must learn to do, move quickly. If she wanted to fit in here, speed seemed to be important, and she did want to fit in here. Oh, she did; and she meant to.

Manuel, happening to look toward her as she bustled about the table, thought, She's picking up quick. Yes, she was indeed. He kept his eyes for a few minutes on the swaying of her skirt as it hung from her slim hips; then turning his gaze to the fire, he looked into the flames that were straining up into the narrow funnel of the chimney and Margee came into his mind again. What had she said? He would eventually come to riches. Why should he think of Margee at this moment? Perhaps because she could see pictures in the fire. Was this house going to have some effect on his life? Well, he now glanced toward Agnes Fairbairn as she was going down the long room, her arms laden with dishes, and he thought wryly his fortunes wouldn't be favored by the daughter of the house as she was about to marry, so that fairy tale was ended before it began. But why should the feeling of Margee be strong on him at this moment? Would he meet somebody here? A woman, perhaps. Why was he asking such silly questions of himself when he knew he wanted to meet no woman?

Deep inside his mind he knew what he wanted. Impossible as it was, he knew what he wanted. But enough of all this fey thinking; for the time being he was well set. They were a grand family this, and no matter what work they expected of him, he knew he wouldn't change his opinion of them from what it was now, and if he had his way, he would stay as long as his predecessors.

What about Spain? It was Margee's face in the flame that was looking at him, and her voice seemed to shut out the laughter and chatter that surrounded the fireplace, and he answered her within himself, To the devil with Spain! I've come into a good harbor. I'm not sailing out of it unless I must, so prod me no more, Margee, and worry over me no more. Go now and rest easy.

4

The Plane Farm was so named because it was situated on an open piece of ground and had little or no shelter from the winds from whatever direction they came.

The farm carried a hundred and fifty head of cattle, at least two-thirds of them milking cows; sheep, pigs, geese and hens; there were fields that gave potatoes and beets in plenty and other vegetables to meet the requirements of every month in the year.

The farmhouse itself and fifty acres had been in the Fairbairn family for eight generations and these were stated in the Bible that lay in the center of the table in the parlor, but Mr. Fairbairn maintained there had been a cottage here for hundreds of years before the farm took shape, and it had housed Fairbairns.

The rest of the land, which ran to three hundred acres, was leased from Lord Stonebridge, whose home was Falcon House two miles away, built on the moors above the River Wear and within galloping distance of the town of Stanhope.

Within three days Manuel had got the lay of the land. He had fallen into the daily routine of the work as if he had been at it for years, and his liking for the Fairbairn family as a whole had deepened. The sons he termed "grand fellows." Their ma he would have liked to address as "Mother," as he had done Amy. Her daughter he termed a "fine lass," and his employer himself "a man, a real man."

What added to his pleasure a thousandfold was the fact

221

that there were six horses on the farm altogether. They weren't animals to be classed with those he had left back at the House, but nevertheless they were horses, each with its own characteristic likes and dislikes; four were big bushy-footed shires; one, an eighteen-year-old gray, ungainly and nothing to look at by horse standards, still retained the temperament of a sprightly young lady. The sixth was a young horse scarcely broken to farm work. But each gave him a particular joy, and Michael, whose job it was to see to the horses, was pleased and grateful at Manuel's interest and both amused and surprised at the way the animals responded to him, especially when he made the sound in his throat.

And then there was his house. It was a farm laborer's cottage, but to Manuel it was a house, for it was twice as big as the hovel that Skillen had provided, having four decent-sized rooms, all wood-floored except the kitchen, and a loft space into which, he surmised when looking along its length, you could get four beds, children's beds.

The last two nights he had lit the fire in the kitchen and Annabella had come over and given him his lesson. There was no set meal at night except when Mr. and Mrs. Fairbairn went to market. The usual procedure was breakfast at half-past seven, a smoke and a drink at eleven and dinner at half-past two which was so good and plentiful that it made you feel disinclined for work afterwards. Then in the evening there was a pan of broth always simmering on the hob from which you helped yourself, and from the cold meat, cheese and new bread that was left on the long shelf below the delft rack.

He was finished at six each evening, but every other evening he was on call until ten o'clock. His personal routine was that he would wash himself and change his shirt, placing his dirty one in a bucket of water to be rinsed out later. Then he would go across to the big kitchen and into the family atmosphere that warmed it. But after the second night sitting on that settle smoking his pipe, he knew that he was wasting his time, and so he startled the whole family when, addressing Mrs. Fairbairn, he said, "Would it be in order, missus, if Annabella came over to the house of a night for an hour or so to give me me lesson?"

They had all stopped what they were doing, talking, laughing, sewing, and stared from him to Annabella, who herself was sewing the beginning of a new work dress, for Mrs. Fairbairn had said the thing she was wearing would insult a scarecrow.

"Lessons?" Mr. Fairbairn's upper lip had squared from his teeth, and Manuel explained, "I'm learnin' me letters, sir."

"But you signed a good hand to your bond?"

"That's only a beginning, sir; I've a long way to go yet."

"Well, I never!" Agnes stared at Manuel, then gave a little giggle, only to be chided sternly by her mother, who, her needle still flying, her eyes attentive on her work, said, "Suit you better if you had all stuck to your lessons. Twenty books there are in the parlor and not one of them been touched for years. What books you reading, girl?"

Annabella swallowed before answering, "We—I haven't any books, only a newssheet, an old edition, and a slate and pencil."

"Well, if those in there are any use to you, you take them, girl." The eyes had not moved from the needle and Annabella, getting to her feet, said, "Oh, thank you, missus. Thank you so much."

They had all watched her go hurriedly across the room and into the parlor, and Sep, muttering to no one in particular, said, "She makes me sort of nervous, that one, you know; every time she opens her mouth she makes me nervous. Aw" —he glanced quickly at Manuel—"I don't mean no harm, I just mean—"

Manuel smiled at him, saying reassuredly, "I know what you mean. I feel the same at times."

"Sure?"

"Aye, sure."

They both grinned at each other now.

"Fancy being brought up in a convent and then having to—"

"You get on with your shift, our Agnes, unless you want to go naked across the moors come February."

At this there was a loud burst of laughter from the men and a protest from Agnes, saying, "Oh, our ma, fancy!"

And the young men had all cried together, "Fancy!" followed by another roar of laughter.

Manuel realized there was a liberty in this family that was unusual and refreshing.

When Annabella came back into the room, she had two books in her hand and it was Mrs. Fairbairn who, still without looking up, said, "What did you pick, girl?" and she answered, "One is *Gulliver's Travels*, Dean Swift's *Gulliver's Travels*, and the other is the fairy tales of Grimm."

Now it was Mr. Fairbairn who cried, "Ah, Grimm. My father, he bought me that one Christmas. Gave it as if he

223

were giving gold dust. Cost a penny or two, that I can tell you. Children's book it was supposed to be, scared the innards out of me. I was howling in the night until my mother threatened to light the fire with it. This lot"—he waved his hand around his family—"don't think one of them's opened it." He now nodded toward Annabella, saying, "Get you to read a story out come Christmas, girl. Snow on ground and fire roarin', plenty to eat and drink inside you an' listening to a story, like those old pictures. Yes, come Christmas, we'll do that."

Annabella inclined her head toward her master; then amid silence she and Manuel left the room.

When Annabella first saw Manuel's house, she had been as delighted as he was with it. "Wouldn't it have been wonderful," she said, "if this had been at Skillen's?" And he agreed with her.

They sat through one whole candle, and he scratched on his plate: rat, bat, cat, mat, sat and fat; then she made him use his tongue as he had never used it before when he said the word "cat," clicking it, snapping it, like a cat's claws themselves, at the roof of his mouth, not dawdling on the word with a gentle pat against the roof as when he pronounced it in his own way, as "caat." She also gave him a short homily on the use of "teach" and "learn," saying, "I can teach you, but only you can learn. I cannot learn you, you understand?"

He stared into her eyes as he nodded. Then he watched her lips as she went on, "Repeat, you teach, I learn." And automatically he said, "You teach, I learn," but somewhere in the back of his mind a voice was saying firmly, "It should be the other way round: I teach, you learn, learn the things I know of, the things you need to know to become whole, to become a woman." She was beginning to worry him when he had time to think about her, as now, and when he was abed.

The following night the boys chided them, saying to him, "Can't you learn here? Good light, everything, table there," and he had laughed back at them, saying, "Me face is red enough repeating 'cat,' 'mat' and 'sat' to the teacher." He thumbed toward Annabella. "I'd be dumb afore you all, or split me sides laughin'."

They went out in a gale of laughter.

Then came the dinner hour, when Annabella caused the greatest gale of laughter that already merry house had ever known. It happened that one of Annabella's duties was to carry the vegetables from the side table where Mrs. Fairbairn scooped them from pans into covered dishes. The biggest dish of all was one that held about twelve pounds of potatoes. Filled for the first helping, Annabella hurried with it to the top of the table, intending to place it between her master and Mr. Willy, but as she bent forward, Mr. Fairbairn in high good humor cried, "Ah, that's it, girl," and at the same time did a little manipulation with his fingers on the part of Annabella's anatomy that had never before been touched, except by old Alice or the nursemaid. With a squeal like a cat whose tail had got caught in the mangle—this was Michael's description later—she seemed to throw the dish of potatoes up into the air, causing them to rain on the heads of Mr. Fairbairn and Willy, then catch it again, after which feat she leaned against the table, shivering amid the cries and shouts.

"What ails thee, girl? Did you ever! Stop that cursing, Mr. Fairbairn. And you Willy, you're not dead."

"No, Ma, only scalded silly."

"Out of the way, girl. What happened to you anyway?"

"Not her fault. Not her fault." Mr. Fairbairn was now knocking the last remnants of potato from his shoulder as he stated flatly. "Pinched her backside; not used to it likely."

"P-p-pinched her b-backside." Sep, from the bottom of the table, looked at Annabella, his face contorted with glee; then slowly there rumbled up out of his thick chest a great laugh, and as it mounted he pointed to the top of Willy's head, on which still reposed, embedded in the thick, sandy hair, a piece of potato.

They all now looked at Willy, and as his fingers extracted the last segment, his body, too, began to shake.

Then Michael joined in.

Mr. Fairbairn fought against it for a few minutes but soon he, too, was leaning on the table, his head in his hands.

Now Agnes was roaring, her mouth wide. Then to cap all, Mrs. Fairbairn, dropping onto a chair, lifted her apron up to her face to smother her laughter.

But the last person to let go was Manuel. To hear of anybody nipping Miss Annabella Lagrange's backside would have been funny enough, but to be present at the incident—it was the most laugh-provoking thing he had seen in many a year. But because she was no longer Miss Annabella Lagrange and because he knew just how she was feeling at this moment, he had tried to restrain his mirth. But now, the whole family convulsed, he dropped his chin on his chest and, covering his eyes with his hand, he joined them.

It was too much for Annabella. She hurried from the room through the scullery and into the washhouse, and there she pressed her hands over her face, her fingers on her eyeballs to stop the rush of tears that threatened and which she considered would strip her of all dignity. For the moment she forgot about the kindness of her new employers; she forgot that this very morning she had awakened thinking, I could be happy here, that is, as long as Manuel stays, for now she couldn't visualize a situation where Manuel wouldn't be present. Why had this happened to her? she asked once more. Not just the fact that her master had taken a liberty with her, but that she had been put in a position where this could happen. Oh, she wished it was a year ago and she could have died before she was brought to this humiliating experience.

The latch of the washhouse door lifted, but she didn't turn round. She knew by his silence that it was Manuel. When, taking hold of her arms, he turned her about she would not look at him.

"Come on, he meant no offense. He's more troubled than you are and—and just as surprised." The ripple in his voice made her want to tug her arms away from his hands, but she remained still. "Come on; they're waiting for you."

"I—I don't want any dinner, thank you."

"Now look." His tone became serious. "They're good people, but they'll be offended, and you must remember we're in no position to offend them. They're wantin' their dinner; they're hungry, but they're waiting for you, so come on."

His tone brought her eyes upwards. There was no vestige of laughter on his face now; he was telling her who she was, and retaliation in any form was not for her.

After a big intake of breath that swelled the white skin of her neck above her collar, she turned from him and went out, and when she entered the kitchen she saw that they actually were waiting for her, and this very fact humbled her.

As she took her seat, Mr. Fairbairn looked down the table at her, saying, "No offense meant, girl," to which she answered, her head bent again, "I'm sorry, sir; it was my fault."

"Well, no more talk, get on with your dinners." Mrs. Fairbairn was in command again, and they all ate their dinners. But Annabella was aware that the laughter, although not in evidence, was still rumbling through the bodies of the three sons, if not of the father, because, should they happen to look at her, they would flick their glance quickly away and, their shoulders hunched, they would attack their food with vigor.

But before the day was out she was even smiling at the

incident herself; smiling, not laughing. It was when Agnes, going through the daily routine of the work with her, was showing her the ropes. This being Friday was parlor day; they were brushing plush chairs, shaking antimacassars, dusting dozens of little ornaments, and finally sprinkling the carpet liberally with wet bran; after which, starting from each end of the room, they swept it up again, so cleaning it and bringing up the pile. It was during this labor when they met in the middle of the room that Agnes turned her big body from her knees and, sitting down, began to rock herself, saying, "I'm still seeing you, you know. It was the funniest thing ever happened in that kitchen. If Betty had done that every time me da's pinched her backside, we wouldn't have a dish left. Was it first time you had your backside pinched?"

Annabella stopped her sweeping; she became still on her hands and knees as she looked at Agnes, then slowly she began to smile, then just as slowly she admitted, "Yes, it was the first time."

"Fancy that now. Wait till I tell Betty. Aw, I wish Betty could have been there; she would have laughed louder than any of us. You'll like Betty. Nice girl, Betty; jolly and willin'."

They finished the carpet. Then Agnes demonstrated how she cleaned the mantelpiece. "Strip everything off first," she said; "all the vases and the miniatures and, mind, be careful of the miniatures because Ma wouldn't mind how many vases got broken, but she'd go mad if one of these was scratched."

The miniatures, Annabella saw, were small paintings of children. There were thirteen of them and because they all had a similarity about them, she asked, "Are these relatives?" and Agnes replied, "Relatives! I should say. They're all our family, our brothers and sisters."

"But—but thirteen?"

"Yes, Ma's had thirteen of us, but all the rest died atween five and ten, mostly with the typhoid. She just managed to rear us four."

This piece of news reduced Annabella to a staring silence. That little woman in the kitchen had lost nine children between the ages of five and ten. It didn't seem possible.

"They're all buried over at Stanhope. Every Sunday, rain, hail or snow, that's if the drifts are not too high, after church Ma goes up to the graves and she has something for each. It might just be some holly berries but always something. Don't look like that—it's all right; she's over it. The last one went nigh ten years ago. You're not crying, are you?"

"No. No."

227

"Ma never cries. Well, if she does it's in the night; I've never seen her cry. Ma's a great woman."

"Yes, yes, I'm sure she is."

They were at the spinet now and Agnes said, "Always take care to lift the lid and dust the keys; and be careful, there's a loose one in the base." Then looking at Annabella brightly, she said, "You know I learned this. I had lessons for a whole year. One day a month I went into Hexham. It took a full day to get that hour's lesson. But it was a waste of time; I hadn't the hands for it, nor the mind. Did you learn an instrument in your convent?"

"Yes." Annabella nodded her head. "The pianoforte."

"Really! Well then, you'll be able to play this. We've got stacks of music up in the attic. Me granda, him that used to read the books"—she pointed to the shelf—"he could play this, and Da keeps it tuned; he has the man coming once a year. Would you like to play something now?"

"Oh no, no, not while I'm working."

"Go on, Ma wouldn't mind."

"No, I'd rather not. Perhaps later."

"Tomorrow night." Agnes's face was one big beam. "We always have a get-together on a Saturday night. Dave comes over, that's my young man, that's his night for coming, Saturday, and Michael goes over to the Pranks to see Lizzie and he generally brings her back 'cause they're a doleful bunch, the Pranks; and Sep's girl, Sarah, she comes over in the winter, but in the summer they go into the town. But now, just think, if you'd play the piano, we could have a bit of a do. I love a bit of a do." Agnes moved her head widely. "At New Year we always have a good do. Can you play dances, do you think?"

"I could play waltzes."

"Oh, that would be grand. Later on I'll tell Ma and see what she says. By the way—" Agnes raised her finger warningly now to Annabella, saying, "Tomorrow night when they're all here you'd better be prepared because somebody'll tell about the day's do; the lads will do anything for a laugh, so you mustn't be offended. Now will you?"

Annabella's eyelids drooped before she said, "No; it's all right, Agnes. I won't be offended."

"Good girl." Agnes nodded at her now; then attacking the work with renewed vigor, she ended, "By! I'm going to look forward to tomorrow night; I'll get the lads to go up into the attic and rake out the music. Ee! fancy being able to have a do in November. I'm glad you've come, Annabella, I am that. I knew I'd be when I first clapped eyes on you."

"Thank you, Agnes, thank you."

And they had "a do" on the Saturday night. Annabella and Manuel were introduced to Dave Pearson, a young farmer and Agnes's husband-to-be, and Miss Lizzie Pranks and Miss Sarah Percy, simply by "Here you Dave, you Lizzie and Sarah, this is the girl, Annabella, and the man, Manuel." This was followed by a nodding of heads, then a complete ignoring of them for the time being while the visitors vied with each other to tell of this happening over at Stanhope where Miss Percy lived and the doings of the week in Woolsingham from Miss Pranks. Dave Pearson talked loudly to Mr. Fairbairn and was definitely out to impress. Annabella thought that he didn't seem nice enough for Agnes; it also came to her that, of all the five men present, not one of them looked as well as Manuel, although Michael, Sep and Mr. Pearson were in broadcloth and Mr. Fairbairn and Willy, who, because they had to do a last round of the animals, were still in their knee cords but had donned fresh shirts and coats, while Manuel was wearing cords, freshly washed and showing it, as cords did after contact with water. His shirt and neckerchief were clean but his coat was stained here and there, yet he carried these clothes as none of the other men did. There could be no doubt that she herself was the shabbiest of the women, yet, the Miss Annabella Lagrange not quite dead in her, she felt a certain superiority to them, not perhaps over Mrs. Fairbairn and Agnes, but decidedly over the two prospective brides, one of whom minced and aimed at being "refeened" and pronounced her words wrongly—this was Miss Lizzie Pranks.

When Agnes, grabbing Annabella up from the corner of the settle where she was quietly sitting, watching and listening, said, "Come on into the parlor, Annabella, and do your pieces," the visitors stopped talking and stared at the new girl, and Agnes cried at them, "She plays! Wait till you hear."

And in the parlor Agnes, picking up one of the pieces that had been set apart on top of the piano, whispered, "Play this first, just to let them see."

As Annabella sat down at the piano, she smiled inwardly as she thought that Agnes looked upon her as an asset. It wasn't everybody who had a housemaid who could play the pianoforte—"hard bits" as Agnes had dubbed them last night,

229

when she had played pieces from Beethoven and Mozart. The piece Agnes handed her now was Mozart's *Sonata in A Flat minor*.

As Annabella began to play, Agnes ran to the parlor door, crying, "Shut up, will you! Listen. Listen."

And they listened, and gradually they came into the room, awkwardly at first, and seated themselves near the fire; but they all looked toward the spinet and Annabella, and when she had finished and turned slightly toward them, and they still looked at her and didn't speak, she said, "I'm—I'm slightly out of practice."

"Coo! I wouldn't mind being out of practice and play like that, what do you say?" Michael pushed his fiancée, and Lizzie Pranks answered somewhat stiffly, "It was a very nice execution," and on this Annabella had to turn quickly toward the piano again before she was tempted to say, "Well, I will try to kill this one, too." When she played "Gigue," the crossing of her hands impressed the company as much as the music, but her talent also embarrassed them a little, and Manuel was aware of this. He was the only one who hadn't seated himself. He was standing to the side of the piano a few feet away and near the wall and, as she played, he never took his eyes off her. The music aroused in him a tender sadness, and at the same time a wild, deep longing that took on the form of a pain, not only because of the hopelessness of it but because of the sight she presented to him, her sad face crowned with that mass of gleaming brown hair and her body covered with clothes that any decent maid would be ashamed to own.

He must buy her some things. Why hadn't he thought of it before? She was making that dress but it would be weeks before it was ready. He'd buy her a dress, and shoes. What matter if it lightened his belt? He should have done it when they were in Hexham.

They were clapping now, and he clapped with them, and the sons were all exclaiming their praises.

"Why, Annabella girl! Never heard anything like it."

"You could play on the stage."

"Seems a pity you have to do housework when you can play like that." Willy was the last speaker and he stood looking down at her, his eyes shaded, his lips slightly apart. Manuel watched him. He knew the signs when a man was taken with a woman, and his stomach muscles contracted and his thoughts started to gallop.

"If you could catch taters as fast as you could play, Annabella, you would have done a juggling trick yesterday; did you hear about it?" Willy turned now, laughing widely, saying, "Aw, I've never laughed so much in me life."

Ten minutes later, the joke against her exhausted, at Agnes's request she played a waltz, and out of time and rather ungainly the three couples hopped around the kitchen table, while Manuel and Willy watched her, and Mr. and Mrs. Fairbairn sat comfortably back and enjoyed the performance as a whole.

The dance over, amid laughter and clapping, they ate from the dishes on the sideboard, and drank parsnip wine. Then it was Mrs. Fairbairn who said to her son, "Get your whistle out, Willy, and let them do the de Coverley. Can you do the de Coverley dance, Annabella?"

Could she do the de Coverley? Yes, and the mazurka and the minuet. She said quietly, "Yes, missus."

"Well then, you take Manuel and get into your places."

And so for the first time she danced with Manuel, and felt strangely and deeply excited.

When nine o'clock came there were great exclamations on how the time had flown. Warmed with hot soup, the visitors took their leave. Accompanied by Michael and Sep, they crowded into the trap amid hilarious laughter.

Back in the house, Annabella and Agnes cleared away the debris of dishes, then they tidied the parlor, for they couldn't leave it until the Monday, for on a Sunday there was no work of that kind done, Agnes explained, except what was absolutely necessary for eating.

Manuel went out with Willy to take a last look round the cattle, and not until they were finishing their round did Willy say, "It's been a grand night, Manuel!"

"Yes, Mr. Willy, it's been a grand night; best I've known in a long time."

"Same here. Your cousin, she's a very accomplished girl."

"She is."

"It's a great pity."

"What is?"

"Well, I mean that she should be in the position she is with all her accomplishments; great pity her folks died. Must have been a blow."

"It was. Yes, it was."

"Good-night, Manuel."

"Good-night, Mr. Willy."

Manuel went straight to his house. It was dark and cold. The evening's enjoyment had faded. He lit a candle and got quickly into bed, but not to sleep. He lay staring into the blackness and after a time he said aloud, "Good-night, Manuel. Good-night, Mr. Willy."

It was the end of a train of thought that had been very revealing.

5

On Sunday they all went to church with the exception of Manuel, who was left to look after the place. In the break, Willy sat next to Annabella and on the journey he pointed out different places of interest to her. That was Bolt's Burn; over there near Rookhope there were some fine waterfalls, grand sights; and at Tunstall there was good fishing; and had she ever been round the castle and caves in Stanhope?

She liked Willy; he was kind and it went a long way to make up for his coarse looks and equally coarse voice.

That he should have taken his seat next to her in the church was not lost on the family, and Agnes, while sorting the enormous pile of washing which was the Monday morning's chore, laughed as she said, "You know something, Annabella, our Willy's smitten with you." Then "Oh my! you've gone the color of beetroot."

"Please, Agnes, you shouldn't say—"

"But I do say, 'cause it's true. Be funny if you should cotton on to him, wouldn't it?"

As Annabella stared at the daughter of the house, she realized she was utterly devoid of any feeling of class distinction and that were she herself to become—smitten by Willy she would be accepted by this family. It was very strange, for they were not poor farmers like the Skillens.

"Mind you, if it were the case, it wouldn't be smooth going, not with Betty here it wouldn't. She's had her eye on our Willy this three year back, but he don't take no notice of her. Well, not much; laughs with her like 'cause it gets lonely out here at times in the winter. I'm glad you've come, Annabella, I'm glad you and Manuel have come. Manuel's fine-looking, isn't he? I wished my Dave looked a bit like him." She giggled now. "But Dave's all right and he's doing fine; seventy-five acres he's got now and all his own. It's a marvelous start. Come February I'll be gone, can't believe it. Anyway, by that time you'll be doing all this with your eyes shut." She lifted up a dozen flannel shirts and thrust them into

232

a tub of soapy water, then taking a heavy possing stick, she wielded it as if it were a wooden spoon, and as she pummeled the clothes, she said, "Mind you see that Betty takes her fair share with the wash; she doesn't like washing, Betty. Doesn't mind anything else, kitchen, dairy, anything, but she doesn't like washing. She should be here tomorrow."

To all this Annabella smiled inwardly and thought that Agnes talked exactly like her mother; and she wondered a little about this Betty, but she felt that if she was a girl whom all the family liked, then she must have some quality and she herself couldn't fail to like her.

On the Tuesday night Betty arrived at half-past eight, but Annabella didn't meet her then for she was in bed, Mrs. Fairbairn having packed her off a half an hour earlier because her nose and eyes were running and she was sneezing. The alternation between the steaming-hot washhouse and the bleak field where she hung out the clothes yesterday had given her a cold.

After being given a dose of cough mixture that almost choked her, and a jar holding goose fat, which Mrs. Fairbairn said she must rub on her chest, she had come upstairs. But not to sleep.

It was almost an hour and a half later when, wide awake and curious, she head Agnes's voice long before she reached the attic landing, and she was saying, "Your bed's in the same place; we put her over by the window. You'll like her; we've all taken to her. An' what do you think about him, Manuel? He's something, isn't he? He's got good manners for a cowman, don't you think? Still, it's 'cause he hasn't been a cowman long, was a coachman for years. Bit a mystery about him, I think, like her. She's different. 'Twas the convent as I told you, but you'll like her, oh you'll like her."

The door opened and the candlelight flickered over the ceiling and Agnes whispered, "You see, she's not in your way. Good-night. You'll sleep like a top."

"Good-night, Agnes. Ta. I'm glad I'm back."

"So's we."

The door closed. There were soft footsteps across the room. The bed became illuminated with light. She stared upwards into the eyes above her, and the eyes stared back at her. They were screwed up, narrowed in perplexity while her own were wide and stretching wider as memory thrust her back down the years to when this face had been prominent in her life. It was fatter now, older, but it was still the same face,

233

the face of Watford. Staring as if hypnotized, she watched all its features registering the incredibility of the situation. She watched the candle go higher and Watford's face come closer to hers; she watched her drop backwards onto the foot of her bed, and then she heard her whisper, "In the name of God, Miss Annabella! It is, isn't it, Miss Annabella? You've hardly altered."

Annabella did not speak; she was leaning back on her elbows now, still and taut, and she remained like that for minutes until Betty said, "I heard you'd been lost. They said you'd been drowned after you were thrown out—"

Annabella pulled herself up and leaned against the wall and she watched Watford's features smooth themselves out and into an odd smile, and it was with the smile that the fear erupted in her. Watford was talking low and rapidly now, "Well, I never! Funny how things turn out, isn't it? My God, the times I've cursed you, specially during those first two years when I couldn't get a decent place 'cause I hadn't got a reference. Why did you leave your last place, they said? 'Cause I called the daughter a 'bastard.' Could I say that? No. I had to lie like a trooper. I was in seven jobs durin' those two years. Do you know that?" She now poked her head forward.

There was another silence before she began speaking again and again prefaced with the words, "My God!" She was shaking her head widely now. "I just can't believe it, you playin' at bein' dead, and alive and kickin' here. Me da told me you were in the papers and the police were lookin' for you all over. An' it's true what he said an' all, the mighty are always brought low: old Lagrange breakin' his neck or somethin', the business gone flat, the place all shut up. Aye, aye, how are the mighty brought low. But here, wait a minute." Her voice rose and she straightened her body, put out her arm and placed the candlestick on the top of a low chest of drawers, then hitching herself slightly up the bed, she leaned forward again. "This cousin business, him down there, that Manuel. He's no relation, never heard of him. He's not a gentleman. How come the cousin business?"

Annabella tried to speak. She opened her mouth twice, but the words wouldn't come. She was staring at Betty as a rabbit would in its last seconds before the ferret choked it, and here was a ferret. Betty had always been a ferret, and a talker, a gossip.

"Look! you're no longer Miss Annabella so you can drop your airs; I haven't to wait any longer to speak afore I'm

234

spoken to. I've just asked you a civil question. Who's this cousin you've dug up?"

"Oh! Oh! Watford, I can exp—"

The bed creaked with the sharp movement of Betty's body, and her voice was equally sharp as she muttered, "That's enough of the Watford. The time's past when you can call me 'Watford,' me name's Betty, and failin' that, I'm 'Miss Watford.' I've got a name if you haven't, and I'm not sorry for sayin' it, either. I've suffered enough at your folks' hands, and yours an' all, quiet, underhand, sneaky little brat that you were. . . . Well, who is he?"

Annabella pulled herself from the wall and, joining her hands tightly on the coverlet, she bent forward. She was overcome with a feeling of helplessness and fear. She could see Betty downstairs tomorrow morning telling them all the whole story. She could see herself and Manuel on the road again, tramping, tramping. She had only been in this house six days, yet it felt like six years. She had touched on the fringe of a happiness and contentment that she never knew existed, and now this chance encounter could be the end of it. Her voice held a deep note of pleading, pleading for understanding as she said, "He's—he's not my cousin, Betty. We—I had to say that because we were traveling together. He was the groom. He came just after you left. He taught me to ride and was good to me, so when the catastrophe—" She paused. "When it happened, I left the House."

"Aye, you did an' all." Betty now nodded her head. "And you went down to Crane Street, didn't you? It was all over the place, me da said, and what you found out there made you do yourself in, so the story went. Everybody's sorry for you, but they wouldn't be if they knew where you were. But why did you come on the road with him? Did you plan it, eh?"

"No, I didn't plan it. Of course, I didn't plan it."

Betty could almost hear Mrs. Lagrange speaking and she pulled her chin in and compressed her lips as Annabella went on, "I was ill, I didn't know what I was doing. I must have lain on the moors for two nights and then a cottager took me in. It happened that she was a friend of Manuel's and—and so as I wanted to make my way to London and he was going that way, I—we—well we journeyed together."

"I'll say you did." The words were weighed with insolence. "But why did you stop afore you got to London?"

"We—we wanted a little money and—and a place for the winter."

235

"And so you landed here on the Plane."

It was as if she had said, "And God has delivered you into my hands." Annabella closed her eyes and bowed her head, but only for a moment. Looking at Betty again, she implored her now, "Please, please, Betty, don't say anything, don't tell them who I am. I—I couldn't bear it."

"It remains to be seen, doesn't it?" Betty got to her feet. "They're good folks these, none better. There's not many families kickin' round like them. But one thing they don't like is liars. I found that out early on. Speak the truth and shame the devil, the mistress says, an' that's what they stand by, the lot of them. Cousins! How long have you been on the road with him?"

When Annabella made no reply, Betty gave herself the answer. "June it happened, didn't it? And now here's November. Five months, long time to be traveling around together, ain't it, a young lady and the groom?"

Another silence followed this statement; then Betty was speaking again. Her tone, no longer lightly jeering, was bitter now as she said, "It's funny, God works in strange ways, He does that. The night when I got home after what happened on the road I thought I would have died. I daren't tell me ma or da 'cause they wouldn't have believed me. They would have said I'd been havin' me fling and that's why I got the push, an' it would have been no use tellin' them to ask me Aunt Eva Page 'cause she was finished with us. Do you know what happened to me that night—MISS ANNABELLA?" She waited, then went on, "A man attacked me, an old, dirty, filthy man. I took shelter in a field barn 'cause it was pourin' whole water and he was in the straw and he practically tore me clothes off me back. I had never been with anybody in me life, keeping meself, I was, for when the right fellow come along, and then this filthy old beggar. I was bad for over a month and I nearly went mad thinking of what might come of it. Oh, I've got a lot to thank you for, Miss Annabella. Me ma always used to say, afore she died, God rest her, that the mills of God grind slow, an' they surely do, but they grind all right."

In the deep, deep silence that fell on the room, Annabella lay taut, and, as Rosina would have done, she was asking God why He was allowing these things to happen to her. She had done no wrong, yet she was being made to pay for other people's sins. Why? Why? And how was she to go on living in this house with Watford hating her like this? She couldn't, she just couldn't. She'd have to tell Manuel that she couldn't.

It was seven o'clock the following evening when she told Manuel that she couldn't stay. Facing him across the table in the cottage, she said, "I just can't stay here, I just can't. Today has been terrible."

He had guessed there was something wrong at breakfast time, and after dinner, back in the cow sheds, Michael had said to him, "They're not going to take to each other. Now isn't that a pity? Two nice lasses and not hitting it off." He had laughed then and said, "The reason's likely because they praised Annabella up to the skies afore Betty hardly got in the door. 'Well, all right,' she said, 'but what's she like at her work?' and our Agnes said, 'Oh, she's as willing as a puppy.' And Betty came back with, 'Well, I'm an old bitch and she'd better be careful.' But then she had gone upstairs laughing. And now Ma says she's been acting like an old bitch toward the puppy all day. Ma's troubled at the situation. She liked the house happy."

With his forearms on the table and his hands joined tightly and his head poked forward, Manuel peered through the candlelight at her and slowly he began to speak. "Now, listen here, Annabella, let's get this straight right away. I'm not leavin' here and you're not leavin' here. The winter's on us; it's going to be long and hard and cold. Where would we find another position at this time of the year? And if that were possible, would the people be anything like these folks are? No, no, you bet your life they wouldn't; these are one family in a thousand. I told you, I feel settled here and they like the way I work, and we have plans, the lads and I. We're going to pave that yard; in our spare time we're going to start cartin' the stones from Brank Quarry. We're going to make a road like I did at Skillen's. What I'm sayin' is I'm set here. I know when I'm on a good thing. I want to work for these people, I want to settle here for good, you understand?"

She was gazing at him, her lips slightly apart. "You—you mean for life, all your life?"

"Aye, yes, if need be."

She looked down at the books on the table, the slate and pencil, and she said, "You don't want to get on, rise, be—be your own master in some place?"

"Huh!" His head went back on his shoulders. Then bringing it forward again and tapping his finger on a book, he said, "You're talking like him, Mr. Grimm and his fairy tales. How would I become me own master? I haven't a trade. The only thing I could be master of would be a tinker's cart. You know,

237

I'll tell you something." His head came nearer to hers. "Deep inside I've always objected to workin' for another man, and I've had what you call"—he again tapped the book—"a phrase, that's what I suppose you'd call it, a phrase, and it went, 'I'm me own man'; always in times of strain or trouble I would yell inside meself, 'You're your own man, Manuel Mendoza,' and I made meself believe I was me own man. But what I wouldn't face up to was I would never be in a position to have any men under me. Now these past few days I've said, 'To hell with being me own man. I'll be Mr. Fairbairn's man. I'll settle here.'" He stopped; then his voice dropped to a soft murmur. "I had plans all made out to settle in this house, to make it—me home." He now raised his head and moved his eyes about the room. When he brought his gaze back to hers, he held her eyes but didn't speak for a moment, and when he did, he said softly, "I'm twenty-seven years old, Annabella. I need a wife."

She felt her body slowly recoiling from him. Her stooped shoulders straightened. She was sitting upright but he hadn't moved, and like that he said, his voice slightly louder now, "Don't look so shocked, it's natural."

"I'm—I'm not shocked, and as you say, it's natural."

"Yes, as I said, it's natural."

Her eyes still stared into his. "Then if you married I—I could go—?"

"Yes." He pulled his body up straight. "Yes, of course, you could go." His voice sounded airy now, careless. "But not until the spring; an' I'm not going to marry tomorrow or the next day, for that matter, or next week. I—I'll have to look around. I'm particular, always have been where women are concerned. I've been able to pick and choose; I've been fortunate in that way."

Her head was hanging deeply on her chest as if in defense against his bantering tone and the dejection of her brought him to her side. Gripping her hands, he said briskly, "Look, no more of this. We'll fix her somehow, I'll get round her." He shook her hands, trying to bring her eyes up to his. "I'll tell her some of my tales. I'll turn on the old Irish charm. It's a bit rusty because I haven't used it for some time, but I'll have a go. I'll bring her round."

Her head remained bent. His proposal didn't please her. She didn't like the idea of his telling Betty tales in order to bring her round. When she was still silent, he dropped her hands and said harshly, "Well, what the devil! Let her tell them. We'll tell our side, all except one thing." His voice dropped. "The last night at Amy's." He paused before going quickly on, "But for the rest, I think I've weighed these people up well enough to know whose side they'll be on; they'll all be for you when they know."

"No, Manuel, I couldn't bear it, not—not for them to know about my beginnings. You see"—she shook her head in a desperate fashion—"you don't understand how it has affected me, is still affecting me. You don't realize what a divided parentage like this can—can mean."

"Don't I?" He was sitting opposite her again now, and, his head nodding slowly, he said, "You know what you've got to realize is that all this has happened afore, and to dozens, hundreds, thousands of people. You're not the only one who's got shaken up in the breeding bag." He stared at her, looking deep into her green eyes, willing her not to shutter their gaze; then he asked a question, "Do you like the name 'Manuel Mendoza'?"

The movement of her head was impatient and suggested that she didn't want to play games, but after a moment she answered, "Yes; I think it is a very attractive name."

"So did I the first time I heard it. You know what me real name is? It's Tommy—Tommy McLaughlin. Yes." He moved his head downwards. "Me name's Tommy McLaughlin. The other I picked for meself one day on the quay in Dublin. It's true. It's true. You can believe me on this. I had been brought up by the McLaughlins, but I knew I wasn't of them. Margee, the one I told you about, well, her mother was a midwife of sorts, and one day a girl comes into the village on a carrier cart an' she was well near her time. The carrier didn't know where she came from; he had picked her up on the road a few miles back. Within eight hours of her stepping down, I was born, and this is no Irish story I'm telling you. It's the truth. She was no great shakes, Margee said, meaning 'no class,' but she had money on her, enough to pay for the laying-in, and quite a bit over. Anyway, when I was ten days old, she walked out. No one saw her go or heard of her after. She left me there, together with ten golden sovereigns. Margee's mother took the sovereigns and brought me up, and when she died, Margee took over and I was known as 'Tommy McLaughlin,' until this day on the quay. And there we were walking along, Margee and me. I was about ten at the time, and down a gangway from one of the boats stepped a man. He was tall and dark and foreign-looking; he could have been an Italian or a Spaniard or anything. We didn't even notice him in passing, he was just another man, and he was some distance away when another figure appeared at the top of the gangway and yelled, 'Manuel! Manuel! Manuel Mendoza there!' There was something songlike, something catchy about the name, 'Man-u-el Men-doz-a.' It had a sort of swing, 'Man-u-el Men-doz-a.' I said to Margee, 'What would that man be?' and she said, 'Oh, a Spaniard likely with a name like that.' I said to her, 'Do I look like a Spaniard?' and looking at me, she said, 'Aye, a bit. You do a bit. But then I've known blond Italians and in parts of Ireland there are faces like yours as thick as blades of grass.'

"But I had already decided to be Spanish, so she didn't put me off. And I said to her that night, 'I'm going to take the name of that man, I'm goin' to be Manuel Mendoza.' And she clipped me ear affectionately and said, 'You're Tommy McLaughlin, you're as good as me own.' But inside, from that day, I was Manuel Mendoza." There was a long pause before he added, "I likely haven't any more Spanish blood in me than you have, I'm bastard Irish; but bastards need something, something to lean on, a crutch of some sort."

"Oh, Manuel!" There were tears in her voice. "You make me feel ashamed."

"I'm glad of that." He pushed his chair back and got to his feet, his voice airy again. Then swiftly stooping toward her, he said, "Leave it to me, I'll see to her. She won't say anything, I promise you; and if she should get under your skin too much, stand up to her, you know, like you did to those two fellows a week gone. Don't bash her with your bundle but give her some tongue; it's the only thing her type understands—give her some tongue."

Again she said, "Oh, Manuel!" and this as a protest against the possibility of her giving Betty some tongue. Yet before another week had passed she had done just that.

It was fortunate, Annabella considered, that she hadn't to work with Betty, for then the strain would indeed have been too great. They met only at mealtimes and in the evening when, returning from Manuel's cottage, she would take up her sewing and sit on the settle and speak only when she was spoken to.

But there were times when she saw Betty from the windows. The sons' rooms overlooked the back of the house and the farmyard, and from the window she had seen Betty laughing with Manuel in the yard; and another time she had seen them coming out of the dairy together, and Betty had pushed Manuel playfully with the flat of her hand. The gesture had indicated that Manuel was doing as he promised—seeing to Betty. And she was surprised that their apparent familiarity should vex her. But it was this that caused her to use her tongue.

It was on a Friday night just before she went to bed. The day had been trying in the extreme. Manuel and Sep had driven in to Hexham around noon, taking in half a dozen pigs to a pork butcher whom Mr. Fairbairn supplied, and they were picking up shopping for Mrs. Fairbairn, and, as it turned out to be Betty's half day, she had gone with them. When they returned at six o'clock in the evening, they were all singing loudly, and when they entered the kitchen loaded with parcels, they were laughing and talking as if they had been on a great spree. Annabella did not look at Manuel, nor did she go across at seven o'clock to give him his lesson, and Betty, while they were both in the scullery, taunted her, saying, "What! you not goin' to learn the child his letters the night?"

Annabella had forced herself to remain silent and she had excused herself from the kitchen early and gone up to her room, not to get into bed, but to sit fuming on the edge of it until Betty entered. And then she had startled her with her attack.

Betty had hardly closed the door behind her when Annabella, springing up and standing at her tallest, said, "I'm standing no more of this, *Watford*." She laid stress on the name. "I give you permission to go down now and tell them everything."

"You give me what?"

The answer came back as if from Miss Annabella Lagrange. "You heard what I said. I give you permission to go down now and tell them everything. Everything, do you hear me?"

"Oh, do you, madam? Well, I'm gonna tell you somethin'. I'll pick me own time when to tell them."

"All right, if you won't, then I will." On this she marched toward the door, only to have Betty bar her way, hissing under her breath, "Don't be daft! What will they think?"

"I don't care what they think. Whatever they think will be preferable to putting up with your tyranny, your blackmail."

They were close enough to feel their breath on each other's face. Betty, looking at this transformed Miss Annabella, didn't need time to think out the situation; she knew that if Annabella went downstairs and told the family the truth, she herself would come badly out of it, not only for harassing her but for the real reason why she had to leave the Lagrange

241

household. It was a different tale altogether from what she had told. Her tale had been that she had been persecuted by the master, and through this she had instantly gained their sympathy.

She also knew that no matter what her feelings were with regard to Willy, he thought nothing of her except to have a laugh on the side. But this Manuel now, he was a different kettle of fish, and he was taken with her, he had made that plain. And with the insight of her kind, she guessed that this was the reason why madam here was on her high horse, because she couldn't have traveled with him all these months without getting attached in some way, high lady that she still thought she was, for he was a likable fellow. Oh aye, and different somehow from the ordinary run. So if she let her go downstairs now, the outcome would be that they would both go off and that would be the end of that; and her position in this house would never be the same again. She'd have to go wary. Like it or not, she'd have to put a different face on things, so with an effort she made herself droop her head and say, "I'm sorry I plagued you; but you would have done the same in my place. You don't know what it was like those first two years tryin' to get settled with no reference; driven from pillar to post I was, 'cause they couldn't keep me at home; nine of them there."

The stiffness gradually went out of Annabella's back, her neck muscles slackened and her head drooped. For the moment she forgot that just a short while previously Betty had come in singing with Manuel. She forgot her taunting as she thought, She's right. I don't really know what it would be like, even with the rough experience of the past months, because during all the vicissitudes she'd had Manuel with her.

Slowly she turned away and walked toward her bed, and Betty toward hers. An uneasy truce had been effected.

6

Christmas came with knife-edged winds and flurries of snow which made Mr. Fairbairn prophesy, "We're in for it, and it's going to be long and hard. These winds will harden the ground and the snow will lie for weeks. So mistress, you'd better think two months ahead when making the list out for the town."

The house was gay and warm and the atmosphere happy.

Everybody laughed and joked, and they all, with the exception of Betty, tried to draw Annabella into their gaiety. But, as Mr. Fairbairn said to his wife when in bed, "Her face is getting more like the alabaster head in the parlor every day. No movement in it, and yet when she first come, there wasn't a livelier miss. It's to do with Betty. There's been jealousy atween them right from the start, but more so since Manuel turned his eyes toward the elder. And you can take me for a fool if that Annabella's feelings are just cousinly toward him. For my part it don't matter which either one gets him so long as he stays, for there's never been a more agreeable man in the sheds, an' he's a real wonder with the horses. And what's more, he can turn his hand to most anything; show him once and he's got it. The cottage is ready: let him make his choice and I'll give him a wedding of which he'll not be ashamed."

"Can't see it," said Mrs. Fairbairn tersely; "if he takes one or t'other, there's going to be trouble."

"Well, there's one thing certain," remarked her husband before turning over and going to sleep; "he can't have both. Pity, but there 'tis." And on this he chuckled deeply.

Manuel had only mentioned Betty once to Annabella since the day following her arrival. "She's let up on you, hasn't she?" he said, and when she didn't answer but just stared at him, he demanded, "Well, hasn't she? She's different, pleasanter?" And to this she answered somewhat primly, "Yes, I suppose you could say that."

"Well, then." He frowned at her. "It's all right, I told you it would be."

Then came Christmas Eve. Manuel had cleaned up the main room in the cottage, the fire was burning brightly, two candles were alight on the table and above the mantelpiece a bunch of holly was tied.

Her face white and straight, Annabella stood facing him. She hadn't come to give him a lesson; she hadn't given him a lesson for over a fortnight because everybody had been busy with the preparations for the holiday. She had come to give him a Christmas present; she had decided to do it this way rather than present it to him in front of everyone tomorrow. When leaving Skillen's farm, she had had twenty shillings in her possession, but after buying a toothbrush and some tooth powder, a piece of linen and silks with which to make a wedding present for Agnes, and some lawn to make handkerchiefs to give as Christmas presents, she had had eight shillings left, and three days ago she had gone into

Hexham in the cart and spent seven and sixpence on a briarwood pipe in a case.

There was no merriment on her face as she handed him the small package, saying, "A merry Christmas, Manuel."

"For me!" He took it slowly from her hand and slowly opened it, and as he looked down at the elegant-shaped, brown wooden pipe, his teeth dropped hard on to his lower lip; then turning to her, he said softly, "All me life I've envied a man who's smoked this type of pipe. I would never have afforded it for meself, even me having the money, yet I longed to possess one. Aw, Annabella!" He thrust out his hands and grabbed her arms, and for one breath-checking moment she thought he was going to pull her into them.

It was the sound of her breath actually catching in her throat that checked him from doing just that. His eyes swept over her face, moving from her hair down to her lips and back to her eyes. "Thank you." He shook his head slowly. "It must have taken most of what you had."

"Not at all." Her tone was precise and he let go of her arms, then said, "Wait a minute, I've something for you an' all. And you might as well have them now. I was keepin' them for the morrow, but—but this is a better place to give them you. Wait a minute."

He hurried into the bedroom, and when he came out he was carrying a long, flat box the sight of which alone brought her eyes wide. Placing it in her arms, he said, "A happy Christmas."

When she made no move to open the box, he chided, "Go on, go on. Don't you want to see what's in it?"

And when she saw what was in it, she put her fingers over her mouth to suppress her tears. After a moment, she slowly lifted out a green cord velvet dress and held it from her; then dropping it onto the table and putting out her hands, she grasped his. "Manuel! Oh, Manuel! How wonderful. Thank you. Thank you a thousand times. It's beautiful."

"It's plain," he said, "nothing fancy."

"It's the fanciest dress I've seen in my life." She looked up into his face as he looked down into hers, and it was impossible for either of them not to read what was in the other's mind.

He now took her hand and drew her down onto the double bench near the fire and, his voice very low, he said, "You've been unhappy, haven't you?" And she answered just as low, "Yes, Manuel."

"Will you understand me when I say there was no need?"

She did not answer for some time, and then she said, "I'll try."

He took one hand between his two now and began to smooth it and he kept his eyes on it as he said, "Do you ever long for the old life, to be back at the House?"

She did not think he would have believed her if she had said, "No," so she spoke the truth, "Yes. Yes, Manuel, I do. But—but only when I'm sad. When I first came here, I thought I'd never feel that way again, but lately I've done so."

"If the opportunity came, would you go back?"

"I can say no to that, Manuel, because I know the opportunity won't arise. Mrs. Lagrange made that very evident."

"What do you mean?" He screwed his eyes up at her now. "You mean the old lady surely?"

"No, I mean the woman I called 'Mama.' You see, she never concerned herself about me. That—that particular day I was in great distress and she never——"

"What are you talking about, girl?" He was on his feet, looking down at her. "Why, she nearly went mad. She flew straight off to Durham to try to put things right there for you; then, coming back and finding you gone, she had me drive the tired horses like hares into Shields. She went and confronted the woman—your mother herself, I know that."

She, too, was on her feet. "You really mean she——?"

"Yes, yes, she did. And what was more, she had me scouring the town that night and all the next day. What made you think she didn't care? She cared so much it turned her brain. The old lady, her mother, it was her who wouldn't have anything to do with you, but not the mistress."

Slowly Annabella sat down on the bench again, and as Manuel looked at her he thought that was a damned silly thing to do, wasn't it, to tell her that. If anything will send her scurrying back, that will. God, but I'm a fool! But there, if she was still hankering in her mind for that life, sooner or later she would make the move, and better sooner than later, and he'd know where he stood and get the fire out of his veins in the usual way, like before this mad business started. He asked now quietly, "Will you go back?"

She had been looking into the fire, and when she turned her gaze on him, the alabaster look was gone and she was smiling as he hadn't seen her smile in weeks. She shook her head slowly, saying, "No, Manuel, no. I'll never go back, but I'm glad to know this. It makes no difference really, but it's comforting to know that she didn't put me out of her mind right away." She thought now that if she herself had been in her right mind at the time, she would have known that the woman whom she had called her mama would never have discarded her on that awful day, for it was against her nature to be cruel. She had a momentary longing now to see her, even if she would not recognize her. She thrust the longing aside. That life was over, finished; there was only the present and Manuel, and he had bought her a new dress.

She got up and went to the table and picked up the dress again, and, holding it in front of her, she hugged it to her, saying, "I cannot wait until tomorrow when I can wear it."

His eyes wide, their color deepening to almost black, his face showing excitement and relief, he stared at her, then said with a laugh, "But the dress is no good without the shoes. I forgot—here they are," and, reaching out to the little delft rack, he handed her a square box, and there inside reposed a pair of soft black leather flat-heeled shoes adorned with buckles.

"Here, take your boots off and try them on."

She had hardly sat down when he was on his knees on the floor by her side, and unbuttoning Amy's boots that were now sadly the worse for wear, he held each foot in his hand as he slipped on the new shoes.

"Do they fit you?"

"Perfectly, Manuel. Oh, they're lovely." She rose up on her toes.

"Go and try the frock on."

"Will I?" She was laughing.

"Yes, why not? Go on." He was pointing toward the door, and, gathering up the dress, she went hurriedly from the room, only to turn round on a laugh and say, "I forgot the candle."

They laughed into each other's face as he handed her the candle.

Alone, he went to the table and picked up the pipe from out of its case. Putting it in his mouth, he struck a pose, walked slowly to the bench by the fire, sat down with his legs apart, then, taking the pipe out of his mouth and holding it in front of him, he bowed slightly to an imaginary figure sitting in the empty chair opposite and under his breath, he said, "To us, Mrs. Mendoza."

The slight rustle of the lining in the gown told him she was in the doorway, and when he turned the sight of her seemed to jerk his heart from under his ribs and knock it against the casing. There she stood, Miss Annabella again.

No, not Miss Annabella, a woman, for when he had last seen her dressed decently, she was a young girl, but the young girl had died in the six months on the road, and there had emerged this woman. It was odd, but she looked older in this finery than she did in her working clothes.

"Do you like it?"

He nodded slowly before speaking. "It's beautiful." Behind the words his mind was asking, If anything should stop me from having her, what will there be for me? He put out his hand in a gallant fashion and she placed hers in it, and like two people entering into a minuet, he led her to the fireplace and, seating her, bowed over her, then raised her fingers to his lips.

He had never heard her laugh like it, except perhaps once or twice far back in their early acquaintance when they had escaped from the grounds and galloped side by side over the fells.

His laughter was joined to hers when a knock came on the door and it opened and Willy entered, only to stop abruptly and gaze at the apparition standing now framed in the light of the fire and candles. It was Annabella who spoke first. "It's—it's a new gown. Manuel—Manuel kindly bought it for me for Christmas." She glanced shyly at Manuel, adding, "He was so ashamed of me."

"More fool him." Willy was staring hard at Manuel and there was a question in the stare. Why play up to Betty, it was asking, if you've got your sights set on your cousin? He didn't like underhand dealings; he was surprised at Manuel; he had thought better of him. Still, he might be mistaken. Yet a man didn't usually buy clothes to put on a woman unless he had thoughts in his head that some day it would be he who would take them off her. There had been similar thoughts in his own mind when he had bought the scarlet shawl that he was to give her tomorrow, and give it to her he would, and that would bring him into the open. He said now, "Will you come and give me a hand with Daisy? Her cough's getting worse; she seems in pain, and she's touchy; she needs two to handle her."

"Aye, right away. . . . You be all right?" Manuel turned and smiled at Annabella, and she said softly, "Yes, yes, of course, I'll be all right." She laughed inwardly. Why shouldn't she be? She had never felt more all right.

As Manuel took his coat off the back of the door and put it on, then pulled over it a burlap cape, Willy, gazing at Annabella, said, "You look very fetching."

With the color swiftly spreading over her cheeks, she inclined her head to him and said, "Thank you."

"Dave is bringing his concertina over tomorrow; it'll give me the opportunity to pick a partner to dance with 'cause I'm either playing the whistle or you're playing the spinet. Be all right?"

It was an invitation. She swallowed, wet her lips, then said formally, as if they were all in the ballroom, "Thank you; it'll be a pleasure."

A minute later she was alone and, sitting down on the bench again, she dropped her hands into her lap, then gazed at them, and slowly and softly she began to laugh, repeating to herself, "Be all right? Thank you, it'll be a pleasure." Oh, Mr. Willy was funny, but nice. But everything was nice, more than nice, wonderful. Manuel had been thinking of her all the time when she thought his mind was on Betty. And to buy her this beautiful dress and shoes! And when he had asked her if she ever thought about the old life, that question had been for a purpose. If only Mr. Willy hadn't come in at that moment, he may have perhaps—She now cupped one cheek with the palm of her hand and rocked herself slightly to the pleasure of her thoughts. He had kissed her hand like any gallant; he could act the gentleman. Give him the clothes and he would pass for a gentleman. Her body ceased to rock. She didn't want a gentleman, she just wanted him. Yes, that's all she wanted in life, Manuel. She stood up, and now she whispered the words aloud to herself, "All I want in life is Manuel. All I've ever wanted is Manuel." What about her cousin Stephen? The question sprung at her and she answered calmly. He was merely someone who existed in that long childhood in which she had lived for so many years. But her thoughts persisted. Hadn't she once hoped to marry Stephen, planned to marry him? Yes, but while she was planning to marry him, hadn't she once said to herself, "When we are settled, we must have Manuel with us; perhaps Papa will let us have him." Right from the beginning, since the morning they had sat on that log together and he had taken away her fear of horses, she must have loved him. That different child hidden under the facade of Miss Annabella had known even then that he was for her.

Like someone in a trance now, she went into the other room and changed back into her working clothes and cloak; then, replacing the dress and shoes in the boxes, she lifted them up and prepared to go out. At the door she paused for a moment and looked back around the room. Some day

248

she would live here with Manuel. He had said he wanted to live here forever; well, wherever he wanted to live she wanted to live. In the meantime it was Christmas.

Annabella's happiness and surprising gaiety, which puzzled the family and which certain members put down to the significance behind the red shawl that Willy had presented her with on Christmas Day, lasted only until the morning of New Year's Day.

Christmas had been gay and lively, but, compared with the festivities on New Year's Eve, it was, as Mr. Fairbairn had prophesied to Annabella, as different as a gooseberry fair from a parson's tea.

The gaiety had got going around ten o'clock, but it was at twelve, when Dave Pearson brought the New Year in, that the real eating and drinking began.

Annabella had drunk only two small glasses of parsnip wine. She didn't need wine to make her feel happy; she had only to look at Manuel and read in his eyes the words he had not spoken yet, for they had scarcely had a minute alone together since Christmas Eve. This was because she had been kept going till late each night, helping with the preparations for the New Year. Never before had she realized that the cooking of food took so much time and energy. Her share in the evenings had been the never-ending washing of pans and crockery while Agnes and Betty helped Mrs. Fairbairn at the table. But apart from being "horse-hog-tired"—Willy's term—she had enjoyed every minute since Christmas Eve. Betty could no longer affect her, and more than once she had been tempted to tell her so, but had refrained, and decided to convey her feelings, as Miss Annabella Lagrange would have done, through her expression and manner.

But tonight she had done no washing-up; she had played the spinet and been loudly applauded. And she had danced with both Manuel and Willy. But this had been before twelve o'clock, for since then the time had been taken up with eating, drinking and singing.

It was around two o'clock when she realized, and not without a feeling of repugnance and dismay, that Manuel was highly intoxicated. Swaying on his feet, his deep voice thick with the Irish twang now, he was singing a questionable song, which went, "In England, the garden of beauty is kept/by a dragon of prudery placed within call;/but so oft this unamiable dragon has slept,/that the garden's but carelessly watched after all./Oh! they want the wild sweet briery fence,/

which round the flowers of Ayron dwell,/which warms the
touch, while winning the sense,/nor charms us least when it
most repels."

She must not have understood the humor of the song, Annabella considered, for she did not think it funny, yet the men
were roaring with laughter, and the ladies with bowed heads
were casting glances at each other while they suppressed their
giggles. And when the song was finished, they called for
more, and he sang and sang and sang and made them join
in the choruses.

It was nearly four o'clock in the morning when the party
broke up. The boys had given their rooms over to the guests—
they had previously taken palliasses into the hayloft—and
they were all staggering when they left the kitchen, Manuel
most of all. He paid no attention to Annabella when he
passed her, although she was within an arm's length of him.
Michael and he had their arms entwined round each other,
and Manuel was roaring at the top of his voice, "I saw thy
form in youthful prime, nor thought that pale decay would
steal before the steps of time and waste its bloom away,
Ma-ry."

Annabella was no longer smiling or feeling gay. Manuel's
behavior over the last two hours had shocked her. When
her papa had drunk a great deal, he hadn't, to her knowledge, acted like this.

But she reminded herself as she went wearily up the stairs
to bed that of course it was only to her knowledge. Hadn't
she heard him laughing loudly with his friends? Manuel, she
felt sorrowfully, had lost something tonight, his dignity, his
natural dignity, and it hurt her; yet he seemed to have im-
proved his standing with everyone present in the house, for
they all hailed him as a fine fellow.

She now asked herself if this new and distasteful side of
him would have any effect on her feelings for him. The
answer did not come immediately, and when it did, she was
almost asleep. It was an occasion, she told herself, that would
happen but rarely, and after all he was a man, very much
a man, and men did these things; and it was the woman's
lot to overlook them. Annabella Lagrange was again speaking.

When she heard the distant thumping, she pulled herself
out of layers of sleep to the fact that it was time to get up.
The thumping on the bottom of the stairs was a signal to rise.

It wasn't until she got, shivering, into her clothes that she
realized there was thin daylight coming through the thick-

250

frosted panes of the little window, and this made her scamper from the room and down the stairs and into the kitchen, where Mrs. Fairbairn was already at work as if it were an ordinary day.

"I'm—I'm sorry I'm late, missus," Annabella began; but Mrs. Fairbairn, cutting thick slices of ham at the corner of the table, said pleasantly, "Not late at all, girl; just had you knocked. Where's Betty?"

"Betty? I—I thought she was down."

Mrs. Fairbairn turned and looked at her, saying, "She's not in her bed?"

"No. She—she must be down."

"Well then, where is she? You go and find her."

"Yes, missus. Perhaps—perhaps she's in the dairy."

"Never knew her going to the dairy without having her tea. The Lord knows where she might be after last night. Had too much mead, full of honey and sauce she was; go and find her."

As Annabella went through the scullery, pulling her cloak from a hook and pulling it round her, she thought, She certainly had too much sauce, for as the night wore on she had lost all decorum, doing the clog dance and showing her legs almost up to the knees. But then, what could you expect? She was merely being herself. . . . Oh, she was out of sorts this morning. She was still very tired and cold, and Manuel's behavior hadn't dimmed with the daylight.

Betty was not in the dairy. She went to the cow shed. There was no one in the cow shed, not even any of the men. She opened the door of the grain room, then went to the hayloft, there to see Michael coming slowly down the ladder, supporting himself with one hand while with the other he held his head.

"Have you seen Betty, Mr. Michael?"

"Betty?" He screwed up his eyes against the light, then shook his head. "Not up there." He jerked his head toward the loft and grinned, then put his two hands to it as if the action had pained him, and he kept them there on his way to the pump.

She trudged through the snow and looked in the stables but could see no one, and as she was about to turn toward the house again, Willy came from the direction of Manuel's cottage. "Hello there!" he hailed her. Like his mother, he was about his work and the past night's gaiety had seemingly left no effect on him.

"Have you seen Betty, Mr. Willy?"

"Betty?" He shook his head. "You lookin' for her?"

"Yes."

"Well, there's two of us then. I can't find Manuel—he's not in his bed."

It was as if her body were being squeezed by an unseen pressure. They looked at each other, and when she turned and walked away, he walked with her. They went through an arch at the end of the stable yard and took the path that was a shortcut round to the side door of the stables. The path was sheltered by the stable wall on one side but open to a paddock on the other. The paddock looked like an unbroken white plane except for the covered wagon that stood by the hedge and about two hundred feet from the stables. The wagon had been used as a playhouse by all the Fairbairn children. It was a gypsy wagon and the wall paintings still showed patches of brightness here and there. Although the wood was rotting in parts and the roof leaked and the front wheels had shrunk from the iron tires, it still looked what it was, a gypsy wagon. It had been the home of a single gypsy for many years and periodically came to rest, with Mr. Fairbairn's permission, in the meadow down by the stream, and its owner would do a turn on the farm and earn a few coppers, especially at the haymaking or fruiting time. Then one day they found him dead in his wagon, and when two years went by and no relatives came to claim the old man's property and burn the wagon, as was the custom, the boys, who had looked after the horse in the meantime, had dragged the wagon up to the field here so that the young ones could play in it.

And now its rickety door opened and down the four worn steps came Betty, and after her Manuel. He, like Michael, was holding his head in his hands, and when he reached the ground, he turned and leaned it against the scroll which supported the hood over the driving seat, and Betty, putting her arm round his waist, leaned her head against his shoulder, and her gurgle of laughter seemed to split the icy air. And then she was leading him up the field by the hedge.

On they stumbled through the snow until Manuel lifted his head, and then he stopped dead, and through his swollen eyes he brought the two figures into focus. Then he flung his head from side to side as if shaking something off. When it became still, his chin was deep on his chest, but when he raised it again, there was no one standing under the shelter of the wall.

252

It was three days later before he managed to get a word with her.

"I was drunk!" he cried. "Don't you understand? I was drunk. I've never drunk like that for over eight months. Every now and again I need to drink and, when I do, I go headlong to hell. That was a short bout; two, three, four days I can be at it, you might as well know. Why did I gather all my days' leave together back at the House, eh? Just so's I could go on a spree. How I came to be in the wagon, I tell you I don't know; you know as much about it as me. There's only one thing I do know. In my right senses I'd never have been there." He waited, then bawled, "Say something! Go on, say something! Ask me what happened in there, anything, only don't stand looking at me as if I'd crucified Christ —I'm a man, and there are things a man needs to ease the urge that eats at him from the bowels outwards. I've curbed the reins for months, and would have gone on because I held a picture in me mind, but I didn't count on the mead, I didn't count on going over me number."

She let him talk until his words ran out, and then she turned from him and walked away.

A fortnight later, Mr. Fairbairn again had something to say about the situation to his wife. "That Betty wants her ears boxed, missus," he said; "an' if I stand to lose Manuel, I'll do the job myself."

"Either way you won't lose him," Mrs. Fairbairn remarked calmly. "He'll take one or the other and the house is waiting."

"And which do you think it'll be?" he asked her.

"If I get my wish, he'll take Betty. Have your eyes been open lately to what's happening to our Willy?"

"I'm not blind, missus. What would you say to his choice?"

"Well, taking all in all I'd welcome it, for neither Lizzie nor Sarah can hold a candle to her. Yet I'm not happy about her; there's something that puzzles me about this convent upbringing. Have you ever thought why they didn't keep her on there when her parents died? A young, comely girl like that, throwing her out into the world and into a family such as Manuel's, for although he's a cut above his class, he comes of working people. It isn't the pattern I've heard that nuns take, especially when they're dealing with young innocents, what I mean is, throw them out on the world. No, it puzzles me, and although I say I would welcome her, I don't think there's much chance of it. She doesn't favor Willy, although she took his shawl. Well, time will tell.

There's one thing evident, and that is she's disgusted with her cousin, be he cousin or no. But I'm not bothering my head about it at the moment for I've got enough on my plate with the wedding looming up, and if there isn't a thaw within the next three weeks, can you tell me how they're going to get to the church?"

All during January the men were kept busy outside from early morning until late at night; day after day, they dug sheep with their lambs out of drifts and carried them to higher ground, and day following day, they cut paths through fresh falls of snow to enable them to attend to the animals, until the snowbanks were head high all around the farm.

The pattern of the evenings had altered considerably. There was no collective sitting round the fire as there had been before Christmas. Manuel never sat in the kitchen at night now. After collecting his supper, he returned to the house or to the stables, where he spent most of his short free time.

As for Betty, she was gay, talkative and very pleasant, at least during the day, but at night, when in bed, she had taken to talking to herself. The first time it had happened, the third day of the New Year, her voice had come out of the darkness as if she was thinking aloud, saying, "I'll likely have a kid. That'll make it October, but we'll be nicely settled in afore that."

Annabella had not slept that night.

Another night, in the darkness came the words, "Some people should start making plans." That was all.

Then once more in the darkness, "Funny, me being your nursemaid when you were a kid, an' him actin' as nursemaid to you when you were a lass, an' then him an' me comin' together. Sort of like two people in the same trade."

Another night the mutterings had gone on for a long while, until Annabella, in desperation, put her hands over her ears. But this action only dulled her acute hearing, and the words stabbed at her, "Tacked yourself onto him. You should be ashamed of yourself. Still, as me da always says, breedin' will out, an' your real breedin' damn well came out, I'll say it did, 'cause you're shameless to go trailing the roads with a man like any tinker's trollop."

Betty's taunting was having a strange effect on Annabella's mind. Each fresh attack seemed to push her back into the past; almost nightly now she imagined herself in the carriage going down Crane Street, and the woman's face was as vivid as it had been on the first day she had seen her. Sometimes she was joined by the man with the twisted nose and she would see herself alone in the carriage, looking first one way at the woman and then the other at the man; they'd each be hanging onto a door as they ran. Then at times she'd hear Manuel's voice saying, "They'll have none of her, let her go back to Crane Street." At other times she would see herself standing before old Alice, looking up at her and asking, "What is a 'bars-tard,' Alice?" Her mind at this point would begin to work along odd lines, for she would shout up at Alice, "But I'm not a bars-tard any longer, Alice. I have a real mama and papa."

And she had a real mama and papa, ma and da, mother and father. Whatever title she had a mind to give them, they were her parents; she wasn't a bastard like Manuel— Manuel was a bastard.

During the day, she managed to keep her mind on her work. Sometimes she would give Agnes a thin smile, and that kindly young woman tried to cheer her up. She had grown very fond of Agnes; she hoped she would be very happy when she married.

Then one day she asked herself what she would do when Manuel married. Would she leave here? Yes, she answered. Yes, she would leave here. In fact, she would leave before he married. She would leave after Agnes's wedding, the day after. When Agnes was happily away to her new home, she would leave.

It was a week before the wedding when the thaw set in, and for a time she was shaken out of her anxiety state when Mrs. Fairbairn said to her, around ten in the morning, "Go and change your frock, girl. Willy's driving into Hexham; I want you to go along with him and do some errands for me."

Obediently, she had gone upstairs and changed her dress; but she didn't put on the green cord velvet but the one she had been sewing at for months. Nor did she put on the new shoes but kept her old boots on. Yet before she donned her cloak, she draped Willy's shawl around her shoulders.

When he helped her up into the front seat of the wagon and saw the fringe hanging down beneath the cloak, he took it as a good sign.

They were both very cold when they arrived in Hexham and the first thing he did was to take her for a meal, and after it was over and there was some color in her cheeks, he took her into the lounge room, and there he ordered coffee and brandy and insisted that she drink it, and for the first time in weeks she felt warmed; and it was at this point he spoke.

"You know why I have brought you out, Annabella?"

She blinked her eyes, saying, "Yes, Mr. Willy, for your mother's errands."

"Don't call me 'Mr. Willy,' Annabella. And I didn't bring you out for mother's errands. I brought you out to ask you a question that's been on my mind for weeks. I'm no good at light talk; I'm just a plain, ordinary fellow and I'm askin' you to be my wife."

She stared at him, her mouth actually falling into a gape. Then her hand went to her throat.

"Oh, Mr. Willy! I mean, it's very kind of you and thank you for the honor but—but I never thought. You see, it hasn't crossed my mind. I'm sorry I—"

"Take your time, take your time. I know that you're fond of Manuel and the way things have gone have upset you, but every man has to make his own choice. I'll be good to you, I promise that, and once Dad goes, the farm will be mine because he's giving Michael and Sep their share when they wed. You'll have a good home and security and no more trailing the roads."

"Oh please, please, I couldn't. I'm sorry. I'm very much aware of the honor but—"

He waved her fine talk away, then sat staring at her for a long while before saying, "Then why did you take me shawl?" He lifted up the red fringe, and she said, "Take—take your shawl? But it was a Christmas gift."

He looked up and then down before he said, "A man doesn't usually give a maid"—his meaning of "maid" in this instance referred to a servant and she realized this—"a present like that, not hereabouts anyway, it has a meaning. But perhaps you didn't know."

"No. I'm sorry, I didn't. I'm afraid I'm very ignorant on a number of matters. . . ." Her voice trailed away.

"If I give you time to ponder it, will you change, do you think?"

She looked at his round, homely face, at his sandy hair, at his thick, strong body, and she thought, "If only I could. Oh, if only I could."

Her silence brought him to his feet and he said stiffly. "Well, we better be gettin' on with the errands; we've got to get back in case it starts again. The sky's heavy."

Manuel was in the kitchen when they returned. He had been answering some question of Mrs. Fairbairn's, and when the door opened he swung round and faced them; his eyes flashed from one to the other looking for the answer, but he

256

could not read it, for Annabella's eyes were downcast and Willy looked as usual. Willy's face rarely gave anything away.

Two days before the wedding, a quick thaw set in, turning the fields into lakes and the roads into bogs, and then, because Agnes said God had answered her prayers, the night before her wedding day a frost descended and hardened the ground and, joy of joys, a weak sun came out in the morning.

The sun shone on the wedding party all through the drive to Stanhope; it shone on the long line of traps and farm wagons on the hilarious return journey. It shone till three o'clock in the afternoon when the newly wed couple mounted the new farm cart, and the groom took up the reins on the two spanking horses, the whole outfit a wedding gift from his father-in-law. It went down as the newly married couple moved off amid cheers and waving from all the guests and members of the household, except one.

Annabella was in the washhouse. She was leaning against the upturned tub which she and Agnes had sweated over every Monday for weeks past. She was crying because Agnes had gone. It was a silent, quiet crying. The tears rolling slowly down her cheeks, she could think of nothing at the moment but that Agnes was gone. Her one friend was gone. Mr. and Mrs. Fairbairn were good, and the boys were good and kind, but Agnes had been more than good and kind—she had been understanding. She had said to her last night, "I know how you feel, Annabella, I know how you feel. You see, I don't love Dave like I did John Bailey. He had a farm over near Bishop Auckland. He used to come out here a lot at one time. He made it plain he was after me, and then all of a sudden he stops and the next thing I hear, he's married the bailiff's daughter from Lord Crosby's place. I was bad for a time after that, I had no interest in anything, and when Dave came along, I thought, No, never, because no one could replace John. But time changes you." She had gone on without pause. "Our Willy's a good man. Annabella; it's a pity you can't favor him, but I understand you won't be able to until Manuel's out of your life. Once he's tied up like John was, you'll settle and your mind will turn in another direction, you'll see."

Dear, dear Agnes. If only what she said was true and her mind would turn in another direction. She was so tired of it all, so weary of feeling like this. But it would soon be over; there wasn't much longer to wait.

The determination to take her own life that had been

growing in her for some time now was not only the outcome of Manuel's defection, or unfaithfulness, or whatever way she thought of it. It was also the revelation of her birth and all it implied; the strain of the past months on a physique unaccustomed to manual labor; and the strong religious upbringing instilled in her by Rosina, which was now telling her that she was being made to suffer because she had been born of sinful people, and as Alice so often said, the sins of the fathers were visited on the children.

The wedding party danced in the long barn, and during all the evening she carried food from the kitchen across the frozen yard to the guests. On one of her journeys she heard Miss Percy say to Mr. Sep, "What's come over Manuel? He won't take a drink. He's not a bit like he was at Christmas." And Sep's reply, "Oh, he's decided to go on the wagon. But his feet are all right; look at him there dancing with Aunt Mildred. Did you ever! She's like a two-year-old."

Every time she entered the barn, Manuel was dancing. Once their eyes met. His gaze was dark, almost fierce, and she looked through it and beyond him. On her way back to the kitchen, she thought men were strange creatures, cruel creatures. Look at her papa, how he had treated her mama. . . . And Manuel could dance. Her thoughts suddenly leaped back to a ballroom in London and she thought Miss Kathleen Wainheart could dance, too; and Stephen could dance. He had danced a lot with Miss Wainheart, she remembered. Three men in her life, her papa, Stephen, and Manuel, and all in their different ways had said they loved her and then had left her. Or had she been imagining that they loved her? Was it her need of their love that made her think that they loved her? Because no one of them had actually said, "Annabella, I love you."

At eleven o'clock the snow began to fall again, and there was a rush to the traps and carts, amid great laughter and shouting in farewells, and by twelve o'clock everyone was gone.

With the combined efforts of the family, the barn was cleared of dishes and the remnants of the food, and everything was in its place by one o'clock.

Before the others had dispersed, Mrs. Fairbairn said to Annabella, "Get yourself upstairs, girl, you look dead beat. It's all over; you can take it easy for a day or two."

Dutifully she went upstairs, and to bed, but she got in it fully dressed. She heard Betty come up and get into bed, and tonight, strangely enough, she didn't talk to herself. She heard the clock strike two, then three, and knew it was almost time to go, but at this point sleep overcame her and she fell into a doze.

When, waking with a start, she rose from the bed, she didn't know what time it was; she only knew what she was going to do. Her boots in her hand, she walked softly out of the room and down the stairs. At the kitchen door she put on her boots but didn't button them, and they clip-clopped slightly as she went across the frozen snow on the yard.

The night was starry and silent, and she could just make out the big door of the grain house when she came to it. Lifting the latch, she pushed half of the door open and went inside. After the snow-laden air, it felt warm. She had brought a candle with her, and now she lit it and looked upwards. There, on the half platform at the end of the room, hung the pulley; over its hook lay a slack rope, one length slanting toward the grain sack around which it was tied. The lowering of the grain from the winnowing room was a simple process. One man tied the sack with the rope, then slung the rope over the U-shaped hook and, hanging onto the other end, let it down onto the cart below, if the grain was going to the miller's.

Holding the candle above her head, she slowly climbed the ladder. Now on the platform, she placed the candle in a niche in the wall that was kept for such purpose; then, going to the rope that was hanging over the hook, she took the end in her hand and looked at it, and as if she were acting this out in a dream, she put it slowly round her neck and tied a knot in it. Then she moved toward the sack of grain that stood balanced on the end of the platform. She looked at it, too, for a time before taking her foot and pushing it off the edge. As the rope tightened round her throat, there passed through her head a great scream and then she fell into deep blackness. . . .

Willy had been coming from the little stable where a cow had just calved and was passing along by the wall when he saw half of the grain door open, and this brought him to a stop because it had only been a short while ago that he had been in there, and he wasn't such a fool as to leave a door open in this weather, particularly the grain door. It was right odd, for there was no wind. It was as he reached out his arm to grab the latch that he saw her in the candlelight above him. She had a rope about her neck and she was about to kick the sack of grain from the edge of the platform. With a warning scream that lifted him from the ground, he sprang to the cart and onto it and, when the sack hit him, it almost knocked him to the ground. But after staggering under its weight for a moment, he steadied himself, and then he began to yell. "Annabella! For God's sake! Manuel! Somebody! Help! Help!"

Manuel had just got out of bed and was getting into his trousers when he heard the first cry. It was distant and muffled but the sound brought him to the door, for it was unusual to hear anything but the animals at this time in the morning. Then he was racing across the space between the cottage and the stable walls, through the arch and in the direction of the shouting.

When he burst into the grain room and took in the situation, he screamed an unintelligible sound and the echo hadn't faded before he reached the platform. His arms about her, he eased her from her toes on which she was balancing, then he tore the rope from her neck, and at the same moment there came the sound of a thud from below as Willy and the sack of grain fell onto the cart.

"Annabella. Annabella." He was on his knees by her side holding her slack head in his hands. "Annabella. For God's sake, don't!—Listen to me—Oh, Christ Almighty!"

Willy, stumbling onto the platform now, gasped, "Is she?" and Manuel, not looking at him, laid his head on her breast; then with his body almost doubled in two as if he were going to retch, he muttered, "She's—she's breathing, just."

"God above!" Willy was still gasping. "That was the narrowest squeak she'll ever have. Another second, just another second."

"Let's—let's get her down; she's—she's cold." He had almost said "dead cold." "Take her legs, will you?"

Willy took her legs, and between them they got her down to the ground floor; then, Manuel carrying her in his arms while Willy supported her dangling head, they brought her into the house, and when they had laid her on the rug in front of the fire, Willy went to the door and yelled at the top of his voice, "Ma! Ma! Come on here, you're wanted."

It was almost half an hour later when Annabella regained her senses. She was still in the dark and she thought she was dead. She imagined for a moment that she was listening to Manuel explaining to God how it had happened, because he was saying, "Well, there it is, that's the true story. That's her name, Annabella Lagrange, and from being brought up as a lady and with the comforts of such, her world was

260

turned topsy-turvy; she's been reduced to pig swilling and even sleeping in a flop house. She came along with me because there was no one else to go along with; nobody wanted to know her, except the woman she had looked upon as her real mother. And then she went out of her mind with it all. An' there were times while we were at Skillen's that I thought she would go out of her mind an' all. But then we landed here, an' I'm tellin' you, it was like heaven to us both. And it would have remained so if it hadn't have been for that one. She was her nursemaid and she got the push just afore I went to the House for calling the child a 'bastard,' and because of that and gettin' no reference, she'd held it against her; not only that, but on her own sayin', her own bragging, she's tormented the life out of her, threatening to expose her for being the offspring of a whore mistress."

"Well, she was, she was. Nothing more or less." Betty, suddenly flaring into self-defense, glared at the faces all staring at her and, the tears running down her cheeks, she cried, "What do you know? What does any of you know what it's like to be put out without a reference? And there was more to it than that, things you don't know. Blame me, aye, you all blame me, but if you"—she was nodding directly at Manuel now—"if you hadn't of played up to me, it would never have got this far."

"The only reason I played up to you, and God forgive me for me stupidity, was because I wanted to keep your tongue quiet, keep you off her. And while I'm on"—he now turned and faced Willy directly, saying—"I'm going to tell you this. I've no more idea than you how I got into that wagon on New Year's mornin'. And something else I'll say while I'm on, begging your pardon, missus." He jerked his head. "When I'm that far gone in drink, I'm no use to anybody, that much I do know, so whatever you think happened atween us, didn't."

The men turned their glances away and looked about the room, definitely embarrassed, but Mrs. Fairbairn wasn't embarrassed. She took the situation in hand by saying, "Well, we'll have no more explanations for the moment. And anyway, keep your voices down all of you, for I think she's coming round." She looked up from where she was kneeling by Annabella's head and said, "We'd better get her out of this and up into bed." Then her eyes turned toward Manuel when he spoke again, directly to her now, saying, "If it's all the same to you, missus, I'll take her across to the cottage. We've shared a roof afore and no harm's come of it. I might

261

as well tell you afore somebody else does that all the time at Skillen's we shared the cottage, and I took the kitchen floor, so now I think I can be trusted to see to her. As I said, if it's all the same to you, missus?"

Mrs. Fairbairn got to her feet and looked up into the dark face of this strange young fellow, who in a way was as mysterious as the girl here. And no, she didn't mind his taking her across to the cottage. At this very moment she was thanking God that things had happened as they had, for should her Willy have taken the girl and her parentage had come out later, she would have died a thousand deaths, for education or no education, she had blood in her that was no good. It wasn't the girl's fault, poor soul, no, and likely she would lead a clean life, but what about the children to follow and their children? Blood would out. She was a great believer in that saying, blood would out. She looked toward her eldest son. What was he thinking? You never knew what Willy was thinking.

At this moment, too, Willy was trying to prevent himself thinking along the same lines as his mother. She was a lovely girl; he still had this feeling for her, but later, when he came to look at things coolly, he knew he'd congratulate himself on having had a lucky escape. The woman he took would have to give him children, and his mind cringed at the thought that in this case, in order to produce a family, his seed, which had come down through centuries of Fairbairns, all good yeomen, would mingle not only with that of a trollop once removed, but a mother of trollops. He now went quickly to Manuel's aid, saying, "Let me give you a hand."

"I can manage, thanks, once she's up."

They placed her in his arms and wrapped rugs around her, and Mrs. Fairbairn accompanied them herself; and she straightened Manuel's tumbled bed. Ordering him to go back to the house and bring over a hot oven shelf, she undressed Annabella and put her between the sheets; and Annabella, opening her eyes at last, looked at her mistress and said, "I'm sorry," and Mrs. Fairbairn, with deep tenderness said, "Go to sleep, child, go to sleep. You have nothing more to worry about, it will all work out. Go to sleep."

And she obeyed her and went to sleep.

She woke up a number of times in the next thirty-six hours, and always there was someone sitting by the bedside, Manuel or Mrs. Fairbairn, and always they said to her, "Drink this." And she drank the hot broth. And then they would say, "Go to sleep. Go to sleep," and she would go to sleep because she continued to feel very, very tired. Once or twice she had tried to speak but found the effort too much. But on the evening of the second day she woke and the tiredness had almost gone. She lifted her heavy lids and looked at the candle in the brass holder on the chest of drawers at the foot of the bed, and then she turned her head on the pillow and looked up at Manuel. She looked at him a long time before she said the same words to him as she had said to Mrs. Fairbairn, "I'm sorry."

She watched him close his eyes tightly and grope for her hand, and hold it against his chest. Then, slipping from the wooden chair, he went on his knees by the side of the bed and did what she should have considered a very strange thing. Her hand still grasped against him, he laid his face on the pillow beside hers and he didn't utter a word, but just lay there looking at her. And after a long while when she said, "Oh, Manuel!" he made a little movement with his head telling her not to speak. And so they lay, his eyes wrapping her in their dark, deep gaze for a while before, his head moving still nearer, his lips touched hers. Softly they lay against her mouth, resting there, waiting as it were, and when her response came, it racked them both. Her pent-up feeling burst from her in an ever rising storm of weeping, during which he held her and rocked her like a child. And when it was over at last, she said to him. "You'll never leave me, Manuel?" and he answered, "Never, as long as there's a breath in me."

The following day the snow fell so thickly you couldn't see the farm buildings from the cottage windows, and Manuel brought the bed from the bedroom and placed it in the kitchen against the far wall and opposite the fire, and when she continued to sleep most of the day, Mrs. Fairbairn said, "Let her be; it's nature's cure."

It was almost a week later when she got up and dressed and began to attend, in a small way, to the chores of the house. She didn't know what was going to happen. Manuel said leave it to him, and that's what she was doing. Only one thing she had made plain: she didn't want to go back to work in the house because that would mean Betty's leaving, and although she would never like Betty, and in fact could still find it in her heart to hate her, she was, in a way, sorry for her.

She sat now by the fire, waiting for Manuel, and when he came, she rose quickly from her chair and went into his arms, and he held her tight-pressed against him.

When he had taken off his coat and his snow-sodden boots and had held out his frozen feet to the fire while drinking a steaming mug of tea, he was all the while searching for the right words with which to give her his news. He was afraid that the very mention of the wagon might create in her a rigidity; yet sooner or later he'd have to explain to her the incident of the wagon, so far better do it now. Leaning forward to place his mug on a chair, he said below his breath, "Before we go any further, Annabella, I want to explain about—about New Year's Day, and the—"

Her hand, slipping through his arm, groped for his fingers, and her head bowed she said, "There's no need."

Gathering her swiftly to him, his face hanging over hers, he whispered, "There was nothing, nothing; when I get drunk like that, I'm dead to the—" Her hand came up on his mouth and she whispered, "It's all right, I know. I must have been half awake the other morning."

"Oh!" He stared at her for a moment, then let out a long, deep breath and leaned heavily against her, muttering, "Aw, darlin'. Darlin'."

Now he was holding her face between his hands and asking, "How would you like to live in a house on wheels?"

"A house on wheels, Manuel?"

"You don't want to go on livin' here."

Her eyes dropped from his. "It—it would be very awkward. Every time I see any of them even in the distance, I'm aware of what they may be thinking."

"That's nonsense."

"No, it isn't, Manuel. Mrs. Fairbairn is a wonderfully kind woman but—but she'll be glad when I'm gone; I've become an embarrassment to her. And I know something else—Willy came in yesterday to see me, and as I thanked him"—her head went lower—"I—I knew that he was no longer hurt, he was cheerful." She lifted her eyes. "Relief makes one cheerful, Manuel."

"You're talkin' nonsense; Willy would give his eyeteeth if he could have you."

"Not now. Do you know he once asked me to marry him?"

"Did he, now?" He pulled a slight face and inclined his head toward her, half mockingly. "But it's no surprise to me. It was the day he took you to Hexham, wasn't it?"

"Yes, it was. And what would he be feeling now if I had said yes? I tell you he's relieved that things have turned out as they have. I know that no one would want to marry me

264

if they knew. I—I have to face up to this; that is, no one except—"

"Well, go on."

Her head drooped again and she said now, "I cannot answer a question until I'm asked it."

There was a long pause before he spoke, no jocularity in his voice now, which came deep from his throat. "Will you marry me?"

Her reply was quiet and firm: "Yes, Manuel; and I consider it an honor you have done me. But—but I want to say something to you." Her head did not droop but her eyes flicked sideways toward the fire as she went on: "You—you needn't marry me, you needn't feel compelled to marry me. I—I am quite prepared to live with—"

"Enough!" He was on his feet, his voice harsh. "I've asked you a question an' I want an answer. I want it again. I asked you if you would marry me, and marrying me means takin' the name that isn't mine; also, it means having people talking behind their hands and sayin', 'How did she come to marry him with "working man" written all over him?' It means that you're likely to be a laborer's wife for the rest of your life. It means being turned out of the saloon end of bars. Remember you've had a taste of it afore. It'll likely mean all the things you've put up with in the last six months over again, but having to now because you'd be no longer a free agent. It'll mean working while you're carrying me kid inside of you. . . . You'd be my wife. Now I say again to you, Will you marry me?"

She got to her feet and her answer came from the woman she had become. She put her hands about him and her mouth to his and held him with all her strength. In return, he held her gently, for there were times, as now, when he had to put a curb on his desires, for like his drinking, once given rein, they tended to consume him.

Drawing her down to the seat again, he said, "We'll have to find a place where we can live for three weeks and then we'll put the banns up. It'll be done right and proper in a church, an' we'll frame the marriage certificate and our children will know who they are from the start."

She said nothing to this, but she laid her head on his shoulder and thought, Oh my dear, dear Manuel. Oh, my dearest, dear Manuel. Then she was asking in a faraway voice, "But where will we go? Which town will we stay in?"

He brought her head up from his shoulder with a jerk.

265

"That's what I aimed to tell you at the beginning of this rigmarole. We can go to any town we like. We can say, 'Gee-up, Dobbie,' and go as far as Bishop Auckland, Darlington, even Stockton."

She stared at him, her eyes wide with inquiry until he said, "The wagon."

"The wagon?" Her eyebrows now moved upwards, and he nodded. "I went to the master and I put it to him. Would he sell me the wagon and old Dobbie. He had said Dobbie was finished and he was going to send her to market anyway. And you know what? He's given them to me, wagon and horse. There's kindness for you. And the lads have all offered to help me do it up, make it livable. And the missus is givin' me stuff to make bed ticks and is hunting out old linen and odds and ends, pans and things; she's all for it. And what's more, the master's given me four months full pay, and you the same. He needn't give us a penny piece because we're bonded for another two months or more, but he's a good man. They're all good, kind people. Now what do you say to that news?"

She shook her head slowly and said, "It's—it's wonderful, Manuel, wonderful. We need never walk the roads again, and there'll always be shelter. It's wonderful but"—she paused and looked searchingly into his face—"I remember your saying more than once that you wanted to live with these people forever, and—and the more I hear of them, the more I can understand that. Is it going to be a great wrench for you leaving here?"

He smiled softly at her as he drew her once again into his arms and, his tone bantering now, said, "You know, if the devil came tonight and said to you, 'Annabella Lagrange, I'm goin' to take you to hell, there to stay forever,' I would say to him, 'You don't get her there without me.' And I'm tellin' you, that's a big thing for an Irishman to say because there's two things that frighten an Irishman, the thought of keepin' company with the devil, an' havin' a potato famine."

"Oh, Manuel! Manuel!" She was laughing now, her hand over her mouth, as she was apt to do when she was happy, and he hugged her to him, saying, "There's one thing I like to hear even better than the sound of the wind, an' that's you laughin'."

Her eyes roamed over his face now as she said solemnly, "Manuel, I—I love you so very much. I've loved you since the day I first saw you, and I'll go on loving you all of my life."

The end of Margee's prophecy came to him. Hadn't she said that he'd come to riches? Margee had always had a funny way of expressing herself: her words had double meanings. A field of buttercups she'd call a golden rug; a light breeze was the flapping of the eider duck's wing. Well, she had promised him wealth, and now he had it and in the only form he wanted it. Margee had been a seer, all right, and God was good.

Book Five

WHITHER
THOU GOEST

1

They had been on the road a week. They had driven through high winds, rain, snow and sleet, but each night when they pulled off the road into a field or by the side of a tumbling stream and Manuel had fed the horse and put him under the best cover he could find, they would sit in the wagon before the little iron stove and eat their evening meal, and after, he would hold her in his arms and ask her the same question. "You happy?"

And always she would answer, "Oh, Manuel! Never, never in my life have I felt like this. If this is happiness, then I could die of it." The question and answer might change slightly, but their meaning remained the same. Then he would smoke his pipe and she would clear the table and bring from the shelf above the end bed the books which Mr. Fairbairn had given her and would give him his lesson.

She, even more than he now, was a stickler for the lesson. They had reached what she called—taking a pattern from Miss Howard's teaching—"syllabification," where she aimed that he should write and speak words of two and three syllables. They laughed a great deal over the lessons, about such things as when he called syllabification, "confuse-and-bemusification." But he was inwardly proud of his achievements so far, for now he could read on his own.

On the seventh day he decided to make for Darlington. His idea was to find work in the town, perhaps at an ostler's, and having no rent to pay, they could save. And who knew, he might find a little cottage and a small piece of land going cheap, and there they could keep some chickens and a cow and grow their own food. The prospect was glowing.

They passed through Winston and Gainford, and it was on a day of high winds and snow flurries that he decided early in the afternoon to call a halt, and so he drove the van off the road and into a field that formed the bottom of a little valley, and after doing his usual chores, he went into the thick copse on the hillside to gather wood.

It was about three in the afternoon when he left the wagon and when, half an hour later, he hadn't returned, Annabella stood on the top of the steps, her eyes fixed on the distant hill, waiting.

When another half hour had passed and he hadn't returned, a feeling of panic seized her. She now ran across the field and into the copse, which formed a long narrow belt of trees, and began to call, "Manuel! Manuel!" but there was no answer except from the rooks. She went on and out into the open again, then climbed to the top of a steep hill, falling on her hands and knees on the way owing to the slippery grass, and all the while her mind was in a turmoil—someone might have attacked him for his belt. But how would they know about the belt? He could have taken ill, but Manuel was never ill. He could have come across an inn and was drinking, but no, he had no need of drink now. No, he would not be drinking.

When she reached the summit of the hill, she stood panting and gripping the sides of her cape because the swirling wind was forming it into a balloon and threatening to take her from her feet. Below her stretched another valley with a wide bottom, and in it were houses and buildings. There was smoke coming from some of the buildings and there was something vaguely familiar about them, but she wasn't interested in them. Where was Manuel? She saw three men come out of a doorway and stand talking; then one of them disengaged himself and moved away. He came across the flat bottom of the valley, and when he began to mount the hill, she was flying down it, crying, "Manuel! Manuel!"

"What is it? What is it?"

She had almost overbalanced him, and now she was clinging to him and between gasps crying, "I—I didn't know what had happened to you; I—I thought all kinds of things. I—I—"

"But I haven't been away all that long, about half an hour."

"Oh no, no, well over an hour."

He held her from him now and looked at her. Then, with a quick movement, he pulled her fiercely to him and there on the open hillside he kissed her as he had never kissed her before, not only because of the wonder of their love for each other, but because in the last half hour he had settled their future. Now, swinging her round and pointing down to the valley, he said, "What's that place down there?"

"I—I don't know. A factory? Oh, yes." She turned to him,

her face alight now, her eyes wide. "It could be a glass works."

"It is a glass works."

"But who would think of putting a glass works out here?"

"It's nearer the town than you think on the other side. And hold on to me tightly while I tell you—I've started work."

"NO! Manuel."

"Yes, just like that." He snapped his fingers. "An' I'll tell you something more; there's a house to go with it. There are four workmen's houses down there, and only two of them filled, one by a Frenchman. Oh, you'll come in handy down there with the lingo. And the man, the owner, a Mr. Carpenter, he's nice, one of the nicest, very civil like Mr. Fairbairn, only different in person. He's a man you can talk straight to, an' I did. I told him I had no experience of glass-making, only what I had picked up in the few months back in Shields, an' I told him I had with me the woman I was going to marry and I was looking for a place where we could settle and call the banns. And you know, he seemed interested, he's that kind of a man. And he was honest on his side an' all, because he said he was having trouble in finding good workmen; once they earned a bit of money, they went off. He said it was the erratic hours of the work that they didn't like, and would I mind what time of the day I started and stopped? And I said I wouldn't."

She was staring at him now, her face straight, and she said, "Manuel, you told me you never liked working in the glass works."

"Well, a man can change his mind, can't he?" He touched her cheek. "About some things, anyway. I get a feeling about people. I think he's a man I'd get on with; I had the same feeling about Mr. Fairbairn. I might as well tell you, Annabella, I never had that feeling back in the House. The only one I ever got on with in that place was Armorer and young Dinning. The others weren't my kind of folk, but"—he smiled widely—"I know you'll like this man. And he says bring the van round; there's a field beyond the cottages where we can settle it and, better still, there's an old stable that will shelter Dobbie. Come on with you, let's get away." And so saying, he ran her up the hill, then down the other side, and he laughed as he ran.

When Manuel presented Annabella to Mr. Carpenter, they both took stock of each other. Mr. Carpenter, Annabella saw, was an old man, with white hair, white moustaches and kindly features. He wasn't what her mama would have termed a "gentleman," more a man of commerce; but it didn't matter what he was, he had taken to Manuel and therefore she liked him.

Mr. Carpenter, on the other hand, had in his early days traveled much and met all types of people. He was, as he laughingly termed himself at times, a student of human nature; that was why he had immediately sensed the honesty of the man who gave the Spanish-sounding name and who indeed looked a typical Spaniard. But his association with this young woman he found strange, for she, from manner and speech, was no traveling tinker's mate. He was further surprised, in fact he was astounded, when, showing them round the small factory, she spoke of processes, qualities of sand; she used words such as "whimsey," "ponty" and "cullet." She stood before a block of wood that they used in place of a table and she watched a boy blowing down a pipe that a gatherer held on it while he turned the molten glass, and she remarked that the "marver had seen some work." There was no forcing of her knowledge: it came out naturally in the course of conversation, and it intrigued Mr. Carpenter. Never had he met a woman who could talk glass before.

Outside of the glass house he asked her pointedly, "Where did you come by your knowledge, Miss——?" and she replied simply, "My relatives had a factory; there were a lot of books in the house concerning glass."

"And where are your relatives now? And where was the factory?"

She paused a while before answering, and then stumbled, "They—they're dead, and—and the factory was on the Tyne, but I'm afraid it went bankrupt."

"Oh, that's easily done with glass these days. Still, I mustn't grumble; this is not a big place, but I've got very good trading alleys."

"Do you export much?"

"Not much, because that means employing agents, but I do very nicely roundabout." Then, nodding at her, he said, "If you would like to refresh your memory about glass, there's a number of books in my house. You are at liberty to take the loan of what you want."

"Thank you."

"And now you'd better see your house. I understand you are going to be married." He looked at one and then the other, and Manuel left Annabella to answer, "Yes, as soon as we've been resident for the required time, and can find a church."

"Well"—he smiled at them—"there should be no difficulty in that, you can have your choice. There's a little church at Denton over there, or one across the border in Yorkshire at Piercebridge. I would say Denton; it's a nice little village and I know the minister." He stopped in his walk now and said, "My wife and I were married there, I mean my first wife, but both my wives are buried there." He moved on again now, adding, "I have a stepson. He comes over at times from Hartlepool; he's a sea captain." He glanced now at Manuel. "He couldn't stand glass. Some men can't, you know, and others can't live without it. Most intriguing thing on earth, glass." He shook his head in wonder. "I hope that you both will come to think that way, too."

They didn't make any answer to this as he was walking ahead into the house, but they looked at each other and Manuel thought, Life's funny. I thought I'd finish up a farm laborer, at best with my own little plot, but here I am starting in glass and who knows where it'll lead? Why shouldn't I become a gatherer? If that lot in there can do it, I can.

And Annabella thought, The tide is surely turning; everything from now on will go well for us. And I can be of use here, I know I can. I wonder who does the books and the accounts? I saw no clerk.

The following day Annabella found out who did the books and accounts: Mr. Carpenter himself, and a very muddled job he made of them. And he admitted that he had hoped his stepson would take to that side of the business besides managing the works, but, as he had said, he had no taste for it.

But it took Mr. Carpenter a full week to make up his mind about employing a woman. The men from Darlington mightn't like it. There were guilds, and these new unions coming up; but when the men were approached, they laughed and said, "Why not? She's a nice miss, ornamental." And Jacques Furnier, the Frenchman, had the last word. "She speaks my tongue," he said. "Not my patois, but an understandable French all right. Yes, yes, indeed."

So Annabella was employed at the surprising wage of ten shillings a week, only half of what Manuel was to receive, but their joint earnings had the effect on them of sudden riches.

Annabella certainly gave value for the money she received, for not only did she keep the books, but she took on self-enforced tasks of checking the glasses and goblets and the assortment of bottles that the little works turned out. And in

275

the evenings she and Manuel would sit in their new house—not so cosy as the Fairbairns' cottage but a place with possibilities and where, as yet, she alone slept—and to the background of raised French voices coming through the wall from next door, she would take him through Mr. Carpenter's books on glass, making him conversant with the different types of crucibles and furnaces. And, as he listened to her, his eyes would stray from the diagrams and he would see her in an entirely new light, and he would become slightly awed by her knowledge. And since he didn't like this feeling, he applied himself more and more to the lessons in hand.

But as his reading became more difficult because many of the words were strange, he wondered at times if this book knowledge was really going to help him in the long run. It was practice only, he felt, that would make a glass man. But still he persevered and knew a strange pride when she, acting as a teacher, would question him on such basic points as types of glass and he would answer like a child repeating a lesson: "From hollow ware you get blown glass and pressed glass; and from blown glass you get bottled glass, tube and lamp glass; then from flat ware you get sheet and crown and mosaic glass, and plate and optical glass."

In the third week of their stay, she was setting him questions such as: "What ingredients are necessary to form glass? What must you add to the rudiments to make finer quality glass? Describe a kiln. How would you recognize good flint glass? What effect do you get when you add an excess of soda in the making of flint glass?" Until one night, suddenly closing one of the books with a bang, he put his hand on it and said, "Enough!" and she raised surprised eyes to him, saying, "What do you mean, Manuel, 'enough'?"

And turning to her he said seriously, "I could never do all these things myself. It isn't necessary to know all this to be a flattener or even a blower. I could have all this in me head and more, but it's the handling of the tools that matters as far as I can see from watching."

She looked at him a long while before she said, "Some men are made for work, Manuel, and some for managing. You have a way with people, a way with men. You can get on with anyone you like, you know you can. And I'm not seeing you as a flattener or a blower. I'm—I'm seeing you as a manager. You can read and write and reckon up. You have memorized as much about glass in two weeks as I did in two years or more. I told Mr. Carpenter that you're studying hard and he seemed very—"

He whirled her up from the table, and, clasping her in no gentle way to him, he narrowed his eyes and shook his head slowly as he said, "You calculating woman, you! You've got it all planned out, haven't you?" And she, her face tantalizingly prim, said, "Yes, Manuel, to the last detail."

Then they burst out laughing and, holding tightly, they swayed together. And now he said, "Come out and let's breathe the air."

Outside, the wind was blowing and the evening was cold, but they both drew it in like perfume, especially Manuel. Taking it deep down into his lungs, he held it before letting it free again. After years of working outside, the hot atmosphere of the glass houses was a trial to him, but a minor one which he told himself he would get used to in time.

They made their way to the field where Dobbie and the wagon were housed. With a stable to shelter in at night and a field of luscious new grass and no work to do, he must, Manuel said, think that he had died and arrived in heaven.

At their approach, the horse ambled toward them, and they petted him and gave him some crusts of bread; and then they went into the wagon, and Annabella, touching the dead stove and the faded painted woodwork, said, "We mustn't part with it," and Manuel, his arm around her waist again, added, "Part with it? I should think not! It's going to be put to the same use as it was at the Fairbairns', I hope."

Miss Annabella Lagrange would at least have blushed at this remark. With eyes lowered, she would have turned away from cousin Stephen even while the prospect he suggested excited her. Annabella Connolly did none of these things. After looking up at him, she laid her head against his breast and the pressure of her arms about him brought a heat and trembling to his body, until, pushing her from him almost roughly, he cried, "Come on." Then tugging her so that she had to jump when halfway down the steps, he ran her along by the field, across a rough, rut-strewn main road, up a steep hillside, and there they were at the other side of the valley from which he had at first spied the Carpenter glass works. But now, looking in the opposite direction, he pointed through the dusk, saying, "Do you see that speck?" and she said, "Yes, it's an early star." And he shook her, saying, "That's no star, it's a street light in Darlington. It could be gas, I don't know; they're putting it into the towns now. But that isn't what I brought you here for, miss. Follow my finger." He moved it to the right. "You see a dark object sticking up into the sky?"

"Yes, sir." Her voice was humble.

"Well, pay attention."

"Yes, sir."

"That is Denton Church, and it's there you're going nine days from today; you won't let it slip your mind, will you?" He was speaking as Lagrange might have done and she answered as a servant might, "No, sir." He now put his hands under the back of his short coat and flapped it like a man might the tails of a dress coat and rising on his toes he said, "You will have to sign the bond, you know that?"

"Yes, sir; I'm fully aware of it."

Still balancing back and forwards on his toes, he went on, "You should not have said you are fully aware, you should have said, 'Yes, sir, that's all right, sir.' You are talking above your station."

"Oh, Manuel!" There was a hurt note in her voice now and, her head back, she said, "Stop playing this game. We've been over and over it. I've told you in a thousand ways. If I haven't convinced you now, I never shall."

"That's the trouble." He was looking down toward the ground. "I doubt if you ever will. You see, I can't believe it. I fear something will happen, I fear you'll suddenly wake up and realize what you're doing, because what you're doing, in fact, is signing a bond to become a servant."

"As long as I'm yours, Manuel, I'll be happy to be that servant."

She waited for him to turn to her and enfold her in his arms again, but he didn't. He just raised his head and stared at her before he said, "I keep wondering, if you had a day, just one day of your old life back again, what your answer would be then?"

"The same."

She had given the answer to this question without thinking, and they both knew it.

They returned to the house by a different way and the journey took them past Mr. Carpenter's gate. Mr. Carpenter's house stood apart. It was a solid, plain house made of granite blocks, and it had an acre of garden surrounded by a picket fence.

At the gate this evening there was a nicely turned out pony and trap and, standing beside it, a man and a woman and Mr. Carpenter.

They had both seen the man and woman before. The man was Mr. Carpenter's stepson and the woman his wife. The sea captain, as Annabella had said on first seeing him, was larger than life, not only in his frame but in the way in which he acted, for she considered that with his overjovial manner and overloud voice, he was like a stage character depicting a rollicking sailor.

Whereas the man was big, burly, and outspoken, his wife on the other hand was thin and reticent, and Annabella, with a woman's intuition, had realized at their first meeting that her employer's daughter-in-law was very much against women's being employed in the glass works. Her displeasure hadn't been conveyed by what she had said, but how she had looked.

"Ah, hello there." The sea captain hailed them now. "Talk of the devil, they say. We were just hearing about you. Going to be married, eh? Well now, well now, never had a wedding at the works, have you?" He turned his head toward his stepfather, and Mr. Carpenter, smiling not at his stepson but toward the couple standing in front of him, said, "No, it'll be our first wedding."

As his eyes moved from one to the other, they thought, in their different ways, He's a nice man, and in their different ways they thanked God for having brought them into his employment. They were lucky; they were lucky all along the line.

The sea captain, as if reading at least Manuel's thoughts, said, "You're a lucky fellow. Do you know that? You're a lucky fellow."

"Yes, I know that, sir."

"A woman who knows all about glass and can take her stand in a glass house with the men and them not down tools, why, it's a miracle. It's almost the same as if my crew were presented with a woman captain. Hah! hah! hah!" His bellow rang out into the darkening night. Then, bending toward Annabella, his face thrust within inches of hers, he said in a very meaningful tone now, "And pretty into the bargain."

"Mark!" The name was like the crack of a whip, but it brought the captain's body only slowly upwards, and now, glancing at Manuel, he said, "If I'm not back for the day, good luck to you; but if I'm ashore, I'll come and drink to you."

To anyone else Manuel would have said, "Do that. You'll be welcome," but he didn't to this man. What he did was to take Annabella's arm and walk away, saying only as he passed Mr. Carpenter, "Good-night to you, sir." And Mr. Carpenter answered flatly, "Good-night, Manuel."

"I don't like him." They had reached the house before Manuel spoke.

"Nor do I. And I don't like her, either. She, I think, would be a very mean woman."

There was a silence between them as she took off her coat and Manuel lit the candle, and when they were seated at the table again, Manuel, voicing his train of thought, said, "We wouldn't reign long if they were here," and she answered, as she put her hand on top of his, "But they're not, and Mr. Carpenter likes you. And you know something, Manuel? I've got a feeling that he likes neither of them, so it all augurs good."

"I hope so."

As he stared into her eyes in the candlelight, Margee's face took shape, and he gave an impatient movement of his head, which made her say quickly, "What is it, Manuel?" and he answered her, "Nothing, nothing." But inside his mind he was troubled and he asked himself why it was that for weeks on end he never gave a thought to Margee, then, as if rising out of the grave, her face would come before him. He had come to look upon it as a sign, a warning. But what could happen now? What could happen here in this out-of-way little factory, from which vicinity they wouldn't move until they went over the hill and into the next valley and to the church a week come Wednesday? Nothing could happen. Nothing must happen. He wished he were a praying man.

2

It was over, signed and sealed and witnessed by Mr. Carpenter and Mr. Furnier. The old minister had mumbled the service. Before he had begun, he had looked at Annabella long and hard, and when he had come to the words "If any man know of any impediment—" he had waited longer than usual for an answer, at the same time knowing that he wouldn't get one, for the chapel held no one, with the exception of Mr. Carpenter, but workpeople and their wives.

Mr. Carpenter had so arranged the firings that it would be late tonight before the gatherers need get to work; besides declaring a holiday, he had told the Darlington men that they could bring in their wives and families, for he was giving the young couple a spread in the sorting shed, and after, there would be a bit of jollification.

Most of the employees had accepted this gesture without question, for their master was known to be an open-handed man, fair all round, but others said among themselves that it would have been understandable if the master had done it for an old hand. But this young fellow, agreeable as he was, had hardly been in the place long enough to cool a bottle, while others said it wasn't because of him the favor was being bestowed, but because of her. She was a kind of curio, for who ever heard of a woman not only doing the reckoning in a glass house but talking glass like she did? And in that voice of hers that was more suited to a drawing room than to a glass-house floor. It was an odd situation, they all agreed, and awkward, some put in, for a man had to mind his language. But least said soonest mended, for the master favored her.

Then one voice had brought the thought that was in all their minds to the surface: How had the Spaniard come to be marrying her? For, after all, no matter how he looked or acted, he was but a workman. There was something queer about it. But it was a wedding and a wedding meant drink and jollification, and who were they to look a gift horse in the mouth?

It was four o'clock in the afternoon when they sat down close together at the head of the long table in the sorting shed. There were forty-two people at the table, and these included Mr. Carpenter's stepson and his wife.

At first, the chatter at the table had been subdued, but by the time the hogshead of beer was half empty, there were loud laughter and quips and innuendoes acting as sauce to the food.

When it was noticed that Manuel kept refusing to have his mug refilled with beer, this caused jests to come flying at him like darts, and among them was the voice of the captain. "Wants to keep his head clear for later on; doesn't want to miss a trick, eh?"

During the whole meal Annabella had been uneasy and embarrassed. She hadn't expected it to be like this. Jolly, yes, but not this frank discussion about this very, very personal matter. She wished, oh, how she wished she could leave the table. But she mustn't; she must keep smiling. A slight feeling of fear came into her body as it had done during the wedding ceremony, for then she had thought, in a panic-filled way, This is forever, forever and ever. But she had known that, hadn't she? She had known she was taking Manuel forever. He had warned her of this only last night. "It's for good," he had said, "till one of us dies. You understand?"

Manuel's stomach muscles were knotting as if a pair of

281

hands were wringing them. He had been at weddings before. There was Agnes's, and there had been two weddings during his time at the House; he had known what to expect. Some of the chaffing would bring a blush to a bull, but the bride and groom had always seemed to weather it. Agnes and Dave hadn't turned a hair. But he knew that Annabella was cringing inside herself; he could feel the tenseness of her body. This thing that he had waited for so long could be marred. His loving her was to be something different, exceptional. All men who loved greatly must feel this way, he knew. They had the illusion that it had never happened before, and that's how it should be, and that's how it was going to be; at least, he had felt this way until they had started their chaffing. And that big, red-faced seaman was putting the cap on the lot of them. He'd like to take his hand and slap his mouth for him.

"Enough talk. Enough talk." Mr. Carpenter had read the danger signs. His stepson, as usual, was drinking too much and his loose tongue was becoming offensive.

The guests were surprised when the bridegroom wasn't called upon to say his piece. But what matter; they were going to dance, and there was still plenty more to eat and drink, and the evening was young.

It was around eight o'clock in the evening and the merriment was at its height. Everybody was very happy; even the captain's wife, after four glasses of wine, had unbent and had actually joined in a dance; and now she was acting hostess and distributing food. It was while she was handing out a glass of ale that she seemingly accidentally spilled the contents down Annabella's green cord dress. What reason she had for doing it wasn't obvious. Perhaps it was because her husband had boisterously whirled the bride twice around the room, or that her dress was too becoming, or that the incident was a slight indication of what she would like to do to this strange girl who was inveigling herself into her father-in-law's affections and who was but a female worker yet gave herself the airs and graces of a lady. Whatever it was, it caused consternation, and mostly to Annabella. This was the only presentable gown she possessed. Manuel had bought it for her and she loved it; it was her wedding gown. She would never get the thick brown beer stain out of it. Anyway, once corded velvet was washed, it was never the same again. To the exclamations of sorrow coming from the thin, dark woman, she answered as evenly as she could, "It's quite all right. I'll go and change," and, skirting the dancers and Manuel, where he was whirling the tubby Mrs. Furnier around the rough floor, she went out into the night.

There was no moon, no stars, but the lanterns that were hung outside the three shops pierced the blackness with an added radiance.

In the cottage she pulled off her wet dress and donned the working one that she had made at the Fairbairns'; then, taking the candle and going out into the little washhouse, she paused for a moment before plunging her wedding dress into the soaking tub. It was like a sacrifice she was making, for she had loved that gown and she had imagined showing it to her children years later, saying, "This is the dress your father bought me and this is what I was married in." But now it would be fit for nothing but working in. Still—she hurried into the kitchen—what did it matter, it was only a dress. They would make money and Manuel would buy her another one. They would go to Hexham to one of the fine shops, and they would sit on chairs, as she and her mama had done, and the materials would be brought to them, and she would say to Manuel, "What do you think about this soft rose, or this violet?" and he would say, if not with his voice, then with his eyes, "Any one of them will be more beautiful when they're on you," for Manuel could be gallant—it was the Irish in him. Soon the wedding party would be over and he would be here with her and the door shut tight. She pressed her hands over her cheeks; then pushing them up over her face she smoothed back her hair and ran out of the house and across the yard and toward the shops.

It was when she reached the third one that the arm came out and caught her. For a second she thought it was Manuel and her cry was half joyous, but it ended in a squealing protest when she saw through the dim light the face of the captain. He was breathing heavily and her struggles seemed to jerk the words out of him. "Ha! ha!—Like a tousle? Every man's privilege—kiss the bride. Always wanted to kiss you, me dear."

"MANUEL! MANU—!"

As his mouth covered hers, she freed one hand and punched at his face, and when this had no effect, she clawed him. Her mouth free once more, she had no breath to scream for a moment, but when she did, it was a high, wailing sound. *"Man-u-el! Man-u-el!"* The second time she called the name, it ended in a shriek as she felt the captain's hand inside her gown, his fingers clutching her breast.

When she was torn from him, she fell back against the wall; her head bounced against it and she slid down to the ground and for a moment everything went black around her. But she was brought to herself when hands lifted her up and dragged her to the side and away from the battling figures.

The captain was a big, strong man and he returned Manuel's blow in the ribs with a punch that sent him reeling against the pile of stacked wood.

Manuel leaned against the wood for a moment. He was in the shadows and he glared with ever-rising fury at the captain standing within the perimeter of the lantern light, his body crouched waiting. Manuel was only dimly aware of Mr. Carpenter clutching at his arm, shouting, "Stop this! Stop this, man!" Nor was he aware of thrusting his arm sideways and almost knocking the old man off his feet. There was only one thing clear in his mind, one desire, to drive his fists into that thick, lecherous face. He had never liked the man, but dislike had no connection with the feelings raging through him now. If he had had a gun in his hand, he would have used it; if he'd had a knife he would have thrown it; instead, he threw himself. His steel fists, flicking in and out between the captain's flaying arms, pounded at the thick body with seemingly no effect until, his shoulder sending his arm straight out, the knuckles caught the man on the jaw; it was the same blow that had felled Lagrange.

The captain now fell back like a great sodden log against the wood pile that had supported Manuel minutes before. Such was his weight and the force with which he hit it that the mainstay of the pile slipped and the big planks rained down on him from all sides.

There was a second of absolute silence from the crowd in the yard, and then the men were tearing away the wood and dragging the captain's great limp body free. There was no blood on his face but his mouth seemed twisted, and his wife threw herself on him, crying, "Mark! Mark!" and when her husband made no movement, she turned her head slowly and screamed up at Manuel where he was standing alone and in a daze. "You've killed him! You beast! You've killed him!"

Annabella now came to Manuel's side, but she was the only one who did. Everybody was crowding round the prostrate man. There was running backwards and forwards; then they lifted him onto a door and carried him into the house.

"Come, come," Annabella whispered, but Manuel stood as if his feet had taken root in the ground. The voices floated about him, sober-sounding now.

"A dreadful thing to happen."

284

"Is he dead?"

"This has been a weddin' an' a half we'll remember for a long time."

"How did it happen?"

"She was yellin', an' he went out and caught him at it."

"No reason to kill a man."

She had to tug hard at him before he moved, and then he stumbled as if he were drunk.

In the cottage he lowered himself down into a chair like an old man, and when she got a cloth and wiped the blood from his cut lip, he made no movement, and she dropped on her knees and put her arms about him and pressed her head against his breast, crying, "Oh, Manuel. Manuel."

He muttered something, and when she raised her head, he looked down into her eyes. "I've done it again, I've killed another man."

"No, no, Manuel, no. It—it was the wood falling on him. But—but he may be all right, we don't know."

"I've killed another man. What is it that is on me?" He pressed her gently from him and looked at his hands, turning them over a number of times as if he hadn't seen them before.

When she began to cry, he did not comfort her. He seemed unaware that she was weeping; he just sat looking at his hands hanging between his knees.

She said now brokenly, "You did it in my defense; he—he was insulting me."

"They used to cut them off in some parts for killing a man." He raised his right hand and examined it again. Then, getting to his feet, he went and stood looking into the fire, and with his back to her and his voice more normal now he said, "I couldn't bear prison. I would rather they hanged me."

"Don't talk like that, please." She dragged him round and pressed him to her, and now, his hand on her hair, stroking it gently, he said, "It's true. I would wither away behind walls. I've—I've been in the open all me life. I couldn't stand it, I know the limit of me strength. I'd rather be hung right off."

"Oh, Manuel." Her head began to roll on her shoulders in despair. "I'm to blame, I'm the cause of it all. I've brought this upon you. If it weren't for me—"

"Be quiet. What has to be will be: the pattern was cut out a long time ago."

"What are we going to do?"

"Wait, just wait."

They waited for another hour, scarcely speaking, sitting

hand in hand before the fire, and then Mr. Carpenter came in. He spoke as he opened the door. "Are you there?" he said.

They got to their feet and stood staring at him, and it was a few seconds before he could speak, for his breath was coming in gasps as if he had been hurrying, and what he said was, "How long would it take you to get the wagon on the road again?"

"He's dead then?" Manuel's voice sounded thin.

"No, no, he's not dead."

"He's not dead?" Manuel's head and shoulders seemed to fall forward over the old man.

"No, he's got a dislocated jaw and his shoulder's out and there's some concussion, I think, but he's far from dead. But even so, it means trouble for you. I've sent for the doctor, but she's sent for the police. At present she's worked up and in a state and I can't do much with her for she's determined to get rid of you. You might as well know, she's jealous of you both; I was foolish in singing your praises. By tomorrow morning I may have made her see sense, but by that time you could be in jail and a charge against you, so my advice to you is to take to the road for a while, for a week or two." He looked from one to the other and smiled at them now. "It won't do you any harm, a sort of holiday. And then make your way back. But don't come straight here; make your way to Darlington first and I'll leave a message for you at the shop if everything is all right, you understand?"

"Yes, sir." Manuel's body seemed to have become deflated with relief. "And thank you, sir. Oh, thank you."

"Well, don't delay now. Pack up what you need and get off. They could be here within the next two hours. But even if she still wants to lay the charge, they couldn't do much searching for you in the dark. I think you'd be well advised to keep moving during the night and keep clear of Hexham and the towns for they could send a runner ahead." He now put his hands in his pocket and, drawing out an envelope, added, "There's what's owing to you both, and a little over. And remember, I'll be glad to see you back."

Annabella came forward now and stood before the old man and, taking his hand, she pressed it tightly in her own, saying, "Thank you for your kindness, Mr. Carpenter. And— and we shall find some way to repay you, believe me we shall."

"It's all right, me dear." He nodded at her, pressed her hand in return, then said sadly, "That this should happen on such a night." Then he turned from her and went out, leaving

286

his words ringing in both their heads. "That this should happen on such a night." It was, Manuel thought, as if God were stepping in at the last minute to prevent him committing a sacrilege. But 'twas no sacrilege; she was not a Lagrange, a high-born lady. She was bred of common people, aye, and very common, and she was his wife.

And Annabella's mind was racing around the thought, I'm fated to bring ill luck to him.

But their thinking did not stop their bustling, and within a matter of minutes they had gathered up their few belongings and their kitchen utensils and bundled them all into the sheepskin bag which they had already come to look upon as a souvenir of those days that were over, and lastly, Annabella wrung out the dress. Then they went cautiously through the back way and to the field, and having harnessed to the wagon a surprised and sleepy horse and lit one small lamp, Manuel led the animal onto the road; and he stayed at its head for the next three hours, and there wasn't a word exchanged between him and Annabella, sitting stiffly, holding the reins on the box seat.

It was around two o'clock in the morning when he drew the horse onto a green siding and said in a voice that sounded like a croak, "I'll rest him for a while, and we could have a hot drink. It's bitter."

When they were in the wagon with the light between them, he looked at her white face. Then, putting his hands out to her, he muttered, "Oh, Annabella!" and she came into his arms and they stood close, but quietly. They did not even kiss or strain to one another; there seemed to be a blight on them both. Pushing her gently from him now, he said, "I won't light the stove, it'll take too long. I'll make a fire outside."

"Where are we now, Manuel?"

"I'm not sure, it's a strange road. I turned north at the crossroads leading to Bildershaw because that way you go into Bishop Auckland. I would say we're some way between Mildridge and Mordon. There's villages and towns around here. We'll have to wind our way atween them."

He went out and she sat down on the bed at the end of the wagon, the bed that could be used as a double bed but which had been hers alone during their days of travel. Now the bed did not concern her. She joined her hands tightly between her knees. It was an attitude she hadn't assumed before, but never before had she been so afraid. In the past she had known fear, but for herself; this fear she had for

287

Manuel was churning her bowels and making her want to retch. What would happen if that woman did send the police after them? The answer her mind gave to this question was not, "What would become of me then?" but "How will Manuel endure it?" As he had said, he had spent all his life in the open and he would not be able to stand being shut in for weeks on end, months, even years. Oh, dear, dear God.

As Manuel came up the steps with the black can of tea in his hand, he saw her for the moment in the lantern light, huddled up, her hands between her knees, her body rocking. Putting the can quickly on the table, he went to her and sat on the bed beside her, then took her into his arms again and pressed her head into his shoulder, saying, "It's all right. It's all right. Everything will be all right. But listen to me, I've been thinking." He now put his hand gently under her chin and brought her wet face up to his. "Now look, this is just in case, a precaution, a sort of precaution in case that woman carries out her threat. I'm going to give you me belt." He stood up now, unbuttoned his coat and pulled his shirt up out of his trousers and unlaced the flannel belt from his waist.

With her fingers over her mouth, she looked at the bare flesh of her husband's stomach as he carried out what was to her a very personal act and she protested weakly, "No, no, Manuel."

What he said to this, and somewhat harshly now was, "Yes, yes. Stand up with you. Now lift your dress up an' your petticoat." She stared at him for a moment and her head made an almost imperceptible motion that meant she couldn't comply; then slowly she was pulling her skirt up to her waist, and then her top petticoat, disclosing her faded and worn silk one that barely covered her frilled bloomers.

Manuel was kneeling on the floor now, his eyes on the belt, but every detail of her stark clear in his mind, making his blood race and his stomach churn and his hands sweat. She was his wife; it could happen now. It was no sacrilege. To hell with such thoughts. But if he should drop a child into her the first time, what then? and she was left alone, for how long? How long would they give him for what he had done? A month? Six months? No, a year more like.

He said without looking up, "See these pockets? They're all round it. There's twenty-seven sovereigns in them altogether. Wherever you go, don't take it off, even when you're sleeping, only to wash, and then keep it to hand. . . . And—

288

and look." He put his hand into an inside pocket. "I'll put our marriage certificate in an' all—it's the safest place."

"But—but Manuel." She had dropped the petticoat down but was still holding the skirt, and she bent toward him now, "But you don't think they will—?"

"No, no." He lifted his head and looked at her. "But it's best to be on the safe side, and I was thinking out there"— he didn't say that the sound of a galloping horse had put the thought into his mind—"I was thinking out there we'll make for the Spennymoor road."

"Spennymoor?" The word was soft and high. "But—but that's on the road to Durham."

"Yes; but there's woods and caves around there. We could hide more easily I think, at least for the fortnight or so as Mr. Carpenter advised. And then we'll make our way back again. . . . Lift your petticoat."

Again slowly she raised her petticoat, now keeping her eyes fixed on the wagon wall where the picture of a long boat was fading away. When she felt his hands go round her waist and his fingers move over the steels of her corsets as he pulled the laces of the belt tight, she shivered. His voice was thick and low as he said, "Wear it near your flesh after this."

She made no answer. She was standing taut. Then his hands came over hers where they were gripping her skirt and petticoat and he loosened them from the cloth, and when her clothes fell down again, he knelt looking up at her. And then, with a swift movement, he laid his face against her stomach and, his arms about her like steel bars, he pressed his face into her while she held his head. But it was over in a minute.

When he got to his feet, he almost overbalanced her, and he did not put his hand out to save her but went to the table and poured out the tea.

Half an hour later they were on the road again.

When the first streaks of dawn appeared, Manuel was sitting on the box, the reins in his hand, and Annabella, fighting off sleep, was supporting herself between him and the ornamental fretwork that was part of the wooden hood. Although they had frequently got down when on a hill to lighten the horse's burden, its steps were dragging now, and when Manuel espied a copse bordering a field, he said, "This is as far as we can go for the present. Anyway, it would be wiser to keep going at night and rest up during the day."

She said nothing, but when they had halted the wagon and Manuel had unharnessed the horse, he said to her, "You lie down while I get us something to eat," and she answered, "I couldn't eat, Manuel; I just want to sleep."

"Well, do that." His voice was tender, his gaze was tender, and he handed her up the steps, but did not follow her.

How long she had slept she didn't know, but it must have been a while because when she opened her eyes the sun was well up. But something had awakened her, not just the light. Then of a sudden she knew what it was and she sprang up from the bed and bent down to the window, and she saw the ugly-looking coach on the road and the three men standing before it. And some distance away Manuel was standing and the men were talking to him over the distance.

When she left the wagon, she ignored the steps and leaped down them as he would have done, and then she was flying toward him. Gripping his arm and speaking under her breath, she said, "What is it? What do they want? Oh, Manuel!" yet all the while knowing what they wanted. Their uniforms told her what they wanted.

He did not look at her but kept his eyes fixed on the men as he said to her, "Listen to me. Now, listen to me. We're not far from Durham. You know the way from there. Make for Amy's. Don't stop for anything or anyone—make for Amy's."

"Manuel!"

"Do as I tell you." He put his hand out and gripped hers that was holding his arm.

One of the men shouted, "Now, we want no trouble with you," but he did not come forward; it was as if he were expecting trouble, were prepared for it.

Manuel said, "What do you want with me?"

"You know well enough what we want with you. Assault and battery of one Captain Weir on the premises of Carpenter's Glass Works. Now are you comin' quietly or do you want us to come and get you?"

"Where do you intend to take me?"

"That's our business."

"If you want me peaceably, where do you intend to take me?"

The man paused a moment, then said, "Durham. We're from there; we were put onto you."

There came into Manuel's mind the sound of the galloping horse during the night. Mrs. Weir hadn't lost much time, damn her, blast her. And him. Oh aye, blast him to hell's flames. He looked down now at Annabella and said, "Listen." He had to grip both her forearms to stop her shivering. "Do you hear? Listen to me. Do as I say, make your way straight for Amy's; you'll be all right there."

"Oh, Manuel, Manuel, they can't, they can't."

"Be quiet; they can—they are." He now pulled her into his arms and held her for a moment; then, putting his mouth to hers, he kissed her once, before pushing her away and walking toward the men.

As he approached them, they spread out, but when he made no fighting move, they closed in about him. Opening the back door of the coach, they pushed him forward, and two of the men followed while the third closed the doors after them. Then he mounted the box and the black, ugly coach drove away, leaving her standing on the verge of the road looking after it.

"Oh, Manuel, Manuel. Oh, Manuel, Manuel." That was all her brain was capable of saying at the moment. "Oh, Manuel, Manuel."

It was a full ten minutes before she moved from the road back to the wagon and then, dropping to the bottom step, she sat staring before her. The horse was grazing peacefully, the sun was shining, on the distant hill there were moving dots that spoke of young lambs; a lark shot from the grass near her and soared straight up into the heavens, its throat bursting with notes. Oh, Manuel, Manuel. What would they do to him in that place? The house of correction was a grim building; she had seen it only once. Her mama had said it was where they housed bad men. Bad men? Manuel wasn't bad, Manuel was good. To the very, very heart of him he was good. What he had done he had done to protect her. But would they take that into consideration when he came before a judge? Her head came up and her shoulders went slowly back. If he came before the judge and there was no one to speak for him, he'd be treated as a criminal. Her body straightened further now. What she must do was to get help, someone to speak for him. She had money. She put her hand on her waist. Twenty-seven sovereigns Manuel had said. But what was twenty-seven sovereigns to legal people? To people on the road, as they had been, it was a fortune, but to people from her old life it was pin money, not even that. She must think, she must think. She'd do as he said and go to Amy's.

But no, that was too near the House. She couldn't bear to be so near the House again. But where would she go? What would she do?

She stood up now and looked about her quickly as if on the point of a run. She knew what she would do; she knew where she'd get help, legal help. She would go to Weirbank House—she would see Stephen. Stephen was in law. He'd know what to do, he would help her.

But could she face Stephen? Of course, she could face Stephen. Why not? She had no pride left. If the journey on the road hadn't taken it out of her, Manuel's plight had. He was all that mattered; getting him free was all that mattered. She would go; she would go this minute.

She ran and got the horse and harnessed him and put him between the shafts, and as she climbed up into the high driving seat and took up the reins, she did not immediately say, "Gee up there!" for her hands were stayed by the thought, How will they receive me? And then she was flapping the reins vigorously, crying, "Gee up! Gee up, Dobbie!" What did it matter how they received her? She knew what her mind had stopped short of saying: How would they receive Mrs. Manuel Mendoza? How would they take the fact that their dear Annabella was now the wife of the groom? Again wagging the reins vigorously, her mind told her she didn't care how they took it because it was a fact and it was something that couldn't be undone. She was the wife of Manuel. For good and all, she was the wife of Manuel; in prison or free, she was the wife of Manuel Mendoza.

3

Half an hour ago she had left the wagon on the road outside the gates of the short drive that led to Weirbank House and when she had rung the bell and the door opened, Frances, the old maid, had screamed at the sight of her, and Bella, the second housemaid, had put her apron over her head and moaned. But their reaction was nothing to when her Great-Aunt Emma had seen her, for she had swooned right away. It was only Uncle James who seemed to keep his head. And now she was sitting on a couch holding Great-Aunt Emma's hand within hers, and the old lady kept staring at her, then shaking her head as if she still couldn't believe that she wasn't looking at a ghost, the poorly clad, sad-faced, changed ghost

of the beautiful young girl she had known as Annabella
Lagrange. And that was another thing she couldn't take in.
This was no longer a young girl; this person sitting by her
side was a woman and she talked like a woman. She remembered that Annabella had been given to high laughter and
slight frivolity, but the face before her looked as if it had
never known laughter or frivolity of any kind; and this as-
tounding tale she was telling was unbelievable, quite unbelievable, and highly unacceptable. The child had been taken
advantage of, that was quite plain.

Her husband was thinking along similar lines and it was
he who voiced both their thoughts as, patting Annabella's
head, he said, "The whole thing's been an unfortunate mistake
from beginning to end, my dear, most unfortunate, but nevertheless it can be righted. After what you have told us, there's
been no real harm done. Manuel, in a way, is to be com-
mended for protecting you, but—but he should never have
gone so far as to force you into marrying him."

"Force me! But Uncle, you don't understand. He didn't
force me, I—I wanted to, I wanted to marry Manuel long
before he asked me."

"You don't know what you're saying, child. You don't
know what you're saying." Aunt Emma was now fanning herself with her lace-edged handkerchief. "You can't possibly
marry Manuel. Manuel is a groom, a workman."

Annabella looked down at the fragile face. Then she spoke
as if she were trying to make a dull child understand some
simple thing. "Aunt Emma," she said, "I have married
Manuel; I'm already married to Manuel. I have the marriage
certificate. It is here, in a belt round my waist." She patted
her stomach.

"Let me see it." It was Uncle James speaking now, and
when she looked up at him and said, "I would have to undress
first," he wiped his forehead and muttered, "Well, well, I must
see it later."

"You shall see it, Uncle James." She disengaged her hand
from the old lady's and, standing up, she looked at the tall
old man, saying, "What I came for, Uncle James, was to
see Stephen and ask him to take up Manuel's case."

"Oh, my dear, my dear. Well now, this is most unfortunate,
and I know if Stephen were available he would do his utmost
to help you, yes, indeed he would, but, my dear, you're not
to know that he was married last week and he's now in Italy
on his honeymoon with dear Kathleen."

She sat down on a chair as if her legs had given way and

drooped her head forward, and Uncle James said practically.
"But there are other solicitors and barristers. We must talk
about this. But first of all, I think we should all have something to eat; it's close on three and the bell is about to go,
I'm sure."

Within a second or so the bell went, and Aunt Emma
raising herself up from the couch, said, "You know what no
one of us has thought about with the shock you have given
us all, dear, is the happiness that you are going to bring to
Rosina again."

"Ma—Mama?" She used the term because she could not
think of any other form of address. "I—I understand she's
very ill and wouldn't know me."

"Wouldn't know you?" It was Uncle James speaking again.
"Who gave you that idea?"

"Well, Manuel went to Grandma's when I was ill. He
wanted to see Mama, but Grandma ordered him away and
said that Mama wouldn't know me if she saw me as she had
lost her reason."

"Oh! Oh! The wickedness of it." Aunt Emma was gazing
at her husband now, and, putting her hands to her face, she
swayed gently as she repeated, "Oh! The wickedness, the
wickedness." Then she added, "I always said that Constance
was wicked, James, be she your sister and dead, I always
said she was wicked, and a stern, hardhearted woman." She
now turned to Annabella, and grasping her hand once again,
she ended, "Rosina, your dear mama, never lost her mind.
She was ill, very ill through losing you, but her reason was
never impaired; she lost the will to live for a time, naturally,
but she is recovered and she's still your dear mama and, as
I said, will be overjoyed to see you and have you back home."

"Dear Aunt Emma, I must make you understand"—
Annabella pressed her thin hands together—"that I'm no
longer the young girl—what I mean is, I'm no longer Annabella Lagrange."

"Come along, come along." Uncle James was now pressing
them both forward down the room toward the dining room.
"We'll talk about this later, but now let us first of all, before
we say grace, thank God that you have been given back to
us, and then we must eat because one cannot reason and
think on an empty stomach."

How often during those first days on the road had she
longed to be back amid the comfort and amenities of the
House; even over the last few days before her wedding the

thought had crept into her mind of how wonderful it would have been if she were going to be married from the House.

Now she was back in the old life—if not actually in the House, in one similar to it, only on a minor scale, there being only ten servants at Weirbank; but the strangest thing now was that she was ill at ease in this environment, as she would have been if she had spent the first seventeen years of her life in Crane Street and then been picked up bodily and placed here.

Twenty-four hours had passed since her arrival and with each hour she was becoming more irritated with everything and everybody. The way the old people spent hours talking about trivialities, even the way the servants moved. She had thought once or twice, They want Mrs. Fairbairn after them, or better still Mrs. Skillen; and then there were the delaying tactics applied by Uncle James. He seemed dilatory even with advice as to which solicitor in the town she should apply to take Manuel's case. When she told him she had twenty-seven guineas and that although she knew that would not be sufficient to cover the legal fees, she would work and pay whatever was owing over this amount, he had laughed, then appeared slightly shocked, and finally said he must have time to consider the matter. And when, later, he informed her that he had considered it and thought it best to consult his friend Colonel Ryson tomorrow when he returned from London, she had startled him by saying, "Tomorrow might be too late," and, what was more, she was going to the house of correction herself to ask if she could see Manuel.

Aunt Emma had actually shed tears at this outrageous statement. "You would never do anything so improper, Annabella, surely? To go to the house of correction on your own!"

It was then she had looked at them and had realized that on the nineteenth of June last year she had left their world forever, and it came to her that they had not the slightest conception of how people lived outside the walls that confined their particular social life. Aunt Emma did good works; she sewed for the poor, and donated quite a lot of money to charities, particularly to the heathen, whose greatest need, she considered, was to be brought to God; but neither she nor yet her husband knew anything of the lives of the ordinary people about them.

She sat waiting now in the small drawing room for her uncle to come and accompany her to the prison. He said he'd had to put many wheels in motion before permission had been granted for her to see Manuel, as the visiting day was still a week hence; and deep in her mind she doubted whether she'd be going to see Manuel today at all if it weren't that she had absolutely refused to return to the House and meet her mama until she had first seen and talked with him, and the not too subtle threat that she would return to the wagon and live on the outskirts of the town until she knew what was going to happen to Manuel finally persuaded Uncle James to "set wheels in motion."

It was only ten minutes' walk from the house to the prison, but they made the journey by carriage. When it entered Stone Street and drew to a stop against a line of cottages, she looked across the road to the grim, high walls opposite and thought, Dear God! He's behind those; that alone will be enough to kill him.

They went through the gate, across a courtyard, through another door, and then an officer was speaking to Uncle James. She didn't take in a word he said, for she was waiting, just waiting.

They went into a passageway, and as the door clanged behind them she started, and Uncle James put his hand on her elbow, and then they were shown into a large, bare room where the officer asked them to wait.

She would not be seated but stood staring at the door until Manuel came through, and there was another officer behind him. And this man came in and stood with his back to the door while Manuel stood looking at her and she at him, and neither of them moved for a number of seconds; then it was she who rushed forward and threw her arms around him and kissed his stiff lips. Then she searched his face with her eyes and said, "Oh, Manuel! Manuel! How are you?"

He swallowed deeply, blinked his eyes, pressed one lip tightly over the other, then answered, "All right—all right."

"This is Great-Uncle James." She turned her head on her shoulder. "I wanted to get help for you. I—I went to see Stephen but—but he's away. But Uncle James is going to help, he's going to get you a solicitor."

Manuel looked at Mr. Dorcy-Grant, as he knew him, but he gave him no sign of recognition or word of thanks, and the old man coughed in his throat and moved from one foot to the other as if it were he who was at a disadvantage; then he said in a pompous tone, "We'll do what we can. We'll do what we can." He omitted the "my man," because he felt that the term might bring this new Annabella storming at

296

him. As his wife had said, she had lost a lot of her nice ways and gained a lot of unpleasant ones during the time she had been absent.

Annabella, gabbling now, said, "We're going to see a solicitor as soon as we leave. Your case is coming up next Tuesday. There's not much time, but—but I have written to Mr. Carpenter and asked him if he can possibly come. He'll be able to explain things, don't you think?"

"Perhaps."

The syllable cut her to the heart and again she was clasping his hands to her, saying, "Oh, Manuel! Manuel! It will be all right. It will be all right. Uncle James knows a good solicitor."

Looking back into her eyes now, Manuel asked, "Where are you livin'?"

She didn't want to give him an answer to this because the answer he would want to hear from her was "I am still in the wagon," but she said as she had to, "I am staying with Great-Uncle James; they—they have been very kind. But—but it's only for a time, until your case comes up."

In the awkward silence that followed, the policeman's voice said, "Time's up!" and she cried at him, "But he hasn't been here but a few minutes."

The man stared at her and repeated automatically, "Time's up!"

It was only now that Manuel seemed to come alive. Taking her in his arms, he held her tightly before turning quickly away and walking out, followed by the officer.

Uncle James was peeved. The fellow wasn't even civil; he had become boorish. He had been a pleasing enough servant, but there was a great gulf between a servant and the husband of Annabella. The quicker he got this business disentangled, the better for all concerned. He was going to take a firm hand—he must.

In the carriage again, he showed his hand by saying, "Annabella, I want you to listen to me. I'm going to do nothing for that fellow until you promise to go and see your mama. Now, it's no use talking, I won't listen. That's my final word. You go and see Rosina and I will set the law into motion on his behalf, but not otherwise."

Her stiff face, her silence told him that he had won this first round. From now on the going should be easy, for once she was back under the protection of Rosina and living to some extent her old life, she would forget this breach of social etiquette, because that's what it amounted to, and during the time the fellow was in prison—for solicitor, barrister, or no, he would certainly do time for his assault on that sea captain —they would see to having the marriage annulled.

4

Both Uncle James and Aunt Emma said they would accompany her to the meeting with Rosina, because it would be a most joyous occasion. Rosina was beside herself with happiness; she couldn't believe the news and she said she wouldn't until she could see Annabella for herself.

That their suggestion should be instantly refused upset them both. Indeed, indeed, dear Annabella had changed, and not, they were afraid, for the better. The circumstances under which she had lived over the past months had left their mark on her. Uncle James had warned Rosina of this. He had also laid their course of action carefully. He had been against Rosina's coming at once to Durham; it would be more advantageous, he said, for Annabella to come to the House, at least to the cottage, as the House was no longer occupied. But anyway, here was the atmosphere of her upbringing; here under Rosina's guidance her nature had been formed, and here, please God, she would return to herself. But, he had warned her, Annabella was no longer the amenable girl that they remembered so dearly. Her manner was completely changed. Of course, this was to be understood when you considered her story. It was a case of not being able to touch pitch without becoming defiled, only in a lesser form. She had, for almost a year now, been mixing, even living closely with menials. Had she not married one? Of course they must not be too hard on Manuel. He had done what he had done to protect her, for Annabella said he had been the soul of honor. But the necessity for his protection was over; Annabella could now return to the life she was made for—at least, he qualified, the life dear Rosina had made for her. And when the publicity and scandal had died—and she must prepare herself for this, for Annabella's reappearance as the wife of their one-time groom would certainly create a scandal—life would pick up where it had left off. And she was fortunate, for the isolation in which she lived would enable her to ignore wagging tongues. So he had comforted Rosina, saying finally,

298

once the trial was over and the case for annulment was put into motion the thing would die, like all nine-day wonders, a natural death.

"Believe me, Uncle James, I have no wish to offend you—you have been so good—but I would rather take this journey alone. I can get the coach to the crossroads."

"But, child!"

"Please, Aunt Emma."

They both stared at this girl who was becoming stranger every hour they knew her, and it was only the fear that she might insist on making the journey to the House in that dreadful wagon that checked their pressure. But Aunt Emma couldn't fail to have the last word. "You can pick up all kinds of things in those public conveyances," she said, then dabbed at her nose with a scented handkerchief. And Annabella wished she could laugh. Then, a strange emotion rising in her, almost touching on ferocity, she had the desire to whisk her Aunt Emma into the room in Reuben's lodging house, into the Skillens' farm, to make her stand in the Market Place at the hirings.

In the hall she almost pushed off Frances's hands as she went to button her cloak for her, then in the next breath she nearly apologized for her roughness, but Frances would not have understood; Frances was happy in servitude, as so many people seemed to be. Yet not all; oh no, not all.

"But the coach does not go for another half hour, my dear." Uncle James was behind her now, and without turning her head she said, "I know, Uncle James, but I have a little errand I would like to do first."

He said no more, but he stood at the top of the steps and watched her go down the drive. He knew what errand she was going on, and he was both annoyed and shocked.

It was around twelve o'clock when Annabella stood against the cottages in Stone Street and looked across at the great stone wall and the ugly buildings behind, and she willed her thoughts to pass through the bricks and mortar and to make Manuel aware of her presence. The gate was opened, and a man emerged. He looked like a workman and she had to stop herself from running to him and saying, "Do you know Manuel Mendoza? Are you going back in there? Would you please give him a message? Tell him I'll be waiting. I told him yesterday but he didn't seem to understand. But tell him I'll be waiting no matter how long."

The man passed along the other side of the road without looking at her. Had he turned his face toward her, she might have been tempted to give him the message.

An old woman at a cottage door said, as if speaking to herself, "Aye, you're not the only one to stand there, lass. But there it is, if they'd done a bit of thinkin' and kept their feet on the right path, those walls wouldn't have seen them."

She felt an anger against the old woman. She wanted to bawl at her, "My Manuel kept to the right path! He's in there because he defended me." Instead, she walked with bent head up to the corner of the market, where the coach would stop, and as she stood waiting she told herself these angry spells would get her nowhere, she must curb these feelings.

The coach put her down at the crossroads at two o'clock in the afternoon and she asked the driver at what time one would be passing this way back to Durham. "Five o'clock," he called to her, "or thereabouts, but you'd better be afore time, We could be ten minutes up, or ten minutes after, no knowin'."

When the coach had rattled away she stood and looked about her. There was the road to Newcastle, there was the road to Jarrow and Shields. It wasn't just ten months since she had run blindly down this road, surely! Surely, it must be ten years, ten lifetimes. For the girl who on that day had been so eaten up with shock and sorrow was someone, she felt, she had never known, someone who had no part in herself as she was now. She had been growing up fast over the last months, but since Manuel had stepped into that wagon, every hour had become a year. And now inside she was an old woman, old and knowledgeable, for she had experienced pain, pain which Miss Annabella Lagrange could never have experienced, the pain of really loving, without the romance attached; the pain of pity and worry and anxiety.

When she reached the lodge gates, she stopped in surprise and stared through them at the grass-grown drive, at the straggly, variegated privet hedge that surrounded the lodge garden and which at one time had been as level on the top as any table.

The gates were closed but not locked and she entered and went past the dark, empty windows of the lodge and up the drive and round the curve, and there was the House as she had never seen it before, for it looked lonely, lost. Always the House had had people in it, and about it. She couldn't remember it without movement of some sort. Servants at one time had been as thick as flies buzzing around it; now there was no sign of life. She felt sad, deeply sad.

She passed by the steps and went toward the stables. The stone flags in the yard were bordered with grass; all the doors in the yard were closed with the exception of one. She went slowly toward it and looked in. The harness room was empty, not only of people, but of saddles and bridles and brasses and bits. She thought, as she looked round the room, that this sight would indeed break Manuel's heart. But then his heart must already be broken, as his spirit was and his body soon would be if she didn't get him out of that place.

She left the yard quickly and went down, through the pagoda walk. At one point she had to push aside the tangle of last year's roses until she reached the gardens, and she had to ask herself, Could a place become so derelict in ten months? The peacock hedges were sprouting branch feathers in all directions, which gave them a drunken appearance. Then she went across the park, and there was the cottage.

Now her step slowed and her heart began to race. How was she to address her? "Mama"? "Mrs. Lagrange"?

She was at the door. She was knocking.

Harris opened it. It was as if he had been standing behind it, waiting, and like the servants at Weirbank he was overcome by the sight of her, and he muttered under his breath, "Oh, Miss Annabella! Miss Annabella."

"Good-day, Harris."

"Good-day, Miss Annabella. May I say I'm happy to see you again?"

"And I you, Harris." Her low voice was cut off by the sight of Alice coming down the staircase. Three steps from the bottom Alice paused for a moment, then, in haste to reach the hall, she stepped onto her long gown and almost fell into Annabella's arms. "Oh, child! Child."

"Hello, Alice. How are you?"

"Oh, my dear! Oh, child, it's good to see you again. I'm all right. I'm all right. How are you? Oh, you've been through a time." Her short, staccato sentences were bouncing one off the other. "She's waiting, been waiting for hours, just sitting waiting. This is the happiest day of her life; I'd swear this is the happiest day of her life." Alice had so forgotten herself as to use the term "I swear," and this was not lost on Annabella. She smiled kindly at the old woman, who for years, she knew, had considered her the product of the devil. Even when she herself hadn't been aware of her parentage, Alice

301

had instilled into her the feeling that she had been born in sin. "Go on. Go on, don't waste a minute." She was pushing her toward the drawing-room door.

Now she had her hand on the knob and she turned and looked at Alice, and Alice, a thin smile stretching her parchment-like face, thrust it forward as if the very act would push Annabella through the door.

Her heart had raced before, but now it was bounding unevenly as if it were being ricocheted from one side of her rib casing to the other.

Now the door was opening and she was entering the room, and there was Rosina, standing as she had seen her countless times, dignified, patient, plain, and the pity that she'd had for the House was multiplied a thousandfold and she had the desire to rush forward and enfold the sadfaced woman in her arms, in her new, strong, protective arms. But she seemed unable to move from the door.

It was Rosina's voice saying brokenly, "Oh, my dearest, dearest child," that gave power to her limbs; and then they were clasping each other, tightly, lovingly.

"Let me look at your face." Rosina pressed her gently away and led her to a stiff upholstered couch, and together they sat down and gazed at one another. And Rosina said, "Child, oh, child, you've changed," and Annabella, her voice picking up the routine of question and answer that had been automatic to her at one time, said, "Yes, Ma—" Then, her head drooping slightly, she said, "Yes, I have changed. It's—it's been a long time."

"Yes, my dear, it's been a long time." Rosina paused, then said, "Why did you hesitate on my name?"

Annabella now raised her eyes and, looking into this pale face that didn't seem to have changed at all, said, "I'm—I'm at a loss as to what to call you."

"What can you call me but 'Mama'?" Rosina said softly. "I was your mama for seventeen years, my dear. It isn't birth that makes a human being, it's environment. I gave you environment; you are my daughter still, I am your mama. Believe me, dear, I am your mama. And that's all I want from life, just to be your mama. You are my child, Annabella, in every possible way, except one, and that is of no matter. You do understand this, don't you? I am your mama."

"Yes—"

Rosina now bent forward, and drawing Annabella's hands to her breast, she whispered, "Say it. Please let me hear you say it."

"—Mama."

Rosina smiled slowly and put out her hand and touched Annabella's cheek. "You are so thin, child."

Looking back at Rosina, Annabella could have said the same thing. "You are so thin." And, now that she was looking at her closely, she saw that she looked so much older than when she had last seen her.

"This is indeed the happiest day of my life. You believe that, my dear?"

"Yes, Mama."

Rosina now in her turn studied the girl before her. Her words were the same, docile, biddable words, "Yes, Mama," but the tone in which she said them was different. Uncle James had warned her of the difference, but that had not troubled her. Only let her be with her child for a short while and everything would be as it had been before; those ten awful months tramping the country roads would be obliterated. Of course, there was Manuel to be considered, but that, thank God, was a matter that could be easily dealt with for the simple reason that the marriage hadn't been consummated. Oh, they were lucky in this, very lucky, and once Annabella had a taste of her old life, she, too, would realize it had all happened for the best. She said now, "You look tired, my dear; we'll have some tea and then we will talk. Alice and Bridget have your room all ready for—"

"I'm sorry, Mama." Annabella didn't actually rise to her feet, but she moved a little along the sofa and again she said, "I'm sorry, but I'm returning to Uncle James; I'm—I'm catching the coach from the crossroads at five o'clock."

"But my child, you've only just come and—"

"I can come again. But until I know what is going to happen to Manuel—I—I know that Uncle has told you all about Manuel and myself—well, until I know what they intend to do with him, I want to be as near as possible to him."

Rosina felt herself freezing as she hadn't done for almost a year now, not since HE had gone. Her mind racing, she thought, Dear God, don't put any more obstacles in my way for I won't be able to bear them. You have given her back to me, let us live in peace. But she made herself say calmly, "Yes, Uncle James told me. But, my dear, you won't be able to visit Manuel every day. And it will surely be harrowing for you, and you've gone through enough."

"I have been through little—Mama. It is Manuel who has suffered, and is still suffering."

"Yes, yes, of course." Rosina's lids drooped. "He has, on the whole, been very good, very thoughtful; if only he could have seen me that day when he called instead of my mama, then you would not have been subjected to all the misery, and this last great mistake."

Annabella slowly withdrew her hands from Rosina's and slowly, but without bitterness, she said, "If you're referring to my marriage with Manuel, Mama, then you have used the wrong word to describe it. It was no mistake, I wanted it. I—I can admit freely now I wanted it long before he proposed it."

"Well, strange as it may seem, my dear, I can understand that, too, because you must have found your position traveling with him almost untenable and you likely saw this as the only proper and decent way out."

"No, Mama. No, Mama." Annabella was shaking her head. "It wasn't like that at all. I—I wanted to marry Manuel because I loved him."

"Oh, child!" Rosina's tone spelled patience and she shook her head slowly. "What do you know about love except from a girlish point of view? You're only eighteen and—"

"I was old enough at seventeen to marry Stephen, if he had been available."

Rosina rose to her feet and walked toward the fireplace and looked down into the fire for a moment before turning and smiling at Annabella, and saying, "My dear, I want you to know that I hold Manuel in high esteem and I don't look at the situation in the same light as Uncle James does. I know that Manuel did the right thing from the very beginning. He not only searched for you, he found you and then he came to tell me. It wasn't his fault that I never got his message, or that he was misled into thinking that if I had received it I would not have understood it. Then he took care of you. Everything he has done, even to marrying you, was, I am sure, for your protection, but now that the whole scene has changed and you are back home, he will, or I'm very much mistaken in him, be quite willing that there should be an annulment of the marriage."

"He won't!" Annabella, too, was on her feet. "He won't. You don't know Manuel. He loves me, he loves me passionately, I know he does. I'm the only thing that matters to him and—and he to me."

Rosina only just stopped herself from expressing her thoughts on this statement which would have been both cutting and revealing. What she said was, "You don't realize you're hurting me, dear."

"I'm sorry." Annabella's voice softened. "I'm really sorry because I'm—I'm so happy to see you. I've longed to see you. But Manuel is in my life, Mama, and he's never going out of it, not if I can help it."

They weren't looking at each other; Rosina was looking toward the floor and Annabella toward the window; then slowly their glances veered toward each other and it was Rosina, woman of patience that she was, who spoke and set the pattern for the future, saying, "All right, my dear, we will let things take their course; we will do all we can for Manuel. I promise you that. In the meantime, you're home, whether in Durham or here, you're home, and I'm looking forward to pampering you and making up for all the long"— she drooped her head and half-smiled—"I must not say 'trials' that you've had, since you tell me you've almost enjoyed them. But come along. Your clothes are just as you left them; Alice and I have attended to them each week even though I thought you would never use them again. So come along and change. . . . That is your old garden cloak, isn't it?" She pointed to the chair where the cloak was lying.

"Mama." Now Annabella came forward, and, taking the two long, thin hands in her own, she said, "Please, don't misunderstand me, please don't think that I am not grateful or that I am not glad to be home, I am. I can't tell you the times that I've longed and longed to be near you, to be back in the old environment, so please try to understand me when I say I can't put on my old clothes—I mean"—she half-smiled—"my elegant clothes again. I could not go and visit Manuel richly dressed. When I know what is going to happen to him, then—then, perhaps, I will take one of the plain dresses and be grateful for it."

"Oh, my dear." Rosina drew in a long, deep breath; then, exhaling slowly, she said, "Very well. As you wish, dear." She made her features move into a smile before she ended, "Now we'll have tea, shall we?"

"Thank you, Mama." Annabella paused, then said hesitantly, "I feel awful saying this, but I would like to take my leave about four o'clock as I want to pay a visit to Amy— Mrs. Stretford—before I go." She could not say, "I promised Manuel I would," but added, "It was Amy who looked after me. She lives along the riverbank. It was she who nursed me back to health. Without her care, I doubt if I would have survived the nights I spent on the open fells. So, if you don't mind, I will leave at four o'clock."

If she didn't mind! Rosina stared now at her child who was no longer a child, who was no longer a young girl, but who was a woman, a woman with authority and poise, a woman whom, she realized, she would no longer be able to mold, or even guide; but strangely she wanted the woman even more than she had wanted the child, or the young girl. But if she was to have her, and the thought of not having her now was so unbearable that she could see herself going to any lengths to achieve her desire, she must tread warily, and when she was returned to her once more, it must not be, it could not be as Mrs. Manuel Mendoza. Oh, no! Even the thought was intolerable. One blessing of God was she was still a virgin. Aunt Emma, in her gentle but probing way, had ascertained that much. And if she had anything to do with it, she would remain a virgin, for all men were vile. She would have staked her life on Stephen, and look how he had acted. No; there would be no man come into Annabella's life from now on if she could help it. Annabella would indeed become a glass virgin. That's what Edmund had called her once in a fit of anger, and now she would see to it that Annabella would follow the same path.

Annabella, this new Annabella, would, for her own good, have to be fought, but subtly, for if she were to lose her again, her second state would be worse than her first. It mustn't happen. She would go to Durham herself, and not only talk with Uncle James again, but see Mr. Fraser and place before him the whole situation. Mr. Fraser was a clever man; he had got them out of a great deal of difficulty when Edmund died. Mr. Fraser would handle the situation, Mr. Fraser would handle Manuel. It needed a man to handle a man, as it needed a woman to handle another woman.

5

The courthouse was crowded, and not only the courthouse but the town itself. Those with time to spare in the town and even on the wide outskirts had taken the trouble to come into Durham on this particular day, if not to hear the case, then to try to get a glimpse of Lagrange's girl who had suddenly appeared from the dead; and that was not all: she had

306

brought back with her a husband, the one-time groom of the Lagrange stable. Now that was a scandal.

A bill of indictment had brought the case up within nine days of the prisoner's being jailed, because the captain wished to rejoin his ship. Those who couldn't read and didn't know very much about the case asked what the prisoner had done besides marrying the Lagrange girl, and they had been told that he had hammered a sea captain and left him for dead.

Why had he hammered the sea captain? Oh, because the man had got a little too fresh with his bride.

On their wedding day?

On their wedding day.

Well then, you could understand a man's losing his temper and hammering another.

Yes, they supposed so; but he was an odd customer, this Manuel Mendoza, a foreigner like his name implied. And it was being said that he had never found favor with the other servants at Redford Hall; there'd always been something funny about him. And wasn't it funny now that he should go off with the daughter of the House? Ah yes, they knew all about her early parentage, but that wasn't any reason why he should take her on the road. Did they know that he had taken her into service on a farm out in the wilds of Muggleswick Common, and God knows where else? He was working her outside Darlington in a glass works when this happened. Had her working in a glass works, a woman, mind, or a girl, for that was all she was when all was said and done.

Was it true that her mother was a prostitute from Crane Street in Shields?

Aye, that's what they said. But that wasn't her fault, was it? But that's likely why this bloke Mendoza took advantage of her.

The conversation among the other classes in the town might have varied but the substance remained the same. There was no sympathy with "the foreigner," and this feeling had seeped into Mr. Justice Lear and had set up a feeling against the prisoner long before he saw him.

He had, this morning, dealt with two cases of housebreaking, and with one of wife beating. A most strange case this, where the husband had resorted to the ancient habit of using a brank on his wife to muzzle her scolding. This case, instead of eliciting sympathy from the court for the woman, had evoked laughter, in which he himself had found it hard not to join.

But now to this more serious case of one Manuel Mendoza, a Spaniard hailing from Ireland. That was a mixture. Yet not all, it would appear, for there was a broad seam of Spanish blood running through many of the Irish.

The report of the prison governor was that the man was a surly customer, but as yet had given no trouble. On the other hand, he had been informed by the clerk that two of the prisoner's employers had come from a distance to speak on his behalf. Well, be that as it may, whatever they said wouldn't diminish that this was a nasty case, and he wasn't thinking only of the prisoner beating this sea captain. That was understandable under the circumstances, it being his wedding day, and the captain wanting to sport with the bride. Ah, there was the point, the nasty taste in the mouth, the bride, the wife, a young girl of gentle upbringing if not breeding. He himself didn't lay much stock on breeding. He had seen many a silk purse cut from a sow's ear. And this girl had had seventeen years of refinement in the Lagrange household and, he understood, was loved dearly by the mistress, whose life, if the stories were to be believed, had been little short of hell until Lagrange decided to fall from his horse but not until after he had exposed the girl's identity to herself. It was this, he understood, that had almost turned the brain of Mrs. Lagrange, and when the girl should have been at her side to bring her comfort, she apparently drowns herself. Then, after months of mourning, the girl returns and brings with her a greater sorrow, a disgrace.

The fact that the man before him now, this one-time groom, should take advantage of such a situation stamped his character as low and cunning and scheming, which scheming had been checked in its fruition by the fight he had had with the sea captain, for, doubtless, had things gone smoothly, he would have returned to Redford Hall and presented himself as the husband of this girl, knowing that he would either have to be accepted, which was an impossibility, or be bought off. These foreigners were wily customers; even the working-class ones seemed to have more guile than those bred on English soil.

Mr. Justice Lear stared at the prisoner from under lowered lids. Yes, yes; he could see how a man like this could fascinate a girl, a young, innocent girl, even make an impression on more sophisticated women. He had an air about him, but he stood too straight; his lips were too thin and tight. He could not see the expression in the man's eyes from this distance, but he had no need to; his whole attitude was expressed in his arrogant bearing.

So thought Annabella as she cried inside herself, "Oh, Manuel, Manuel, be careful. Please, please be careful what you say, and how you say it." She watched his eyes move round the courtroom like those of a man who had walked out of deep shadow into strong sunshine, and then they were resting on her. And as if she were about to rise and go to him, her body bent forward, only to be checked by the gentle pressure of Rosina's hand on her arm on one side and her Uncle James's short, telling cough on the other. When his eyes left her, she followed his gaze and saw they were resting on Amy, and in this moment she would have given anything if she had been sitting side by side with Amy, for then it would have made him feel better; it would have lessened the gulf that was growing between them. She had done everything in her power during the twice she had seen him to lessen this breach, but she knew she had failed.

When next his eyes moved, she saw them widen slightly, for now he was looking at Mr. Fairbairn and Mr. Carpenter, sitting side by side on the raised seats opposite to her. She could never be grateful enough to these two men for answering her plea to come and speak for Manuel; altogether it meant three days of their time, and three days was precious to Mr. Fairbairn, and equally so to Mr. Carpenter.

And now his eyes were resting on the cause of all this trouble. The captain, his head swathed in bandages, his arm in a sling, his disabilities evoking pity, sat next to his thin, peevish-looking wife, where battle and retribution were etched on her every feature.

But now the case was beginning and the proceedings were slow and measured. Manuel was asked his name. The policemen gave details of the arrest, and then the court was told why the prisoner was being charged.

When the defending counsel stood up, he talked quietly and reasonably, too quietly, too reasonably. There was no penetrating force behind his words: they appeared more like an explanation. His client had been in this country for eight and a half years. During that time he had worked for four masters. One, Mr. Edmund Lagrange, was now deceased, but he himself had been given to understand that his late master had held him in high esteem. Next, he had worked as a cowhand on a farm outside Hexham, after which he was bonded to Mr. Fairbairn of Plane Farm, East Allen Dale.

Later, he was employed by Mr. Roland Carpenter, a glass-works proprietor. He would now call upon Mr. Fairbairn.

Mr. Fairbairn was sworn in, and in answer to the counsel's question, he said in his forthright manner that he had found Manuel Mendoza not only a most willing worker but a thoughtful, kindly man, and it was not with his wish that he left his employment.

Next, Mr. Carpenter was on the stand. How did he find Manuel Mendoza during the short period he was at the glass works?

Mr. Carpenter said that he had found Manuel Mendoza an exceptional worker, good-tempered, willing, and very quick to learn.

"Would you say he was of a spiteful, vengeful nature?"

"No, not at all."

"Had he been drinking at the wedding party you provided?"

"No, it had been commented upon, because he refused drink."

"Why do you think he attacked your stepson?"

Mr. Carpenter drew in a deep breath at this point, then said, "Because my stepson took a liberty with his wife."

There was a protest from the prosecuting counsel at this point and an exchange of words between the clerk to the court and Mr. Justice Lear.

Following this, the defending counsel began, "M'Lud, this man had just been married—"

"I think we are aware of that." Mr. Justice Lear seemed slightly bored.

"I was merely going to point out, M'Lud, that on a man's wedding day his perception is heightened and—"

There was a murmur like a ripple, followed by smothered laughter from different parts of the court. Mr. Justice Lear called for order and the case proceeded slowly, wearily, and Annabella thought, Uncle James said this man was brilliant, and there crept into her mind a suspicion that it would be the prosecuting counsel who would be the brilliant one, and in this she was right.

From the moment the defense counsel sat down, the atmosphere in the court changed. The prosecuting counsel's voice was vital, his manner was vital, his gestures were vital. Gowns rustled as women sat straighter and then became utterly silent, their interest riveting their eyes on the man who was "wiping the floor" with the defending counsel.

"The picture that Your Lordship has been given of the prisoner is, in my estimation, a false one."

"I object."

"Objection overruled."

"Of course, he was a worker. There was no doubt that he was a worker; so are thousands of other cowmen in the country. He was a willing man. Yes. Yes. I can endorse that statement, too, for wily people are often willing at first, overwilling."

"I object, M'Lud."

Mr. Justice Lear and the clerk to the court and the defending and prosecuting counsels had a whispered conversation and then the latter was speaking again. "Why did this man, when he knew the whole county was looking for the daughter of Edmund Lagrange, why did he not inform the authorities of her whereabouts? Why did this man take this young girl, this young, innocent girl, on the road with him, as any tinker would take his woman, if he was in the least concerned for her? And then inveigle her into marrying—"

"I did no such thing!" Manuel's voice cut like a giant scythe across the courtroom. "And I'm not on trial for marrying a woman. I'm here because I hit a man—"

The policemen were pulling Manuel back from the edge of the box over which he was leaning. Mr. Justice Lear was calling the court to order and warning the defending counsel to advise his client that such displays would not help his case. He also warned the counsel for the prosecution to adhere to the point of the case, the attack on Captain Mark Weir.

The counsel for the prosecution, now doing as he was advised, stuck to the point of the case, and very effectually. "Wasn't it the custom for wedding guests," he said, "to kiss the bride? And wasn't it the privilege of male guests to kiss the bride? In most cases it was the desire of the bride that the male guests should kiss her; and if they failed in this duty, she would be left with the feeling that she was unprepossessing and not desirable. All his client did was to kiss the bride. He did not deny this; the Captain had been very open about it. He had said quite frankly that he thought she was a pretty girl and wanted to have the privilege of kissing her. But when he was about to do this, he was attacked by the prisoner, his jawbone broken, his collarbone broken, added to this he was concussed—"

"It has been proved, M'Lud, that all but the injury to the jaw was caused by the plaintiff's falling among a stack of wood."

"Yes, after he was knocked into the stack by the prisoner."

"I must warn the defense counsel not to interrupt." Mr.

Justice Lear, at this point, looked severely down on the weary-looking barrister, and the prosecuting counsel finished with the telling words, "The prisoner's actions on that particular day were not those of a happy groom who would take the fact that other men wished to kiss his bride as a compliment to himself, but that of a man suffering under high tension, a man knowing that he had done a mean and underhand thing in marrying this young girl, and we could say it was his conscience at work that made him strike out blindly when the first opportunity provided."

As he sat down, Manuel was again straining over the box, his lips squared from his teeth, their blunt edges clenched. He was glaring at the calm countenance of the lying devil below him, for that is how he saw the prosecuting counsel, not knowing that to him it was just another case, another chance to show off his skill, another opportunity to score over his weak-kneed opponent, Mr. Peebles.

But Mr. Justice Lear was not deceived by either the tactical brilliance of the prosecuting counsel or the inanity of the defending counsel. He liked neither man. Nor did he like the prisoner, but he wasn't here to like the prisoner—he was here to judge him, yet strangely he had a different opinion altogether of him since he had come into the dock. One thing he felt certain of, and that was the man wasn't the rogue that the prosecuting counsel made him out to be. Certainly, he took the young girl with him on the road, but there was that other angle. He understood from a private source that, when that happened, she was no longer Miss Annabella Lagrange but the daughter of a woman of a most unsavory character, and it was doubtful, if she hadn't disappeared, that any of the people who supported her now would have continued to know her, that is, with the exception of the woman who had brought her up. But about this man. Under ordinary circumstances, the case being a quarrel on a wedding day when emotions were running high, he would most surely have dismissed him with a caution if, and the if was large here, his opponent had been one of his own class and not the stepson of his employer, and a sea captain into the bargain, although he himself didn't care for sea captains— brutish, loud-mouthed individuals, little in their heads and all in their hands had been his experience of them. Of course, there were exceptions, but the plaintiff, he felt, wasn't one of them. His wounds, he observed, were overdressed; he appeared as if in swaddling clothes. His wife's doing likely; she looked a shrew.

But the prisoner, what sentence was he going to give him? If he got a long, stiff one, it would certainly meet with the approval of old Dorcy-Grant, because although the girl was in no way related to them, by blood ties anyway, they were taking the whole affair as a personal insult and, he understood, were moving every obstacle they could in order to get the marriage annulled. As the prisoner was the greatest obstacle, it would certainly help if he put him down for two years or more; and he could do that, for he was charged with assault and battery and the blow he had delivered must have been extremely heavy to break the jaw of such a burly man as the sea captain. . . . He sighed deeply. He wouldn't be so severe as that. But, on the other hand, he could not let him off too lightly. He was a workman who had attacked a gentleman—he supposed sea captains came under that category.

He looked at the prisoner now over the top of his glasses, and the whole court became silent, waiting. But no one was waiting as Manuel was, and he held his breath as he listened to the little bespectacled judge now talking in a flat, unemotional voice. "There is no doubt in my mind that you struck a blow that could have killed the plaintiff; fortunately for you it merely broke his jaw. I have taken it into consideration that it was your wedding day and that your emotions would have been somewhat heightened on this occasion. I've also taken it into consideration that two of your employers have come quite long journeys to speak on your behalf, and this has gone some way to making me take a lenient view of your action, so I will not pass on you the sentence that some people might think you deserve but send you to be detained in the house of correction for six months from this day."

There was a stir in the court which covered Annabella's audible groans. Everyone was now looking at the prisoner. He was standing straight but holding his brow with the palm of his hand, and from his attitude it couldn't be detected whether this action was caused by relief or consternation at the sentence. But as the policeman took his arm to turn him about, he gave his body a heave and shrugged the man off, and it looked for a moment as if he were going to leap the box. But again he was just bending over it, staring toward Annabella, where she stood now shaking her head in small movements that left no doubt in the onlookers' minds what she thought of the sentence.

Not until Rosina and Uncle James turned her about and

led her away did Manuel loosen his grip on the edge of the box and allow himself to be taken below.

Five minutes later, Annabella was alone with him, that is, alone but for the policeman standing with his back to the door of the small, bare room. But she didn't mind about the policeman; he wouldn't inhibit her talking as Rosina and Uncle James would have done. Unashamedly, she had her arms around Manuel, holding him tightly, looking into his stiff face, pouring words over him, reassuring words, telling him that she would be waiting for him. "Believe me. Believe me, dear. Don't be afraid. I mean—I mean about me. They can do nothing to change me, I mean change me back into what I was. I—" Her words dropped to a whisper. "I'm Mrs. Manuel Mendoza and that I stay." She jerked him with her arms in an endeavor to get through the dead, disbelieving look that lay buried deep in his eyes.

"Where are you going to live?" His voice was thick and throaty.

"I don't know yet. I would prefer to stay in the wagon; I would, believe me, Manuel, I would, because I don't want to be beholden to anyone but you."

"You'll look after it and Dobbie?"

Her eyes widened slightly. Why was he bothering to talk about the horse and the wagon at this time when the seconds were precious? "Of course, of course."

"There's a weak spot up near the driving seat in the roof; see that the sail canvas is over it."

"Yes, yes, Manuel. Yes, I'll see to it. Of course I will, because we'll need it to go back to Mr. Carpenter's."

The dead look left his eyes now, though it wasn't replaced by one of hope but by a deep, scrutinizing stare. "They're going to try and get our marriage annulled."

"WHAT!"

"Your uncle came to see me."

"Oh, Manuel! Manuel! I didn't know. I didn't, believe me. But listen to me. They won't do it, I won't allow them—"

"You're under age. He said you were."

"But—but that doesn't matter. Don't you realize that Uncle James or Rosina, or any of them, are in no way related to me? The only person who could raise an objection to my age would be"—She made a swift, downward movement with her chin, then continued—"Well, you know who that would be, and I'm sure she wouldn't do it—why should she?"

"She was in the court."

"Yes, yes, I know, but—but only out of a matter of

curiosity, I feel. She made no attempt to speak to me, and for that I'm grateful. But about an annulment—I can't believe it."

"You can believe it, and—and they'll wear you down. They have ways."

"They won't. Oh, Manuel! Manuel!" Her voice dropped almost to a whisper as she pleaded, "Hold me. Hold me tight."

There was a space of time when he gazed at her before he responded to her plea, and then his arms, viselike, crushed her to him, but the embrace had hardly begun when the policeman said, "Time's up." For seconds longer they held together, then, raising her hand and touching first one cheek and then the other, she said to him, "I'll be waiting, just remember that, I'll be waiting; wherever I am I'll still be waiting for you. Good-bye, my dear, dear Manuel." She leaned forward and softly placed her lips on his before the policeman took him away.

6

"It isn't seemly that you should look after the horse, Annabella."

"But, Mama, I have nothing else to do."

"Oh, my dear Annabella! Well, I'm sure I can find you things to do that will be more suitable. But you know yourself that it's a man's work attending to a horse. Look, I will get in touch with Armorer again; I'm sure he'll be only too glad to come back. And, my dear"—now Rosina caught hold of Annabella's hand—"I'm going to mention something that I haven't touched on before, money. I can well afford to have Armorer back and a number of the other servants if I so wish. I'm not living here in the cottage through force of circumstance. I could in fact open up the House again. You see, my dear, Mr. Frazer did some very good work for us after"—she could not now say "your papa," so substituted —"my husband died. He sold the land and the factory to the Cookson firm for quite a substantial sum; I never realized that the land was worth so much. And then, of course, there was all the equipment in the glass works, besides which he got in a number of outstanding debts, so altogether I found myself very well placed, even before Mama died. Her fortune wasn't large, only in the region of thirty thousand

315

pounds, but this will give you some idea that you needn't worry about money. So please, Annabella, do as I ask and let me get Armorer to look after the horse. And what is more"—she spread her hands out now—"we can have another horse and use the carriage again. You'd like that, wouldn't you?"

Annabella got to her feet and looked down at this woman who, over the past weeks, had done everything in her power to make her forget that she had ever left her protection, and she realized that nothing she could say would convince her that she was no longer dear Annabella, pliable Annabella, genteel, ladylike Annabella, but that she was a woman who had worked with her hands at menial tasks, and had seen life as it is lived by the majority of people. She was a woman who was a wife, if in name only, still she was a wife, and she intended to remain a wife. All the new clothes Rosina had bought her, meant nothing. The food she ordered to be cooked, good food, exquisite food, food that a few months ago would have brought the saliva flowing over her lips, now did not even tempt her appetite, for every time she looked at the variety of dishes being passed to her, she wondered what Manuel was having at that moment.

She was worried about Manuel. The whole of her mind was in a perpetual state of worry over him, not only because he was in prison, but because he was changed. She had seen him last week for the first time since the trial and he had looked haggard, even old, but what troubled her most was his moroseness. Hardly speaking, he had just stared at her as if filling himself up inside with the memory of her, storing her away against a vast hopelessness.

And the visit had not been private; they had sat in a room with a score of other prisoners. Most of them had talked, some had even laughed, but the muscles of Manuel's face had not moved.

In her room there was a diary, put there thoughtfully by Rosina, but she wrote nothing in it except that each night she scratched off a date. Tonight she would scratch off the twentieth of June, and tomorrow would be her birthday. Tomorrow she'd be eighteen years old and she hoped, oh, she hoped that Rosina wouldn't give her an expensive present, because, when the time came for her to leave, she would not take it with her, nor all the beautiful clothes she now had and which were of no interest to her at all. The only dress that interested her was the green cord velvet with the beer stain down the front, and one day she would wear it again, no matter what it looked like, and on that day Manuel would be free.

As she walked across the room, Rosina's voice came at her sharply, saying, "Where are you going?"

"To Amy's."

Rosina did not rise from the couch but sighed deeply, then said, "Must you go every day to see her?"

"She lives on her own, as you know, and likes me to visit her."

"What if Uncle James should call? He—he was coming to see you on business."

Annabella's shoulders stiffened and she stared at Rosina for a moment before saying, "I won't be long, and should Uncle James come, I will be pleased to see him, but I have no intention of listening to the business he will wish to discuss. I have already made that clear to him."

Not once while speaking had she used the word "Mama." At one time she had punctuated her speech as thickly as commas with the title, but more and more now she found difficulty in saying it at all. Yet she still cared for this woman; she could say that she loved her. It was a love that was made up of deep gratitude, but it was a love that she knew she would throw aside if she found it acting as a wedge between her and Manuel.

She went out into the hall, where Alice was passing, and the old woman smiled at her and said, "If you're going out, put your cloak on; there's a keen wind blowing. It isn't like June at all." It was as if she had been listening and knew where she was going. Alice was kind to her, gentle with her, but then she'd be kind and gentle to the devil if it meant making her mistress happy.

She took her cloak, a new one, out of the wardrobe, put it on, and, leaving the hood lying slack, she went out, having said no word to Alice; and Alice stood watching her going down the path to the gate, and all the while she shook her head.

Fifteen minutes later, when she entered Amy's cottage, the old woman turned from her ginger-beer making and said casually, "Oh, hello there." It was just as if Annabella had left the room a short time previously. "Well, how's things? I won't be a minute; this is the last bottle I'm fillin'. You look peaked, you eatin'?" She stopped her pouring and, holding the jug in midair looked at Annabella, and Annabella, taking

317

her cloak off and throwing it over the back of the wooden saddle near the fireplace, sat down, saying, "Too much, Amy. That's all I do, sleep and eat."

"Good thing, too. You need it."

"Uncle James is coming over today to talk about the annulment, Amy."

"Oh, aye!" Amy was again pouring the beer into the bottle. "He's a sticker, I'll say that for him."

"They're all stickers, Amy." Annabella sighed. "They think they've just got to give me expensive clothes, good food and the promise of a holiday in Paris, which"—she nodded toward Amy—"they haven't settled a definite date for yet, but will arrange to take place when Manuel is coming out. They've only got to do all this, they think, and I'll forget about him. Amy"—she leaned toward the old woman—"how can people be so widely different? Why have people the power to bottle up their emotions? Mama has. She must have been living under terrible pressure for years but she never really showed it."

"It's trainin'. Like anything else, it's trainin'. Just look back to yourself." Amy was now carrying the bottles into the scullery, and Annabella, getting up from the seat and filling her arms with them, followed her, saying, "Yes, yes, I suppose you're right. I know you're right. It was, 'Yes, Mama. No, Mama. Yes, Papa. No, Papa,' and remembering that young ladies didn't laugh loudly or run, and that one never cried in public. Oh! That was the unforgivable sin, to shed tears in public. It was considered the height of bad form to show emotion of any kind in public. But, you know, Amy." She put the bottles down on the bench and put her hand intimately on Amy's shoulder, and she smiled at the old woman as she said, "I could scream in public now with the best of them."

"I bet you could an' all. Go on." Amy, on a hic of a laugh, pushed her with the flat of her hand, then said, "We'll leave the rest; let's have a sup tea, eh?"

When the tea was brewed, Amy put the pot on a tin tray and took it outside, and they sat on the bench and there Annabella drank the liquid that was so different from the tea back in the House, as she continued to think of the cottage.

Without any lead-up, Amy said, "I dreamed of him last night. It was a pleasant dream, though. He was swimmin' the river and enjoyin' it. Did you know that he used to swim the river here stark naked?"

Annabella bowed her head for a moment; then, slanting

318

her eyes toward Amy, she smiled as she said, "I became acquainted with that habit very shortly after we left here, Amy; and I'm afraid I wasn't only astonished but highly indignant."

They were laughing together now. Annabella drank the last of her tea and leaned against the stone wall. It was nice to be here; she could be herself here, no strain on her, no guard on her tongue in case she mentioned Manuel's name. Here Manuel was a man, alive and vital, an attractive, charming man, but back there he was still the groom, the workman, the inferior being, the prisoner.

She said now quietly, "They just won't believe that I mean to go on with it. They cannot understand that I would give up all they offer, at least all she offers, to go and live in a wagon. I tried to talk to her the other day and tell her that Mr. Carpenter would be only too pleased to take Manuel back, for now he has become entirely estranged from his daughter-in-law and his stepson. In fact, I emphasized that he was looking forward to our return, but she just looked at me blankly as if I were talking in a dream and that, when I woke up, I would see how ridiculous the whole situation was."

Amy didn't answer for a time, and then she said, "Well, lass, whichever road you pick, and knowin' you as I do now I know you're for him all along the line, but even then it's going to be difficult, for he's a proud bein', is Manuel, stiff-necked in a way, and for the rest of your life you'll have your work cut out to make him see that you're carrying no regrets about leaving all that." She nodded back toward the estate. "And it won't be easy. Now mind, I'm tellin' you it won't be easy."

"Anything will be easy after these last two months, Amy, anything. You know I'm eighteen tomorrow?"

"You are, girl?"

"Yes, it's my birthday tomorrow, Amy. But I don't feel eighteen, I feel twenty-eight, thirty-eight, inside. It's a year yesterday to the day that I went into Shields, just twelve months ago, but I seem to have gone through many lifetimes since then. I don't feel the same person at all, Amy. I don't think like the person I was a year ago. I don't even talk like her." Now she smiled as she patted Amy's arm, adding, "And this upsets Mama very much; and Miss Howard would have a seizure if she could hear me at times." Again they were both laughing, but softly, quietly.

"You know, Amy, if this year had never been, I would

never have known what it was to live. I would have gone on being the smug, correct Miss Annabella Lagrange no matter whom I'd married, and I would never have lived. All I would have done would be to extend my education and learn to swoon correctly." She now turned her eyes upwards, put one limp hand in the air, the other under her chin and demonstrated, and Amy laughed out loud, saying, "You've spoken a true word when you say you've changed."

"Amy." Annabella's voice was serious now. "Will you do something for me?"

"Whatever is in me power, lass. Whatever is in me power."

"On the next visiting day will you come to Durham with me?"

"Come with you? But don't you want to see him alone?"

"Yes, but I also want to convince him that they're not getting complete control of me. If he sees you with me, it'll help."

"I'll be only too pleased, lass. But what will they say?" Again she jerked her head back.

"They won't know. Uncle James doesn't offer me the carriage on visiting days. It is pressed on me at other times, but not on visiting days. I go by coach. We'll make arrangements later, Amy."

"We will that, we will that, lass. An' I'll tell him he hasn't a thing to worry about."

"Thanks, Amy. Just convince him of that and I'll be happy, as happy as I can be until he's free."

7

Manuel's time should have been up the last week in October but on the first Friday in October he came unexpectedly to the cottage. It was quarter past three in the afternoon and they were in the middle of dinner. Harris had just served a roast hare and had taken from the housemaid a damson pudding, and it was as the maid went out into the hall that there came a knock on the front door. And when she opened it, there, standing before her, was the foreign-looking groom, the man who had caused all the trouble.

They stared at each other for a moment; then she said, "Yes?" and to this he answered, "Tell my wife I'm here."

Her mouth agape, she surveyed him for a moment, then turned and looked toward the dining-room door. There was

320

no one in view from whom she could ask advice, neither
Harris nor Miss Piecliff, nor even cook. But she knew she must
close the door because the wind was cutting. "Come in,"
she said, and he came in, his hat in his hand. And he stood in
the hall, familiar to him as if he had crossed it yesterday on
his way down that passage opposite to him.

The maid now tapped on the dining-room door, entered,
then sidled up to Harris where he stood at the serving table,
and putting her face close to his she whispered, "It's him."

"What did you say?" The whisper was as low as hers.

"It's him, the man Mendoza."

His eyes moved from hers in the direction of the table,
but he didn't move his head. "Where is he?"

"I've left him in the hall."

Now he was in a quandary. Should he inform the mistress
or Miss Annabella? Well, it was Miss Annabella's husband,
but he must do this tactfully. He went toward the table, and,
standing between his mistress and Annabella, he bent slightly
toward both but addressed his mistress as he said, "There is
a person to see Miss Annabella, ma'am."

Annabella put her knife and fork slowly down on the
plate and looking up at Harris she said, "A person, Harris?"

"Who is it, Harris?" It was Rosina asking the question
stiffly now.

"Manuel. Manuel Mendoza, ma'am."

As if she had been hoisted from the table by a jib, Annabella was across the room and through the door. And there
he was looking toward her, Manuel, her Manuel, free. Her
movement toward him was as quick as it had been when she
left the table. Her arms about him, her head buried in his
neck, she muttered again and again, "Oh, Manuel! Manuel!
Oh, Manuel! Manuel!" Then looking up into his face, she
said, "I didn't know, I thought—"

"It was a remission." His voice was thick, flat, unemotional. He stared down at her face. They were alone in the
hall. They remained quiet for a moment, and then he said,
"Are you ready?"

"Yes, Manuel, yes." Her answer came without hesitation;
then she added, "But—but you must have something to eat.
Just a moment. Look, sit down. I'll—I'll tell her." Her voice
was a low whisper now and she led him toward a hall chair,
but he refused to sit. What he said was, "I can wait standing."

She stared at him again, then turned and hurried back
into the dining room.

321

"It's Manuel." She was looking down at Rosina, but Rosina had her eyes fixed on her plate and she said, "He is earlier than you expected?"

"Yes."

"Well, what do you wish me to do?" Her eyes weren't raised as she asked the question.

"Ask him in to have a meal."

Now Rosina was looking up at Annabella, her face twisted with the incredulity of the request; then she said stiffly, "I can't do that. I can't possibly eat with Manuel; I don't even eat with Alice. You understand, I couldn't possibly eat with Manuel, ever."

There was a pause while their gazes held.

"I'm sorry. Then we'll go to the wagon."

"Annabella!" There was sternness in the tone now. "You can't do this, you mustn't do this. Don't you realize that—that I need you? Don't you realize how much I need you? . . . And after all these months together to—to leave me. You can't—I will talk to Manuel and explain—"

"No, you won't. Oh no, you won't!"

"Annabella! You forget to whom you are talking."

"No, no I don't,—*Mama.*" She laid stress on the word now, then went on, "I don't, and I'm very conscious of all you've done for me, particularly these last few months, but I warned you from the beginning that as soon as Manuel was free I would go with him. I'm sorry, I'm really and truly sorry to leave you, but I must. I am Manuel's wife, but I'm not doing this just out of duty because I'm his wife. I'm doing this because I love him. He is the only person for me, now or ever, and I've told you this before."

They stared at each other a moment longer and as Annabella made to turn away Rosina said brokenly, "Annabella, don't go like this, please. Give yourself time; just stay a little longer till—till tomorrow."

She was at the door now and she turned and, after a moment, said, "Very well, until tomorrow."

When she entered the hall her eyes sprang wide, for Manuel was no longer there, but Alice was.

"Where is he? Where is he, Alice?"

"He's gone. He went off striding through the woods. The door was open; he has ears." Alice's voice was stiff, her manner was stiff. It said, You are an ungrateful hussy, that's what you are.

Without waiting to put on her cloak, she flew out of the door, down to the gate, and through the park toward the

House, calling, "Manuel! Manuel!" But she didn't get him into view until she reached the pagoda walk; and then she shouted at the top of her voice against the wind, "Manuel! Manuel!"

He stopped and waited for her coming, and when she threw herself against him and leaned heavily on him, he supported her with his arm and said stiffly, "It's all right. It's all right. Don't upset yourself."

"It's ready," she gasped. "The wagon. I did as you said, I've kept it watertight, and Dobbie's fit and well. We'll— we'll go in the morning. I want to collect my things." She checked herself. "I mean just a few personal things, the few I came with. Oh, Manuel! Manuel!"

They had stopped on the drive in front of the empty, gaping windows of the House, and now she put her arms around his neck, and he could resist her no longer. Pressing her tightly to him, his hungry mouth fell on hers and they swayed drunkenly as if they were tossed by the high wind.

When they had climbed up into the wagon, they again embraced, holding tightly, silently, now clinging to each other as if fearing the very air would tear them apart; then breathlessly she said, "Look, do you like it? See what I've done." And he looked about him at the interior of fresh white paint, with rabbits and birds picked out here and there, and he said in surprise, "You did this?"

"Yes, yes." She nodded proudly at him. "And look, I made this bedcover in patchwork. And the curtains—I made the curtains and I embroidered them." She lifted one end of the tiny curtain; then, flinging herself on him again, she cried, "Oh, Manuel. I had to fill every hour, every minute, or I would have gone mad. Now tell me." Her voice dropped and she now drew him down onto the side of the bed and asked, "How do you feel? How—how was it there?"

He shook his head and looked at her hands clasped within his own and said, "In a way, like death, because I was shut in; in a way, terrible, because I couldn't get you out of my mind; and in another way, not so bad, breakin' stones, sewin' sail canvas. The work was like a holiday compared with what I had been doing. But I would have been willin' to work twenty-three hours a day just to glimpse the sky above me at night, just to glimpse your face in the open air. I thought at one time I would go mad, an' was for tryin' to break out, but then I thought they'd only catch me and bring me back again, and so I behaved meself, and it paid off in the end: I got remission."

"Oh, my dear." She rubbed her cheek up and down against his sleeve, then asked, "Are you hungry?"

"Well, I could do with something to eat. I've been travelin' since eight this morning when they let me out."

"Oh, Manuel, you mean to say you've had nothing since then? Look." She jumped to her feet. "Stay there, I'll be back. Now promise me you won't move."

"I promise you." His voice was weary-sounding, but he put his arms around her waist and buried his head between her breasts, and she trembled as she held him. Then, kissing him tenderly now, she said, "Lie down, rest and you'll have a meal within ten minutes."

And he lay down, and he rested, but as he waited for her coming, words began to whirl round in his mind, the same as they had whirled back there in prison. But with one difference. Then the whirling words had said, "Will she come with me?" but now they said, "She will come with me, she will come with me. They can't keep her. She knows her own mind, she's a woman, she's a woman at last." And on this thought his body slumped and he fell into a deep sleep.

Back at the cottage, Annabella was again confronting Rosina. "Will you allow me to take him a meal?" she said somewhat stiffly, and Rosina, her face twisted with her inner anguish, murmured, "Oh, Annabella, of course." Then she added, "I'm sorry—I'm sorry, but you see it's the habit of a lifetime."

"It's quite all right, I understand."

"I don't think you do, but—but tell me, what are your plans?"

Annabella remained silent for a moment, her gaze straight. She did not want to hurt Rosina, but there must be no prevaricating; she must speak the truth. "I'm going with him in the morning," she said. "As I've already told you, Mr. Carpenter will welcome us."

"Oh, Annabella!" Rosina was now pressing her fingers across her lips to still their trembling, but when she spoke, the trembling staggered her words. "I had—I had great plans; I was going to speak about them to you very shortly. I—I had discussed them with Uncle James and they were all for your benefit, and—and let me"—she drooped her head to the side—"let me be truthful, for my own interest, also. But—but do you know what I had in mind, Annabella?"

"No—Mama."

"Well, I thought of turning the House, or at least the

324

Hall, into a glass works: Trade, they say, is picking up again and, as you know, you can build a glass works anywhere. And—and I went over the building only yesterday and I could see the possibilities. You see, you said that you had nothing to do, nothing to hold your interest, and I thought that if you were prepared to work in this Mr. Carpenter's glass works, then surely you would be able to work in your own."

Annabella looked into the pleading eyes; then, her own lids drooping heavily downwards, she muttered in real anguish, "Oh, Mama! Oh, Mama!"

"Will—will you stay and consider it?"

The lids lifted. "No, Mama. Thank you, thank you from the bottom of my heart for such a great gesture, but I can't stay anywhere where Manuel is not welcome."

"But, child, what you don't understand is that it is not only I who would not welcome Manuel; it is the neighborhood, in fact the county. Your position would be untenable; you wouldn't be accepted."

"Have I been accepted without Manuel? Have I been accepted over these last months? Who has called, Mama? Tell me, who has called on you once while I've been here? You said you had been very lonely without me, but you'd be more lonely with me, for not once have your friends visited you, or you them. How many invitations have you had to go to eat? Not one, not while I've been with you. As you say the position would be untenable."

"I don't want other people, Annabella." Rosina's voice was deep and heavy now. "I want no one but you. I didn't do much visiting before all this happened. Outside people are of no interest to me; they make no difference to my life, but they will to yours because you are young. You are only beginning to live; you are only eighteen years old, Annabella. You are hardly on the threshold of life yet. So many wonderful things could happen to you."

"One already has, Mama. If only I could convince you of that, one already has. I'll never meet anyone whom I will think more wonderful than Manuel. And Manuel will not always be as he is now. He will rise, I know he will. I mean him to, not for my satisfaction but for his own. He's very quick to learn. He learned to read and write in one-tenth of the time that it would take an ordinary person. When he cares, when his interest is aroused, he is quick to imitate or adopt a manner. Oh, I have no fear, Mama, but

325

that Manuel will rise. But even if he didn't, he would still have my love as it is today. But now, if you'll excuse me, I —I will get him something to eat."

She was trembling with anxiety as she approached the wagon. She had been away so long—more than half an hour. What would he be thinking? When she opened the door and saw him stretched out, relaxed, breathing evenly, the tension left her body. Setting down the tray that had almost snapped her arms in carrying it, she now lowered herself to the floor by the side of the bunk, and, resting her head on its edge, she sat gazing at him. She sat there until she, too, almost dropped off to sleep. Cautiously rousing herself, she put a match to the fire that was already set in the little iron fireplace, then put on the kettle to make some tea.

It was as she laid out the cups that he stirred. She turned swiftly, and when he opened his eyes she was sitting beside him, her hands cupping his face. He stared up at her in wonder for a moment as if he were in a dream, and then, his arms coming round her, he pulled her onto the bed and pressed her close to him, then lay perfectly still, savoring the moment.

Her body was filling with an excitement which would, she felt, at any moment burst from her when he said softly, "Did I see you brewing tea?" The rising excitement was checked. She opened her eyes and stared at him, then drew in a long breath, saying, "Yes, dear, I'll get you some. And your meal is here. You must be very hungry."

"No, not really." He was holding her face now, staring into her eyes. "There's only one thing I'm hungry for, but that will come—later."

She felt the blood rushing to her face and bringing sweat out of her pores, for as he spoke, he looked deep into her, and his eyes spoke even plainer than his words.

When he released her, she got up hastily and poured out the tea, then said softly, "I have your belt safe. It's under the top board of the bed." And to this he said simply, "Good."

Uncovering the tray now, she said, "Come and eat."

At one point during the meal he made her laugh. "Hare," he said, as he took a mouthful from the plate. "Quite good." He nodded as a connoisseur might. It was then she began to laugh, and her laughter rose as he went on, "But not quite up to the taste of a tinker's stew." He was referring to a hare he had trapped and cooked in the black can after they had left the Fairbairns' farm. At the height of her laughter, she spluttered, "You must tell that to cook. She will appreciate it; in fact, you must show her how you did it."

"I will an' all." He was laughing with her but not so loudly, and his laughter had no hysteria in it.

It was their laughter that partly muffled the first knock on the door, and when it came again, they stared at each other. Then Annabella took the three steps down the wagon, opened the painted panel and looked at Rosina standing at the bottom of the steps.

"May—may I come in?"

Annabella checked herself from turning her head to look at Manuel and said, "Of course, of course." Then she put out her hand and assisted Rosina up the narrow steps.

"Good-afternoon, Manuel."

Manuel was on his feet. "Good-afternoon, ma'am."

There was a moment's silence before he indicated the narrow bench on which he had been sitting and said, "Won't you take a seat?"

"Thank you." Sedately she seated herself, having to press down the front of her gown so it wouldn't protrude over the little table; then she looked from one to the other and said most courteously, "Please, please, do continue with your meal."

A little over an hour ago she had said, "You cannot expect me to eat with Manuel," but now she was expecting Manuel to eat with her; and he did just that. He sat down and with apparent calm continued his meal.

Annabella, too, sat down, but she was far from calm. She was searching in her mind to fill the awkward, yelling silence that had settled upon them.

It was Rosina who broke the silence. Looking from Annabella to the stove and back to Annabella again, she smiled thinly as she said, "You have tea made? Do you think I may have a cup?" Annabella swallowed deeply, opened her mouth slightly, then closed it and got to her feet, looking almost wildly round her for a moment. They possessed only two cups and saucers—and both had been used. Now, picking up her own cup and saucer from the table, she dipped them into a bucket of water standing within the doorway, then dried them and took them to the stove. About to pour out the tea, she looked at Rosina and said, "I'm afraid it's strong."

"I don't object to its being strong." It was as if they were in the drawing room.

"There is no milk or lemon."

The thin smile on Rosina's face widened a little to hide her distaste of black tea, but she said, "That is all right. I sometimes prefer it black. It has the same effect as coffee then, don't you think?"

"Yes, yes."

There followed another silence. This was dreadful, Annabella thought. She was right after all. It would be quite impossible for the three of them to exist together. Perhaps that is why she had come, to demonstrate the impossibility of it. If so, her effort was succeeding. Annabella looked down into the black tea. She knew that Rosina had never drunk black tea in her life. She could run to the House and get some milk, but that would mean leaving them alone together. But perhaps that was the thing to do, leave Manuel alone with her; without herself being present, Manuel might be less tense and talk, and if he talked as he could talk, he would charm even Rosina. It was a chance and she took it, saying, "Oh, I can't let you drink this without milk. Look, I'll run to the cottage and get some."

If she had expected a protest from Rosina, none came. What Rosina did say was, "Would you? Well, that will be kind of you, Annabella. Although I can take it without milk, I prefer it with. Or better still, bring lemon." Her thin smile took on a touch of humor as she added, "You won't spill that if you run."

The underlying meaning of these words did not, of course, reach Manuel, but Annabella knew that she was being chided for running.

She did not look at Manuel as she hurried out of the wagon, but his eyes were on her and remained on the door after she was gone.

Again it was Rosina who broke the silence between them. Looking at his bent head as he continued with his meal, she said, "I have never thanked you, Manuel, for taking care of Annabella."

Slowly he placed his knife and fork on the plate, not at right angles, but close together as Annabella had taught him. Then he looked at this woman, at this cold-faced woman. But no, he could no longer call her cold-faced; the eyes that were looking back at him had a straight glance, but deeply, deeply sad, and their expression could only be described as pleading. Yet her back was straight, her hands folded one on top of the other on her lap, her whole deportment refusing to recognize that she was sitting in a wagon and not in a

328

drawing room. As he stared at her, he knew that no matter how forbidding she appeared, he would give her nothing but the truth. She was no longer his mistress; she had no control over him. He was not afraid of her manner or what she might say. Looking back into her eyes, he said quietly, "You're not grateful to me, ma'am, for my association with Annabella; in your heart you consider it a disgrace, especially that I should have married her. And if it was in your power, you would, as Mr. Dorcy-Grant said, have the whole thing severed."

The expression in her eyes had changed slightly. It was as if she had uncovered a stone and found not a slug but some touchable creature. She said softly, "You are right, Manuel; I cannot deny what you say."

There was a short silence again before he answered, "You cannot stop her coming with me, you know that, don't you?"

"Yes, Manuel, yes, I know that. I cannot stop her, but you can."

They were staring at each other, their eyes wide, unblinking; and then she went on, in a hurried way now, "I wanted this opportunity to talk to you. I—I didn't think it would be so easy, I mean Annabella leaving like that. She is determined to come with you, but I feel, and I must say this to you, that her whole reaction is emotional. She is still a very young girl, Manuel—"

"She's not a young girl; she's a woman."

Her eyelids flickered downwards for a moment before lifting to his again. "I hope, Manuel," she said, "that she is still a young girl."

Again they were staring at each other, and then he said, "In the way, ma'am, you mean, she's still a young girl, but in her outlook she's a woman. There's no more connection atween her and the young girl that left here than there is atween me and Disraeli, so to speak."

"You may think that, Manuel; you may wish to think that. It is natural, but environment, early environment has a telling effect. Annabella is still the child I brought up, the young girl I trained into a young lady. She is still that young lady, and in your heart you know this."

"What are you saying to me? What are you getting at?"

"I am saying to you, Manuel, that without the emotion, without the pity, without the romance of—of your coming out of prison, and I am not misplacing my words when I connect romance with prison, because there is something romantic about a woman waiting for a man who has done a term of imprisonment, and in her defense. I am showing you the picture through Annabella's eyes. She may not recognize it herself, but it is a true picture, and if you give it a little thought, you will surely come to this way of thinking."

He had no need to give it thought to come to this way of thinking; deep down in him this had been the substance of his thinking for months past. Yet he would tell himself that she had married him, hadn't she? Yet again the reasoning answer would come back. But under the romance of adversity, because there was something about an adversity shared that created this feeling that this woman was putting over to him. Oh, oh, he knew it; there was no need for her to press the point. But that made no difference. Annabella was coming with him. It would be the years ahead that would prove who was right and who was wrong.

"Will—will you do something for me, a great favor?"

"It all depends what the favor is, ma'am."

"Will you give me a week's grace?"

"A week's grace?" He screwed up his eyes at her now, uncomprehending.

"I'm going to ask you to leave her here for a week longer, just one week, and you go away without explanation, just to go away for one week, and then if she's of the same mind—"

"No, I won't do it." He was on his feet. "She knows her own mind now and a week further on is not going to change her."

"You have just come out of prison, Manuel, you are free. Her thoughts now will not be about a man incarcerated behind walls, which very fact, as she said, was a torment in itself. When she thinks of you now, she'll think of you as a free man able to go where you wish, no longer fettered in any way—"

"I am fettered to her for the rest of me life, whether you like it or no."

"That may be so, Manuel." Her head leaned a little farther back on her shoulders and she paused before she said, "But do you think that she will remain the same? She is only eighteen years old; you are twenty-eight, I understand. You are settled in your mind; you are not going to change, but she is still an impressionable girl—yes, I repeat, a girl. But should she be of the same mind at the end of a week after she has had time to ponder on the fact that you are free and can go where you like, then I'll put no further obstacle in your way. I'll accept that this—" she drew in a deep breath —"is God's will."

He was staring down at her. Then his lips moved from his teeth in what could have been a smile, but the sound he made in his throat had no laughter in it, and he said, "If I had the command of big words, I could explain all that is in me mind; I could explain that I understand your little plan, but at present my words are limited. All I can say is that it sounds too simple, too childish to succeed."

"Well then, if you think so little of it, it shouldn't be hard for you to do."

Christ Almighty; it shouldn't be hard for him to do. His wedding night, to be torn from her for the second time, and after all these months of agony, mind-searing agony. He couldn't do it. He wouldn't do it. Not for this madam or God Almighty. There came a long, blank pause in his thinking as he continued to stare at her. Then his thoughts, moving on again, said, But if he didn't do it, all the rest of his life this woman's words would plague him, and he would wonder if Annabella had come to him out of pity and a romantic feeling, the latter which dies as every man knows, and was she still, underneath her changed exterior, Miss Annabella Lagrange, the girl playing at living.

She was waiting for his answer, but whatever ne would have said was taken from him by Annabella's bursting into the wagon, the lemon in one hand, a jug of milk in the other, saying, "I thought I'd bring them both." She looked from one to the other apprehensively. Manuel's face was stiff and gray-looking, but Rosina looked as she had when she had left them, composed, calm.

Rosina said to her, "Thank you, dear. I think I will have the milk now that you have brought it."

Annabella poured out the stewed tea, then handed the milk jug to Rosina in order that she should add her own to it.

Rosina sipped the distasteful liquid, then looked at Annabella and said, "I was telling Manuel that we are thinking of turning the old Hall into a glass factory because it would be a shame to waste your interest."

"Oh!" Annabella looked quickly at Manuel. The expression on his face hadn't changed. Only his eyes had widened slightly at this piece of news, and she said, "It's a good proposition, isn't it, Manuel? Wouldn't it be wonderful if we could work together here, actually in the old Hall?" She was speaking as if she were trying to sell him the idea, trying to persuade him that it would be good to stay here under any conditions. Swiftly her mind was forming a plan. They could live in the House, at least part of it, and the rest could be

331

storerooms, and they would have horses again—Manuel would love that. Her face was bright, her smile wide as she looked from him to Rosina. That was why her mama had come to the wagon, in order to put this proposition to Manuel, so it would be up to her now to persuade him to stay, because, yes, she must admit it, at the bottom of her heart she didn't want to leave Rosina. Rosina needed her, and if only she were willing to share her, they could be so happy. She would come to like Manuel; she would come to love him as a son, she was sure she would; no one could help but like Manuel once he knew him.

When Rosina, finishing her tea, said, "Will you walk back with me, dear. For if you decide to go in the morning, it will likely be early and I won't see you again." She then turned to Manuel. "You don't mind?"

He stared at her without speaking. She was a devil, a subtle, scheming devil of a woman. No, she wasn't a devil, she was like a god, a female god directing his course. And like a god, she knew what was in the mind; she knew how a man would react, a man of his type. She was a clever woman, was this Madam Lagrange. How was it she hadn't managed her own life so well as she was managing his?

"I won't be long, dear." In spite of Rosina's presence, Annabella put out her hand and caught Manuel's and smiled softly at him before going down the steps first and assisting Rosina to the ground. Then she did what she hadn't done since she had come back. She put her arm through Rosina's and together they walked into the parkland as they had done so often of yore. And Manuel watched them.

Rosina had lingered on the journey to the cottage. She had talked about ordinary things lightly, even brightly, and when they reached the house, she had suggested what Annabella should take to add to their comfort, and Annabella, a little puzzled, had said, "But, Mama, back—back in the wagon I thought you were hoping that Manuel might be persuaded to stay. I—I mean, if you are going to carry out this idea of the glass house."

Rosina turned away from her now, saying, "It is up to Manuel, my dear. But I doubt if he will. But come, we will talk as if you were going in the morning. What about that small set of china?" She pointed to the glass cabinet in the corner of the room.

"But, Mama, that is Coalport and it could quite easily get broken. No, no; thank you all the same, but I couldn't take it.

But I know what I would like: the blue mugs from the kitchen, the ones with the flowers on. You know? I would love one or two of those."

"Take them, my dear; take anything you want. And—and about clothes. Now, you won't be able to take all you have, but you must take a suitable wardrobe."

"Oh, Mama." Annabella threw her arms around Rosina and laid her head on her shoulder and laughed gently as she said, "You are sweet to me, you know, you are so sweet to me, but I won't need a wardrobe as you call it. I'll be working most of the time and Mr. Carpenter won't be entertaining at the end of the week, I can assure you."

Rosina answered nothing to this little bit of frivolity, but she held Annabella close to her, then said airily, "Well, come along, we will sort out what you can take."

The sorting out took much longer than Annabella had anticipated. This, that, and the other was suggested and rejected, and at last she decided on four of the plainest dresses, two shirtwaists and skirts and a considerable quantity of underwear, then she exclaimed, "But I'll never be able to carry all these. I'll get Manuel to come and fetch them, shall I, Mama?" She looked at Rosina pleadingly and Rosina, her head turned away, said, "Yes, yes, do that, my dear. As you say, you'll never be able to carry them."

So having hugged Rosina again, Annabella sped out of the house, through the park and to the paddock where she had first learned to ride, and at the gate she stopped quite dead. The wagon had gone.

Her mouth dropping into one long gape, she gazed about her. Then, the name spiraling up and seemingly coming out of the top of her head, she screamed, "Manuel! Manuel!" and lifting her skirts, she raced toward the stables, on to the drive and down to the main gate; and there, standing like a bird poised for flight, she turned her head swiftly to the right and then to the left and peered through the deepening twilight. Which way had he gone? Which way? She was now running in the direction of the crossroads and when she came to them, the two main roads, one leading to Newcastle, the other to Jarrow and Shields, were, as far as the light allowed her to see, empty. The road opposite to her, a byroad to Rosier's village, was also empty. Suddenly, her body slumping, she buried her face in her hands and wept, and as she wept, she cried to herself, "Why, Manuel? Why?" and for answer there came into her mind the face of Rosina. Why had she come to the wagon? What had she really said to

Manuel? She remembered the look on his face when she had come back with the milk and the lemon. He had looked strange when he had come first this afternoon, but this was a different strangeness, a tense strangeness that hadn't been there when they had begun their meal. And that touching little scene back at the cottage; the suggestions over and over again to take this or that. It had all been a sort of delaying tactic. Oh, how could she? How could she?

Now she was running breathlessly back to the drive, up it and across the parkland. But she had to stop and rest before she reached the cottage, for she was out of breath.

She was half-running, half-walking when she burst into the house. Rosina was in the drawing room. Gasping, Annabella stared at her, glared at her, then she cried, "You knew! You knew he was going. You sent him away. What did you say to him? How could you! Well, it won't do any good. I'm going, I'm going to find him."

"Annabella! Annabella! Be quiet. Be calm, please."

"I can't be calm, I don't feel calm."

"Manuel has done this for the best."

"Manuel would never do this for the best. You have forced him."

"I did not force him. I made a suggestion to him."

"You—you made a suggestion to him? Then you knew he was going. You purposely delayed me."

"No, I did not know he was going. As I said, I merely made a suggestion to him. I hoped he would carry it out, but—but it isn't final. I—I asked him to go away for a week and leave you here with me—"

"For a week? Leave me?" She was speechless for a moment. "But I've been here months with you. What do you mean, leave me here for a week with you?"

"You were here with me under stress. He was a prisoner all the time you were here; you thought of him as a prisoner. Now he's a free man and can come and go as he pleases, and —and do all that a man of his type usually does."

"He's not a free man; he is married—and to me. I'm his wife; he should stay with me." Her voice was breaking now. "And I should stay with him. I am going to stay with him. Manuel needs me, I know he does. And what do you mean, all that a man of his type—?"

"Child, if you'll give yourself a little time to calm down and look at things clearly, you'll realize that Manuel is no longer in prison; and you'll also realize, as he does already,

334

V-M CORPORATION

EV 26   Zenith

that your union is one of oil and water. Still, if at the end of a week he should come back——"

"*If* he should come back? You know that he won't come back; you've sent him away. You talked as only you can talk, and made him feel small. Well, it's finished. It's finished." She turned now and flew from Rosina and up the stairs and into her room. Tearing off the soft pink woolen dress she was wearing, she dragged open a drawer and pulled out from layers of paper the green cord dress. She was thrusting her arms into it when Rosina appeared in the doorway and, her voice holding deep agitation now, said, "Where are you going?"

"Now, where would I be going?" Annabella didn't turn round as she spoke. "I'm going to find my husband, wherever he is."

Rosina swallowed deeply. "Annabella, please, please listen to me. Please be reasonable; you can't go out at this time of night, and alone."

"I can't? But I can, and I am." She was now pulling open the wardrobe door and taking from it her old cloak that she had prevented Alice from burning. She put it on, and not waiting to gather up any of her small belongings, she went toward the door. But there Rosina blocked her way and with her hands now joined tightly against her flat breasts she pleaded, "Annabella, my dear, my dear, please don't go. Don't leave me. I need you—you don't know how much I need you. I've only begun to live again since you came back to me. I'll wither if you go. I cannot bear to live without you. Please. Please."

Annabella never thought she could look coldly at this woman, but now she did, and her voice was icy as she said, "I feel the same way about Manuel. I cannot bear that he should leave me. I feel that I would die if he should leave me. Now do you understand? And should anything happen to separate me from him for good, I—I shall hate you: Can you understand that? I shall hate you. Now, please, will you allow me to pass? Because I am no longer Miss Annabella Lagrange, or Miss Annabella Connolly, but I am, with or without Manuel, his wife, Mrs. Manuel Mendoza."

There was a moment's silence as if following a blow, and then Rosina moved and leaned against the frame of the door, and Annabella passed her, walking stiffly. She passed Alice on the landing, standing shaking her head as if at some sinful being. She went down the stairs and when Harris

335

paused before opening the door for her she looked at him, and he said, "Oh, Miss Annabella!" and then slowly he withdrew the bolt, and she went out into the black night.

She was outside the gate when the door closed and for a moment she knew panic. Which way should she go? Along the riverbank to Amy's, or to the crossroads again and chance that he would be making his way to Gateshead, then Low Fell and in that direction to Darlington?

But no, she'd go to Amy's; it was more than likely he had called there, more than likely. He wouldn't come this far without seeing Amy. But she'd better not go along the riverbank in the dark in case she fell in; she'd go by the road.

She had to grope her way through the park, but she ran when she reached the drive and most of the way along the main road toward Amy's house. And now she was hoping against hope that she might find the wagon there.

She was some distance away when she saw the gleam of light from Amy's lamp, and then she was knocking on the door, crying, "Amy! Amy!"

"God, lass! you gave me a start although I was half-expectin' you. Come in, come in."

"Have you seen him, Amy?"

"Yes, lass, I've seen him. Sit yourself down."

"No, Amy, no, I can't, I can't wait. Where is he?"

"Sit down I say." She pushed her into a seat, then said, "Get your breath and listen."

"But tell me first, how long has he been gone, I mean away from here? I want to—"

"I know what you want, lass. You want to find him, you want to be with him, so listen. It's nigh on an hour since he left here and he only paused for a few minutes, an' would hardly get down off the cart. He was in a tear, but I made him drink a glass of beer and got out of him as much as I could. It seems like he's been put on trial, but he's havin' none of it. He's had enough, you know, has Manuel; with one thing and another he's had enough. First there was the business of Lagrange, and then there was you. And you were the biggest handful. And then these months in Durham. And now when he comes out he's told he's got to give you more time to consider whether you want to stay with him or not."

"But I had nothing to do with it, Amy. I didn't know a thing about it. I was astounded, nearly mad when I found he had left. She did it unknown to me."

336

"Yes, I know that, and he knows that, but at the back of his mind he's still not sure of you, so it's goin' to be up to you to make him sure, isn't it?"

"I will, I will, if I only knew where he was. Do you know, Amy? Do you know?"

"I've a good idea. But he said that if you came after him to tell you to go back home and that he would come for your answer at the end of the week. But if he's got to wait that long, I doubt if he'll come back; the further he gets away, the further he'll go. I know Manuel. He's a strange man. He's straight and honest, but strange; he has a code all his own. He said he'd be making for Darlington and that he'd be travelin' all night. But he didn't go by way of the crossroads but straight on down this road here, and it's my mind he's passing the night in old Jacob's field."

"Jacob's field?"

"Aye, you know it as Bluebell Meadow, but the land belongs to old Jacob, a farmer over near Pelaw. Well, it's a long shot, but here's what I would do. I'd take this lantern— and fancy comin' out a night like this without a lantern. How far did you expect to get?"

When Annabella didn't answer but rose to her feet, Amy went on, "It's—it's a good half hour's walk along the road from here, about a mile and a bit I should say. Now, if you shouldn't find him there, you'll come back. You'll promise me that, won't you?"

"Yes, Amy. Oh, yes, I'll come back. Anyway, I couldn't go on walking all night, but—but I'll leave again tomorrow. I'll go by train to Hexham and start from there."

"Yes, you could do that. But anyway, here you are. Come on, take this now." She picked up the lantern she had just lit, and moistening the tips of her fingers with her tongue, she nipped at the end of the candle, saying, "There, that will give you a good light, an' if you're not back here within the next two hours, I'll know you've found him. But don't go on past there now, will you?"

"No, Amy, no, I won't." Bending forward she kissed the old woman, saying, "Thank you, dear Amy, thank you. I don't know what we would have done without you, ever."

"Get away with you. Go on. Go on." She pushed her toward the door. "Aw mind, I'll be waitin'. Be back within two hours at the latest. Are you warm enough?"

"Yes, Amy, thank you. Good-bye."

"Good-bye, lass."

337

She was walking on the road in the black of the night with only the lantern for company. The wind was high, the trees thrashed and at times wailed, creatures scurried across her path, and although she started and at one time cried out loud as an animal she took to be a stray sheep bounded before her, she wasn't really afraid. The only thing she was afraid of was not finding the wagon in the meadow.

Amy said that it was a little over a mile; a little over two would have been nearer the mark, but she knew she was close to the meadow when the lantern light glittered on the pond to the side of the road. The pond was the reason a lot of road travelers came to rest in this particular meadow. The pasture was a walled field with a gap for a gateway, and in the opening she lifted the lantern high and her heart leaped with it when she saw Dobbie tethered under a tree, half-hidden by the rough tarpaulin shelter.

There was no sound within the wagon, nor a sign of light, but gray smoke was coming from the little chimney. She went up the steps and opened the door and again lifted the lantern high, and it shone on him raised on his elbow on the bed, his eyes wide, startled.

"Annabella!" With a spring he was up. "In the name of God, at this time of night!"

"Oh, Manuel! Manuel!" She put down the lantern, then flung herself into his arms, crying now, "Why? Oh, how could you leave me? You should know by now—don't you understand? Even yet?" She dropped her head back onto her shoulders and gazed up into his face, at the dead look seeping away, and all he could say was, "Oh, Annabella! Annabella!" Then, after a moment, he cupped her face in his hands and said thickly, "It was madness coming out in the dark."

"Well, you're to blame." Her voice was still breaking. "Anything could have happened to me on the road, anything." She shook her head widely now. "And you would have been to blame, leaving me like that. When I went to the field, I nearly went mad. Manuel, don't you understand?"

He stared at her through the diffused lantern light. Then his head slowly nodding, he murmured, "Yes, yes. Now I understand all I want to understand." And his voice suddenly rose almost to a shout as he cried, "Yes, I understand!" And he jerked her to him and held her fiercely before he kissed her. And they clung together until they swayed and fell backwards onto the bed, and all the while she still had her cloak on. Laughing, his hands trembling, he undid it, and when he saw the green velvet dress with the beer stain still in evidence, he gathered up the skirt in his hands and buried his face in it.

Now, as he had dreamed of doing so often, he took off her garments one after the other, as a man should be privileged to do on his wedding night, and then they became married as only two bodies of those who love can marry, and when it was over, she did not lie in his arms relaxed, but sobbed unrestrainedly, and he soothed her with words that he had never used to her before, such as "my darling," "my dearing," "my beauty," "my lovely," and all the while she cried. But he was not disturbed by her crying because he knew that this was the way that happiness took a few women, women who, having reached an ecstasy, found it unbearable.

When her crying ceased, she laughed tentatively, softly; and then they ate the remnants of the food left over from the meal, and some bread and pork fat, and drank the herb beer that Amy had pushed into the wagon at the last moment. And once more they loved; then they slept until the dawn.

It was just coming into full light when they put Dobbie between the shafts. Then Manuel, lifting her up in his arms, kissed her hard on the lips before thrusting her onto the seat. When he climbed up beside her, he drove out of the gap and in the direction of Darlington and Mr. Carpenter's.

For the first mile they alternately laughed and talked; then of a sudden Manuel became quiet, so quiet that she bent forward and looked up into his face and asked, "What is it?" She felt so close to this man now that she was almost in his mind. "You're sorry about something?" she asked.

"Yes. Yes, I am." His face was straight as he nodded at her. "I'm sorry about her."

"Mama?"

"Yes, Mam-ma." The word had a lilting sound on his lips. "Aren't you sorry for her?"

"Yes, yes, Manuel." She was looking ahead now, her own face straight. "Deeply, deeply sorry. But she would have separated us, and yesterday when I was beside myself after I found you gone, I said something dreadful to her."

"You did? What was it?"

"I said if I didn't find you, I would hate her all my life."

"You shouldn't have said that."

"No, I know I shouldn't, for she has been so good to me,

but—but you were all that mattered, and it's true, if she had parted us I would have hated her."

"But she hasn't parted us." He pushed the reins into one hand and, putting the other around her waist, drew her tightly to his side. But his face was still straight as he said, "I've got something to thank her for, for, you know, if we'd come together back there, I would always have been a little unsure of you. Yes, yes, I would. You can shake your head, but I would. Deep in me heart there'd have been a doubt. But now I can say that neither man nor woman, God nor the devil, could shake me faith in you."

"Oh, Manuel! Oh, my dearest Manuel." She rubbed her cheek against his shoulder, and as they came to a turning in the road he pulled on the right-hand reins and Dobbie paused, then marked time before turning round, and the wagon followed. Now, pulling herself from him, she asked, "What are you doing?"

"I'm going back; we're going back."

"But. Manuel!"

"Gee up, there. Gee up, Dobbie." His head was up and his eyes were fixed on a point between the horse's ears as he said, "She can't touch me now; she has no power to separate us, no matter what she does. Where I go, you go, I know that, and so I can go back. . . . An' you know what, Mrs. Mendoza?" He now jerked his head toward her and grinned down at her. "I am going to run her glass house."

"Oh! Oh! Manuel. Manuel." She was laughing loudly, her mouth wide.

"Yes, that's what I'm going to do, Mrs. Mendoza, I'm goin' to run her glass house. And another thing I'm going to do, Mrs. Mendoza."

"Oh, Manuel. Be quiet, do."

"No, I won't be quiet until I tell you. An' listen to me, because you're hearing aright. I'm going to woo her."

Now Annabella let out a most unladylike squeal, and Manuel went on, "It's going to be a difficult job wooing Mrs. Rosina Lagrange. The wooing of you will be child's play to it. But woo her I will." Then, his jocular manner fading away, he turned and looked at Annabella and said quietly, "She's a lonely woman, a lost woman; without you she'll just pine. I saw that yesterday when she put up the fight. It was her loneliness that defeated me. Loneliness is a terrible scourge to the spirit. It's bad enough for a man, but it's much worse for a woman."

Again she laid her head on his shoulder, and now she

whispered with tears in her voice, "If I had never loved you before, Manuel Mendoza, I would love you at this moment."

Gee up there, Dobbie! Gee up! An' God rest you forever, Margee.

SPECIAL OFFER: If you enjoyed this book and would like to have our catalog of over 1,400 other Bantam titles, just send your name and address and 50¢ (to help defray postage and handling costs) to: Catalog Department, Bantam Books, Inc., 414 East Golf Rd., Des Plaines, Ill. 60016.

ABOUT THE AUTHOR

CATHERINE COOKSON achieved worldwide success the hard way. Born in 1906 in Tyneside (in the north of England) to a tragic, alcoholic mother and a father she never knew, young Catherine bore the sting of illegitimacy and poverty from childhood. Though she worked at a variety of menial jobs, she had always wanted to write. (When she was seven years old, her grandfather told her that she was a born writer because, as she says—"I was the biggest liar he had ever come across.")

Today, Catherine Cookson is the most popular of all contemporary English writers: in a 1979 survey—"Who is your favorite author?"—she ranked Number One . . . far ahead of the venerable Agatha Christie, Victoria Holt and even Georgette Heyer!

Her romantic melodramas—featuring beautiful, resourceful heroines who battle hardship and heartbreak to achieve their goals—are translated into many languages. (Particularly popular with Americans are *The Mallen Trilogy, The Girl, Katie Mulholland, Feathers in the Fire* and *The Glass Virgin.*) Small wonder, then, that Catherine Cookson is acclaimed as "the author with 20 million friends around the world!"

Catherine Cookson lived for many years in Hastings on the south coast of England (as far away from Tyneside as possible). But she has recently returned to the north, setting of her childhood and her novels, where she now lives with her husband.

Catherine Cookson

For years a best selling author in England, Catherine Cookson's readership today is worldwide. Now one of the most popular and best-loved writers of romantic fiction, her spellbinding novels are memorable stories of love, tragedy and courage.

☐	13935	**KATIE MULHOLLAND**	$2.75
☐	10355	**THE DWELLING PLACE**	$1.50
☐	14187	**THE GIRL**	$2.25
☐	13937	**THE GLASS VIRGIN**	$2.50
☐	13932	**THE MALLEN STREAK**	$2.50

Buy them at your local bookstore or use this handy coupon for ordering:

Bantam Books, Inc., Dept. CC, 414 East Golf Road, Des Plaines, Ill. 60016

Please send me the books I have checked above. I am enclosing $_____ (please add $1.00 to cover postage and handling). Send check or money order —no cash or C.O.D.'s please.

Mr/Mrs/Miss_____

Address_____

City_____ State/Zip_____

CC—4/81

Please allow four to six weeks for delivery. This offer expires 10/81.

BRING ROMANCE INTO YOUR LIFE

With these bestsellers from your favorite Bantam authors.

Barbara Cartland

☐ 13942	LUCIFER AND THE ANGEL	$1.75
☐ 14084	OLA AND THE SEA WOLF	$1.75
☐ 14133	THE PRUDE AND THE PRODIGAL	$1.75
☐ 13579	FREE FROM FEAR	$1.75

Catherine Cookson

☐ 13279	THE DWELLING PLACE	$1.95
☐ 14187	THE GIRL	$2.25
☐ 13170	KATIE MULHOLLAND	$1.95

Georgette Heyer

☐ 13239	THE BLACK MOTH	$1.95
☐ 11249	PISTOLS FOR TWO	$1.95

Emilie Loring

☐ 12947	WHERE BEAUTY DWELLS	$1.75
☐ 12948	RAINBOW AT DUSK	$1.75
☐ 13668	WITH BANNERS	$1.75
☐ 13757	HILLTOPS CLEAR	$1.75

Eugenia Price

☐ 13682	BELOVED INVADER	$2.25
☐ 14195	LIGHTHOUSE	$2.50
☐ 14406	NEW MOON RISING	$2.50

Buy them at your local bookstore or use this handy coupon:

Bantam Books, Inc., Dept. RO, 414 East Golf Road, Des Plaines, Ill. 60016

Please send me the books I have checked above. I am enclosing $_____ (please add $1.00 to cover postage and handling). Send check or money order —no cash or C.O.D.'s please.

Mr/Mrs/Miss_____

Address_____

City_____ State/Zip_____

RO—4/81

Please allow four to six weeks for delivery. This offer expires 10/81.